Finding Home

The Lost & Found Series

Kristen Casey

The Lost & Found Series

Girls Night Out

Finding Home

Finding Love

Lost in Love

Lucky in Love

Christmas in Cambridge

Finding a Husband

Heroes & Husbands

Finding Forever

Forever and a Day

Forever Starts Now

The Flynn Sisters Box Set

The O'Connell Sisters Box Set

About This Book

Getting Away Was Supposed to Fix Everything.

Divorce might have thrown Morgan's life into a tailspin, but at least she had a plan for recovery. Going on a girls' trip—as far away as possible—was supposed to be just the thing to pull her out of her funk and get things back on track. But when tragedy strikes before she even makes it home from the safari, Morgan finds herself unable to return to the broken life she knew before. Instead, she stays put and takes a safe, unassuming job as one man's housekeeper—Owen, an intriguing game warden with a sticky problem of his own.

Caught up in dangerous forces they don't understand, Morgan and Owen work together to unravel what—or who—is killing a rare animal in Owen's nature preserve. They can't deny the growing attraction between them, but when foes look like friends, the couple is pushed to the brink and threatened with consequences worse than either is willing to contemplate.

Will they learn the truth in time to save the last of the gazelles, and themselves? Or will they fall victim to the treachery surrounding them, and lose their hopes for a new life together?

Only time will tell.

Prologue

MORGAN PUSHED THROUGH the glass front door of the British liaison office in Victoriaville and stepped into a chilly front room that immediately put her off with its sterile officiousness. It reminded her of a dentist's office back home, only without the magazines, fake plants, and aquarium.

This was no doctor's appointment, however, even if it felt like it could be. If Nina was to be believed, this meeting was all about cowardice, plain and simple.

Shaking herself, Morgan forced herself to walk toward the receiving window, where a stern-looking woman sat glaring at an ancient computer. The receptionist was the only break in the monotony of the room, besides a couple of tattered posters and some orange plastic chairs lining the wall.

Morgan cleared her throat. "Hi, I'm, uh…I'm Morgan Flynn. My tour guide, Conrad, said he would call over for me?"

The woman barely looked up. "Yes, ma'am," she said. "Please have a seat and I'll bring you back shortly." She spoke English with a clipped, indefinable accent which, Morgan was quickly learning, was usually the product of the missionary-run primary schools scattered across the area.

The longer Morgan stayed here, the more those little remnants of colonialism stuck out to her. They gave her an odd sense of dissociation. She had the distinct sense that she wasn't *supposed* to notice this stuff. She was only supposed to visit, marvel at the sights, and then leave again—like all the other tourists.

While she waited, she remembered watching the Olympics with Chip, years ago. They'd thought it was so odd when the delegation from Zimbabwe had included a white female athlete, but neither of them had considered why that was. At the same time, it'd seemed totally unremarkable when most of the Western countries had advanced Black athletes.

Troubling, in retrospect, all the things she'd never stopped to think about, nestled in her cozy former life. Race. Privilege. *Chip.*

Morgan shuddered, the frigid air conditioning turning the sweat on her skin clammy. Her damp shorts and shirt clung uncomfortably, and the unwelcome memories sat like rocks in her brain.

She felt very awkward perched on her orange chair in stained safari gear. It seemed an offense to be this grimy and disheveled in such a temple of efficiency.

She scrubbed her hands down her face and tried to smooth back the strands of hair coming loose from her ponytail. She really had to pull herself together if she expected this plan to work.

"Mrs. Flynn, you can come back now." The receptionist held open a door Morgan hadn't noticed before and handed her a clipboard as she passed through. "You can sit in here while you fill out the forms. Dr. Bing will be with you in a moment."

"Thank you."

Morgan sat at the battered old table and studied the single peeling travel poster on the wall. *Why Turkey?* It seemed an incongruous destination choice for east Africans, but what the hell did she know?

She was coming to suspect that the answer was, "not a lot."

Morgan looked at the forms and abruptly realized she hadn't been given anything to write with. She rifled through her backpack, searching for a pencil to no avail.

When she approached the reception desk a second time, she felt exactly like a problem child, who'd arrived at school without the proper supplies. Worse, in her anxious effort to be polite, she spoke too quietly and had to repeat herself twice before she managed to get the secretary's attention.

"I'm sorry to bother you," Morgan said, once the lady finally looked up. "May I please borrow a pen? I don't seem to have one."

The woman peered over her bifocals, then handed Morgan a worn-down old pencil without comment. Morgan returned to her room and stared at the thing. The yellow paint was cracked, and the eraser was shiny and hard with disuse. She hadn't written with a pencil like this in years—maybe not since elementary school.

She smiled briefly, thinking about how things could change so much in such a short time. Two months ago, she'd done nearly everything on her smartphone, and now look at her— wielding this grade-school pencil in dust-caked boots. She couldn't say it was a downgrade, though.

When she'd had a closet full of matching shoe boxes, containing elegant heels of satin, suede, and crocodile skin, she hadn't been happy, either. Maybe somewhere, she still had those shoes—maybe her sister Meg was boldly wearing them out to nightclubs all over Boston.

Now that Morgan had seen real crocodiles up close, though? She didn't think she'd ever want to wear one's skin again.

She'd be completely fine in these hiking boots forever. They'd carried her this far, after all.

Her eyes fell to the pages of questions and snagged on one in particular. *Why are you seeking employment in this country?*

Morgan rubbed at the pencil, and the old chew marks in the wood felt rough against her thumb. How could she answer that simply? She could wax poetic for fifteen paragraphs, and even then, she might not make a dent. As it was, her life story was dangerously close to becoming some celebrity's book-of-the-month, and that was before she even wrote this next chapter.

Fortunately, the liaison came in then, a reassuringly gray and rumpled old man who reminded her of her grandpa.

"Ah, Mrs. Flynn. My condolences on your sad loss," Dr. Bing said, elegantly settling himself in the chair across from her.

"Thank you." Morgan couldn't help but wonder, however, which loss he meant. At the moment, she had quite a few to pick from.

"Conrad told us a little about what happened," Dr. Bing began. "It must be difficult to make decisions at a time like this."

"Somewhat," Morgan admitted ruefully.

"My concern is…well, I must say I'm not entirely sure why you wish to stay here in Victoriaville." The liaison's voice remained courtly and kind, but his confusion was evident.

Morgan was on intimate terms with confusion herself, these days. "Honestly, I'm not exactly sure myself," she replied self-consciously. And then, "That probably sounds ridiculous."

"I could give you a whole spiel about Africa getting into one's blood and so forth," he smiled, "but I don't suppose you'd buy it, now. I should think after your experiences here, you'd be rather eager to leave and never return."

"I know that's what most people would do. I just… I can't, um…I don't know how to say this," Morgan stuttered. "I just can't bring myself to go back right now. I know it's strange, and I realize I can't stay here *forever,* but for now…"

The liaison nodded as if he understood perfectly. Morgan didn't believe it. Undoubtedly, she was baffling him more with every word she spoke.

Perhaps this was all a big exercise in futility. For all she knew, she could've already ruined her chances. Maybe she hadn't even had a chance, to begin with.

Dr. Bing picked up the pencil from the table and examined it thoughtfully. Morgan had the abrupt, irrational fear that he would think she'd been the one to chew it up. It would be one more mark against her, to add to all the others.

Eventually, he set it down precisely and mused, "A woman of your education and skills—I'm afraid there's not much finance work at your level, here. Not in our little corner of the world."

"Oh, that's okay. I wasn't expecting anything like that," Morgan rushed to assure him.

"Perhaps one of our larger cities would afford you more opportunity in that regard?"

"No, I—I'd prefer to stay here." The liaison peered at her, his rheumy gray eyes unreadable, and she rushed to amend, "If that's possible, I mean."

Morgan really hoped she wouldn't be reduced to begging him like a child.

Dr. Bing let out a long, slow breath. "Right. Well..."

"I can do a lot of things. A lot of, um, homemaking things," she stammered. Morgan nodded at him as she blundered along. "Like domestic jobs. Are those an...an option? I'm not afraid to work hard."

The liaison looked dubious, but allowed, "If that's the case, we might have more to work with. I know of a few open positions around here, but my concern is that the families would want someone quite experienced in running a household in the local ways."

Morgan inhaled deeply, unsure of how much to commit herself. She had no idea what *the local ways* might entail, and if she got in over her head...

She laughed bitterly to herself. Who was she kidding? She'd been in over her head for so long now, she barely knew which way was up.

Dr. Bing looked her over for another minute, considering. Then he rose abruptly. Sprier, it seemed, than he looked.

"You know, I've just had a smashing thought. Why don't you finish up those forms there, and I'll pop out for a minute and check up on something. I may know of exactly the right job for you."

"Okay. Thank you, Dr. Bing," Morgan said shakily.

A job meant a work visa, which in turn meant she could stay here for months longer without having to go home. That had been her plan when she'd marched in here today—and that was *still* her plan. So why were butterflies suddenly swooping around her stomach, making her queasy?

The liaison ducked out, and Morgan straightened the mimeographed sheets in front of her. *They already know how strange this is*, she thought, *Nothing I write is going to change that.* All she had to do was tell them what they wanted to hear.

For example, she could answer, *I want a chance to fully experience your lovely geography and culture,* as the reason she wanted a job, but then she might be tempted to add, *and never return to my own private hell of a life.*

Maybe it was better to start small, and at the beginning. Morgan picked up the old yellow pencil and printed carefully, *Flynn, Morgan Theresa,* on the first short line.

FORTY-FIVE AGONIZING MINUTES later, Dr. Bing returned. "Mrs. Flynn, I must apologize. Thank you for waiting here so patiently."

"Of course. It's no trouble," she chirped, though she'd started to wonder if her neck would ever be the same after so much time spent beneath the vent overhead, spewing out artic air like this was a meat locker and not a crossroads in her life.

As omens went, it wasn't terribly encouraging.

"I hope the delay did not inconvenience you," Bing said as he sat down.

"I have nowhere else to be," Morgan tried to joke. "In fact, Conrad is probably dying to get rid of me by now."

"Not at all. He'd hire you himself if he didn't think it would be too uncomfortable for you."

She smiled politely but quickly had to shift her gaze away to hide the sudden, unexpected stab of pain she felt. It wouldn't help to dwell on it, though. Morgan had to push on if she wanted to live through this.

Dr. Bing was quiet for a moment, studiously rearranging some papers he'd brought in while she regained her composure.

When she looked up again, he continued, "The position I had in mind for you has indeed remained open. The employer, Mr. Owen Hargreave, had a local woman working for him for quite some time, but she has left to care for her own family. Quite pregnant, you know."

"Okay. What kind of job is it?" Morgan asked with some trepidation.

"Well, domestic, naturally. And I am somewhat acquainted with Hargreave. He works at the Preserve, north of here. Do you know it?"

She thought she might have heard something during the tour but couldn't be sure—everything from those weeks had run together, into a blur she'd rather not examine too closely.

Morgan shook her head.

"It's one of the only parks left in the country that's still in private hands," he said, "And British hands, at that."

"How is that possible?"

"Let's say…my countrymen can sometimes be a bit too clever for their own good," he smiled ruefully, "and for everyone else's, as well." The liaison checked his notes briefly, then went on to explain, "Hargreave is the head game warden there. Oversees anti-poaching, I believe. Things of that sort, anyway."

"I see," Morgan said, though she wasn't quite sure she did. She kept quiet, hoping for more details.

Bing obliged immediately. "No wife or children that I know of. He came over from New Zealand originally…must be ten years or more, by now. Since he's a bachelor, I presume the household will be smaller, and simpler to mind. Let me see…" Dr. Bing trailed off, reading his paper again.

"Sounds do-able," Morgan told him. A single guy would probably be easier to handle than some micromanaging housewife—as long as he wasn't looking for an in-house sex slave or anything, that was.

That thought gave her pause.

"The only small consideration is that his home is quite out of the way—not in town, but several kilometers out on the west road." Dr. Bing sighed and looked forlorn to be sharing this unsatisfactory detail with her.

"All right," she hedged, growing more unsure. Isolated, alone with a strange man…that could blow up in her face, and then some.

"I'm sure he would provide you with some sort of transportation, though. We've made him aware of your circumstances," the liaison assured her. He sounded as if he was trying to reassure himself.

"I see." Morgan contemplated what she'd heard so far. The potential for disaster was inching upward, but it wasn't high enough to make her back out yet. The thought of going home was still much, much worse.

"Really, the only other issue I can see is that Hargreave is often away from home. If you were to need assistance, being so far out…" Dr. Bing frowned but shook it off quickly. "Well, as I said—I'm certain he's considered that and will provide means for you to get around. If you got into a real jam, you could always phone the Twospeaks or even one us here in the liaison office."

"So, he travels a lot? For work?" Morgan confirmed.

"Yes, the Preserve is quite large, you know, and his duties apparently send him to the further reaches with some frequency."

"Huh." Somehow, she had stumbled into a no-brainer of a job, for one person who was never home. What were the chances that he was normal, and not some psycho? Could her luck really have changed so dramatically, so fast?

"Well then, there isn't much else I can tell you. If you want to go ahead, he's willing to pop over now. Hargreave can fill you in on his specific requirements then if you'd like."

Morgan swallowed. *This was it. Time to put up or shut up.*

Dr. Bing noted her hesitation, and said gently, "I feel compelled to tell you, he's a decent sort of man. The women who've worked for him in the past have given him good reviews. Plus, I think you'll find the accommodations comfortable, and the pay quite fair."

Morgan nodded, her mind made up. "Piece of cake," she said, smiling at him.

Here we go, she thought to herself, then. *Here we go, not going home.*

July 9

Back in college, when I had friends from all over the world, I learned about their countries and cultures and I longed to expand my own narrow horizons. I ached with the need to transmute my mundane self into something as exotic as them—to trade my cardboard for their embroidered silk. So why did I ignore my dreams and make such safe choices? Before I knew it, I was married, and they'd flown out into the world, wings fluttering like a beautiful horde of butterflies, disappearing on the breeze. I'd only flexed my wings once or twice before the glare of routine had reduced them to ash. So, I sat on my windowsill, stuck behind glass, stuck watching. But now—I'm flying now, and the reality feels much scarier than I ever imagined it would. Not at all like soaring, but like one great, wingless leap down into the unknown. Down here, I don't have the comfort of being anonymous, or unremarkable. I'm the stranger, the oddity to be dissected. I have to believe, in the end, it will be worth it. The alternative is way too grim to contemplate.

Chapter One

MORGAN WAS SULKING—she knew she was. It wasn't like it was any great surprise. After all, she'd been wallowing for months, now.

There was just something disconcerting about this new apartment of hers, though. It was too quiet, too empty. Shadows lingered in the corners in the evenings, and completely creeped her out.

However, the problem could simply be *her*. This new Morgan—the one walking around in her skin ever since the divorce—was nothing like the woman who'd existed before.

She was hollowed-out. Numb. Frozen.

As Morgan sat there alone, the clock on her bookshelf ticking off the minutes until she could reasonably retreat to bed for the night, she knew she had to do something to pass the time. Staring off into space was accomplishing exactly nothing, and frankly, she was beginning to annoy herself.

She heaved herself up and marched over to the box of books still parked on the floor next to her shelves—in the exact same spot she'd dropped it months before. She ripped into it and found the photo albums she was looking for, took them back to the couch, and set them on the coffee table in front of her.

Morgan contemplated them. Was she really going to do this now?

She'd had this habit for a long time. Whenever she'd grown dissatisfied with her current situation, she would comb through her photo albums, and try to determine where she'd gone wrong—as if looking at old pictures might help pinpoint how she'd ended up somewhere she didn't like.

Somehow, she'd convinced herself that leafing through images of the people and places that had impacted her would give her insight. She always hoped she'd discover that things weren't as bad as they seemed—or at least figure out what she needed to do next, so she could move forward.

Instead, what Morgan often learned was that the pictures of her supposedly happy events usually papered over a hidden twist—like a memory of a botched holiday meal, an anniversary argument, or some seething inner resentment masked by a blinding smile for the camera.

People said that cameras didn't lie, and in her old photos Morgan could see the stark realities of innocence lost, dreams unfulfilled, and disappointment by the bucketload. Why was she still so meticulous about keeping these things? Why didn't she stick them in an attic somewhere, where they couldn't hurt her?

True, it might have been a harmless pursuit, if not for the fact that Morgan got into such dark moods, and that she seemed to be baking up a seriously nasty side dish of masochism along with them.

The notion that her life was surely happier *before* was a dangerous one. Did Morgan really need to torture herself by seeking out irrefutable evidence of that supposed bliss in her old albums? If she found it, she'd only wallow in its loss. What was the point?

She leaned forward, grimly set aside her wedding album, then steeled herself and cracked the cover of the next book in the pile. A faded image of her and Meg looking into the camera, with identical expressions of teenage boredom, stared up at her.

Yeah. It looked like she was really going to do this now.

MORGAN WAS ALREADY deeply invested in the operatic tragedy of her evening when her phone began ringing a while later. She let the answering machine pick up. In her current frame of mind, she'd undoubtedly say something prickly to whoever it was, and cleaning up that mess on top of the current one held zero appeal.

After the beep sounded, Ruth's voice called out, "Morgan Terrrrrrry, quite contraaaaary?" She drawled out the ridiculous college nickname in an irritating singsong, and Morgan couldn't help sneering at the machine.

Why did she still maintain a landline, anyway? That had been something Chip insisted on. Not her.

There was a pause, and then, "Oh, for god's sake—stop screening me, woman."

Morgan scowled at the machine, its little red light blinking slowly while it recorded this nonsense.

"Like you had anywhere to be tonight," her friend continued wryly. "Even if, by some chance, you let yourself get roped into something, you're still too lame to actually *go.*"

Morgan rolled her eyes and crossed her arms over her chest, feeling sullen. Ruth didn't have to be so blunt.

And now, she was in a fight with a recording. This was her life now.

"Fine. Do your Eeyore routine. Depressing bitches aren't invited, anyway," Ruth said, then hung up.

Morgan glanced at her cordless phone, snug in its cradle on the kitchen counter, and then looked quickly back at the photo albums piled in front of her. She picked up her wine glass and drained it.

Then, exactly like Ruth had known she would, she dove for the kitchen, grabbed the receiver, and dialed.

When the call connected, Morgan didn't bother with preliminaries. She simply asked, "Invited where?"

"God, you are so predictable!" her friend huffed.

"Come on—where are you going?" Morgan was in no mood to be placatory. Ruth was lucky she was even playing along tonight.

"Forget it. You screened me. I'm not telling." The petulance was almost, *almost*, believable, too—but Morgan knew this woman too well. She could hear the excitement simmering underneath the words.

When Ruth stayed silent, Morgan muttered, "You are such a cow," then hung up once she heard her friend's gasp of outrage.

They'd done this dance a thousand times over the years, and its steps were as familiar as breathing. When Morgan stomped back to her couch, she was already smirking, and she brought the phone with her.

It rang right away. Without preamble, Ruth announced, "Nina and I are going back to Africa."

"Really? *When?*" Morgan didn't have to feign surprise—this was totally unexpected news.

"In two months. Are you coming, or what?" Ruth's impatience was intended to goad her into making a hasty decision, but Morgan had been down *that* road with her before. Many times, in fact.

"I can't afford it," Morgan bristled. Unfortunately, she also asked, "How long are you going for?"

Ruth snorted, clearly recognizing she now had the upper hand. "Four weeks. You know you want to."

A month-long safari—was Ruth insane? The very thought filled Morgan with dread. She immediately felt guilty about her anxiety, however. Someone in her position *should* do something like this. She had no husband to worry about anymore, and certainly no children. Morgan had a good job, a safe home, and few responsibilities.

If she hadn't turned into such a coward lately, this would be her big chance to finally do something interesting with her life—something like she'd envisioned when she'd been a wide-eyed college student, watching her wealthier, more intrepid friends jet off to semesters abroad and summer backpacking trips. Something her ill-fated marriage had taken away from her.

Morgan would have the added bonus of going with people who had been to their destination before, too. Ruth and Nina had both done Peace Corps stints in Africa, so they actually knew what they were getting into. They could show her the ropes.

"Hello?" Ruth's voice yanked Morgan out of her spinning thoughts.

"I'm here."

"Please, please come with us, Morgan. You could really use this."

She hated how her friend was treating this like a quick jaunt to Nantucket, instead of a swan dive off a high, sheer cliff. That's probably all it was for Ruth—nothing more than a blip in her long parade of awesomeness.

"Have you lost your mind?" Morgan asked, feeling every prick of her inadequacy like thorns in her skin. "Trekking around Africa after you two is hardly what I call a vacation."

"Maybe that's your problem," Ruth snapped. Her tone segued quickly into wheedling, however. "Listen, you're really sinking into a rut. You need to break out of it, before you get stuck there."

"Ruth, I have a *job*. How am I supposed to take off for a whole month?"

Ruth was exasperating, that's what she was. Morgan was a grown-up now, and adults didn't just up and leave whenever they felt like it.

Or did they? Wasn't that what Chip had done?

"Come on, Morgan," her friend argued. "You probably haven't taken a day off work since your freaking honeymoon. You probably have eight months of vacation time saved up. Call it a…I don't know. A sabbatical, or something."

Morgan actually had closer to three months of leave saved up, and she'd been banking it seemingly forever, in preparation for the baby's arrival. A baby who had never arrived, if they were being strictly factual about things.

"Okay, well—how am I supposed to pay for it?" Morgan countered. She paused, then asked, "How much does something like this cost, anyway?"

The panic beginning to ice her veins was so pervasive, Morgan was willing to grasp at anything to hold it off. Over the long tenure of their friendship, Ruth had cajoled her into doing a host of inadvisable things, but there had to be some way to hold the line against this newest scheme.

"We have a whole guided package for $6,500," the woman said, utterly matter of fact.

"What! Ruth, I just went through a divorce. I had to cough up a deposit for this stupid apartment, and I haven't even bought real furniture yet. You know I don't have that kind of dough," Morgan complained.

"It's a bucket list thing. Put it on a card."

Morgan sighed. Ruth's father must have been bankrolling this exploit for her. Given the woman's patchy employment history and his wealth, it tended to be the only viable explanation for these things.

"Besides," Morgan continued, "If I were going to rack up seven thousand dollars in debt, I'd go to Italy—or somewhere else in Europe. Somewhere I studied, for crying out loud!"

"Look, you only say that because you don't know what you're missing. Trust me, by next year you will be thanking me for this," Ruth said calmly. "This safari will be so much better than all your little nature calendars and pretty screensavers, Morgan. I promise—Africa will take your breath away."

The utter conviction in Ruth's voice made Morgan hesitate, because it often appeared when she was trying to paper over something tender underneath. Morgan needed to face the other factor at play here—her accidental discovery of Ruth's scary diagnosis last week.

Suddenly, this crazy trip took on a connotation it hadn't had before.

"Where exactly are you guys going?" Morgan heard herself ask.

"The works, babe! Victoria Falls, the Serengeti, Zanzibar, *blah, blah, blah*. Mostly Tanzania, though."

"In two months?"

"Yes."

"For four weeks?"

"*Yes!*"

Damn it, Ruth was starting to sound downright cheerful. That meant she knew she'd won.

She'd always been an infuriatingly pleasant winner.

"Ruth, I don't think—"

"Yup. Stop right there. Don't think. Just do it, Morgan. Just…*go*. Don't analyze everything to death. Don't *decide*. Just jump."

"Let me think about it."

"No. I am emailing you the itinerary and everything right now. All you have to do is call and give the travel agent your card number in the morning. I'll tell her to add you to the tour first thing."

"Ruth, honestly—I can't," Morgan protested—weakly, but it was still worth a shot.

"Yes, you can. I need you there. Call me tomorrow." And Ruth hung up.

I need you there. That was a low blow, and Morgan supposed Ruth knew it.

Somehow, against all odds, her evening had gone from bad to worse. Morgan flopped back on her rented couch and groaned.

No photo album foray was going to fix this disaster. She well and truly screwed.

SHE LAY AWAKE all night, paralyzed with indecision. How could she simply leave for so long without any fallout? It was so much money, too, when Morgan really didn't need another big expense on top of the ones she was already juggling.

While Morgan tossed and turned, a host of statistically unlikely terrors paraded themselves through her mind. There was plenty to consider. Diseases, dangers of all kinds—hell, Morgan could end up getting herself kidnapped, and then where would her sister Meg be? Stuck managing their folks alone when she hadn't even finished college yet?

It was exhausting, but by the time morning rolled around, Morgan was happy she could stop trying to fall sleep.

She got up, got ready, and headed into the office. And when the inevitable email arrived in her inbox a couple of hours later, she was too sleep-deprived to think very clearly or put up much of a fight. Morgan simply rolled over and let Ruth win. She was going to Africa.

If she was going to keep this from turning into a royal disaster, she had a ton to do—but the most important thing on the list was to make sure Meg would be okay without her.

Morgan shut her office door, then fished her cell phone out of her purse.

Her sister picked up on the first ring, sounding as excited as she always did. "Morgan!"

"Hey Meggie."

"Hey! How are you?"

Morgan couldn't seem to make her mouth work. She sat trying for so long that her little sister had to prompt her with, "Mo? What's up?"

Morgan decided on a tried and true line. "Yeah, so...I've got good news and bad news."

"Why do people always say that?"

"It's tradition. But listen, I wanted to tell you that I'm going away for a few weeks. A month, actually."

The fact that Meg laughed told Morgan all she needed to know about how her sister viewed Morgan's current state of mind.

"All those bad checks finally caught up with you, huh?" she joked.

"No, really. I'm serious. I just...I can't even believe it, but I just signed up to go on a safari with Ruth and her friend Nina. We leave in May."

Now it was Meg's turn to go quiet. Eventually, though, she managed a weak, "Morgan, that's...wow. *Wow*."

"I know."

"But...are you sure that's a good idea? I mean...a safari isn't exactly something they have over in Dorchester." What went unsaid, of course, was that Morgan might easily have gone around the bend for good this time.

"Meggie..." she sighed. Morgan was not even a little sure this was a good idea, but she'd never felt comfortable sharing her inner doubts with her little sister, and she wasn't about to start now. "I've got to do *something* to get back to normal. Short of taking up tennis, I've tried everything else."

"Yeah, but a safari? That's a big deal."

"Maybe *big* is what I need. I can't live like this anymore."

"I get that." Meg sighed too, then added, "I'm not sure whether that was the good news or the bad."

"The bad, you goofball. The good news is, I want you to come crash at my place while I'm gone."

It was an impulsive offer, but it had potential. Maybe by the time Morgan returned, Meg could accomplish what Morgan hadn't been able to—maybe she could make the utilitarian apartment feel more like a home.

"Really?" Her sister's squeak of elation was hard to miss, and Morgan was relieved that she'd called.

Her sister had been putting up a good front for months, pretending she liked subletting in that old house with her friends, when Morgan could tell it wasn't working out. Meg was not the college commune type, and the alternative—going home to live with their crummy parents for the summer—well…no one in their right mind was *that* type.

"Yes, really. Ditch the party people while I'm gone. *Mi casa, su casa,*" she said. "And you know what? You should come hang out this weekend, too. It'll be like old times."

Meg giggled, not even trying to resist. "Thanks, Mo. I'd love that."

Morgan was relieved it was that easy. Leaving her sister for so long had been the biggest thing bothering her, even if they barely saw each other these days. Morgan had been avoiding her, trying to hide how destroyed she was so Meg wouldn't worry.

For some reason, she still felt like she had to take care of her, even though Meg was basically a grown up now, and Morgan desperately needed to take care of herself if she ever expected to leave the last, miserable year of her life behind.

"Then it's settled. Pack up your stuff and I'll come get you Friday night. Okay?"

"Yeah. This is great!"

"Let's hope so. Just…don't ask me what could go wrong. I don't want to know."

AT THE END of the day, before shutting off her laptop and locking it in her desk, Morgan downloaded a stock photo of

Victoria Falls and made it her screen saver. The image was vibrant and lovely, a wonder of the world she'd assumed she'd never see.

She might die there, Morgan thought melodramatically, but at least they would have something better to put in her obituary than, *Alone, at her home, after a long and totally uneventful existence.*

Of course, if she didn't die, there would be the credit card bill to contend with, and the work backlog, and who knew what else.

That was the thing about friends like Ruth, though. At any given moment, you could love them or loathe them, because— just by being themselves and being in your life—they forced you to live, too.

Whether you were willing or not.

March 7

I didn't expect Ruth to kick a girl when she was down, but there I was, lying defeated in my gutter of a life, and instead of stepping over me or tossing me some pocket change, she took complete advantage of my inability to defend myself. I'm like the walking dead, animate but empty inside. Why did she choose this moment to make me pantomime adventurism and joie de vivre? She won't stop poking at me, refusing to let me blow away in the wind even though I'd like to. I hate her. And weirdly, I also love her—I love her for not giving up on me, even when I have.

Chapter Two

WHEN HIS OFFICE door banged open, Owen looked up to find Thom striding across the room. With a groan worthy of a hippopotamus, he dropped into one of the old wooden armchairs facing the desk and sent a fake grin Owen's way.

"Well, *good* morning, mate," Thom said, in a voice as cheerfully false as the smile.

"That seems bloody thick for 8 a.m.," Owen commented.

He sighed at the intrusion. His first hour in the Preserve office was *usually* his favorite: the air was warm and still but not yet humid, the street outside was quiet as a mouse, and the dust motes drifted lazily through the rays of sun that slanted through his window blinds.

Owen liked to drink his mug of coffee and let the caffeine slowly but efficiently clear the cobwebs from his brain while he decided what needed to get done that day. If all went well, the second hour at the office would then be his most productive.

That had been his routine ever since Owen had been promoted to head game warden, and it worked for him. He was a creature of habit. He didn't like to be disrupted.

He supposed he might have felt more charitable if it was anyone other than Thom interrupting his peace and quiet. Thom was an acquired taste at the best of times, but today he was almost vibrating with nervous energy, too high-strung to sit still or leave Owen alone for very long.

Best to get this over with. Owen raised an eyebrow and inclined his head toward the dog-eared file Thom held in his lap, suspecting it was the reason for this visit.

Thom grinned for real this time and said, "I knew you couldn't resist me."

"For the love of god. Let me see it or rack off."

His friend handed him the file and adopted a more serious demeanor. "That's the second dead Rathbone this month," he said.

"Where did the scouts find it?" Owen asked, flipping slowly through the folder and scanning the pages.

"B Quadrant. Odd place for poaching."

Owen frowned. "Yes, it is," he said, then set the file carefully to the side. "Listen, I've got to finish this report for TANAPA first, but I promise I'll look at it again as soon as I'm done."

One crisis at a time, he thought. If Owen couldn't convince the government to slide a little more funding their way, the Preserve was going to have bigger problems on its hands than figuring out why a few endangered gazelles had suddenly kicked the bucket.

"Maybe it's a new cat moving into the territory. A leopard or something. You want to head up there?"

Owen looked up. Thom's eyes were skittering around the room while he scratched absently at the birthmark on his forearm, then picked at his dirty fingernails. His casualness felt...studied, which was weird. Thom usually had no problem whatsoever slouching his way through life.

"Yeah, we should probably check it out," Owen told him. "Just let me take another look at the file before you ring up there."

Thom sprang up, satisfied with that, for now. "Aye, aye, Captain," he drawled, then let himself out.

Owen blew out a breath and massaged his forehead. When Thom had come over from Australia six years ago, he'd seemed at first like a kindred spirit—so much like the young men Owen had grown up with in New Zealand that he may as well have been a blast of home. These days, the man was different. He was cagey and hard to read.

It could be that Owen was the one who'd changed, though. Lately, he'd been feeling antsy and restless. He felt out of place, and that was new.

Hell, he'd moved to Tanzania eleven years ago, willingly leaving his safe park ranger job behind to dive into this land of sweeping panoramas and big game, and he'd never once doubted his decision. Not until recently, anyway. It made no sense.

For some strange reason, Owen suddenly couldn't stop thinking about home. The time that had elapsed since he'd left Christchurch had begun to feel like an enormous weight, and the number of family events he'd missed, an incalculable loss.

Owen missed his parents and his siblings. He missed the way his dad's sheep dotted the green hills of the family farm, and the way the sun sparkled on the water of Pegasus Bay. He felt alone, and not in a good way.

However, the fact that Thom had just dropped a new headache in his lap—to add to all the others already brewing—meant that Owen didn't exactly have time for a massive existential crisis right now.

Eventually, he'd have to shine a light on what was going on inside his head. He was going to have to decide what to do. *Later.*

OWEN DIDN'T GET another chance to look at Thom's file until late the next day, but it was in the back of his mind the whole time, stewing. Something about it was bothering him.

So, when he finally pulled the thing in front of him again, Owen paged through the sheaf of handwritten reports slowly. As usual, the scouts had filled out the mimeographed forms hastily, with all manner of writing implements, on all kinds of writing surfaces.

Each sheet had started out a crisp, pristine white when Thom had copied them, but the scouts did unspeakable things to the papers as they reported on their daily rounds of the Preserve. Some pages were crumpled around the edges, and some were stained and creased before being tucked away in field packs and pockets. By the time they made it back to the Preserve's main office in Victoriaville, they were a certified mess.

Owen was used to that, though. He generally gave these biweekly compilations only a cursory glance, relying on his scouts to highlight any serious anomalies for him with special missives.

This set of reports was different, though. For one thing, several scouts had found something peculiar about the most recent Rathbone death. In their reports, they described returning again and again to the site of the gazelle's demise, simply to "check things out again."

Interestingly, none of them seemed able to articulate *what*, specifically, was out of the ordinary with the dead animal. They all had hunches, though, and Owen knew better than to ignore those.

Evidently, Thom had noticed their unease, too, summarizing the scouts' concerns in a cover note that he'd slipped into the folder, as well.

Owen chewed on his lip and stared at the words, then spun his chair around to pull out the prior biweekly folder, and the one before that.

Lo and behold, the same amorphous questions hung over a carcass in those earlier reports, too. He hadn't thought much of it at the time, but two Rathbones biting the dust in a row could be a real problem.

Usually, it would've become clear by now if a new predator had expanded its territory into the park, or if something had pushed the humans who lived nearby into unusual behavior. So far, there was no indication that either of those things was a factor.

So, what was it? Could it be a new cat, as Thom had suggested, or some really ballsy—or really stupid—poachers? Neither theory seemed to fit.

The Rathbones were a dwindling subspecies, and the small herd that Owen and his team watched over was part of what made the Preserve so distinctive. But the gazelles weren't usually fodder for traditional medicines, and their hides looked so much like other breeds that they were unlikely to fetch a high price on the black market.

Thom was right, he decided. Owen was going to have to go up to B Quadrant and investigate what had happened for himself.

He paged through the folders again, shaking his head and frowning even more. *Strange, indeed.* He gathered everything up, pushed out of his chair, and walked to the door of his office.

Thom sat in his customary spot in the front room, his boots propped on the edge of his beat-up desk while he drank a bottle of soda and paged through a magazine. When Owen cleared his throat, he smiled sheepishly and tossed the magazine into a drawer.

He eyed the folders in Owen's hand, then catalogued his expression. "So, what do you think?" he inquired.

"You're right, we need to make a run up there. I could blow off losing one to bad luck. Not two, though."

Thom's ruddy, freckled face lost some of its good humor. "When do you want to go?"

"First thing tomorrow. Can you ring the field station and let them know we're coming?"

"You betcha." As quickly as it had left, the cheer returned.

Owen checked his watch. His housekeeper, Nadra, was running errands in town, and wouldn't be ready to head out with him for another forty-five minutes.

"When you're done, why don't you meet me across the street," he told Thom wearily. "I'm knackered and I want a beer."

"Thought you'd never ask," Thom grinned. "Give me ten minutes and I'm there."

Owen suspected he'd be the one buying again, but that was hardly a surprise. Thom made a decent salary, but he was perennially short of funds. It was supposedly part of the reason he'd come to Africa in the first place. He'd said he wanted to make a better life for himself than the one he'd left behind, but he'd never been inclined to get too specific, and Owen had never wondered enough to pry.

AN HOUR LATER, he *was* wondering, though. Owen sat outside Charlie's, the café across the street, nursing his warm beer and pondering what might have become of his erstwhile coworker while Nadra and Kisima, the office's cleaning woman, chatted by his truck.

He finished off his beer and called over to the ladies. "Be right back," he told them, then trotted across the packed dirt road to see what foolishness had waylaid Thom this time.

The Preserve office was, however, quite empty. Owen checked in every corner, but it didn't take long to scout out the place and determine that Thom, along with Thom's car, was gone. Completely miffed, he rang the man's cell and the call rolled directly into voicemail.

Owen locked up and walked slowly back to his truck, frowning. How had he missed Thom leaving? The bloke was rubbish at office work, but he wasn't that dodgy.

Owen thought back over the last hour. He'd been drifting in thought, sipping his beer and people watching, but he hadn't been so out of it that he wouldn't have noticed Thom's loping stride and gangly figure…*if* he'd left by the front door. And if he hadn't left by the front door, why hadn't he at least stopped by to say something?

Nadra was waiting for him by his truck, absently rearranging the folds of her colorful dress across her stomach. Owen held the door for her while she jumped up, but he was definitely peeved as he drove toward home—bumping over the pocked road a little too fast, and grumbling at the way the ruts were slowing them down.

Nadra gripped the passenger door for stability and eyed him with an arch expression. "What's the matter, boss?" she finally asked.

As it was meant to, his housekeeper's tone caught his attention. Owen looked over at her and smiled. She had a pointed way of calling him *boss* whenever he was getting too big for his britches, and it was probably one of the reasons they got along so well. Nadra kept him from taking himself too seriously, and clearly that was a necessity.

"Just stewing," he tried.

She snorted.

Owen had always assumed that if Nadra was this deft with adults, her four kids probably posed no problem at all for her.

Four kids and *counting*, perhaps. He'd been noticing some signs lately and had intended to ask if she was feeling all right— but then she'd headed him off with her own question, and he decided to hold off.

The thought of having to find a new housekeeper, yet again, made him want to groan. He couldn't face it tonight.

Instead, Owen cleared his throat and asked, "Okay, then how about this? Did you and Kisima happen to see Thom leave the office before?"

"You mean just now?"

"Yeah." Owen stared at the road ahead, the curving path cutting a narrow swath through the brown grass and brush.

She thought for a moment. "No, I don't think so. Was he in the office today?"

Owen nodded. "He was supposed to meet me at Charlie's, but he never showed. And, given how ecstatic he looked at the prospect of a pint…"

"You think it's strange."

"I do." Owen might have been able to overlook Thom's increasing laziness, or his new, unreadable moods—but he could never ignore the outright odd. He simply wasn't wired that way.

And Thom slipping out the back of the Preserve office, instead of coming over to have a beer like they'd planned? That was as odd as things got.

He and Nadra drove on in silence for a while before she said, "I don't understand. We were all standing out front."

"I know." None of it added up.

She fell quiet again, a frown knitting her brow. It probably should've made him feel better that she couldn't decipher it either, but it didn't.

"Do you think he's all right?" she asked finally.

"I don't know," Owen said at last. "I really don't."

And he thought, *Add it to the list.*

Chapter Three

WHEN MORGAN FINALLY staggered off the plane in Arusha, she was definitely a little loopy. It had taken the women more than twenty-four hours to travel from Boston to Tanzania, and she was so tired she couldn't think straight—or think, period.

In retrospect, their stopovers in Amsterdam and Zanzibar might not have helped the situation, but they'd certainly sounded like excellent ideas at the time. What did people say? Go big or go home? Ruth was determined to become the principle's living embodiment, and to drag Morgan and Nina along with her.

Morgan still couldn't believe that she'd gone through with this crazy plan, but when she stopped and eyed Mt. Meru— looming through the window of the low-slung arrivals building, its apex wreathed in drifts of clouds like a surreal dream—all the headaches seemed worth it.

Soon, however, she was stumbling ahead, swept along with everyone else from their flight. There was a knot of people waiting at the other end of the terminal, but it took several minutes for the signs they were waving to penetrate the fog of her sleep-deprived brain.

Eventually, Nina spotted a man holding a placard for their tour group, and the three of them headed over. The clutch of young Irishmen who'd flown with them from Amsterdam was already clustered around him, and their pronounced hangovers brought back memories that Morgan wished she could've slept through.

She dropped her bags nearby and tried not to breathe the funky smell wafting off them. Morgan didn't feel so terrific herself—she was sticky, hungry, tired, and irritable, and the combination did not exactly spell out *Vacation Goddess*.

But soon, a tall, strapping man arrived, and in a booming voice introduced himself as their tour guide, Conrad Twospeak. Two things were immediately clear: one, he relished his job, and two, he was undoubtedly well-rested. Morgan stared at him and felt herself die a little more inside.

Next to her, Ruth breathed, "Babes, we are *doing* this thing! Isn't he great? This is going to be amazing." Despite her grin, she, too, looked a bit peaked, but Morgan didn't bother mentioning it. Ruth would never admit it.

Nina, also wan, asked, "Can I get some sleep first? *Before* being amazed?"

Morgan sank down on top of her big, wheeled bag and dropped her head into her hands. The enormity of where she'd landed was beginning to sink in. She wasn't in New England right now, or even in Hawaii—she was in *Africa*.

What was she thinking? It wasn't like she could just change her mind and go home now. Well…she could, but even she wasn't that much of a loser. She was well and truly stuck on this trip.

Right on cue, Conrad belted out, "Welcome to Tanzania, people. Gather around and prepare to be amazed!"

Morgan—along with the Irish guys beside her—groaned. He just had to be the theatrical type.

SOMETIMES, WHEN MORGAN got this tired, her brain fell into a weird loop, like an old record player with a skipping needle. In the grip of exhaustion, her mind latched onto phrases or ideas, and replayed them over and over until she finally got some rest.

Morgan usually found it comforting, a mantra lulling her to sleep. The chant was often random and nonsensical—which, while admittedly odd, presented no problems. No worse than counting sheep, anyway.

Sometimes, though, the chorus was different. If Morgan was anxious, sad, or uncertain, that looping idea could end up being awful. Then, instead of drifting off into peaceful slumber, she'd lay awake wondering if something was really wrong with her.

The first day of a freaking month-long safari couldn't be a worse time for *that* to happen, but as Morgan slumped on her bag and stared at her boots, her brain began whispering, "*I lost my baby. I lost my baby. I lost my baby.*"

At one time, that might have meant Chip. Except, Morgan had not really lost her ex-husband, so much as willfully ousted him. This was about her real baby, and the horrible refrain in her head would have made her cry yet again if she weren't so numb—if she hadn't already cried so many great wracking sobs that she was probably as arid as a desert for all eternity now.

Morgan lifted her head and glanced around, afraid that her friends would notice her mood, but Ruth and Nina were poring over an itinerary that Conrad had handed out, and the Irish guys were propped against each other, looking green.

She swallowed thickly and let herself remember. Last year, when she'd first realized she was pregnant, she'd greeted the news with mixed emotions.

On the one hand, she'd been aghast—they'd rarely spent time together that didn't feel forced, so it was a wonder that they'd managed to get knocked up at all. How could the awkward mechanics that had passed for their sex life have resulted in something so monumental? Plus, she and Chip had definitively *not* wanted to conceive yet. She knew he was going to lose it.

On the other hand, however, Morgan had stupidly allowed herself a tiny measure of hope. She'd thought it would be good for them. They'd intended to have children someday, after all, and a baby would force them to slow down and reconnect to what was important. Being parents could help them resurrect their relationship and return to being a couple that had once loved each other enough to marry.

Hope was a treacherous thing, though, and it hadn't helped Morgan find the right words to say to him. She'd agonized for weeks, dreading what Chip would do, then stuttered it out apologetically, like she'd somehow shamed herself for failing to remain childless.

Chip had played his role perfectly, hadn't he? Morgan gripped the handles of her carry-on and snorted quietly to herself. He'd been the very picture of a betrayed male—wild and irrational, stomping around after work with an inch of bourbon sloshing in his glass, bellowing and berating her.

He'd dragged out the inevitable, alternating between rage and cold silences while he made up his mind. The longer it had gone on, the more Morgan's tension had grown, curdling into an awful poison in her soul.

She'd convinced herself it was going to harm that poor fetus. For weeks, she'd walked into her checkups on eggshells, waiting to hear that something had gone wrong—but somehow the baby survived those first days.

At the four-month mark, Morgan could no longer button her suit pants, and Chip finally packed up his own suits and moved out. Soon after, the doctor had informed her that the baby was dead. She'd made it sound like a common thing—like babies simply stopped growing, stopped developing, stopped *becoming* all the time.

However, Morgan had known that they had killed it with their bitterness. It made no logical sense, but the certainty had been there, deep within her.

The rest was still a blur. At some point, she'd signed papers agreeing to the divorce, then laid in bed watching the sunlight move in slanted rectangles across the walls of her room. Morgan had suffered through both losses alone, the emotional and physical pains so intertwined that they were impossible to tell apart.

I lost my baby, I lost my baby, I lost my baby, went the refrain in her head. She stood up abruptly. She had to get out of here.

Why were they all still sitting around? Morgan scanned the tour group and wondered if she'd missed something while she'd been stewing. Everyone else looked as weary as she felt, though, zoning out while Conrad paced near the doors and hollered into his phone.

Last year, by the time Morgan made it through her miscarriage and divorce, she'd felt completely ruined, inside and out. She still did. Maybe—even after gallivanting halfway around the globe on a safari—she would never feel whole again.

She was standing next to luggage that was filled with the ridiculous purchases of someone with too much money and not enough sense, she was about to see a part of the world that many people only dreamed of, and she might as well be an automaton for all the excitement she felt.

Naturally, Conrad—curse his cheerful soul—chose that moment to march over and marshal his troops. "All right, everyone! Up you get. Time to board our transport and be on our way!"

There was a collective groan as everyone staggered to their feet. Their tour guide was not impressed.

"None of that," he scolded. "You're paying me good money to be here. Chop, chop!"

Morgan blew out a breath and thought of the cheesy inspirational posters that had hung in her old office's break room. *Dreams Don't Work Unless You Do,* one had said, and the other, *The Journey is the Reward.* She had a feeling she was about to learn different lessons than those.

OUTSIDE, THE PORTER loaded their gear into an ancient minibus that looked like it could have had air conditioning at some point in its lengthy past, but definitely didn't currently.

Through it all, the man managed to smile at Morgan with startling frequency and enthusiasm, while she tried—unsuccessfully—to avoid eye contact.

Finally, he simply planted himself directly in front of her and placed his hands on his chest. He announced, "I am Laurent," so sweetly, that she just couldn't bring herself to be mean.

She smiled back, and told him, "Nice to meet you. I'm Morgan."

Laurent the porter nodded and grinned again, eyeing her up and down. "You are a very beautiful American." He stroked his hips, abruptly turning lewd. "Call me. We can go party."

Laurent then pressed a grimy and dog-eared business card into her hand. Morgan pocketed it and looked up at the sky, as if someone, somewhere up there, might suddenly have mercy on her.

She hoisted her tired, aching carcass into the bus, and told her giggling friends, "Don't say a word." Across from her, three of the Irishman revived with unfortunate timing and burst into bawdy laughter.

And so it begins, Morgan thought. *Looking* so *promising, too.*

AS THE BUS trundled down the crowded streets of Arusha, and then on into the outskirts of town, Ruth and Nina fell asleep, and Morgan was left with her memories once more.

It seemed pitiful now, the way she'd festered on her couch for so long after everything that had happened. She'd been disconnected and depressed and had felt lightyears away from any dream she'd ever aspired to. All she could manage was looking out that window and wondering if life was passing her by.

But now, surrounded by the unfamiliar, Morgan was perfectly willing to let life take a detour around her. There didn't seem to be any harm in continuing to exist on autopilot in this corner of the world where so much was directed at survival and not consumption.

She was even more disconnected here than she'd been in Boston—from the languages, the cultures, and the landscape. The streets passing outside the bus window were an elaborate montage of sights, smells, and tastes, but they didn't have anything to do with her.

As far as she could tell, this trip was going to require almost nothing of her at all. For the next month, Morgan would only have to wake, eat, look, and then sleep again—whenever and wherever she was told. Africa wasn't going to connect her to the living, breathing world any more than Boston had, even though Ruth insisted it would.

The only thing this trip could do was get rid of the constant, painful reminders of her failure to achieve a normal, grown-up existence at home. *Home.* The thought of it was already as totally alien as the country she was barreling through.

Morgan tried, but for the life of her, she couldn't remember the color of that rented sofa in her new apartment. She could barely recall the name of the market, or the stores where she liked to shop. Out of context, their names seemed like comical, made-up brands from some alternate cinematic universe—not the routine things she'd taken for granted a week ago.

Was it normal to feel like this? Morgan had been in purgatory in America, and she was in purgatory here, but at least in Africa, she was relatively anonymous. It was a staggering relief.

Probably because there'd been nothing anonymous about the way her marriage had tanked. The judge had been a friend and the lawyers, family—and it seemed as if all their acquaintances had gossiped for weeks when the "perfect couple" they'd known for years had broken up.

All things considered, she and Chip shouldn't have fought tooth and nail like they had. Separating as quickly and as painlessly as possible ought to have been their greatest mutual goal, but instead, they'd made it a grueling endurance test from which Morgan had barely walked away.

Lesson learned.

Since then, it felt like even her bones were exposed to an icy wind. Sometimes, Morgan worried that her wounded soul would end up cannibalizing her from the inside out if she couldn't pull herself together soon.

Cue the reckless, Hail-Mary trip to Africa.

From the front of the bus, Conrad drawled, "*Africa,*" with a dramatic flourish. "Who's ready to fall in love with her?"

Nina muttered, "Right now?" and even Ruth—well-meaning and oblivious Ruth—snorted in amusement.

June 3

I've awoken from a terrible dream to find myself a million miles from home—so far away, that I couldn't describe it if I tried. Some days, I'm not even sure I am awake. I just ride along in the back of this rickety bus and watch life pass me by through the grimy windows.

I don't feel a thing. I can't feel a thing. Why am I here? Why hasn't someone put me out of my misery yet? And why, with so many people all around me, do I feel so alone?

Chapter Four

IN THE FRONT room of the Preserve office, Owen sat in Thom's chair and watched the sky gradually grow brighter through the window blinds.

The birds, so raucous in the hour before sunrise, were already beginning to quiet down. To pass the time, he tried to pick out the calls of a few—*mourning doves*, he thought, some *cisticola*, and maybe a *boubou*.

Not like it mattered. Owen was hungry, impatient, and irritable, and it was only getting worse the longer he waited.

He dropped his head and stared at the scarred wood desktop, and his eyes fell on a bent fishhook resting next to the dish of paper clips on the blotter.

It made him think of the last time he'd been fishing with Thom, who'd insisted they go when problems at the Preserve had begun to vex him.

"You're a tad tense, mate," Thom had said, that half-drunk smirk and tongue-in-cheek tone speaking volumes about how ridiculous he found him.

Still, the memory made Owen smile. For so long, it had been pleasant to have a compatriot here—a partner in crime, so to speak. Only now, in the face of what was perhaps a real crime against the Rathbones, the turn of phrase made him flinch.

"*Damn it,*" he grumbled, hoisting himself up and walking out the front door. "He's probably sleeping one off."

Owen stood outside with his hands on his hips for a few moments but didn't hear a sound—not a snapping twig or a clearing throat, or even a beat-up car approaching.

He sighed and weighed his options. If he waited here (maybe indefinitely) for Thom, he might have to postpone the trip up to B Quadrant until tomorrow—and whatever evidence remained near those Rathbone carcasses would grow even more degraded.

Owen could try to go fetch him, he supposed, but Thom's place was several kilometers outside of town. Even if he left now, it would still take him a while to get there, roust Thom, and then haul back to the road that led to the northeastern edge of the Preserve.

If they hurried, they might be able to make the bulk of the trip before midday, but they probably wouldn't hit the field station closest to where the gazelles had died until late afternoon. Which likely meant, no hiking out to the sites themselves until tomorrow morning.

However, something about Thom's odd disappearance the evening before still nagged at him. What if Owen got all the way out to Thom's and he wasn't even there? Then, the trip would definitely be a wash for today.

He looked around the empty street, debating about what to do. He expected the trip to be fairly routine, but the situation in B Quad still required a two-person team. If he couldn't make the foray alone and Thom was a poor bet at this stage, who else could accompany him?

After some though, Owen at last remembered Joseph Teleki. The man had scouted for the Preserve a while back, before moving down to Victoriaville for family reasons about two years ago. He still stopped into the office to chat occasionally, and he'd always struck Owen as a practical guy.

While he wouldn't be a barrel of laughs on a long road trip, he'd certainly get the job done. *If* he was available, that was, and *if* he was still living at the place Owen remembered—conveniently right on his way.

He had nothing to lose by trying. Mind made up, Owen went inside and straightened up the front office, then locked the door and walked out to his truck. He checked his packs one last time. He'd brought enough gear for two people, but the scouting station could fill in with any other necessities if Joseph needed them.

So, Owen slid behind the wheel, turned the key in the ignition, and drove to the edge of town, where a packed dirt track led out to the Teleki property. Before making the turn, though, he hit the brakes and put the truck in park.

A lot could happen to a man in this part of the world, especially if he didn't keep his wits about him. What if something had happened to Thom—something more than forgetfulness or slacking off? What if his friend was sick or hurt? As far as Owen knew, no one but him would even think to check on the guy.

He gritted his teeth, weighing whether to scrap everything, go now, or to wait and see if he heard from Thom later. Owen could swing by his place on the return trip in a few days, but if Thom needed help now, that might be too late.

"*Damn it.*" He hit the steering wheel, blew out a frustrated breath, and threw the truck into gear, turning left toward Thom's. He'd never forgive himself if he didn't at least check.

As he drove, Owen watched the sky and tried not to dwell on how light it was getting. He was probably crazy to attempt this, but he had to try. He'd already wasted a week after those first reports had come in.

At this point, there might not be a whole lot left to see, but if there was, Owen would find it. If Thom couldn't rally and come with him, he'd just have to find it with Joseph.

BY THE TIME Owen reached Thom's bungalow, the morning was already turning hot and humid. He parked under a tree and got out of the truck, and immediately had to wave away the swarm of gnats that surrounded him, sticking to his face and the sweat on his arms.

He'd never seen so many out here before. Thom wasn't near any bodies of water, which probably meant he should be checking around for a dead animal or something—but Owen was a little surprised the man hadn't already taken care of that.

As he looked around, his misgivings grew. The place looked deserted, with no sign of Thom's car and the house standing dark and quiet. Owen checked his watch and walked closer, listening carefully.

By now, pretty much anyone in these parts would be up and about for the day, even someone sleeping off a bender. It was too damn muggy to sleep comfortably, especially without air conditioning, and Owen knew for a fact that Thom did not have air conditioning. He barely had a fan that worked.

He climbed the stairs, his field boots clomping heavily on the wood, and pounded on the frame of the rickety screen door.

"Thomas! Hey mate, you in there?"

The birds called high in the trees and the insects buzzed in the underbrush, but inside the bungalow, there wasn't a sound.

He rattled the handle. "Thom? Time to go, mate. Wake up!" Again, nothing.

Owen pulled open the screen and tried the doorknob, but it was locked. He walked down the stairs and glanced around, then skirted the small building. At the back, he dragged a bucket from the shed over to the window, upended it, and climbed up.

Thom's window was grimy and cracked, but Owen smeared away some of the muck with the side of his fist so he could peer inside.

The back bedroom where his friend usually slept was dim and still. Messy, but nothing out of the ordinary.

The bed was rumpled, its utilitarian sheets and pillows stark white in the gloom. Thom wasn't in there.

Owen stepped down and carried the pail to the side of the house. He stood on it again to look in the main room's window.

Sometimes, he knew, Thom had enough to drink that he passed out on his couch, his gawky limbs dangling off at awkward angles and the radio crackling softly in the background.

The living room was empty today, though, and somewhat neater than usual. None of this felt right.

The hair on the back of Owen's neck was standing up, and a shiver worked its way down his spine. He glanced uneasily around the small yard.

Something was watching him.

He didn't think Thom was here, which was probably a good thing because suddenly, Owen felt the need to get out of there fast. Every instinct he possessed was tingling with warning.

He left the pail where it was and stepped briskly back to his truck. He fumbled with his keys, dropping them into the dirt twice before managing to get his door open.

Owen turned the truck on, winced at the way the engine seemed to reverberate through the trees, then drove a little too quickly back out to the main road. From there, he turned right and tore away from whatever had caused that atavistic fight-or-flight response in him.

It took some maneuvering, but Owen eventually got himself headed in the right direction, and he was hoping to find Joseph's place sooner rather than later.

He'd feel a lot more comfortable with some company right now. Owen was not entirely sure what had just happened, but he couldn't remember the last time he'd felt such a visceral urge to flee. It was almost a little disgraceful how spooked he'd been.

There'd been danger at Thom's house. Owen would bet his life on it. The question was—why?

OWEN EVENTUALLY SPOTTED what he hoped was still the Teleki spread, maybe twenty kilometers past where he'd thought it would be.

The land had been mostly left alone, except close to the house—where the vegetation looked neater and more orderly than if it hadn't been touched. The trees and shrubs were pruned, and the grasses cropped short. Birds and smaller animals could still make homes there, but more dangerous wildlife wouldn't want to linger.

The house itself was a compact, raised concrete structure, with a newer-looking addition extending off the back and large trees clustered around, lending their shade. Everything seemed tidy and well-kept.

Owen approved.

He turned in and parked at the mouth of the driveway, so he wouldn't risk running over one of their chickens—or worse, a child—before he'd even greeted anyone.

As he strode up the path, he caught the sound of goats out back, and spotted movement off to the side. He called out a friendly, "*Hodi!* Good morning!"

His presence sufficiently announced and noted, he stopped and waited for whoever lived here to acknowledge him.

In short order, a rapid-fire discussion took place inside the house, followed by an amiable-looking young woman opening the door and greeting him.

"Good morning," she called.

"Morning. How are you?"

"*Nzuri.* And you?"

"Fine, thanks. Sorry to pop by without calling first," Owen said. "I'm Owen Hargreave, from the Preserve office in Victoriaville. Is this still the home of Joseph Teleki, by any chance? Used to be a scout for us a few years back?"

"It is," she replied. "Shall I tell him you're here?"

"Please."

She turned and looked into the house, then stepped aside when Joseph came out the door. He hurried down the steps and greeted Owen warmly.

"Mr. Hargreave, it's been too long. To what do I owe the pleasure?"

"Please, call me Owen. And I'm sorry to just drop in on you like this."

"No worries. But let's have a seat over here in the shade," Joseph said, leading him to a bench by the side of the house. "Can I get you something to drink?"

"I'm fine. I've got water in the truck."

Joseph eyed him, and his smile fell away. "Is everything alright?"

"Not exactly. I'm in a bit of a fix." Owen glanced up at the sun's position and checked his watch. It was already so late. "I didn't know who else to ask," he admitted.

"Ask what?" Joseph watched him, looking concerned.

"To be honest, I need a scout. Badly. I'm on my way up to B Quadrant right now, actually."

"Alone?" Joseph frowned, his disapproval evident.

"Not if I can help it. We've got some Rathbones corking off for no reason and I need to run up there to look into it." He took a deep breath, trying to gauge the other man's reaction, then barreled on. "You remember Thom Hannity, from the office?"

Joseph nodded.

"He was supposed to come with me, but he's missing in action at the moment."

The scout studied his face, but his expression didn't give much away. "You don't know where he is?"

"No, I don't," Owen replied. Something in the other man's tone made him wonder, though. "Do you?"

Joseph rose to his feet and looked at Owen oddly. "No," he said firmly, "But I can help you." He turned and walked toward the house, calling over his shoulder, "Wait here while I dig out my gear. I can be ready to go shortly."

"I'd hate to leave your family in the lurch. Are you sure?"

"Absolutely."

Owen sagged with relief. "Thanks, mate. Much appreciated, believe me."

"Don't mention it," Joseph replied, then disappeared inside.

Chapter Five

ANOTHER DAY DAWNED on the safari and with it, another outing in the hope of seeing big game. Morgan tried to muster up the proper degree of excitement, but they'd already endured plenty of discomfort on their hikes to date and there was no reason to assume today would be any different.

She snorted to herself. *Discomfort*, indeed. Grossly understating the many complaints that weeks of trudging across Tanzania had engendered might as well have been their new hobby.

She, Nina, and Ruth had somehow morphed into a gaggle of ultra-polite grandmothers—speaking delicately of topics such as intestinal distress, biting creatures, and aches and pains.

All of them probably would have preferred to curse a blue streak, but the gracious demeanors of their guides had somehow worked this odd trick on them—it felt shameful to be whining when the tour employees were working so much harder without a single peep of protest.

Besides, the group already had several people filling the *Ugly American* roles. It seemed like overkill to add three more.

Regardless, Conrad had arranged today's excursion with the expectation that all his group members would attend, even though he wouldn't be joining them. So, here Morgan was.

At the moment, the guide Conrad had left in charge—who'd introduced himself as Modest, though he appeared to be anything but—was organizing what would remain of their base camp, as well as directing the packing of what would come into the bush with them for the next few days.

He'd already carefully explained how they'd be expected to eat and drink during the trek. Morgan guessed that was to avoid any problems with dehydration or heatstroke, and naturally they'd all agreed. They'd been trained into very good little soldiers.

But now, as they stared balefully at their breakfast plates, she wondered if compliance would even be possible. Déo, the porter who had filled in as cook for them that morning, stomped over to glower at them.

"We leave soon. Eat," he said.

Unfortunately, Ruth and Nina picked that moment to launch a mini-rebellion—or at the very least, test the man's English skills.

Nina asked, "What is this lovely breakfast, anyway?"

"Is good," Déo replied stoutly. "You eat."

"Is it a buzzard?" Ruth inquired, poking at a grayish-brown lump with her fork.

"Yes," the porter confirmed.

"Or maybe it's a sock monkey," Nina said. Her tone was cheerfully sweet, but *sweet* coming from Nina could be deadly ground.

"Stop it," Morgan hissed, scowling at her and receiving an epic glare in return.

"Don't mind me," Ruth announced, not dissuaded in the least, "I'm going to eat my yarn animal now."

Déo looked momentarily puzzled, but to his credit, he didn't lose heart. "Yes. Is good! You eat now."

Morgan shook her head at her friends, disappointed in their antics. The mean-spirited game was beneath them—especially given the years they'd both worked in neighboring countries.

"Quit acting like spoiled brats," Morgan told them.

Nina stuck out her tongue, but Ruth serenely gestured at Morgan's plate. "Perhaps you'd like to go first, darling," she said. "Put up or shut up."

Morgan shrugged and gingerly took a bite, then tilted her head and frowned when she realized that the food truly was unidentifiable. It could even, she supposed, have been made from a knitted puppet.

Déo nodded encouragingly at her. Ruth and Nina waited to see if Morgan could swallow before they waded in themselves. While she tried to transform the mouthful into something she could actually force down her gullet, Morgan looked at them and they looked at her.

Déo wandered off, apparently satisfied that the women would now be following orders appropriately.

"Well?" Nina demanded, once he was gone.

"Don't do it," Morgan advised. "Starvation would be better."

THE EXPEDITION ITSELF was their most difficult yet. Morgan and Nina only got halfway up the mountain before calling it quits and begging a guide to bring them back to camp—and they only made it that far because they'd had a contraband flask of whiskey and secret protein bars stashed in their pockets.

Ruth, who had eventually capitulated and eaten what she was told to, managed to complete the full circuit with a only few of the other tourists. However, when they returned a couple of days later, her face was gray.

She tried to make light of it, asking, "Who doesn't love a big helping of misery on their toast?" before she headed straight to bed. Morgan thought about those test results she'd seen back in Boston and worried, though.

Nevertheless, she and Nina were more than happy to crowd into Ruth's tent that evening to *ooh* and *aah* over her photographs, and to wish they'd been able to muster up the fortitude to accomplish what their friend had.

Ruth looked on, eating her dinner quietly, and seeming—for the first time in Morgan's memory—completely uninterested in making anyone else happy.

She looked like Morgan felt.

How long had Morgan been wandering through life as a virtual robot, anyway? It was as if the recording had skipped or been inexpertly spliced somewhere along the way.

There was a baby, and then there wasn't. There was a husband, and then no one. Once, there had been Morgan, and then...

Then. Then came this barely alive shade, sitting in a tent half a globe away from home, eating strange things in the company of strangers. She looked around and thought maybe she ought to be making sense of this—that maybe it wasn't safe to not pay attention here.

However, the truth was that she really didn't care whether she died here with Modest, Déo, and their maybe-meat. Her little sister Meg might miss her, sure, but hardly anyone one else would even realize she was gone. Morgan was a failure and a joke—and that was all.

June 13

I used to marvel that there could be so many shades in the palette of human skin. My skin fell on the paler side, but there were so many others, notching tone by tone toward another, darker end. It was interesting, but not problematic to me—which makes sense, given my position of privilege.
I had enough self-awareness to recognize that not all immigrants came to my country willingly, but at the same time, I was naïve enough to believe

that the existence of interracial couples and biracial children all around me meant that things were changing for the better.

Surely, my people were evolving and becoming better humans if they could find common ground and unity—even love—after such a horrifying history of enslavement and oppression?

Being white in America, I had the luxury of believing it was that simple.

In Africa, though, I'm not a member of a privileged majority. Here, my lack of melanin is not an asset, but an infirmity. I'm a pale ghost, worthy of ridicule—a weakness in this formidable land of strength.

In Africa, it seems, I am not only a symbol of oppression, I'm an anomaly—a creature that doesn't belong. Perhaps that was the case at home, too, but I just never knew it.

I've realized, however, that we should all be so lucky as to experience this humbling sense of Otherness. After feeling it, I think the injustices we used to ignore would no longer be allowed to stand.

THEIR CONVOY OF trucks had been bumping along a rutted track through the undergrowth for miles now, and Morgan was already beginning to feel the now-familiar aches starting up.

That morning, Ruth and Nina had lobbied hard for Morgan to come on one final outing with them. Eventually, she'd had to concede, albeit wearily, that not seeing any leopards would have left things somewhat incomplete.

She was regretting that decision now, however. What were leopards, after all, except panthers in a different color scheme? Did the group really need to see every cat bigger than a tabby here? And for Pete's sake, why couldn't the elusive leopards hang out somewhere more accessible?

Only Ruth seemed content and calm as the trucks pushed deeper into the trees along the river. Morgan and Nina were tense and grouchy—along with everyone else, it seemed.

Somehow, Morgan had gotten through three whole weeks of this trip, and the break from Boston had been—much like Ruth predicted—good for her.

Courtesy of Conrad's staggering enthusiasm and thoroughness, she'd seen so many of Tanzania's natural wonders that they were beginning to run together into a big, lovely blur. Even the animals—who'd been so amazing to behold at the beginning of the trip—were starting to bore her.

While Morgan thought she might never visit a zoo again, Conrad continued to maintain his cheerful demeanor no matter what befell them. She was in awe and, frankly, starting to hate him a little for it.

Somewhere amidst all that, though, she'd found peace. Morgan was ready to return home now. She wanted to soak in her own bathtub with loads of hot water and nice-smelling bodywash, sleep in her own bed for about ten years straight, and then then figure out what came next for her. It was time.

WITH EACH BOUNCE and roll of the truck tires, Morgan could feel her neck and shoulders and jaw locking tight, while she tried in vain to brace herself against the door.

She could tell she'd have a splitting headache before long, one that the oppressive humidity and persistently unfamiliar food would only exacerbate. Even her butt was beginning to hurt.

And of course, an odd refrain was stuck on replay in her head. Over and over, her brain murmured *Home is for lovers. Home is for lovers.*

Yeah—because she hadn't been miserable enough.

Morgan wished home was as easy to procure as a wink and a smile but suspected that was too much to hope for.

When they finally came to a stop, she was tired, cranky, and sore—and in no mood to sit silently in some truck forever, waiting for a mysterious animal that might never show.

Nina had been complaining for half an hour that she needed to go to the bathroom, and even Ruth—seizer of all opportunities—begged for a chance to stretch her legs. Fortunately, with Conrad off the roster again, the guides were exasperated—but not terribly inclined to be strict.

No one seemed to be expecting leopards, anyway.

The groups in the other two trucks decided to stay put, so the guides from their truck armed themselves casually, then handed Morgan, Ruth, and Nina three old and ineffectual-looking rifles to carry. They didn't bother to ask if they knew how to shoot, and it was the first time on the trip anyone had done it.

Morgan wondered whether it could possibly be standard procedure.

"Don't point at people," one man warned, prompting Ruth and Nina to snort at each other.

With bored waves, the guides moved slowly into the forest, the three women clustered close behind them. Gradually, the trucks disappeared, obscured by the dense underbrush.

The guides turned their backs while Nina crouched in a large clump of bushes to relieve herself, and when she returned, they started back to the convoy.

"Do we have to?" Ruth wheedled. "There's nothing out here but a bunch of birds. No one will care if we walk in a little circle, will they?"

The men conferred in Swahili for a bit, then nodded reluctantly. They set off on a path that seemed to sketch a broad circle around the trucks, hacking at low branches and watching the trees all around them.

Morgan trudged after them, staring at the dirt so the brim of her hat would block out the glaring sun. She was numb with fatigue, hungry, and her head throbbed—and she didn't give two shits about the dangers that were undoubtedly teeming in the forest around her.

At the beginning of the safari, she'd been so conscious of the threats lurking around every blade of grass and tree trunk—of the insects, reptiles, parasites, and carnivores just waiting to do her harm.

Sometimes, every nerve-ending had tingled and each fine hair on Morgan's body had stood on end, when her subconscious had picked up on dangers her eyes couldn't see. It was almost as if her emotional disassociation had somehow thrown her body's visceral fight-or-flight response into overdrive.

She was inured to all that now. Morgan couldn't care less what wanted to bite her, sting her, or maul her. She just wanted to leave—and that made the ostentatious beauty crowding in on all sides offensive, somehow.

She'd only endured this last jaunt because it brought her one step closer to her ultimate goal—putting the trip of a lifetime firmly in her rearview.

All day, she'd been fantasizing about returning to the lodge, so she could begin packing up for the long trip back to the States. Even Paris, where Ruth and Nina had decided to stop for a couple of days on the way home, held no allure for her.

Morgan wondered whether Boston had grown unfamiliar in her absence—that sterile apartment she hadn't lived in long enough to fill, the empty bed, the handful of possessions, the quietly humming air-conditioning.

It didn't matter. None of it mattered.

After a while, they turned back toward the safety of the trucks, presumably to wait out the leopard family that supposedly lived nearby. In her haze, Morgan heard Ruth announce cheerfully, "I'd like to partake of the facilities, too, if no one minds."

The request barely registered. They'd been joking about the stilted way they made these type of requests for weeks, and her friend probably would've sounded the same if she'd been asking for a spare kidney. Morgan hardly bothered listening anymore.

Once Ruth explained to the guides what she'd meant, they rolled their eyes, but they did stop their progress and wave toward some bushes.

"Watch for snake," one muttered.

While they all turned their backs again, Morgan searched through the trees for some sign of the dirty white Range Rovers, and the rest of the tour group.

The familiar fog of an impending migraine was settling in, so she'd trusted the guides to keep them oriented, but now she couldn't decide if the convoy ought to be close by or not. Morgan had a fuzzy grasp of the size of the trucks, the distance they'd moved away from them, and how much time had passed. Surely, they'd circled most of the way back by now?

Morgan's sluggish brain wrestled ineffectually with the particulars while she stared off into space. Her headache had her disoriented, and she couldn't seem to come to any logical conclusions.

Luckily, no one was relying on her to lead the way. She was firmly in the follower category and intended to stay there.

A loud report sounded suddenly behind them, accompanied by an oddly bright flash. Morgan grabbed for the arm of the guide closest to her, instantly terrified. He wrenched his sleeve away, pushing her and Nina toward one of the other men, while he shouted in Swahili to the third.

They crashed through the undergrowth, heading toward the sound, instead of away. Not wanting to be left behind, Morgan grabbed Nina and tried to follow.

The guide beside them pulled them back, holding the women in place but refusing to meet their eyes. Morgan and Nina craned their necks, trying to see the others—one of whom appeared to be staring at the ground in horror while he yelled into his two-way radio.

When he finally paused long enough to listen, loud static crackled through the trees. He took something from his pocket and bent to hand it to the guide squatting near his feet.

Morgan and Nina tried to get free of the man restraining them, peppering him with questions he stoically refused to answer. He still wouldn't look at them.

Suddenly, Nina's face turned the color of paste. Her mouth worked silently for a moment before she finally blurted out, "Oh god. *Ruth*. Ruth? Morgan, where is Ruth?"

Chapter Six

B Y THE TIME Owen and Joseph decided to stop for food, the field station they were heading for was still pretty far away. Owen had hoped to reach it well ahead of supper, but Thom's disappearance had blown that to hell.

Unfortunately, Joseph had spent his scouting days in a different quadrant of the park, so he wasn't familiar with the outlying villages here on the eastern side, and Owen hadn't been up this way in quite a while.

If he'd been alone, he'd have pressed on—but he already felt indebted to Joseph for agreeing to come along on such short notice. As it was, he'd be keeping the man from his home and family for almost three full days. He hated to inconvenience him further.

And so, rather than waste time they didn't have, Owen rang up the head scout in the area for suggestions. Instead of listing local cafés, however, the man told them to cut west and cross into the Preserve.

The scouts that patrolled the region would be checking in for a meal and a shift change soon, at an outpost about fifteen minutes from their current location. He explained that the men were bound to have enough food to share, and that it would be well worth the detour.

Joseph warmed to the idea immediately. "It will give us a chance to hear their accounts of the Rathbone deaths," he said, "before we check out the sites ourselves."

"The rapidly deteriorating sites," Owen pointed out.

Still, he made for the nearest Preserve entrance, amused as he always was by the quaintly British predilection for tidiness that gave the park its ridiculous borders—these squared-off quadrants that defied actual topography but looked smart on paper, and the firm schedules that revolved around tea time.

Tea that they'd taken at great cost to one of their other colonies—*not* so amusing.

So few of these little pockets of colonial hubris were left in Africa, and that was for the best. Owen had never understood how the Preserve had survived as long as it had in English hands. It didn't seem just, but it also didn't seem sporting to point that out to the people signing his paychecks.

Someday, though, when he was on his way out, he just might.

While Owen navigated the narrow lane, his thoughts circled back to Joseph's odd tone at the mention of Thom this morning. It'd been curious, to say the least.

As casually as he could manage, he mused, "I can't imagine where Thom got to this morning."

Joseph rode shotgun in silence, glancing at him only briefly.

"Damnedest thing, don't you agree?" Owen prodded.

His stoic passenger raised his eyebrows, but didn't seem inclined to comment on that salvo, either.

It appeared subtlety would get him nowhere, and if he wanted to know the man's thoughts, he'd have to dive right in. Joseph might try to stonewall him, but perhaps he'd let some small detail slip in the effort.

"So, mate," he inquired, "What do you think? Do you know him well?"

"Not as well as you." The former scout paused, weighing his words carefully. "Though our paths have crossed periodically over the years."

"Really?"

"Mm-hmm."

Owen wanted to groan. This wasn't going well. "How so?" he prodded.

Joseph looked at him quizzically. "At the Preserve. Obviously."

"Of course," Owen nodded, like that explanation had cleared it all up.

In reality, he was more puzzled than ever. If the only time Joseph saw Thom was at the Preserve, he'd have no reason to dislike the man. Thom might not be the world's most efficient office manager, but he was nearly always gregarious with the other employees.

Teleki clearly didn't like him, though, which made Owen wonder what the scout wasn't saying.

After several minutes, driving past tree branches that encroached on the path and occasionally brushed along the sides of the truck, Joseph changed the subject.

"We should be getting close now."

"Should be," Owen said. There was a brighter gap in the vegetation up ahead.

"I have an idea," the former scout announced, rubbing his chin. "What if I try to get the story from these guys in Swahili, instead of English?"

Owen wasn't sure he liked where this was going. "Well…I can speak some, but I can't really pick up on nuance well enough to follow along."

"Hargreave, you must know you can trust me to translate everything accurately," Joseph replied, a note of offense creeping into his tone.

Did he know? Owen wasn't so sure. They pulled into the small clearing beside the outpost, and he wondered, "Why do you want to interview them in Swahili?"

"Because some words…they don't always have perfect translations."

"Right—"

"And the men are often writing up their reports in a hurry, with English as their second language."

Owen nodded, catching on.

"We should make sure we get whatever details they remember absolutely right," Joseph finished.

Owen nodded again, allowing himself to be convinced. "Sometimes it's the smallest thing."

"Exactly," said Joseph. "And if I take the lead in Swahili, then maybe…"

"Maybe we'll get what we need," Owen finished.

The scout shrugged, his face grave. Owen toyed with telling Joseph that he wanted to record the conversation but decided almost immediately against it. He didn't want the man to tailor his questions accordingly, and he certainly didn't want the assistant scouts to hold back critical information.

Owen didn't know why gazelles were dying or who might be behind it—and therefore, he couldn't be too careful.

Two junior scouts came out, waved, and motioned them inside. They'd obviously been told to expect them.

Owen got out of the truck and eyed the steeply pitched thatch roof, and the deep shade of its eaves, with affection. Sometimes he missed the days when he'd been just another lowly scout, working full-time in the bush with his mates.

When he took a deep breath and smelled the aroma of homecooked food, though, his feet carried him swiftly inside.

Introductions were made as everyone clustered around the rough table in the center of the main room. Teleki didn't appear to know any of the men personally, but Owen recognized most of their names from their weekly reports.

Before he could explain the purpose of their visit, they began tearing into a communal meal with gusto. There was *ugali*—delicious roasted chicken in a thick tomato sauce—and fried plantains, along with several other side dishes. It was an impressive spread for a humble outpost. That head scout had not steered them wrong.

As he dug in, Owen wondered if the men had cooked the food themselves or brought it from home. Nadra was a perfectly fine cook, but her recipes tended to be utilitarian at best, and his own repertoire remained pathetically small. This feast was an unexpected, but welcome, treat.

There was no time to dwell on it, though. The men ate quickly and efficiently, then cleared the table with dispatch. Then, the group sat back down in unison and stared at them, waiting for one of them to make the first move.

Joseph glanced at Owen, stood, and began speaking.

Owen made a show of sorting through his pack for a Preserve map to lay on the table, so he could tap the recording icon on his phone screen. He slipped it carefully onto his lap and held it carefully out of sight.

When Joseph paused, he nodded at him and smoothed out the B Quad plat—and attempted to follow along. Owen understood the gist of the conversation but that was all, so instead of focusing on particulars he watched the body language of the scouts and tried to determine their personalities.

Gradually, it became clear that one of the senior scouts, Sully Temba, was the older brother of an assistant named Andrew. Joseph seemed to be zeroing in on them, but they all spoke too quickly for Owen to register why.

Andrew was getting pretty emphatic, however, and Owen watched as his older brother placed a steadying—or perhaps restraining—hand on his shoulder.

Owen caught Joseph's eye and arched a brow, but the man only gave him a brief nod of acknowledgement before launching into rapid-fire Swahili himself. It looked like he was intrigued by what he was hearing.

Suddenly, he paused, held up his hand, and asked Owen, "How much of this are you following?"

"Not a lot," Owen admitted. "What are they saying?"

"These two are the ones who found the most recent kill," Teleki explained. "They're telling me they didn't like the look of it."

The brothers nodded warily, looking from Joseph to Owen. In English, Sully said, "It wasn't...normal."

Andrew shook his head. "Nothing was right," he agreed.

"I could tell that from the photos you sent," Owen told them. He'd been hoping he'd learn more, however.

Unfortunately, Joseph switched back into Swahili to ask his next several questions, and all the men took turns answering him. They kept busy as they talked, washing dishes and putting away food, leaving nothing out of place for when they returned to the field.

Their break was drawing to a close, and their departure imminent.

Owen understood their need to be on their way—the scouts would have a lot of ground to cover before the next crew took over tomorrow morning—but he was disappointed, too. Joseph couldn't possibly have discovered anything important in the little time they'd had.

When Owen had planned this trip, he hadn't expected to have so little input into this part of the investigation. It chafed. What if Teleki had forgotten to ask something important, or had focused on the wrong things?

Owen was frustrated by his inadequate language skills and hoped his recording would be clear enough to make up for it.

The scouts were standing around expectantly, waiting for Owen and Joseph to take off so they could leave, too. They thanked the men for the meal and said their goodbyes. Joseph seemed upbeat.

As Owen pulled onto the wide track that would bring them the rest of the way to the field station, he asked him the most important question.

"So? What did we learn?"

"You know, the Temba brothers are interesting," Joseph commented. "The others didn't have much to add, but those two..." He trailed off, apparently deep in thought.

"Did they tell you anything newsworthy?"

"Maybe," Joseph said. "I'm trying to digest it all so I can make sure I explain it clearly."

Owen tapped his fingers against the steering wheel and frowned. "Was it that complicated?"

"Not exactly. I think it was the way they told the story." He stared out the window, rubbing his chin again.

They rode in silence for a bit, and Owen worried that Joseph might not say any more. He prompted him with, "Sully seemed like he was trying to rein the kid in a bit."

"I agree. I wish I could have talked to Andrew alone first." Joseph toyed with the wrinkled cargo pocket on his leg, bending the flap up and down. "Just to see what he would've said, you know?"

"Do you think they could've been lying?" Owen asked. If unsavory types had infiltrated the Preserve's scouting system, that would be more than a little concerning.

"No, not blatantly, though maybe by omission. I'm not sure yet."

"Could they be trying to cover something up?"

Owen kept his voice steady and his eyes trained on the darkening road ahead, hoping no animals would decide to choose this moment to dart in front of the truck.

"I can't decide. Let me think about it some more, and I'll go over everything with you later." Joseph's words sounded thoughtful as he gazed into the trees beside the track, but his tone was awfully final.

Owen told him, "You got it, mate," but he felt even more frustrated and impatient than before.

Why would the man insist on a delay? Could he be holding something back about the Rathbones?

If he were Thom, Owen wouldn't have to wonder if he was being manipulated. The Aussie couldn't keep a secret to save his life, and Owen could use that kind of transparency right about now.

The Preserve was one of the last remaining parks in the country to shelter a Rathbone herd, and since Owen was its head game warden, the survival of the rare gazelles rested almost entirely on his head.

It was an important job that he took very seriously, so he'd rather not have to also worry about Thom going inexplicably missing, or about Joseph having hidden agendas or allegiances.

After riding for several more minutes, lost in thought, Joseph suddenly blurted out, "There must be something else."

"We'll find it," Owen said, trying to sound confident despite his lack of conviction.

However, the meeting at the outpost had left him feeling like an outsider, and he was concerned that he might miss something crucial because of it.

If Joseph was as reliable as Owen hoped, he'd be an asset to the investigation. On the other hand, if he was crooked, they might never learn what had happened to those damn gazelles.

THEY FINALLY ARRIVED at the B Quadrant field station well after dark. The low, squat building looked deserted.

The scouts on the day shift had likely already eaten and retired for the night, anticipating an early start tomorrow. The night shift was gone, too, no doubt having left for their rounds an hour before.

Owen and Joseph convened in the station's mess hall to eat a light supper before they snagged a couple of spare bunks and turned in themselves. Joseph was still being regrettably circumspect about those Temba brothers, and Owen was still impatient to get more details.

When it became clear that Joseph wasn't going to offer up the goods on his own, Owen inquired once more, "So, what do you think? Did those scouts give us a good start today, or what?"

Joseph raised his eyes from his plate, and a knowing smirk flitted across his face. He knew what Owen was about.

His voice, when he replied, was cautious, however. "I think so," he said. "A small one, anyway. Hopefully, we'll learn more tomorrow. It will help to see the actual sites where the Rathbones died."

"The Tembas seemed particularly invested, to me. What was their story?"

Owen watched the muscles in Joseph's jaw tense. "The younger one—that was Andrew—had a lot to say, but it was hard to get around his brother. I tried."

"That was Sully, right? You think he was holding his brother back?"

"I do," Joseph concurred.

There was another side to all this that Owen didn't really want to bring up, but maybe hitting the nail on the head would nudge Teleki into sharing more information.

He cleared his throat. "It appeared that Sully wasn't too happy to have me there, in particular."

Joseph's head snapped up in surprise, and something flashed in his eyes that told Owen he was definitely on to something.

When he quickly schooled his expression and said, "No, that wasn't an issue," his tone was steady, but his hands gave him away. When he refolded his napkin and set it beside his plate, the man's fingers trembled just a touch.

Something was off here.

As soon as they returned to Victoriaville, Owen would have to find someone to translate his recording, and it had to be a person he could trust—like Kisima, or Nadra. Handing it over to some random person, just because they spoke fluent Swahili wouldn't work anymore.

"Alright, well…when do you think you can have a full translation written up?"

"I'll write it up before I go to sleep tonight," Joseph assured him. "Don't worry."

"Good. That way you won't forget anything," Owen remarked, but he caught the other man's gaze and held it.

Joseph didn't falter at all. He simply stared right back at him, his expression inscrutable, and asked, "Why would I do that?"

BRIGHT AND EARLY the next morning Joseph handed over his handwritten translation as promised.

His timing wasn't great. Owen was busy dodging the scouts going through their shift change and preparing his gear for the hike out to the Rathbone sites—but he still took a minute to scan the pages.

It was impossible to ignore the document's brevity. There was no way the transcript included everything that had been said yesterday. He would have to play dumb for now, though, and hopefully, Joseph would show his cards soon.

Was he only covering for the Tembas, or were others involved? Even more importantly, what was going on that required such secrecy?

Owen sighed as he packed up his gear, then hung back and watched Joseph banter easily in Swahili with the scouts passing through.

Owen had lived in Africa for so many years now, he sometimes forgot that certain people still viewed him as an interloper. And why should they trust him? Families had lived and died in this corner of Tanzania for generations untold— what could they possibly feel they owed to a man who looked just like the colonizers who'd done wrong by them?

Owen had done his best to be a conscientious steward of the Preserve and its treasures, but the fact remained that it was a privately held park in the hands of a British citizen, and its entire management team was comprised of non-African white men.

It didn't take a genius to understand how that might irk any number of individuals—both in the government and in the surrounding towns.

When a situation rankled long enough, Owen knew, angry folks in these parts took matters into their own hands.

Chapter Seven

MORGAN OPENED HER mouth to say something—anything—but no words would come out.

She took a step away from Nina and stared at that guide, agitatedly shouting into his radio. She couldn't understand a word he was saying. It was as if she'd been swaddled in bubble wrap, and everything around her had plunged into silent slow motion.

Morgan forced her eyes down, looking for whatever had the guide so upset. But even though every leaf and branch on the way stood out in vivid, high-def color, nothing seemed out of place on the ground.

Finding only weeds, her gaze began to drift away, until suddenly, snagged by the subconscious recognition of a piece that didn't fit the puzzle—a color too bright to be vegetation, a shape too mechanical to be foliage—it shot down once more.

Morgan stared for what felt like an eternity, as her brain unraveled the outline of an old, useless rifle, and the length of nylon fabric the same shade of blue as Ruth's trendy hiking pants.

On the ground. Not moving.

Morgan fell abruptly to her knees, then sank awkwardly back on her heels. A garbled, choking sound bubbled out of her throat.

Nina dropped down beside her, sitting uncomfortably close. While they watched the impossible—the unthinkable—unfold, each of them gripped a rusty old gun in her lap.

AT SOME POINT, the guide's tirade petered out. He clipped his field radio to his belt and came back over. Reaching down, he hauled Morgan to her feet first, then Nina. Together, the men marched them in a wide arc around the place where the commotion had begun, and the underbrush was all flattened out.

Their truck appeared out of nowhere, and Morgan and Nina were urged into its back seat. Once they were safely stashed inside, one man stood guard at the open door, while the others rummaged through the back compartment, then tramped back into the forest with their arms full of gear.

Through the windshield, Morgan could see the faces of the other tour members, like pale moons peering through the glass. She looked away from the fear in their eyes.

The guide blocking their exit looked away for a moment, then said haltingly, "Your friend, she…uh…" He shook his head, unable to summon the words he wanted. "She, with the gun—"

Morgan blinked at him and attempted to find some logical link between her dull haze from before, and her current whirling feeling of unreality.

Why couldn't she remember this guy's name? She'd known it ten minutes ago, but now he might as well have been a total stranger.

She thought she might have to throw up.

Beside her, Nina was growing frantic. She cried shrilly, "She *what* with the gun? Did she drop it? Or did something attack her?"

The man shook his head. "No animal, Miss."

Nina sobbed, "Then tell us what's happening! What is wrong with you?"

The guide's face stayed stonily impassive as he watched his coworkers struggle with the nightmare on the ground, over where Ruth had disappeared.

When they finally returned, they carried the same materials they'd left with, only different, somehow. Bulkier.

They opened the back hatch of the truck and laid their bundle on the floor, then secured most of their guns in the racks on the side. Then they slammed the door, stalked around the truck, and slid two more rifles behind the front seats.

Those guns, at least, looked like they'd been maintained perfectly.

The guide corralling Morgan and Nina motioned for them to buckle up and shut them in, then climbed into the passenger seat up front, next to his buddies.

The engine revved, and they pulled away, the other two trucks in their convoy falling into line behind them.

Morgan wondered why they were leaving. If something bad had happened, shouldn't they wait for the authorities? Surely the police would want everything left the way it was for their investigation.

Nina had fallen eerily quiet, so Morgan would have to be the one to say something. She needed to open her mouth, and make words come out. But just as she was gathering the courage to do that, Nina elbowed her hard in the side, and jerked her chin toward the back compartment of the Range Rover.

Behind their seat lay that terrifying bundle, and with every bump of the truck the tent material covering it slipped further askew. A dusty suede boot was now exposed, still looking expensive, after four weeks of stomping around Tanzania.

Nina bit her lip but didn't look away. "Oh, no," she whimpered. "Oh, Ruth."

When a limp hand came into view, Morgan wrenched her body back around, but she couldn't stop herself from vomiting violently between her feet. As they drove on and on, back to the lodge and back to people who presumably could help them—

people who would know what the hell to *do*—she couldn't seem to stop retching.

LATER, THE LODGE'S manager summoned a translator for Morgan and Nina, and along with a pair of local policemen, he tried repeatedly to explain the mechanics of guns to them— specifically, the one Ruth had been carrying.

Because they were convinced that it couldn't have discharged by mistake, the authorities seemed to have decided that the accident hadn't, in fact, been an accident, and that Ruth had intended to kill herself all along.

The guides received a mild slap on the wrist for allowing the girls to leave the truck, and for giving them guns they weren't trained or licensed to carry.

To Morgan, the bigger issue appeared to be that they'd removed Ruth's body before the cops had arrived, but no one seemed to care about that.

Nina struggled to grasp the finer points of what they were being told. She got progressively more belligerent—accusing everyone from the tour guides to the bell hops of malfeasance in some form or another—but all Morgan did was sit quietly and watch.

Nina threatened legal action and bodily harm, and it was all to no avail. And Morgan, sitting in numb silence beside her, began to think.

She began to drop the supposedly meaningless little comments and actions that Ruth had made over the last few months into their proper places.

AFTER TOO MANY hours of mute shock, Morgan finally summoned the strength to lay her hand on Nina's arm and say, "Nina, stop. I think they may be right."

"What? What do you mean?"

"I mean, I think they're right. Ruth meant to do it."

"Are you *nuts*?" Nina cried, instantly incensed. "How can you say that? You and I both know she would *never* do something like this on purpose!"

"Nina," Morgan sighed, resigned to spilling Ruth's secret. "Before we left, Ruth saw some doctors. Did she tell you?"

"Yeah. What does that have to do with anything?"

"Do you know why she went?" Morgan tried to keep her voice from cracking. It shouldn't matter anymore, but she still felt like she was betraying a confidence

She guessed the dead got to keep some secrets, but not all of them, though.

Nina stared into her face and wavered a little. "She had the flu, or something."

"No, she didn't. She'd fainted a few times, and said her fingers kept trembling. That's not the flu."

"But if her blood sugar was low—"

Morgan shook her head. "She was diagnosed with early onset Parkinson's, Nina. She hadn't admitted it to me outright yet, but I saw some papers at her apartment, before we left."

"Are you kidding?" Nina gaped at her, incredulous.

"I asked her about them, and she said a lot of weird stuff, trying to explain," Morgan said. "I should have put it together earlier, but…"

"But *what*?" Nina looked like she was ready to commit violence.

"But I guess it all makes sense now. I thought maybe Ruth was in shock, saying all kinds of nutty stuff while she tried to process the news. I mean...it was...I acted like it was no big deal. I thought if I played it cool, then Ruth would feel more comfortable telling me on her own, eventually."

The translator had been sipping tea at a table nearby, lingering in case they needed help filling out the police forms, but now he interrupted gently. "Ma'am. Mrs. Flynn. If you'd be willing to tell us—"

"Of course," Morgan nodded.

Nina screamed, "What is *wrong* with you people?" then threw her pen aside and stomped off.

BY THE TIME the investigation was closed, and Ruth's body was released by the authorities, Morgan and Nina had stayed on in Tanzania for three weeks past their original departure date.

Fortunately, their avuncular tour guide, Conrad, had done his level best to help them. He'd comforted the women and encouraged them to vent about that horrible day, instead of bottling up their feelings.

He'd shepherded them through the questionings and bureaucratic red tape, eventually insisting that they move out of the lodge and stay with him and his wife, Christine, while the details of sending Ruth's remains back to the States were worked out.

However, despite his hospitality, and the compassionate efforts of his wife, Nina was routinely awful to everyone.

That day, in particular, she'd been nursing a particularly foul temper, over fees the airline had charged her she changed her return ticket. Because of it, everyone in the household had been walking on eggshells for hours.

Morgan had quickly grown weary of the drama and had tried to avoid the other woman. But that meant she hadn't yet found an opportunity to mention that she'd made a decision of sorts—even if that decision had largely come about through inaction, rather than any real courage on her part.

She'd come out to sit on the Twospeaks' back porch, watching the insects buzz around in the afternoon sun while she debated how to handle things. Christine was still inside, bustling around her kitchen, when Nina finally found Morgan and plopped into a nearby chair.

Morgan heard their host stop what she was doing and move closer to the window over the sink, giving them space, but understandably curious, too.

Nina announced sourly, "Part of what is irritating me so much today is how blasé you're being about these fees. I mean...don't you find it even a little insulting? We *know* they're supposed to give us some sort of...you know, bereavement discount, or whatever—"

Her voice broke, and she stopped for a moment, fighting back the same tears she hadn't been able to stop for days. "Instead they're charging us *more* money for changing our tickets. I mean, what the hell is that?"

Morgan sighed, "Nina, I'm so sorry this is happening. It's really awful."

"Well, it's not *your* fault," she snapped. "But honestly, it's like you don't even care."

Morgan restrained the urge to lash back. There was so much the woman didn't know about her. They'd never been friends independent of Ruth, and now they'd been forced into this strange kind of intimacy against their will.

Someday, when all this was over, Morgan didn't think either of them would choose to continue their acquaintance.

"I *care*," Morgan assured Nina testily, "Of course, I care. I'm just...in shock, I guess."

Inside the kitchen, the telephone rang. After a moment, Christine called out, "Nina, honey? It's for you."

There were only so many people it could be, and Morgan tried to brace herself for the coming storm. In all likelihood, she'd lost the chance to come clean with Nina herself. Any minute now, the cat would be out of the bag.

She leaned back on her hands and listened to Nina's rising hysteria. Christine came out and sat beside her, leaning over to rest a sympathetic hand on top of Morgan's. The woman already knew what was about to happen—Morgan had pulled her and Conrad aside the night before and told them what she planned to do. They didn't necessarily understand her reasoning, but thankfully, they'd pledged their assistance.

Still, when Nina stormed out onto the porch again, Christine rose quickly and went back inside.

Nina stomped her foot to get Morgan's attention, then shrieked, "I am so *sick* of this stupid place! Those people keep saying I'm the only one taking Ruth home tomorrow. I keep trying to tell them we're both going, but they won't listen. They said they've got all this stuff for me to go sign." She stopped and stared at Morgan.

Morgan stared back at her.

"Morgan, you'd better go call them right now. They think I'm the only American on the flight."

Morgan swallowed hard, then sighed, "Nina, you *are* the only American on the flight."

"What?" she screeched. "Why?"

"Nina, I'm not flying home tomorrow." Morgan had to choke it out, but she said it.

There was a long, terrible pause. "*Why. Not.*" Nina's voice went dangerously quiet.

"I never changed my tickets," Morgan explained.

"You're kidding. You said—"

Morgan shook her head, and Nina tried again, "But you said you called right after I did."

"I didn't call," she admitted. "I meant to, but I…I just couldn't make myself do it."

Nina blinked rapidly, trying to process the incomprehensible. "But what are you going to do?" She was working herself into a real panic, but Morgan couldn't help her now.

"I don't exactly know, to be honest. I just know I can't go home yet," Morgan murmured.

"So, you'd rather stay *here*?" Nina gaped at her.

Morgan forced herself to smile, but she didn't attempt to defend herself. The truth was, there wasn't anywhere she wanted to be. She only knew where she didn't want to be—and that was Boston, where there was no way she could get lost in anonymity.

"You're freaking nuts," Nina spat, then stalked off.

Morgan stayed where she was, wondering if Nina could be right. She searched the Twospeaks' tidy yard for answers, and though it was comfortingly tame, it also looked so normal it was nearly painful. Perhaps someday, she could say the same about herself.

Inside, Christine walked quickly across the house, heading for the guest room where Morgan and Nina had been staying. Flies buzzed in the still air, alighting here and there in the grass.

Then, from a distance, came the sound of a car approaching. It stopped before it got close to the house, but the voices of a man and woman gradually became clear. They were talking quietly as they came nearer, flirting, but also *not*.

They came to a stop beside the house, around the corner from where Morgan was sitting.

The man said, "Anyway, that's the whole story. I swear haven't seen her in months."

"A little too convenient, if you ask me," the woman replied.

"What do you mean?"

"Oh, come on, Thom. Somehow, you knew exactly when I was getting in today, but you couldn't figure out how to reach me when I left?"

"I told you, love—Conrad wouldn't give me your number. To be honest, he seemed testier than usual this time."

"Imagine that," she said.

Then, their voices dropped lower, some suspicious rustling followed, and finally, a burst of giggling that Morgan didn't want to think too hard about.

Eventually, the woman sighed, "Fine! You win. Are you happy now?"

"Very."

There were a few more minutes of indistinct conversation before the mystery man announced quite clearly, "By the way, if anyone asks, say I picked you up yesterday, not today."

There was a long pause, and then the woman snorted, "Jesus—it's always the same with you, isn't it?"

"Not this time. I promise this gig is the real deal."

"Yeah, well, you've said that before. Besides, what am I supposed to tell my sister? She'll lose her shit if I'm just sitting around the house all day. I'm going to have to get a job or something."

"So, go to the liaison's office in town. They always know who's hiring."

"Right. And would you like to guess how long it'll take for my boss to start complaining that I never show up? Christine and Conrad will definitely be asking questions then."

The man was quiet. "Okay, then how about—"

She cut him off. "Don't start. I agreed to this stupid plan of yours. I'll figure this part out myself."

"Good girl. Now, when can we meet again? Tomorrow?"

"I don't know. I'll call you."

"Carol, my darling, I can hardly wait." His voice trailed off as he walked away.

Carol. Christine had mentioned that her sister Carol would be arriving for a visit sometime today. Sure enough, a moment later, Morgan heard the woman trudge around the house, open the front door, and step inside. "Anyone home?" she called out.

A door slammed and Christine went running. "Carol? Is that you?"

"Hey," the woman sang out. "God, it's good to see you."

"You, too—but I didn't think you were getting in until later. How did you get out here?"

Morgan stood up and started for the back door, just as Carol mumbled, "You'll never guess."

"Oh, no," Christine groaned.

"Oh, yes. He was waiting for me at the bus depot."

"But how did he find out?" Christine cried. "We were so careful."

"Damned if I know," Carol muttered, "But you know Thom. He works in mysterious ways."

"Don't remind me."

Before Morgan could overhear any more, she cleared her throat and stepped into the house. Christine beckoned her over.

"Morgan, come meet my sister, Carol."

Morgan stuck out her hand. "Nice to meet you," she said, and got a wary shake in return.

"Carol, this is one of the girls from the tour I told you about. Nina's in the guest room, but I'm sure she'll be out for dinner."

Carol looked over, then murmured, "I'm sorry about your friend."

"Thanks," Morgan said. "So am I." What else could she say? It was the truth, after all.

No one seemed to know what else to say. Carol shifted on her feet, glanced down the short hall with its closed guest room door, and blurted out, "So when do you leave?" at the same time Christine wrung her hands and began, "Morgan and Nina are sharing the guest room, but—"

Carol and Morgan stared at each other.

Christine started over. "Morgan's going to be staying with us for a little while longer. Nina is accompanying the body home tomorrow by herself."

Carol looked a little green at that news. "I see."

Morgan thought about the hushed conversation she'd just heard in the yard. "I'll get out of everyone's hair as soon as I can," she assured them. "Don't worry."

"There's no rush," Christine said, with far more confidence than Morgan felt. "You just need time to process, that's all."

Carol looked dubious, probably because she had plans she didn't want company for.

Morgan stood there enduring her scrutiny for as long as she could, but the urge to flee was overwhelming. "I should probably go check on Nina," she said and bolted for the hall.

"But you're still joining us for dinner, right?" Christine tried for chipper, but she sounded a little strained.

"Of course," Morgan agreed, glancing at Carol again. "I'll come help you set up in a few minutes."

"Don't bother. I can do it," Carol retorted quickly. "We'll let you girls know when it's ready."

Morgan turned away, resigned to the task of mollifying Nina again.

"Morgan?" Christine called. "I meant to tell you before—Conrad said he'd poke around in town today, to ask about jobs for you. He said you should be hearing about your work visa soon."

"I appreciate that."

"I'm sure he'll have more news when he gets back tonight."

Morgan looked between the two women, and suddenly remembered something she'd heard that man say outside.

"I was thinking…on our tour, Conrad mentioned the liaison office in town. Would they know of any openings I could apply for?"

Carol glared at her, so Morgan kept her eyes trained on Christine.

Her host shrugged. "That's not a bad idea. We'll ask him about it when he gets home."

"Great."

"One more thing." Christine fished in her pocket and pulled out a locket on a silver chain. "Is this yours? I almost stepped on it, out on the porch earlier."

"Oh, shoot," Morgan exclaimed, rushing over. "That's definitely mine. In all the fuss with Nina, I didn't even realize I lost it."

Morgan took it and smoothed it out on her palm, rubbing the locket fondly. The clasp looked a little bent, but it seemed to still work.

Good thing, too—her sister Meg had apparently saved up for months so she could give it to her before this trip. Morgan would've hated to lose it.

She fastened it safely around her neck, sent a weak smile toward her host, and then trudged off to placate Nina one last time.

June 25

I can't stop thinking about the fact that Ruth's diagnosis didn't have to be an immediate death sentence. Why did she choose to make it one? Didn't she consider that she'd be burdening us with bringing her home—or realize I'd be too weak to see things through? Lucky for us, Nina is angry enough to carry the load for everyone.

Still, it's one more blot on a year that's stained my soul beyond belief.

I don't yet know if my life will remain permanently surreal—I only know that, right now, I can't function on any level approximating who I used to be.

I feel nameless and anchorless—a spirit form, adrift among real people.

Can they tell that I'm a shadow, a shell, a husk? Will they forgive me for my empty, barren soul?

Chapter Eight

THE SUN WAS hanging low over the tops of the thorn trees in Victoriaville's town square by the time Owen turned his truck into the lane, then pulled up alongside the Preserve's main office.

It had been an exceedingly long, hot day—encompassing a final, fruitless dissection of the degraded Rathbone sites, as well as the lengthy drive back.

He and Joseph had barely spoken during the last stretch of road, each lost to their own thoughts. Now, however, they dragged themselves from the cab and groaned in unison, cracking their backs and stretching their legs.

Defeat felt like a heavy weight, pressing down on them.

Owen told him, "If you want to leave your gear in the truck, I can run you out to your place after I check in."

"To be honest, I'm tempted to hike home," Joseph said. "I've been cooped up in this vehicle for far too long, today. I need some air."

"It'll be pitch dark before you even get halfway there."

"The dark doesn't bother me. Besides, I could probably find my way with my eyes closed," Joseph smiled.

"That's not what I'm worried about." Owen shook his head and grinned back at him, though. "Before you set off, come in and have some tea. Then decide."

"As you wish," the scout conceded.

Joseph was so easygoing, it was hard not to trust the man. The little matter of his translation notwithstanding, he didn't seem the least bit devious. That could be the point, however—maybe all the *gentle* and *kind* going around was just a great big smokescreen.

Owen headed for the door, and finally registered that it was propped open with one of the office chairs. It was strange for someone to even be here this late, much less optimizing the evening airflow.

Joseph stopped beside him and they frowned at each other in concern.

Inside, Thom was bustling around the room like it was all perfectly normal, filing scouting reports from the looks of things.

"Hey, mate! How's it going?" the man beamed. "We were starting to miss your grumpy mug around here, but don't tell the boss I told you."

He jerked his chin to the side. Owen turned and saw that Nigel's door was open and his light on, though the director hadn't deigned to emerge with a greeting yet.

Owen's door was still closed at least, and hopefully as locked as he'd left it.

"What's he doing here?" Owen asked quietly.

He'd *thought* Nigel was going to be in Dodoma all week, meeting some Parliament member about funding or licenses, or whatever—though naturally he'd been vague when Owen had tried to ask about it.

"Beats me. The old git put in a full day for once, though," Thom said. "Pissing and moaning like usual."

He finished with the reports and plopped happily into his desk chair, then peered over Owen's shoulder. "Who's that with you?"

Owen moved aside so Thom could see Joseph. "You remember Mr. Teleki, I assume."

The scout stepped forward, his eyes locked on Thom, and his face went blank.

"Mr. Hannity. Imagine that."

A look crossed Thom's face that Owen had never seen before. He nearly snarled, "And Mr. Teleki. Who would've guessed."

Before Owen could ask what that was all about, Joseph turned to him and announced, "You know, I think I'll be on my way, after all. My sister lives a few blocks away. I'll have supper with her, and she can run me home afterward." His voice was carefully neutral, flat without being outright rude.

What in the world? Owen studied him but couldn't figure out what he'd missed.

Still, he could use a few minutes alone with Thom, since his friend had some explaining to do.

"Sounds good," Owen told Joseph. "I'll keep you posted if I hear anything about those Rathbones."

"Please do," Joseph replied, then turned and walked out.

Through the window, Owen watched him haul his gear out of the back of the truck, sling it onto his back, and then stroll easily up the lane.

Owen shook his head and turned back to Thom, eyeing him critically. He didn't appear to be a flight risk any longer, but Owen had clearly been wrong before.

Thom asked brightly, "So? How'd it go up north?"

Owen sat on the edge of his desk. "Interesting question. Why don't you tell me what the hell happened to you that morning, first?"

Thom blinked at him, the very picture of innocence. "What do you mean?"

"I mean, you were supposed to be the one who went with me, not Teleki. If he hadn't been available, I would've had to scrap the whole trip. So, where were you?"

Thom smirked, coy as a teenage girl. "Ah. Well, mate—as it turns out, Conrad's sister-in-law came back to town."

"So, you were with Carol," Owen confirmed. "Because I ran by your house before I left, and no one was around."

"It's good that Teleki guy could go up with you instead, right? I thought he'd retired, though. How'd he work out?"

The deflection was smooth—almost seamless. Unfortunately for Thom, Owen was not in the mood to be managed.

He set aside his concerns about that interview translation and said, "Teleki's still a good scout, and you're lucky he was available. Doesn't explain why you ditched on our trip, though. Did you forget to call, or what?"

Thom laughed. "You know me," he said, getting up and ambling around his desk. He clapped Owen on the arm as he passed. "Anyway, keep an eye on that guy. He can be a right bastard when he wants to."

Owen watched Thom leave the office, cross the lane outside, and get into his dusty little Toyota. It took a few attempts, but he finally got it started, waving cheerfully out his window as he sputtered away.

Owen sat there, completely mystified for a while, before he pulled himself together and went to see what the boss was up to at this hour. If Nigel was in a snit about something, it was entirely possible he was in there waiting for Owen to pay homage.

However, when Owen walked over and stuck his head in the door, Nigel's office was quiet and still—and quite, quite empty. Hadn't Thom mentioned that Cotton was there?

Nothing else seemed out of the ordinary, though, so Owen switched off the light, turned the lock on the inside of the doorknob, and pulled the door closed.

Owen might not be getting out in the field as much as he'd like to lately, but he was fairly sure his skills hadn't degraded to the point that a 58-year-old man with a stick up his arse could sneak by him easily.

Which meant Thom had lied, right to Owen's face. *Again.*

Owen was just testing the knob on his own office door when a rapid knock sounded behind him. He turned and found his housekeeper Nadra grinning at him.

"I passed Joseph on his way to his sister's," she said. "Are you as happy to be back as he is?"

Owen sighed, weary to the bone. "Yeah. We drove a long way to find out exactly nothing. I'm knackered."

"Do you want me to follow you home, *Bwana*? I can get you settled in tonight, and then run to the market on my way over tomorrow."

"That sounds great," he admitted. "But you don't have to. I appreciate the offer, though." The thought of fresh sheets and a hot meal sounded like heaven at the moment, but Nadra had her own family to worry about.

"Don't be silly," she scoffed, "I could use a break from the children, and you pay better than they do. Besides, my husband doesn't mind. He feels sorry for you, you know."

Owen snorted. He could only imagine. Lately, he'd begun feeling a little sorry for himself, too.

For instance, when he was eating a delicious home-cooked meal at a Preserve outpost, and remembering how empty his own home usually stood, he did not exactly feel like he was winning at this whole "life" thing.

He'd always intended to have a family of his own, after all, it simply hadn't manifested itself quite yet. He had only himself to blame, though—he hadn't exactly exerted himself to meet new people in recent years. Little hard to meet The One under those conditions.

He shook his head and took a last look around, then ushered her out. He'd meant what he'd told her. Nadra *had* been good to him—the best of all the women who'd worked for him over the years. She'd become a friend.

As she walked beside him to his truck, he remembered the recording he'd made. "Nadra, how well do you know Joseph, would you say?"

"Pretty well. We grew up together, and his wife Patricia and I were at school together in Arusha for at least a year or two, as well. She's a couple of years older than me, though. We lost touch until she and Joseph got married and moved back here."

In the past, Nadra had always found a way to warn Owen about people, when it was warranted. He wanted to give her an opening now, just in case.

"So…anything I need to know about him?" he wondered.

"He's straight," Nadra said, then stopped. She looked like she wanted to say more.

"That's it?" Owen prodded.

"That's it," she said firmly, then slapped the truck's door. "You can trust him. Now go home. I'll come by tomorrow morning."

Owen slid behind the wheel, and his eyes fell on the phone he'd left sitting on the dashboard. Whether he could trust Joseph Teleki, or not, remained to be seen. He could trust Nadra, though.

"Hey, do you have another minute?" he asked. When she nodded, he gestured for her to get in on the passenger side.

Once she got settled, he tapped the wheel with the phone in his hand and glanced over at her. "I need your help."

Nadra eyed him suspiciously. "And?"

"It's business," he explained. "If you can't…" Owen trailed off, not wanting to make a big deal.

"Can't what?"

"If you can't keep it quiet, say so, now."

Nadra's voice grew warier. "Is it about Joseph?"

"Maybe. I'm not sure." Owen trained his eyes out the windshield. Perhaps bringing Nadra into this wasn't the right thing to do.

She chewed on a nail, then toyed with the edge of her bright yellow head scarf while she considered it. Owen held his breath, expecting her to turn him down.

Instead, she said, "All right. Tell me."

"I need you to listen to this." He put his phone between them and called up the audio file. "And translate, word for word."

Nadra looked from him to the phone, then back again. "I can try."

The first few minutes proceeded almost exactly the way he remembered them, but once the Temba brothers began their rapid back-and-forth with Joseph, Owen lost the thread of what they were saying again.

Nadra translated rapidly, though, periodically reaching out to stop the recording so she could catch up.

"What else did you see?

Some men in the woods. Maybe the day before? I'm not sure.

Where?

Close by. Very near those first two animals. Too close to be a coincidence.

Were they Bantu?

No, Bwana. *Outsiders. Why do you think we were suspicious?*

Andrew, don't say that!

Why, Sully? Joseph needs to know…

Was it…this man here?" Joseph's voice asked carefully.

"Not him. One of his friends, though.

Stop, you little idiot. You're going to lose your job—

Okay, stop. Just describe the men you saw."

Nadra continued, translating the younger brother's description. *"One of them was Sully's height, with dark curly hair. A real smooth city man. Who knows why he was out there.*

And the other?"

Nadra paused as the recording did, interjecting softly to herself, "That was Joseph."

Then Andrew Temba began speaking again, and she quickly repeated, *"The other one was taller. Slim, with short red hair. Spotted skin. You know how the really pale ones look. All those freckles everywhere."*

Owen recognized Sully's reluctant voice next. Nadra dutifully translated his words, *"And the mark."*

"Yes. He had this big brown birthmark, right here, on his arm." Andrew agreed.

Owen slammed his hands on the wheel, then blew out his breath and dropped his head back against the headrest. Nadra looked worried as she translated Joseph's final words.

"Don't tell anyone else. I'm going to have to report this, but I'll come to you later with further instructions."

The recording ended and Owen grabbed his phone, closing out the audio file and buttoning the device into his shirt pocket, where he could keep it safe.

Beside him, he could feel Nadra's eyes searching his face. He gripped the steering wheel and tried to come up with a reasonable explanation—anything other than what it had sounded like.

After a while, Owen glanced at Nadra, saw the look on her face, and forced his eyes forward again.

She put a tentative hand on his arm. "Was it really him?"

THE FOLLOWING DAY was predictably frustrating, with Thom bumbling around in his usual klutzy way, and Owen attempting to catch up on all the work that hadn't been done in his absence.

He hadn't gotten much sleep the night before, turning the questions he had over and over in his mind, and by late afternoon, about all Owen could manage was to slump at his desk and grip the armrests of his ancient leather swivel chair, while he stared balefully into the middle distance.

At some point, he recognized how tightly his jaw was clenched, so he stretched his mouth wide, trying to relax the muscles. But then, in the main room, he heard the sound of Thom spilling his coffee again, followed by the inevitable farce of him trying to mop it up.

Thom would, no doubt, do a terrible job—and Kisima would never let them hear the end of it. Owen cringed.

He knew he ought to just call it a day and go home, since he felt a bit like a sitting duck, parked here waiting for something else to go wrong. However, the thought of leaving Thom out there alone didn't exactly fill him with warm and fuzzy feelings, either.

Owen had been hoping to wait him out, and he wasn't the only one. His housekeeper was also sitting in the front room, along with Kisima, who was finishing up for the day.

Nadra had arrived a while ago with Owen's groceries for the week, and while she seemed to be perfectly content chatting with Kisima, he knew they were all waiting for him to get his act together.

It was like some kind of weird standoff, but all he had to do to end it was get up, walk out there, and leave.

He kept sitting there.

Kisima was nothing if not practical, however, and she knew how to prod the men around her into action. In English and loud enough, naturally, for Owen to hear, she announced, "Don't worry, *mama*, I'm sure he'll be ready to drive out to the cottage soon."

She then switched into Swahili to add quietly, "He's been stewing in there for an hour. Probably not a good day to ask for a raise."

That, at least, got a smile out of him.

Suddenly, Owen heard a little cough, then the scrape of chair legs on the floor.

Kisima called, "*Mama?*" as Nadra, presumably, flew into the small office washroom and slammed the door.

Owen dropped his head into his hands and groaned. *Here* was the rotten turn of events he'd been expecting.

"Oh no," he whispered to himself. "Not again."

He'd experienced this exact situation twice already, and it always started the same way. There was no doubt in his mind that Nadra was pregnant. *Shit.*

What was this for her? Kid number four? Five? An embarrassment of riches, surely.

It might take months for her to admit it, but once she did, Owen would either have to fend for himself, or line up a new housekeeper until Nadra decided to come back—*if* she decided to come back this time.

In the meantime, he'd have to navigate morning sickness that lasted all day, but Nadra tried like hell to hide. There'd be lightning-fast mood swings, and, if past experience was any indication, there would be tears. Great torrents of them, perhaps for many weeks to come.

It killed him to watch her go through it all, and he was only her friend. How much worse must it be for her husband?

Still, Nadra shouldn't have to worry about cleaning up after his sorry hide when she had much more important things to worry about now. Waiting would only prolong her misery.

Owen sighed and reached for his desk phone. Maybe Dr. Bing, over at the liaison office, would know of someone he could hire temporarily.

Another small commotion in the front room made him pull back his hand.

"Mr. Cotton! I didn't know you'd be in today!" Kisima exclaimed.

Owen heard her jump up and begin to bustle industriously around, straightening things. Mainly for effect, he imagined—she'd already cleaned the place within an inch of its life this afternoon.

Owen strolled over and leaned against the doorjamb of his office, watching the show. As he did so, Nadra emerged from the WC, and looked immediately sheepish when Nigel's eyes fell on her.

She squared her shoulders but stared down at her shoes. "Mr. Cotton, how are you?"

"What are *you* doing here?" he demanded.

"Waiting to accompany *Bwana* Owen back to his cottage," she demurred. "I'll go sit in the park until he's ready."

"Wait, *mama*—I'll go with you," Kisima offered.

Owen wasn't surprised. Nigel, stiff-necked prig that he was, had made disparaging comments about the women's socializing in the past, and they'd grown wary of provoking him.

If they happened to cross paths with the Preserve's director now, they managed to put on a completely believable pretense of submissiveness, even though neither of them possessed an iota of natural subservience normally.

Owen was impressed with their acting skills, but it still bothered him. Why should two of the strongest women he'd ever known—who both sassed him regularly, and with good-natured relish— behave like caricatures in the face of one stiff and irritable Englishman?

He understood but appreciated that they didn't pull that crap with him. The *Bwana* had been a bit much, even for Nadra. It sounded like something his mother or sister might say, when they needled Owen about living here for so long.

The thought elicited a little pang in Owen's chest. He should call them, later, to see how they were. It'd been a while.

Nadra and Kisima slipped deferentially out the front door. In response, Nigel only scowled—but somehow still managed to give it a pompous, superior spin.

Owen strode over to shake his boss's hand, hoping to distract him from whatever tirade he was about to unleash. "Nigel, we weren't expecting you today. To what do we owe the pleasure?"

Over Nigel's shoulder, Kisima was rolling her eyes at him through the front window. Owen attempted a glare in return, but it was probably undercut by the smirk tugging at his mouth.

"Bad luck, I'm afraid. I've got some new photos for you." Nigel glanced distractedly at Thom, then gave his leather attaché a shake before moving to unlock his office door.

"Be with you in a moment," Owen told him, then stuck his head out the front door to call for Nadra.

The women had settled on a bench in the shade of a large thorn tree down the lane, but his housekeeper scurried over once she saw him.

"You still have my keys?" he asked her.

He'd given them to her earlier, so she could put the nonperishable groceries she'd bought for him in his truck. The other things were still stuck in the small refrigerator they kept in the storeroom.

"I do."

"Why don't you go on ahead, then. I might be a while," he told her. "I'll bring the cold food out before you go, and then Thom can bring me home once we're done."

"Are you sure? I don't mind waiting."

"Yeah, nah. Go ahead. I have no idea how long this is going to take, and I don't want your husband to get mad at me for keeping you out too late."

She laughed. "Don't try to act noble. You just want to make sure your dinner is on the table once you get there."

"Maybe," Owen grinned back. He reached out to touch her arm. "And Nadra? I know it's not my business, but it might be time to break out that ginger tea again."

Her face went slack with shock, but soon she was smiling again. "You great big oaf. Why do I even put up with you?"

"I assume it's because you think I'm pathetic. Let's figure out what you want to do once I get home, though, okay?"

She nodded. Now that her secret was out, she'd probably milk his sympathy for all she was worth.

Nadra was a lovely woman, but she held a pretty firm belief that pregnant mothers could pretty much do whatever they wanted. She was probably right.

However, Nadra wasn't a blue-ribbon chef at the best of times, and her culinary efforts tended to take a marked nosedive when she wasn't particularly keen on eating, herself. She'd told Owen before how the smell of food could turn her stomach, so he wasn't terribly optimistic about what she'd come up with for him tonight.

He'd already eaten stale bread and cheese for last night's dinner and this morning's breakfast, though, so he was willing to take his chances. Surely Nadra would remember that, after eating on the fly for days when he was in the field, Owen was often desperate for a decent meal by the time he returned home.

He watched her face grow tight, and then her hand flew up to press over her mouth. Nadra backed away to sink onto that bench again, and Owen knew he was probably destined for yet another sandwich.

At that depressing thought, he walked back inside, sent Thom out with the groceries, and headed dejectedly into Nigel's office—where the director was busy laying out a gruesome array of snapshots across his desk.

Chapter Nine

"MORE RATHBONES DOWN?" Owen's heart sank when he scanned the grim display. "Where did it happen this time?"

"Quadrant C. Maybe five kilometers southwest of the last one," Nigel said.

Owen nudged the corner of a picture, delaying the moment when he'd have to look closer. "Do the scouts know why?"

"No. But I'm not certain we're looking at poachers. Something about this is quite…" he trailed off for a moment, then shrugged, "…unusual."

Owen took a deep breath and leaned in to examine the photos arrayed before them, and immediately shook his head. "Definitely not poachers. They would've come back for them— at least for the horns, if not the hide or the meat." He straightened and studied the other man's face.

"A witch doctor, then. There's probably plenty of those chaps lurking around out there."

Owen picked up photo after grainy photo, looking for the parts of the gazelles that might be used in traditional medicines and concoctions—and even some not-so-traditional ones.

He was no expert but, "I don't think that's it, either. Whatever did this left all the most important bits. Plus, from what I can see, these kills are worse than the B Quad ones. At least there they took the horns."

The Preserve director cocked his head. "You're sure?"

"Yeah. For one thing, the others were bucks, and these all look like does," Owen murmured, truly perplexed. "I don't...I don't get it."

"Alright. Now look at these." Nigel eyed him narrowly, gauging his reaction as he laid out a few more photos.

"A fawn, too. *Jesus*," Owen groaned, dismayed. "When did this happen?"

"A week ago."

He blinked at Cotton's matter-of-fact tone. How could the man be so untroubled by this? What did he have to worry about, though? Nigel's job was only to point out the problem to Owen. Owen and his scouts were the ones who would have to fix it— and then bear the brunt of the consequences if they couldn't.

Speaking of which, how had Nigel come into possession of these pictures, in the first place? Why hadn't they been sent to Owen and Thom with the regular field reports?

He thought of the recording biding time on his phone and swallowed hard.

"Maybe they're just falling ill," Nigel suggested. "They're delicate creatures, aren't they? Probably why the little suckers are going extinct."

"Uhhh…"

"What about a cat? Or some other new predator?"

Owen scowled, baffled at the suggestion. They'd all know if a new animal was carving out territory up there—it was their business to know.

"Not bloody likely," he said. "For one thing, a cat would've dragged the remains someplace safe, so it could work on its leftovers later."

Owen frowned some more, thinking about that. "It does beg the question, though—where were the scavengers? None of them came for these guys?"

"Not a one. Your men in C Quadrant said that no other animals went near them."

Nigel studied the photos, then absently tapped them into perfect alignment with his fingertips, like he was making a morbid collage instead of troubleshooting a life-or-death problem.

"That almost makes it sound like poison," Owen responded. "But the scouts patrol regularly. They'd know right away if—"

"I agree it's bizarre," Nigel interjected calmly. He flipped through a stapled sheaf of field reports until he found the one he was looking for, then added "But this report echoes what we see in the snapshots."

Owen reached out slowly, accepting the pages.

"I think we need to consider that the little buggers might be poisoning themselves," Nigel announced. "Perhaps they're eating something they shouldn't. It would explain why nothing wants to touch what's left once they bite the dust."

Ignoring that silly conjecture for the moment, Owen continued to examine the pictures. He didn't even know where to start—there was so much that troubled him about this.

Eventually, he asked, "Who took these photos, anyway?"

"How should I know?" Nigel huffed. "The forensic fellows, most likely. Why?"

Owen frowned. "Damned peculiar angles."

Nigel was getting impatient, however, and therefore irritable. "By the time those teams hear from your scouts and get out there, they never have much to work with. You know that. Besides, those blokes are hardly high-caliber fashion photographers—they're just hacks, documenting lousy evidence so we don't run afoul of the bastards at TANAPA."

Owen could argue, but he knew it wouldn't get him very far. Instead he asked, "So…poison, aye?" He sat down and studied two pictures in particular. "Or rather, *self*-poisoning, wasn't it?"

Nigel rocked on his heels, jammed his hands in his pockets, and nodded.

Owen mulled over Cotton's words, trying to determine why the man would want him to come to that conclusion. Concocting hare-brained theories before they knew all the facts wasn't the way they did business—but at the moment, he felt a bit like a bull being led by the ring in its nose.

"Right, then." Nigel brushed his hands together, clearly declaring that his part in this farce was at an end. "Read that report. Look into whether someone's been spraying chemicals in the area."

Owen nodded.

"In case you haven't noticed, Hargreave, we've now got a two-quadrant problem," Nigel said, staring him down. "And you're going to figure out what to do about it."

DAYS LATER, OWEN received a phone call at his desk that was as unexpected as it was welcome. He spoke to the caller for a few minutes, then hung up and walked out to the main room.

Thom looked up from a chart spread across his desk, and Kisima stopped watering the plants she kept near the front window. They waited expectantly.

"Funny thing just happened—Dr. Bing, over at the liaison office, called." Owen smirked at the immediate shift in Kisima's expression. "It seems he's found me a new housekeeper. *Already*."

"Nadra will be so relieved to hear that," she told him stoutly.

"Will she? Because she and I discussed her working for another couple of months yet."

"Wait—so why did you already call around town?" Thom asked in surprise.

"I never had the chance," Owen pointed out. "Because someone seems to have put the word out already." He eyed Kisima again, who spun quickly around to poke at her plants.

"Clearly. But is the liaison office a good idea?" Thom grinned lazily then sat back in his chair. "You dirty dog. Let me guess, word has spread to all the local girls about you, hasn't it?"

Owen rolled his eyes at that absurdity. "Sure. Let's go with that."

"Well, don't hold out on us. Where's she from?" Thom asked—a little too avidly, as Owen saw it.

He told them, "The States," then braced for their reaction.

As expected, Thom laughed outright. "You're kidding!"

Owen shook his head. "Apparently, she's been camped out at the Twospeak place. I'm a little surprised we haven't run into her yet, to be honest."

"Ohhhhh…wait a minute. I'll bet I know who she is," Kisima groaned, turning around with a pained grimace on her face.

Owen and Thom stared at her curiously.

"You heard about it," she prodded. "Remember? The American girl from Mr. Conrad's tour a while back?"

Thom's expression contorted instantly. They'd all heard about *that*. "The one who shot herself?"

"Yes!" Kisima exclaimed.

Owen was confused. "But I thought she died."

"Oh, she absolutely did," Thom confirmed. Owen scowled at him, wondering why he was so certain about that detail.

"Don't you see, though? This girl is probably one of her friends," Kisima explained with wide eyes. "Who else could it be?"

Owen sank into the closest chair. "So, we think they're giving me not only an American woman on a temporary visa, but a traumatized one, too?"

Thom chuckled, "Sure sounds like it, mate."

"But why would she want to live with me? Kisima, haven't you or Nadra got any cousins who could do it?" Owen pleaded. "I promise I'll be nice."

"*Monsieur*, I'm afraid you've already run through all my cousins," she fired back.

Owen flushed. "That wasn't *me*—it was him!" He pointed at Thom.

Thom merely shrugged, "Told you word got out."

"Well, I'm going over to meet her," Owen announced, getting to his feet. "Now, actually. I'll be back shortly."

"I'll come with you!" Thom popped up instantly, coming around the desk and wiping his palms on his pants.

"Is that really necessary?"

"Yes. It really is." Thom took Owen's arm and led him outside.

They walked up the lane, and then turned left when they reached the square. A gargantuan baobab tree shaded the far side of the road, but they strolled through the sunshine—past the alley that ran behind the buildings, and onto the liaison office's street.

Victoriaville's British Liaison Office was vaguely Mediterranean in design, with concrete arches across its facade that glowed white in the sun. Flowers spilled from big pots set on either side of the door, and a small group of people stood outside chatting.

As they got closer, Owen quickly picked out Conrad and Dr. Bing, as well as Conrad's wife Christine. The second woman was easy to identify as well—she resembled Christine in both coloring and build, and she stood up straighter and tossed her hair when she noticed Thom approaching.

Undoubtedly, Conrad's wild sister-in-law Carol.

Only the third woman in the group remained. She was young and more petite than the other two and shifting nervously on her feet. Her back was stiff, her arms were folded tightly across her stomach, and her eyes darted over him as fast as a hummingbird.

The liaison broke away from the knot of people and extended his hand warmly. "Ah, Mr. Hargreave—so nice to see you again."

"And you as well," Owen replied. "Thanks for the call."

He couldn't imagine how old the man must be by now, but he seemed to be as hale and gracious as ever. It was impossible not to like him.

Conrad and Christine shook hands as well, then gave Thom a significantly chillier reception.

Owen doubted he noticed, however, since he was already attempting to flirt with Carol and at the same time, check out the new housekeeper.

Dr. Bing gestured regally. "Mr. Hargreave, may I introduce you to Mrs. Morgan Flynn?"

Owen stepped closer and let his first impression take form. Physically, she looked delicate—and about as ineffectual as a plucked bird or a wet cat.

She smelled store-bought, too, with a distinct floral scent wafting from her in the warmth of the sun that was definitely artificial. Her posture was positively brittle, and her skin was so pale and smooth, that Owen knew she hailed from someplace easy.

An American, and then some.

"Pleased to meet you," he said, then grasped her outstretched hand.

Mrs. Flynn's handshake was all business, and the instant they made eye contact, he revised his initial opinion.

Fierce eyes, he thought. Interesting.

"Likewise," she murmured, but her expression said it all.

This female might look small, but she was no doormat. Not quite as young as Owen had assumed, either—a woman, not a girl, despite those trim legs sticking out of her shorts, and the smooth, glossy ponytail hanging down her back.

Conrad spoke up. "You'd be doing us a big favor if you give Morgan here a fair shot, Hargreave."

"I'm always fair," Owen protested. Conrad raised a skeptical brow.

Christine merely smiled and grasped the woman's arm, leaning in to say, "He just means that we've grown very fond of Morgan. We only want her to be happy."

Owen looked between them, a little confused about why everyone was acting like he was some kind of ogre.

But then liaison interjected, calm as ever. "If you'd like to see Mrs. Flynn's resume, I'm happy to provide it."

Owen held her gaze and tried to envision having that face in his home every day. "That won't be necessary."

"Right. Then let's give some thought to when you might want Mrs. Flynn to start."

Finally, Owen caught the *Mrs.* attached to her name, though a rapid inspection uncovered no ring on her finger.

So, was she a wife, or not? What's more—what on earth was she doing out here alone, and trying to extend her stay?

Mrs. Flynn was busily trying to size him up, as well. Owen watched her large hazel eyes surreptitiously examine him from head to toe and wondered what kind of conclusions she was drawing.

He squared his shoulders. It didn't matter.

"Actually," Owen announced, "Nadra would like to leave as soon as possible. So, whatever's convenient for you, works for me."

Mrs. Flynn turned and smiled sadly at Christine. "I think I've imposed on these people long enough. I'm ready whenever you are."

Keen to leave, Owen decided, and not terribly surprising given that Carol had reappeared in town.

"Alright. Then why don't I come collect you the day after tomorrow?" he suggested. "That should give us both plenty of time to prepare."

Owen knew that was soon, but the memory of that terrific meal he'd eaten at the outpost kept bugging him. Nadra might be an adequate cook—but Bing had told Owen over the phone that this woman claimed to be a great one.

"Sounds good. And thank you," she said, with more than a little relief.

Perhaps Conrad and Christine had already reassured her that Owen was a decent human being, or perhaps they had simply smothered her so much that she didn't care. Whatever it was, Mrs. Flynn didn't seem to be finding anything strange about her sudden employment.

"Well, that's settled, then. Glad I could facilitate," the liaison smiled. "And now, I need to break up our little soiree and get myself back inside before I burn to a crisp. Hargreave, I'll have Lucy walk the forms over to your office in a few minutes."

"Thank you."

"Mrs. Flynn, will you step inside before you leave, to sign off on a couple of things?" Dr. Bing inquired.

"Sure," she replied, casual and chipper and so unbelievably *American*.

Why was that needling Owen so much? He didn't have a problem with Americans in general, so it made no sense why he'd be faulting Mrs. Flynn for her nationality. Where she came from shouldn't matter, in the general scheme of things.

Owen watched as the Twospeaks congratulated her, and though she smiled back at them, her expression looked a little forlorn.

His eyes lingered on Mrs. Flynn's mouth—she had even, straight, beautifully-white teeth—and he found himself picturing what a full-wattage grin might look like on her.

Beside him, Thom snickered and bumped his shoulder, jostling him from his thoughts. Owen wrenched his gaze from Mrs. Flynn's lips, but it was an effort.

Didn't matter, he reminded himself. He had bigger problems to worry about.

Chapter Ten

MORGAN SHOULD'VE KNOWN it was too easy. The perfect job that just happened to be available when she needed one…the employer who everyone seemed to like and who happened to be ready to meet her on the fly…

Even Mr. Hargreave's willingness to hire her on the spot and let her start two days later should've been an omen that it was all too good to be true.

However, everything else had run so smoothly that day, so she'd let herself believe it was a sign. She'd made the right decision in staying here.

After all, Morgan and the Twospeaks had had no issues taking Nina to the airport. She'd watched the plane take off, and she'd bid Nina—and also Ruth—a final, silent goodbye.

They'd stopped in Victoriaville on their way home so Morgan could meet a man named Dr. Bing, who, according to Conrad, might know where she could find a job.

The Twospeaks had split off to do some errands and meet up with Carol, and Morgan had gone her own way, intent on finding the liaison office herself.

All of that had been simple. Routine, even.

She just hadn't expected things to move so quickly once she got there. One minute she was filling out her forms and speaking to Dr Bing, and the next thing Morgan knew, they were all gathering on the street, negotiating her transfer like she was a farm animal instead of a grown woman.

And that was before they'd even gotten to the flirting part.

At the end of the meeting, the Twospeak family had already started for Conrad's truck when the man hovering next to Morgan's new boss pointedly cleared his throat and nudged Mr. Hargreave's arm.

Hargreave had rolled his eyes and laughed, saying, "Forgive me, Mrs. Flynn, it seems I've neglected to introduce my colleague, Thom Hannity."

"Nice to meet you, Mr. Hannity," she'd said, shaking his hand briskly.

But the man had held on, leveling a charming wink at her and declaring grandly, "The pleasure's all mine, I promise you. And please, call me Thom."

Morgan had been happy to dispense with all of the gracious formality wafting around, so she'd smiled and told him, "I will. You can call me Morgan, too, if you like."

Mr. Hargreave had tried to regain control of the situation by inserting himself between them and shouldering Thom aside. "I wish I could say you won't be seeing much of Thom," he'd explained ruefully, "but he seems to follow me home with disturbing regularity."

And then her boss had given her a crooked little grin that made Morgan's breath whoosh out of her lungs like she'd been punched.

She'd figured out within three seconds of meeting him that Hargreave had the kind of tall, strapping build that made her heart go pitter-patter and her body want to make a love connection, but that smile…that smile was not going to be good for her mental health.

She'd looked from her boss to Thom, trying to figure out their relationship before things got further out of hand. Hargreave had said they were colleagues, and they appeared to be friends, but her boss had also seemed none too pleased about Thom's interest in her.

Not exactly the kind of good first impression she'd set out to make.

Morgan had squirmed a little, acutely aware that she was the local curiosity. And she'd dithered a bit, too, because something about that Hannity guy had seemed familiar.

"Until Friday, then?" she'd asked Mr. Hargreave.

"Until Friday," Thom had purred, cutting off whatever her boss had started to say. "Bye, love."

It wasn't until Morgan had turned to go back into the liaison office that she saw Carol glowering at her from the passenger seat of Conrad's truck. Morgan had understood a little more, then.

Thom's teasing alto was the one she'd heard with Carol, in the Twospeak's yard the other day. Morgan would have to steer clear of him, she knew, even if he had seemed friendlier than her new boss. *Complication number one.*

Problem two, of course, was that her new boss was inconveniently gorgeous. His rugged features and big, strong frame—coupled with that general air of capability he'd exuded—had awoken all kinds of female molecules in her system that Morgan had assumed were dead and gone.

Luckily, even though Hargreave had been hotter than a four-alarm fire, he'd come off as reserved, the type to leave her to her business. That was a good thing, because heaven knew that the overbearing solicitude of the Twospeaks was becoming exhausting. Morgan desperately needed some space to just…think.

The final, most troubling issue, however, was her lingering sense that Hargreave hadn't quite approved of her. Still, it'd been far too late to back out, so Morgan had willed herself to push through the doors of that liaison office, holding her breath and praying her galloping heart stayed inside her chest.

Here we go, she'd thought to herself. *Here we go, not going home.*

ON THAT DAY, and in the thirty-six hours since, it had felt like a Herculean task to go through with this thing.

So, when some woman named Kisima showed up at the Twospeak home to deliver a note from Morgan's boss, she didn't exactly find Morgan in a flexible frame of mind.

No, Morgan had barely made it to her start date, and was itching to get out of there as soon as possible. If she'd thought that staying with the Twospeaks—virtual strangers mere weeks before—had been awkward with Nina stomping around the place, it was doubly weird now that Nina was gone.

With only Morgan to focus on, Christine's sympathetic pity had stopped seeming kind, and begun to feel oppressive. Add in the fact that Christine's sister Carol had been treating her with surly suspicion ever since that meeting with Hargreave and Thom, and Morgan simply could not stand another day of life with the Twospeaks.

Morgan faced down Ms. Kisima and made a snap decision. "Thanks for letting me know," she said, "But I think it's best if I head over there and get settled in like we planned."

"But Mr. Owen won't be there," Kisima sputtered, turning first to Conrad, and then to Christine in obvious consternation. "He said she shouldn't come."

"Conrad, would you mind driving me over right now?" Morgan asked. "I'm all packed and ready, and I know Carol would love to sleep in a real bed tonight, instead of on the couch again."

"Ah…" he hemmed, looking from their visitor, to his wife, to Morgan, while he tried to decide.

"This will work fine," she assured him. "Christine shouldn't have to take care of an extra person any longer—especially not with you leaving on a new tour tomorrow. I'll be fine for a few days by myself. Mr. Hargreave's note said he'll be home by the end of the week."

"This goes against my better judgment," Conrad said.

"It'll be okay. I promise. And if something goes wrong, I'll just call Christine. Or Dr. Bing," Morgan announced, moving toward the door where Kisima stood paralyzed in horror.

"Well—"

Morgan eyed the woman. "Do you have the key to his house?"

She seemed too stunned to lie. When she nodded slowly, Morgan asked her, "Do you have time to ride over with us and let me in?"

"Yes, but—"

"Good. Then it's settled," she said brightly.

Conrad sized her up with a frown, and then his gaze slid to his wife, and on to Carol. Morgan knew she had him then, because Carol was even more of a handful that Nina had been.

"Let me get my keys," he said.

The capitulation sent Kisima into a tailspin, and she began to pace around, muttering, "This is *not* what Mr. Owen intended. He is not going to be happy about this."

Her efforts to corral Morgan in the Twospeaks' family room were stymied by Conrad, however, who—now that he'd made up his mind and found his keys—was cheerfully herding the women out the front door, protests be damned.

Christine looked forlorn. "Morgan, honey, won't you reconsider? I'm worried about this." She didn't sound very convincing, however.

Morgan could feel freedom like a blast of fresh air, though, so she held her ground and calmly marched outside to load her things into the bed of Conrad's truck. Then she climbed into the narrow back seat of the extended cab and sat waiting patiently while Conrad and Kisima debated the issue a little more in the packed dirt drive.

Finally, Kisima shot her a death glare but gave up the fight and climbed in next to Morgan. With any luck, she'd shake off her resentment by the time they got there and impart enough information for Morgan to stay alive until Mr. Hargreave returned.

Conrad got behind the wheel and turned to smile at Kisima. "Morgan's a stubborn mule, no doubt about it. But you have to admit, it's kind of endearing."

Kisima looked dubious. "I'm just hoping it doesn't get her into too much trouble."

"Don't worry. I'll have someone look in on her before Owen gets back," Conrad soothed. Whatever his worries had been before, he was apparently free of misgivings now.

Christine got in next to her husband, and Morgan allowed herself a small smile of triumph.

This was going to be good. She actually felt...*excited*. And her anticipation didn't wane as they rode along, not until they drove past the square in the center of town.

That's where they came upon Thom Hannity walking quickly along the side of the road. He turned down a small street as they passed, giving them a friendly wave as he did so.

Kisima turned to watch him, but he didn't go far. He ducked into a building just a few doors down the lane.

"That's odd," the woman murmured. "I thought he was supposed to go with Mr. Owen this morning."

"Oh. Well, maybe Mr. Hargreave didn't leave after all," Morgan said.

Abruptly, she wondered what, exactly, she was walking into. It seemed much easier to move into an empty house than one containing a large, overly handsome game warden.

"No. Hargreave would have come around to rescind the note if he'd stayed," Conrad replied. "He probably just took someone else."

Kisima frowned but held her tongue. Morgan's trepidation grew.

"Anyway, you'll be alright, just like you said," Conrad called. And the man kept driving, clear out of town.

THEY TRAVELED ALONG the narrow, pocked road for longer than Morgan expected, but eventually Conrad turned onto a dirt track leading through a stand of acacia trees. After a while, they came to a clearing, and Hargreave's cottage.

The wooden building was low and wide, with a steep thatched roof, deep porch, and shuttered windows. Morgan glimpsed stretches of water between the trees and realized there must be a river or lake behind the house.

Conrad parked and they all got out of the truck.

"Wow, this is lovely," Morgan exclaimed. The pretty building was a surprise after seeing so many utilitarian concrete structures around town.

"He designed the place himself," Conrad explained. "Used local workers and materials and all that, but drew up the plans on his own. Took him quite a while, as I recall."

They stood in the yard gazing up at the house, and Morgan contemplated that new bit of information.

Kisima broke away and climbed the stairs, unlocking the front door with a key she retrieved from under a box on the porch. Morgan stepped inside after her and looked around.

The main room was large, with a vaulted ceiling crisscrossed by thick beams overhead. Bookcases lined the far wall, and a small kitchen was tucked into the corner beside the door. The back wall held two large shuttered doors and several windows that opened onto an elevated patio, surrounded by an intricate railing. Past that, a deck extended toward the water.

Opposite the kitchen, there was a campaign desk and chair set up to face the view. Deep couches with carved wood frames and thick cushions surrounded a low coffee table in front of the windows.

There were shelves everywhere, holding a fascinating collection of books and artifacts. Morgan walked across the glossy parquet floor, deeper into the room. Two doorways led into rooms off to the right.

Kisima followed her gaze and explained, "The front room is Mr. Owen's. I think the back room is supposed to be yours. No one else uses it."

Morgan peeked in, surprised by the size of it. The furniture was spare but sturdy and looked antique. There was an iron bed with canopy rails draped in mosquito netting, a nice nightstand, and a large, heavily carved mahogany wardrobe.

Like the main room, the plaster walls were painted white, in stark contrast to all the dark wood everywhere. Kisima stood in the doorway next to her and pointed to another door in the back corner.

"The washroom is in there, between the bedrooms."

Morgan walked back to take a look, noted the simple sink and toilet, and then what appeared to be an enclosed shower area with either skylights or some other openings that let in the sunlight.

A door on the opposite wall opened into the front bedroom. The bathroom was shared, then.

That seemed...intimate.

"Is this the only bathroom?" she asked.

"No, there's another small one on the other side of the house. For visitors," Kisima explained, watching her face.

Morgan thought about the way Mr. Hargreave had strode toward them at the liaison office, and tried to picture him leaning over this sink, wearing only a towel while he shaved the planes of that tanned, square jaw.

Then she gave herself a firm mental shake. Thoughts like that were *not* going to help matters. She banished the image and looked around again.

The polished wood walls reminded her of a sauna, but instead of trapping the heat from outside, the room felt cool. As a matter of fact, the whole house felt cool—and it was really nice.

Probably something to do with the high ceilings. She'd ask her boss about it sometime, but right now, she had a more pressing question.

Morgan cleared her throat and hoped she wouldn't sound stupid. "So…there's running water here, right?"

Kisima stepped aside as Conrad entered the room and put some of Morgan's things on the floor next to the wardrobe.

"After a fashion," he said. "There's a cistern outside that can use rainwater or water pumped from the well, and that runs into the house. I would go easy on using too much of it, especially until you get a feel for how it works. Not sure what kind of filters he's got on the system. Until you can ask him, you probably want to boil it and treat it before you drink any. But the toilets definitely flush."

Morgan nodded, not wanting to inquire where the sewage ended up after those flushes.

Christine called out from the main room, so the three of them went out and gathered around the back doors with her.

"Would you look at that?" the woman said. "There must be ten egrets out there."

"It's really beautiful," Morgan agreed. "Why don't more people live around here?"

Kisima shrugged, looking unimpressed as she gazed out at the lake.

"Hargreave's off the power grid here, not that that's unusual," Conrad said. "But I heard he had to fork over a pretty penny to rig it with solar power. Knowing him, he probably has a generator or two hanging around somewhere, as well." He elbowed Kisima, who snorted in agreement.

"Mr. Owen always keeps plenty of kerosene and batteries on hand," Kisima told Morgan. "They're in the kitchen."

"Okay. So, other people don't live around here because of the power issue?" Morgan asked, confused.

"Well, no. Lots of folks don't have electricity. But a body of water like this one has pros and cons," Conrad said. "Christine and I feel more comfortable where we are."

Morgan nodded, but she still didn't quite get it. She looked around out there, trying to uncover what the hidden hazards might be. Malaria, maybe, or parasites in the water?

Or...*crocodiles*, she remembered, her mouth going abruptly dry.

Kisima took one look at her expression and steered Morgan away from all those windows. "Come with me. I should probably show you the kitchen and what not before we leave."

Chapter Eleven

MORGAN SAT OUT back, enjoying the sun on her face and the warmth of the deck planks under her feet, and breathing a deep sigh of relief. The food poisoning seemed to be behind her, at last.

Now that she'd gotten past it, she'd finally caved and called Christine for help that morning. The scraps of food Mr. Hargreave had left in his kitchen were clearly not fit for human consumption anymore, and if Morgan didn't want to die of botulism before he got back, she needed to buy some fresh food. *Soon.*

Unfortunately, Christine hadn't been the one to answer the Twospeak's phone—Carol had. So instead of some reassurance and the promise of rescue, Morgan had only received a cursory, *I'll see what I can do.*

Eventually, she'd decided to give the woman a few hours to come through for her before trying the liaison office, so she'd taken a quick, bracing shower and combed out her hair, then come out here to let it dry in the sun.

When she'd moved in, she'd blithely assumed that no one would let her starve out here, but maybe that had been too optimistic. She'd nearly exhausted the food that was left, and no one had checked in on her even once.

Morgan swallowed past the knot in her throat and tried to relax. Most of the time, she didn't think about her vulnerability out here, but that was stupid. If anything wanted to get to her, there wouldn't be a whole lot she could do about it—even if that thing was on the microscopic level.

She closed her eyes, and let herself doze off for a few minutes, since she'd been up and down for the last two nights. But when a flock of egrets suddenly took flight in front of her, swooping over the lake in a great noisy cluster of squawks and flapping wings, she jerked awake again.

Morgan blinked at them as they wheeled around and around, bright white against the blue sky, before they settled back among the reeds along the opposite shore, one by one.

Something had startled them, that much was clear, but whether it was a human visitor or an animal one remained to be seen. Morgan rushed inside—a little light-headed but determined to prepare for either outcome—and put on her socks and boots.

"Noisiest birds I've ever heard," she muttered, yanking her laces tight, and then felt her face get hot.

For some reason, she'd started talking to herself here. Maybe it was the absence of the constant media onslaught she was accustomed to at home, or maybe this was the longest stretch of time she'd ever spent by herself, but still—it was getting kind of weird. Even without a soul around to hear her, she was still embarrassing herself.

With a huff, she stood and held still, straining to hear any other sounds that might indicate what was out there, but it was eerily quiet in her room. Morgan edged into the main room instead, heart thumping fast. Should she find a weapon? There wasn't much more than a bunch of books and a carved letter opener in here.

Maybe…she was getting ahead of herself. Maybe those birds did that kind of thing all the time. Stretching their wings, probably, or doing a fun bird dance.

It was still really quiet outside, though, like the world was holding its breath. Abruptly, it occurred to Morgan that if someone *was* coming, it might very well be her boss.

He had to be coming back soon, but would he even bother to warn her that he was on his way?

No, of course, he wouldn't. He probably didn't know her number and Morgan wasn't even supposed to be here.

Speaking of which, in addition to eating him out of house and home—and nearly dying in the process—she hadn't exactly worn herself out scrubbing the baseboards while he'd been gone.

She looked around wildly, wondering if the place looked clean enough for a single guy who'd left town with his bed unmade.

Morgan swallowed hard and forced herself to move from where she'd frozen in place. She was clearly overreacting.

If someone was really on their way here, it was almost certainly because Carol had asked them to come. Instead of frantically rushing around, trying to do days worth of cleaning in a matter of minutes, Morgan simply walked to her nightstand and slicked on some lip gloss.

Then she winced at her vanity.

Maybe it wasn't a six-foot hunk of handsome heading her way. Maybe that woman Kisima had roused the birds. The Preserve's cleaning woman had seemed like an efficient type— if Morgan had to bet, she'd put money on the woman doing the shopping herself, then simply dropping off the bags.

If Morgan was wrong about that, though, she needed to get her act together. At minimum, people were going to expect her to know what she needed from the market, so she rushed to the kitchen and began rifling through the meager remaining contents of the icebox, shelves and cupboards.

If she was lucky, her possible savior would let her tag along to the store. It couldn't be *that* different from what they had at home, right? She was bound to find some inspiration for meals there…but how often could she expect to go? Back in Boston, Morgan had usually shopped for food once a week. But here, without a car, that might be too much of a hassle.

She'd have to get enough to last two adults, one of whom looked like he would have a pretty decent appetite, for a few weeks at least. Mr. Hargreave would probably be desperate for home-cooking after eating trail mix for days on end.

Morgan paused, considering that.

She didn't actually know what he did when he went "into the field." For all she knew, he could have a five-star chef on call, and spend his evenings eating all kinds of gourmet, alfresco meals.

Her complete ignorance would not help her determine how much food she needed to get, or what kind. Morgan had met her new boss exactly once, and they hadn't had a chance to discuss what kind of meals he expected or enjoyed. She had no idea if he had sensitivities or allergies, or if he followed some kind of wacky caveman diet to stay so buff.

Worse still, her former life with Chip provided her zero frame of reference. By the end, they were rarely eating together.

In retrospect, Morgan realized that she'd never really gotten the chance to cook for him. She considered herself a decent cook, but her ex-husband had preferred to eat sushi and salads way more often than one man should—and he'd usually done it at work.

Not exactly a helpful body of experience to apply to her current predicament.

Morgan sighed. It was her own fault. She deserved this, coming here uninvited like she had.

If she didn't want to be fired and packed off for home, however, she couldn't throw in the towel without a fight. So, she dusted off her hands and hoisted herself onto the thick, polished wood counter, then brought down the tins and canisters that were stowed on the highest shelves.

Once she was on the ground again, Morgan pulled off lids, but most of the containers were empty of everything but dust and crumbs. Only one was half-full of something—a small brown grain that she didn't recognize. She smelled it, but only got a whiff of earth.

Mysterious. Morgan eyed what was inside the tin and figured she was looking at a really high-fiber breakfast cereal of some kind, but when she fished out a kernel and pinched it between her fingers, she decided it was far too hard to eat as it was.

She dropped the little nugget back in the container, and that was when she noticed the surface was shifting, almost imperceptibly.

"*Gross.* Bugs," she muttered, and tossed the can into the trash.

Just as quickly, she pulled it back out again. Maybe Mr. Hargreave knew what the tin contained—maybe he'd meant to save it, like some kind of compost. She'd better check with him before getting rid of it. Morgan screwed the lid back on as tight as she could and set it far off to the side.

It was no use trying to put together a grocery list, anyway. She needed everything.

Morgan darted back to her room, found her purse, and pulled the strap across her chest. The small pocket of embroidered silk was just big enough to carry an ID, some cash or credit cards, and maybe a key or two.

She'd gotten it on vacation once, but it had always seemed too impractical to use at home. There was no room for a newspaper, an e-reader, or a bottle of overpriced water. No room for lipstick, hand cream, a brush, or files from work.

Fortunately, Morgan didn't need any of that stuff here, so she slipped in the TZs that Dr. Bing's secretary had exchanged for her, the housekey that Kisima had left with her, and her passport. She wavered about bringing her work visa, too, not sure if she might need to present it on demand.

She really should've paid more attention when Dr. Bing had been going over all this stuff.

Morgan folded the document and tucked it in, just in case, then went back out to the main room to look around. If Kisima had already shopped for her, she decided, she would ask for directions to the market anyway.

That way, she could walk there herself whenever she needed something, instead of depending on others. She could meet people, even. Maybe make some friends.

She couldn't just cower in this house by herself all the time. Morgan was fluttering around right now like a total dork. She needed to get out more.

She chewed on her lip and contemplated the idea. Would hiking it be safe? There were animals to consider, after all, and humans, too. As far as she knew, this area wasn't very dangerous, but there *had* been bombings in Arusha, not too long ago.

Hell, even her neighborhood in Boston could be tricky if she didn't keep her wits about her. Out here, Morgan would be the easiest mark on the planet. She was totally clueless.

Her chest started to feel tight, and her breath started sawing in and out, in shallow little spurts. What the heck did she think she was doing? Morgan wasn't merely alone out here—she was exceedingly, conspicuously vulnerable.

There was the sudden crunch of car tires on the gravel outside, and Morgan jumped. Heavy boots clomped up the stairs. No way was that Kisima.

"Mrs. Flynn?" a man called out. "You home?"

Morgan tiptoed to the door and tried to surreptitiously peek through the slats on the front window, only to jump out of her skin when Thom Hannity's face was right there, smiling like a loon from the other side of the glass.

"Mr. Hannity! What a surprise!" Morgan gasped, opening the door and trying to calm her racing heart. "I expected Kisima. Or Christine."

Maybe she shouldn't have been surprised, though. She'd asked Carol, this man's girlfriend, for help, after all.

"Stuck with me, I'm afraid. And please, call me Thom." He looked her over, from her boots to her cross-body bag, and added, "Going somewhere?"

"Hopefully," Morgan grimaced. "I really need to get some food."

"Ah," Thom smiled, "Of course. You've been stranded out here with a bachelor's pantry, haven't you?"

Then he gave her another, more blatant once-over, his eyes lingering on her undoubtedly glossy lips. Morgan cursed herself and wished Carol had come with him.

"Yeah, about that—do you happen to know if Mr. Hargreave will be returning soon?" Morgan asked. Maybe a little reminder of what she was here for would deflect his interest.

"I believe he's due back in a couple of days." Thom stepped into the kitchen and squinted at the tins on the counter. "What are you running low on?"

Morgan quickly smoothed her hair into a ponytail and felt her cheeks to see if they were warm. Hopefully, she hadn't already turned beet red in embarrassment, but Thom's pointed notice was throwing her off her game.

Morgan hadn't felt this conscious of her appearance since she'd arrived in Africa. She'd just been an anonymous tourist on vacation with her girlfriends and knew that the lions and hippos couldn't have cared less what she looked like.

It figured that the one man she'd resolved to avoid was throwing out serious come-hither signals.

Morgan laughed at his question, though. "I'm low on everything," she told him. "I found this, but..." She opened the half-full tin and showed Thom its contents. "Who knows if it's breakfast, dinner, or bait."

Before she could warn him, Thom reached in and popped a grain into his mouth. He spit it out quickly, however, and proclaimed, "Stale."

Peering closer, he noticed the bugs and shook his head. "Trash," he announced, laughing. "You're worse off than I expected. I'd better take you to the big market outside town."

"Great," Morgan said, and pulled open the front door. "Let's go."

Thom stood where he was, looking bemused.

"What?"

"You probably need to bring some bags, to carry home what you buy." Thom's eyes traveled down her legs, frankly appreciative of them, if not her planning skills.

"Right," Morgan said, trying to look like she knew what she was doing. "I'll be right back."

She walked to her room and swung the door most of the way closed, hoping it would seem like she was searching for the required bags behind it.

As quietly as she could, she tried to shake off her looming panic. This was good. This was okay. Thom might not be the first person Morgan would've picked to take her to the store, but at least Carol had come through with someone.

Morgan had a ride there, and soon she'd have some decent food. It was progress.

She took several deep, calming breaths, then casted around, before eventually grabbing a large straw tote she'd purchased in Zanzibar before Conrad's tour. It was probably too fancy for the job, but it was all she had.

Morgan paused, remembering how Ruth had chosen a similar one for herself. What had become of it? Had it made the trip back to Boston in Ruth's luggage, along with Nina and the body?

She shook off that morose thought and rushed out of her room again. "Sorry. This is all I could find."

Thom stood up from Mr. Hargreave's desk chair and laughed, "I was beginning to wonder if I might have to go in after you."

"No…nope," she stammered, "I'm right here."

He shifted nearer. Morgan edged around him and made for the front door, fussing with the bag's handles so she could pretend she didn't see the way he was looking at her.

"After you," he drawled, trailing behind.

They left the cottage and tooled down the long dirt drive, then turned onto the paved road. As they rode along in Thom's small battered Toyota, Morgan reflected on the fact that she had not had nearly the same reaction to that bus driver hitting on her at the airport as she did just now to Thom.

She wanted to think that was because she'd known she would never see the driver again. He was a passing connection, someone destined to remain a stranger, whereas Thom was someone she was likely to see frequently—a friend of her boss.

Morgan wouldn't be able to ignore him or blow him off easily. At least, that's what she hoped was the problem. Because if it turned out that she was really some "Nice White Lady" with a hidden, biased underbelly, that would really suck.

Morgan had enough wrong with her already, without adding that to the list. True, she'd never considered herself racist back home, not by a long shot. She'd thought she was both progressive and inclusive of all kinds of people, but here in Africa, she was suddenly the odd one out—the one who didn't fit in. It'd given her perspective, for sure, but was that enough?

The politics jerky people argued about at home seemed so artificial out here. As she saw it, most humans were simply trying to live and love the best they could. It shouldn't be so hard to give each other a fair shake.

Morgan cringed in her seat, wishing it were that simple, and knowing it wasn't. How was she ever going to be accepted in this place, where her skin color and cultural conceits felt wildly unnatural, even to her? How could she spend one more minute worrying about some dude ogling her, when she clearly had bigger fish to fry?

"Almost there," Thom smiled over at her, perhaps thinking that her discomfort had to do with the heat or worries about food.

If he only knew.

Morgan looked around and realized she'd lost track of time. She asked him, "How far is this place, anyway? Could I walk there?"

Thom laughed and shook his head. "No, that's not a good idea."

Morgan didn't get a chance to ask him to elaborate, however, because just then they pulled up to a big clearing with a cluster of tarps and mats spread on the ground, and a few makeshift tables and canopies set up among them.

Thom gestured expansively. "Behold your market, my lady."

It was definitely no American grocery store. It wasn't even the vision of open-air commerce that Hollywood might have conjured up. In fact, as she sat there staring like a fool, Morgan was a little shocked by the scrappy, kind of disreputable nature of things.

Thom got out of his car and strode to the edge of the gathering, then waited for her to pick her way across the rocky ground, too. Several of the vendors closest to them broke off their conversations and stared balefully at her.

Morgan hovered at her companion's side, trying to peek at what was for sale without making eye contact or looking too oblivious. She was achingly conscious of how she must appear.

She was also completely ignorant of what to do next.

At least she had Thom with her. He could smooth the way and explain things, and Morgan could watch how people interacted with each other without making a complete mess of things. Before long, the expected protocol would surely reveal itself to her.

Except, it felt like no one was resuming their previous activities. Everyone seemed to be waiting, to see what she would do.

Thom broke the awkward silence first. "You've been here before, haven't you? With Christine, maybe?"

"Nope," Morgan admitted.

Her eyes darted around, registering more detail. Some of the vendors looked pretty aggressive, with flat stares and angry frowns. Some of the shoppers looked sketchy, too, and the vibe was…a bit scary, truth be told.

Morgan was clearly a total fraud in the adventure department and her whole internal dialogue in the car weighed even more heavily on her. They were just people, out here buying food, for crying out loud. No more, no less. Nothing to be afraid of.

Thom clapped her on the back. "Okay, well—take your time. Get whatever you need, and I'll meet you back here when you're ready to go." He began to stroll away, but called over his shoulder, "If there's something you don't see, just ask around for it."

He didn't offer any further advice or assistance, only paused for a moment, watching her. His cheerful smile was beginning to fade.

"You okay?"

She nodded, and off he went. Maybe he was testing her, she thought mournfully. Maybe this was the way new people got hazed.

But honestly, how much trouble could she get into, trying to buy rice? She took a few steps into the fray and saw that most of the sellers had prices scrawled on paper near their wares. She wouldn't even have to ask how much things cost, and if she got ripped off too badly, she'd simply offer to split the difference with her boss.

Morgan headed toward a table with a pile of what looked like squash but stopped when someone pushed past her, knocking hard into her shoulder in a way that could only have been purposeful. She glanced around warily.

A few young men in bright polo shirts and ball caps swaggered by, eyeing her with disconcerting stares. Steps away, they exchanged money and little paper packets with another group, shooting her sly smirks through the entire exchange.

They gave Morgan one more challenging stare, like they were daring her to say something, then melted back into the crowd. Morgan had lived in the city long enough to know a drug deal when she saw one, but what was she supposed to do? Chase the guys down?

She didn't even know if she was supposed to haggle over the price of eggs or not.

She didn't speak Swahili and didn't want to insult anyone by assuming they would understand English. Somehow, she doubted that any of these vendors would feel sympathy because she was trying to be helpful.

Morgan probably had *gullible* written all over her right about now.

She looked for Thom, and spotted him moving through the crowd, calling out greetings and shaking hands. He didn't glance her way, so she turned back to the tables around her.

One of the salesmen called out to her, beckoning Morgan over to his table. He gestured grandly to his assortment of beaded Masai jewelry, arranged across his table in a riot of color, then tapped the sign with his prices.

Morgan had already bought tons of this stuff, though—for herself and every other woman she knew back home.

With what she hoped was a polite smile, Morgan told him, "No, thank you," and prayed he would understand. He rapped on the price sheet again, she shook her head, and then had to turn to acknowledge the woman tugging on her arm.

That lady tugged Morgan over to a table piled with a selection of vintage t-shirts, belts, and shoes, as well as stacks of colorfully dyed fabric.

Morgan shook her head once more, but the woman began lifting things up and trying to press them into her hands.

Morgan didn't need a belt, though—she needed food. She found Thom in the swirl of people again and tried to catch his eye, but he was too busy flirting with some woman. *Shocker.*

Morgan wracked her brain for the pointers Conrad had given them at the start of the tour, when they'd visited a tourist market in Arusha before leaving town.

"*Apana…asanti…sana,*" she tried with the t-shirt lady, hoping she'd remembered the phrase correctly. "No thank you."

She pantomimed eating, hoping that might help, but the woman only watched her silently for a moment before shrugging and turning away to straighten her piles of cloth.

Morgan turned and took a few more steps, and that was when the floodgates opened. Suddenly, people were crowding around her, all yelling at once. They pulled on her arms, and jostled each other out of the way, trying to get her attention.

She couldn't understand a word anyone was saying. Morgan was hot, hungry, and a little dizzy after days of food poisoning. No one seemed willing to help her, they just seemed like they wanted to take advantage of her ignorance.

And worst of all, she'd made this bed herself.

Morgan blinked back the sudden wash of frustrated tears stinging her cheeks and tried to push through the knot of people to head back to Thom's car. The crowd stared at her but wouldn't give way.

"Excuse me," she tried. "Can I please—? Let me—"

All at once, Thom appeared in her peripheral vision, jogging over with a worried frown on his boyish, freckled face. He fired off a barrage of Swahili, and the people dispersed as quickly as they'd come.

"What's going on, love?" he asked. "What's the matter?"

Morgan swiped at her damp cheeks, totally humiliated. "So, fun fact—I have no idea how to do this."

July 12

I have never felt so stupid in my entire life. Virtually everything is a struggle. What water do I use to bathe myself? Where does the trash go? I'm starving and I need to eat (no, you can't casually throw around the word "starving" here, you twit), but where do I find food?

This shouldn't be so hard, but I don't even know the right questions to ask. What's more, I've put myself at the mercy of others, people who couldn't care less whether I sink or swim.

It's a bed of my own making and I am lying in it, alright.

Chapter Twelve

IT WAS CLEAR and cool on the morning Owen and Thom were supposed to go investigate the latest Rathbone deaths, though it promised to get much warmer later in the day.

Owen parked in front of the Preserve office and rolled down the windows in his truck, then reclined his seat and scrubbed at his face. He needed to wake up a little more if Thom was going to be riding shotgun. No telling what state the man might show up in.

He laced his fingers behind his head and watched the dark sky for signs of dawn. The early morning birdsong soothed him, as it always did.

Before long, though, the birds were taking flight from the baobab tree in the town square, and Thom's car was sputtering up behind Owen's truck, the racket jarring a resigned sigh out of him.

Thom tossed his gear in the back, then climbed in yawning. He nodded once, leaned as far back in his seat as he could, and closed his eyes—like he intended to go right back to sleep again. Judging by the fumes wafting off him, he'd definitely enjoyed a boozy night before he'd passed out in his clothes.

Terrific.

"Hello to you, too," Owen muttered, and started the engine.

He made a quick U-turn on the lane but didn't get much further before Nigel's dusty old Mini roared into the spot they'd just occupied. Owen elbowed Thom and threw the truck in park.

They got out of the truck, and Nigel opened his door—but then the passenger door of the Mini opened, too, revealing the very unexpected sight of Mr. Joseph Teleki.

Owen asked, "What's going on?"

"Glad we caught you. I'm pulling Hannity off the trip," Nigel announced brusquely. "Teleki will join you instead."

"Why?" Owen wondered. "What's happened?"

Joseph was watching Thom, so Owen turned to look at him, too. The man had grown decidedly more alert than he'd been moments ago and had a curious glint in his eye.

He was not, however, the least bit confused, and remained uncharacteristically silent as he reached into the truck bed for his pack.

Owen scowled and turned back to the Preserve's director. Nigel had never done something like this before. Normally, he concerned himself with the business side of things and left day-to-day operations to Owen—as it was supposed to be.

Nigel said, "Long story, I'm afraid. I can tell you more when you get back. Hannity, meet me back here at ten and we'll go over what I need from you." He paused, then added, "And for chrissakes, clean yourself up before then."

He hit a button on his key fob, and Joseph moved to pull his gear from the boot of the Mini. Once he stepped toward Owen's truck, Nigel got behind the wheel and pulled away a moment later.

"What the hell just happened?" Owen asked Thom.

Thom rolled his eyes. "Like I know?" he shrugged. He tossed his pack into the back seat of his car and got in. "Bon voyage, boys," he called, "happy hunting." He snapped off an insouciant salute as he pulled away.

Owen and Joseph stared at each other. "So…how's retirement treating you?" Owen wondered.

Joseph chuckled as he pulled open the passenger door. "You know, it's not quite what I expected."

Owen shook his head and got in, intending to ask him how he'd gotten saddled with this duty again. They'd only driven a block before his phone buzzed with a reminder, though.

Owen glanced down, saw what was on his screen and slammed on the brakes. "Damn it," he cursed, banging on the steering wheel. "God *damn* it."

Joseph looked at him quizzically, and he swore again, more profanely this time.

"What's wrong now?" the scout inquired, calm as always.

Owen exhaled, and scrubbed his palms over his skull. "I forgot that I'm supposed to bring that Flynn woman out to my place today. She is…" He trailed off and shook his head.

Not going to appreciate the delay.

"Flynn woman?" Joseph prodded.

"Sorry. She's this American from one of Conrad Twospeak's tours. Apparently, she's staying in the country for a while, so Dr. Bing asked me if I had a job for her."

"Ah, of course," Joseph said, understanding dawning. "I'd heard Nadra was working on another child."

"She sure is," Owen agreed grimly. "But she feels pretty awful right now, which means I'm in the market for a housekeeper."

Joseph sat looking at him patiently. Owen tried to think of some way to make it all work, but short of going over and pulling the poor woman out of bed right now, there was no finessing it.

"I'm not going to be able to fetch her before we leave, am I?"

"Probably not."

Owen groaned. "She's going to think I abandoned her."

"Could you leave a note with the Twospeaks?" Joseph wondered, "To let her know what's going on?"

He sighed. It would be another delay, but it probably had to be done. And yet, "With Conrad gone, everyone else will definitely still be asleep. I don't want to disturb them."

"You could leave the woman your key," Joseph mused, "and let her make her own way over."

"I have no idea what she even knows how to do. Plus, she won't have access to a car if she needs one."

"So, she stays at the Twospeaks until you get back. Surely she won't make a fuss?"

"I wouldn't think so. She didn't seem the type, but she *is* American," Owen pointed out.

Joseph snorted.

Owen looked back at the office and decided, "I'll leave a note for Mrs. Flynn with Kisima. She likes Christine—she won't mind bringing it over there after her shift later."

With a bit of a pang, Owen remembered that look of relief Mrs. Flynn had given him two days ago. There was nothing to be done for it, however. She'd have to wait to escape for a little longer.

With that sorted, Owen threw the truck in reverse and left the engine running while he unlocked the office and dashed inside. Five minutes later, he and Joseph were on their way once more.

THE DAY WAS long and full of annoyances, but Owen and Joseph finally arrived at the field station closest to the newest Rathbone deaths late that afternoon.

They shared another meal with the C Quadrant scouts—not nearly as mouth-watering as the last had been—then spent the night on some spare bunks before heading out into the bush early the following morning.

Though they'd inquired at dinner, and again at breakfast the next day, the scouts here did not seem familiar with the Temba brothers, or what had happened in the neighboring sector of the park.

Owen had longed to ask if they'd seen Thom or a dark-haired stranger, but that would've meant tipping his hand about what he knew. However, between the translation anomalies and Nigel's odd actions yesterday, Owen wasn't at all sure how much to reveal, or to whom.

He didn't want Teleki to know he'd translated the recording on his own, yet—especially until he determined the nature of the man's connection to Nigel.

Owen thought about that as they trudged quietly through the underbrush, but had to put it aside when a fetid, unmistakable smell alerted him to their arrival. A moment later, Joseph pointed out the yellow plastic ribbons tied to some of the trees, fluttering innocuously in the breeze as they marked the scene of the slaughter.

Except for the buzzing of the insects, it was oddly bereft of other noise here. No birds sang, no small creatures rustled in the underbrush, nothing—just a terrible, unnatural quiet.

Owen suspected that whatever animals lived in the area had simply paused to assess their arrival, but even so, Nigel's words floated back to him. *None of the other animals went near them.*

Owen stayed alert, listening for anything else that might be out there with them.

"Let's fan out," he told Joseph. "Look for where the forensic team investigated."

Joseph discovered the space first. "There," he said, pointing out the little red tags dangling from bushes and tall weeds, sketching a broad circle nearby, close to the ground.

Nodding to each other, then combed the patch of earth within, but didn't find anything that hadn't already been covered in the scouting reports.

Owen straightened from his crouch and huffed in frustration. Then he picked his way to a spot just outside the perimeter, pulled out Nigel's latest set of photos, and compared them to the real site, searching for any indication that something had changed since the original investigation.

The angles of the photos still seemed strange, with less-than-straightforward composition and cropping. These were not the routine photos Owen was used to seeing in these situations. He could feel it in his gut, but it was hard to define why.

When Joseph came to join him, he handed over the prints. "What do you think?"

Teleki looked between the pictures and the grisly ground. "Perhaps…the carcasses have been moved a bit since these were taken?"

"I saw that. My guess is a jackal came in for a look—it must not have liked what it was tasting, though. Looks like it let go pretty fast."

Joseph went closer and bent to get a better look.

"These two have bite marks on the neck. But look here, on the rump of this one—no claws or bites. I don't see the prints of whatever took them down either," he said, clearly perplexed.

"Maybe it rained." Owen pulled some notes from the pocket of his vest and consulted them. "The reports don't mention the bites."

Joseph nodded. "Not surprising. These look more recent," he mused, "They don't look like they were running away when it happened."

"True," Owen agreed. "Which means something other than our usual predators killed them." He folded the report and shoved it back into his pocket. "So…what did?"

Teleki straightened and braced his hands on his hips. "Why does the ground look so clean? There are no signs of struggle. It's like the Rathbones simply laid down on their own."

"I can't tell if it was mucked up in these," Owen replied, tapping the photos in his hand. "Grass is in the way." He shoved the useless prints into his pocket, too, and looked around.

"What do you say we have a little look around outside the perimeter?" he asked.

Joseph nodded, and together they walked a pattern through the high grass, meticulously moving out from where the carcasses lay. Two vultures wheeled low in the sky above them, their shadows skating over the ground below as the two men searched.

Owen suppressed a shudder. *Not* his favorite critters.

Joseph murmured quietly, "How many dead does this make now?"

"This is the sixth site in two months," Owen told him. "We've lost twelve Rathbones altogether. Never this many at once, though."

And never, in his entire tenure at the Preserve, had he come across something quite this troubling.

He scowled as they moved along, trying for the umpteenth time to puzzle it out.

Joseph shook his head, looking as troubled by the numbers as Owen was. But then he stopped short and stared at his feet. A second later, he beckoned Owen over and grabbed his arm, pointing down.

The earth under the scout's boots was stained a dark, rusty brown that looked an awful lot like blood that had soaked into the earth several days ago. It lay at the center of an area of flattened grass and broken twigs, almost exactly the size of a small gazelle.

"Apparently, I was right," Owen commented. "It hasn't rained."

Stepping carefully, they combed the nearby grass and rapidly found three other areas that looked the same. Joseph's expression was stormy.

"There's no excuse for this. Why didn't Forensics find these?" he growled, showing more emotion than Owen had ever seen from him.

Owen could empathize. He knew for a fact that his teams were trained better than this. It was infuriating. Someone had done a half-assed job up here, and then some.

He tried to reign in his temper. "They sure as hell should have. But what I want to know right now is…" He looked over the spot to where the carcasses currently lay. "Why move the bodies way over there?"

Joseph peered closely at one of the stains, then strode over to the bodies and examined them once more. When he stood up, though, he still looked baffled.

"Perhaps they were trying to hide the blood? The amount that's on the ground looks consistent with a gunshot wound, but…none of these animals appears to have been shot," he said.

Owen went to stand next to him. "Maybe the wounds are hidden underneath. These bites sure aren't big enough to make stains like that," he commented.

They both looked back and forth, and Owen knew the other man was measuring the distance, like he was.

After a moment, he commented, "I find the distance they were moved very interesting."

"I agree. Just outside the perimeter that Forensics will search." Then Joseph held out his hand. "May I see those photos you had again?"

Owen handed them over and watched as Joseph stepped carefully around the marked site, holding up the pictures to estimate the cameraman's vantage points.

Eventually, he announced, "Well, they were obviously trying to keep the original locations out of their shots."

Something about the scout's pronouncement made Owen peer more closely at him. Was he being handled right now? It was hard to tell.

"Perhaps," he hedged, "But the quality of the photos is so poor. It's a wonder they even bothered."

He cocked his head and gazed down at the nearest animal. Was there something strange about the position of the head? Or maybe the jaw?

As if he'd read his mind, Joseph handed back the pictures and pulled out a pair of latex gloves. Next thing Owen knew, the man was probing at the animal's neck and prying open its mouth.

"Hang on," Owen told him.

He slipped off his pack and dropped it near his boots, but before he could bend to dig out his own gloves, a bolt of white-hot agony seared into his shoulder.

He grunted and dropped into an unsteady crouch, knocked off-balance by the force of it. *Christ.* Had he been *shot?*

Joseph hit the dirt and brought Owen the rest of the way down with him. Three more gunshots echoed across the field in quick succession but didn't find their marks. He and Teleki were probably hidden by the tall grass, sprawled flat amidst the stinking, rotting carcasses as they were.

Owen pressed on his shoulder and stifled a groan. He *had* been shot. What the hell was going on?

Teleki dragged himself closer. "Where did it come from?" he hissed, trying to peer through the vegetation.

No one could fake that look on his face, and it told Owen all he needed to know about the man's allegiances—that was a win, at least.

"Don't know," Owen muttered, trying to raise himself up on his good arm so he could look around.

He ended up rolling onto his back instead, however, beginning to feel a little queasy. "Damn it. Those bastards got me good."

"Stay down," Joseph scolded, holding Owen in place with a firm hand on his chest.

Owen took shallow breaths and watched ragged shreds of clouds skate across the sky above them. No vultures, at least, but how long before they scented him?

He and Teleki held still for several long minutes, but everything stayed quiet.

Joseph said, "I guess someone wasn't too keen on us poking around. But what did they expect us to do? Have a picnic out here?"

Owen didn't answer, too busy fighting down the bile trying to work its way up his throat.

Joseph narrowed his eyes at him. "Hargreave? Are you okay?"

Chapter Thirteen

OWEN CRANED TO get a better look at his shoulder, then swore a blue streak when the effort sent a burst of pain through him. "I think they might've just clipped me. Hurts like hell, though."

That was an understatement. Owen pressed on his shoulder with his free hand, but he didn't like how fast his fingers were growing wet. He'd had to wipe them on the grass a few times already, and they were rapidly getting sticky again.

He didn't want to think about it, though, so he wondered, "How'd they even know we were going to be here? Were they fucking *waiting* for us?"

Joseph gestured for Owen to pipe down and stay put, then wriggled a short distance away. Slowly, he raised the butt of his rifle up out of the grass, but if the shooter was still there, they didn't take the bait.

Joseph looked back at Owen, a question in his eyes. Owen shrugged, then winced when the pain flared. He was as baffled as anyone. That damn shot had come out nowhere.

Teleki sighted through his scope and panned around the clearing but didn't seem to find anything useful out there.

"They could be moving," he whispered, echoing Owen's thoughts. Joseph paused, then added, "If they're good enough that we missed them coming in…"

Owen completed the thought for him. "…then we won't find them now." Especially with him out of commission.

Whoever was out there knew exactly where Owen and Joseph were, however, and they could start taking potshots whenever they damn well pleased.

It was obvious to Owen who they were dealing with, but just to confirm his suspicions, he asked, "So, what do you think? Locals? Or professionals?"

"Locals," Joseph answered without hesitation, "No question."

"Yeah," he agreed, "But were they lying in wait, or did they follow us in?"

Teleki didn't have a ready answer to that. His gaze was roving over the grass and brush, searching the terrain with a practiced eye.

From his position, Owen only spotted two small lovebirds, flitting among the low tree branches and the grass. That was it, the sum total of fauna activity.

They waited for an eternity, watching and listening while the normal signs of life gradually returned to the clearing around them. Nothing seemed out of the ordinary any longer—nothing but the dead animals staring Owen in the face.

With low ugly squawks, a couple of vultures landed a short distance from Owen, flapping and hopping around. Thankfully, they didn't seem inclined to get closer to the carrion—or him—with an able-bodied man so close by. There were still questions to be answered about that man, however.

Owen studied Teleki. There was no denying he'd been as shocked as Owen when the lead started flying, but how had he ended up on this expedition to begin with?

As they'd driven out of town the day before, he'd only said, *"Mr. Cotton briefed me on the way over."*

In the moment, noncommittal had been the best Owen could manage.

So, he'd said, "*No worries,*" and then drove for many more miles before curiosity got the best of him. Eventually, he'd inquired, "*When did Cotton tell you about this trip?*"

"*Early yesterday. He sent someone over,*" Joseph had explained, placing the contact at hours before Owen himself had learned of it.

Things had gotten even stranger when Teleki added, "*I didn't expect him to pick me up himself, though. I figured the other guy would do it.*"

Owen had been confused. "*Did you know him? The other guy?*"

"*No. I've never seen him before. Young man, named Stephen.*"

Joseph had searched Owen's face for a reaction, but his own expression hadn't given anything away.

Owen had searched his memory for every one of Nigel's cronies he'd ever met but had come up empty. "*That's odd. I have no idea who that is. You sure his name was Stephen?*"

"*Didn't catch his last name,*" Joseph had said. "*You don't know him?*"

"*No, I don't.*"

Owen had been baffled then, and he was still baffled now.

Victoriaville was too small a town to contain any strangers, but suddenly, it contained two—Owen's inconveniently-attractive new housekeeper and this mystery man, connected in some way to the director of the Preserve.

That had to be a coincidence. Right?

OWEN BLINKED AND shook himself back to the present. He'd hoped Joseph would prove to be an untainted ally in this investigation, but between his abridged translation and Nigel taking a shine to him, Owen wasn't sure what to think anymore.

The closer Teleki's links to the Preserve director became, the less Owen felt like he should trust him.

Still, the man had him at a bit of a disadvantage out here, and he'd done nothing to exploit it. Instead, Joseph seemed to be doing his level best to protect him.

Perhaps that was how he intended win Owen over, though.

And…now the blood loss was making him paranoid.

Owen snorted. He already had plenty to keep himself busy worrying about Nigel and Thom. There was a new dynamic developing between them that he couldn't quite identify, but the thought of them getting chummy strained the imagination.

They clearly knew more about the Rathbone situation than they were letting on, and Owen was at a loss as to what it was. While he was lying in a field and leaking like a sieve was not the time to figure it out, however.

"You think we're clear?" he whispered, eyeing those glossy black vultures, edging closer.

"Looks like it," Joseph replied. "I bet the shooter headed out the same way we came in. That's the most direct route to the closest road."

"I hope you're right, because…I should get back too," Owen said, as calmly as he could. "Think I'm…losing a bit of blood over here."

He attempted to hold off the darkness trying to creep in at the edges of his vision, while he fumbled his phone out of his pocket.

Joseph scuttled quickly over. Owen handed him the phone and listened to him call the field station for help.

The biggest Rathbone doe lay inches away, its sightless eyes aimed right at him. Owen stared back at it as Teleki recited their coordinates to the scouts, until something out of place caught his eye further down the neck. He peered at it, then pulled his pack closer so he could get a glove and probe the wound.

Joseph ended his call and crawled closer, just as Owen pulled a small, blunt metal object free.

"Well, well. Would you look at that," he said, holding it up for Teleki to see. "Someone clearly forgot this."

Joseph squinted at it, then reached quickly into his own pack for a sterile evidence bag. He held it open so Owen could drop his discovery inside.

Pain momentarily forgotten, Owen continued examining the gazelle's neck and mouth for the rest of the tranquilizer dart that he knew had to be there—but sadly came up empty.

Frustrated, he rolled to his back, but the abyss beckoned a little too insistently from that position. So, he hauled himself awkwardly into a sitting position, making himself dizzy with the effort and nearly vomiting from the pain.

Joseph finished noting the details on the bag, then sealed it and handed it over. Owen zipped it into an inside vest pocket, where he could keep it safe.

"Should we check the others?" he asked.

Teleki pointed at the spreading stain high on Owen's sleeve and shook his head. "No time. We have to get you out of here. Hold still for a minute."

He pulled a field kit from his pack and set to work peeling back Owen's vest and shirt so he could bandage the injury. "Think you can walk?"

"Maybe. But not very far," Owen admitted. He braced his hands on his knees, submitting to the scout's treatment while his head swam. He couldn't quite keep himself from flinching every time Teleki had to touch his shoulder.

Fortunately, the other man was quite adept, finishing his ministrations in short order and pulling Owen's clothes back into place. As usual, Owen couldn't read his expression.

"How bad is it?" he asked.

Joseph dug out a plat of C Quadrant and pored over it, not making eye contact. "I've seen worse," he hedged.

"Listen, we shouldn't go back the way we came. The gunman could be there," Owen said. His thoughts were getting muzzy, though. "How many of them were there?" he inquired, followed by, "Do you suppose they took my truck?"

Joseph looked up and studied him critically. Owen wondered if he might be going into shock.

Teleki shook his head. "We would have heard the engine." He returned his gaze to the map on his knees. "The medics are going to meet us at this outpost," he said, indicating the spot. "It's slightly farther than the other one nearby, but the terrain looks easier. Just a few-minute walk. You think you can make it?"

"Bloody hell," Owen breathed, trying to steel himself.

One glance told him it was more than a *few-minute walk*, but at least Joseph wasn't lying about the ground being flat.

He muttered, "Yeah, alright. Let's do it."

He clamped his teeth together and forced himself to a standing position, swayed precariously once he was up, and eyed his companion. Owen had several inches on the man, and probably outweighed him by twenty kilos or more.

Owen didn't have any choice but to make it, not unless they wanted to split up, or wait who knew how long for help to get to them. And besides, even if his truck was still parked where they'd left it, he wasn't going to chance starting it until they were sure it hadn't been tampered with.

He swayed again, trying to process all the variables.

"Okay, off we go." Joseph steadied Owen's good arm and urged him into a walk. As they made their way slowly through the bush, Owen staggered along in a daze, refusing to stop and rest for fear he wouldn't be able to get up again.

It seemed to take an eternity, but miraculously, his legs kept moving even after the rest of him had pretty much checked out. By the time they made it to the outpost, though, Joseph was nearly carrying him up the stairs.

Owen had to hand it to the man, however—Teleki was stronger than he looked. He got Owen onto the porch, Owen took two steps, then slumped bodily onto a bench, giving in to the faint he'd been trying like hell to avoid.

He had no idea how long he was out, but when he drifted back to consciousness, Joseph had removed his shirt and vest and was checking on the wound in his shoulder, the outpost's emergency medical kit spread out on the ground beside them.

"Where's everybody?" he mumbled—or tried to, anyway.

"On their way."

It occurred to Owen, kind of foggily, that the shooter could easily have followed them here or intercepted the medics en route.

He also had no idea how much time had passed, and that was troubling. Owen had to struggle to stay awake as Joseph braced him on the bench, trying to hear past the blood whooshing in his ears for the sound of vehicles approaching.

Not like he could do anything about it. Owen felt about as solid as a beached jellyfish at the moment.

At last, however, the big yellow medic truck came crashing through the brush on the narrow dirt track. Owen noted its arrival with relief, but the passage of time felt off, like the minutes were skipping around, rather than proceeding in an orderly way, like they were supposed to.

Joseph kept popping up in unexpected positions—one minute sitting next to him, the next trotting up the porch steps, and the next coming out of the outpost's front door.

Owen wasn't quite clear on how or when they'd gotten him strapped to a collapsible stretcher, but before long, the medics were hoisting him and moving him to the bed of their truck.

One of them climbed in the back with him for the ride to the field station, and Owen's eyes drifted shut again, blocking out the sun glaring through the treetops.

We need to get those animals into the lab for autopsies. Had he managed to say it out loud? It was impossible to tell. He couldn't see Teleki anywhere.

The medic beside him had rigged up an IV at some point, and as Owen studied the fluid dripping through the line, the urgency drained clear out of him. His limbs had gone boneless and he was teetering on the verge of unconsciousness again, when he looked out the back of the truck and suddenly spotted Joseph.

He was standing on the outpost porch, his expression inscrutable as he watched the remaining medic gather his gear. Then he glanced around, reached to the floor, and carefully stuffed what looked like Owen's shirt and vest inside his pack.

Teleki slung it on his shoulder and dashed down the stairs in the medic's wake. He cast one last, worried glance around before he passed out of Owen's field of vision.

A moment later he was climbing into the passenger seat. The medic got behind the wheel, barked something unintelligible into his radio, and Owen finally succumbed to that beckoning oblivion.

Chapter Fourteen

MORGAN STOOD NEAR the kitchen of the cottage, feeling foolish and on edge. She had been here for days and, other than keeping things tidy, she still had no idea what she ought to be doing on a daily basis.

She'd been hired to be the housekeeper. She was supposed to cook and clean, that much was obvious—but was that *it?*

Morgan had been so impatient to get away from the overly attentive Twospeaks that she hadn't thought to ask any important questions when they'd dropped her off.

That wasn't like her. She was more of a *think it through* type than a *jump first* kind of woman—not that anyone here would guess that.

It served her right that the only human being who'd expressed any concern over her well-being since she'd moved in was the one person she'd intended to avoid.

Morgan supposed Thom had a boyish charm that might have grown on her eventually—*if* she'd been able overlook his somewhat glaring "quirks." However, it hadn't taken long to figure out that he was definitely a guy who fudged lines here and there, and likely crossed some, too.

Out of nowhere, Morgan wondered what her ex-husband would've said about him. Chip would probably have accused her of being too uptight to *get* Thom, she decided. He'd always been inclined to side with…pretty much anyone over her.

It seemed odd, in retrospect, that she'd never put up much of a fuss about that. Morgan took a deep breath and sighed, the last few years weighing heavily on her as they always did.

She didn't need to worry about them anymore, though. She was far from the past and far from Boston. She could choose her own way forward, starting right here in this cottage.

Still, as she stared into the small, neat kitchen, she had to admit that her first few steps had been somewhat disappointing.

On her trip to the market with Thom, she'd been way out of her depth. The vendors hadn't been the least bit friendly—even after Thom had come to help her—and instead of feeling inspired by all the fresh ingredients, Morgan had only gotten overwhelmed.

Then, when they'd come back here, Thom had given her a brief rundown on how to prepare the foods she'd purchased, but he'd run through everything so quickly that Morgan was no longer sure what got peeled, what got boiled, or what got sautéed.

It made her wonder how many frozen dinners she'd been microwaving back home, anyway.

Too many, it seemed. Morgan stepped into the kitchen and ran her hand over the polished wood counter, looking at the sweet potatoes and eggplants in the baskets against the wall. There was chicken in the fridge now, and eggs, too. Simple ingredients. Things she'd eaten a thousand times.

She would be able to figure this out, Morgan thought irritably, if she would just get out of her own way. She needed to stick to the basics until Mr. Hargreave got back, instead of getting tangled up in thoughts of what he might expect of her.

She didn't even have to be a mind reader. Once her boss returned, she could find out everything she needed to know by asking him directly.

In the meantime, taking cooking advice from a young and probably reckless bachelor wasn't her most brilliant plan. For all Morgan knew, Thom had no idea what the heck he was talking about.

She peeked in the fridge and pulled out the cup of water she'd left for herself earlier.

She wished she knew what Mr. Hargreave was used to. Had his last housekeeper coddled him with special dishes and treats? Had the woman left a spoiled mama's boy for Morgan to contend with?

She groaned and left the kitchen, pacing slowly around the living room. She'd dusted and straightened everything she could reach and had arranged the kitchen neatly. She had swept the floors with the broom she'd found and kept the porch and the patio clean.

One time, Morgan had even tried sweeping the packed dirt in front of the house, like she'd seen women doing from the tour van. That dirt was so perfect now, no one would ever be able to tell where Thom had parked his car.

She'd felt completely ridiculous doing it, but at least no one had been around to see her creating the pint-sized Zen garden.

Despite everything else she'd tackled, however, Morgan had left Mr. Hargreave's room largely untouched. She'd made his bed, and that was it.

Absent his explicit instructions, she hadn't felt comfortable violating any more of his personal space than she already had—probably because she was ravenous for details about the man, and a simple dusting could easily turn into a stalkery examination if she wasn't careful.

Luckily, Thom had told her that, even though Mr. Hargreave had "run into a snag," he should be returning in a day or two. Morgan would undoubtedly get her marching orders then, and she wouldn't have to worry so much about screwing up unwittingly.

The only glaring issue with that was, her presence here at all was bound to be a bit of a shock, and Morgan did not want to be caught with her feet up when her boss finally came through that front door.

She sank onto the couch and tried to picture how it would go. What would she say? Should she have some kind of snack ready?

Her grandma—like all grandmas, probably—had always said that the way to a man's heart was through his stomach. So if Hargreave found Morgan cooking upon his arrival, maybe that would smooth things over.

Which…brought her right back around to the food conundrum. How could it be so hard to guess what the infernal man liked to eat?

Morgan blew out a long, frustrated breath. She was getting nowhere by just sitting here. She had to burn off this restless energy, before experimenting with some of that food for dinner.

At least there were plenty of spices in that kitchen. Once Morgan figured out which ones went together best, she'd be well on her way to creating something edible.

With a plan of sorts in place, she wandered into the bathroom, figuring she'd give it another wipe-down before attacking her cooking experiment. As she'd done every day, Morgan held a rag under the faucet, then ran it over the sink, until a sudden movement two feet in front of her face made her spring back with a gasp.

A large, colorful lizard slowly sauntered across the mirror, like that was a perfectly normal place for it to be. Morgan pressed a hand to her chest, trying to calm her galloping heart.

No way could that thing stay in here. She'd never be able to shower again. Unfortunately, it was moving at a snail's pace, and wouldn't find its way outside until next year at this rate.

Morgan had to do something. She tried to shoo it toward the shower area with the rag, but the reptile froze in place, opened its weird little mouth and hissed at her.

What a surprise. Morgan was standing here snapping her rag at the lizard's backside like this was a high school locker room—no wonder it was getting angry.

She didn't think it was dangerous, but who was kidding who, here? Morgan hadn't been doing a lot of *thinking* in general lately.

And, since the lizard was proving more resolute than she'd anticipated, Morgan decided that discretion was the better part of valor. She beat a tactical retreat to the kitchen, to see if she could find something better than a rag to aid her cause.

In all the commotion, she hadn't even heard the truck pull up outside.

She did, however, hear the two heavy sets of boots on the front porch, as well as the deep voices that went with them.

Hell Lizard forgotten, Morgan backed warily toward her bedroom. A key turned in the lock, the front door swung open, and an African man that she did not recognize stepped inside.

He spotted her quickly, and seemed just as surprised to see Morgan as she was to see him. He hesitated for only a moment, though, before turning to help the second man through the door.

Morgan exhaled in relief. At last, her long-lost employer had returned.

"Mr. Hargreave. Welcome home," she called, wringing her hands.

She tried to channel her inner housekeeper—culled from hours of TV sitcoms in her childhood—and smile nicely, but capably, at them.

The first man looked at Mr. Hargreave, and her boss looked at her. No, not looked—he blinked rapidly and *gaped* at her. He opened his mouth to speak, then closed it again. Struck dumb, apparently, by her presence.

His companion cleared his throat, looked between them again, then went quietly back outside. Maybe he was getting a gun. Maybe he was getting their stuff from the truck. Maybe he was a smart man and wanted to flee all this awkwardness.

Her boss leaned on the door jamb and recovered his composure enough to ask, "Mrs. Flynn, what on earth are you doing here?"

"Oh. Well…" Morgan bit her lip, and nervously smoothed the stray hairs back from her forehead. In all her ruminating, how had she not worked out an answer to this most obvious of questions? "I, uh…I had Conrad and Kisima bring me…over," she stammered.

She glanced from Hargreave to his friend, who'd slipped back in. "Um, they brought me over here last…last week?" Morgan held her breath and forced herself to make eye contact. "Please don't be mad. I kind of steamrolled them."

Her boss's gaze was unwavering. "But I left word that I would pick you up when I got back," he said. He was piqued. Of course, he was.

"Yes, I know that. I—" she swallowed hard and forced the rest out, "—I thought I might be more useful here."

Morgan knew that was a weak excuse, and she couldn't help glancing nervously at the other man. They might not know each other, but maybe he could save her from herself.

Hargreave noted the look. He said immediately, "Forgive me. This is my colleague, Joseph Teleki. Joseph, this is my new housekeeper, Morgan Flynn. From America."

Joseph raised an eyebrow but then smiled graciously. He scrubbed his hand quickly on the leg of his pants and reached out to shake hers.

"A pleasure, Mrs. Flynn," he said, in pleasantly soft voice. "Likewise."

Her boss straightened from the door jamb and reached out to relieve Mr. Teleki of the pack he was still holding, but he winced and swayed with the effort.

"*Kuwa makini*," Joseph chided. "Be careful."

"I keep forgetting," Mr. Hargreave replied, shaking his head. He relinquished the bag and grabbed the doorframe, ruefully massaging his shoulder.

Morgan frowned. "Mr. Hargreave, are you okay?" He didn't look very steady and his friend was busy with their bags.

She crossed the room and reached out to take her boss's arm, but hesitated inches from that big bicep. This was probably a terrible idea. If he decided to go down, he would definitely take her with him.

"Yeah, but I'd better sit down," he said, smiling a little sheepishly at her. Morgan ducked under his arm and helped him shuffle the few steps to his desk chair, the nearest available spot. He dropped stiffly into it.

She stood beside him, paralyzed by shock. Hargreave was a large, warm, strapping male, and he smelled incredible. Wrapping her arm around his waist had sent an electric jolt of awareness thrumming through her that was…completely unprofessional. *Crap.*

Joseph seemed utterly unaware of her sudden bout of insanity. He asked, "Why don't I make some tea?" As amiably as if he were the housekeeper in this equation.

Morgan shook off her ridiculous stupor. "I can do it, but," she hesitated, "I'm not sure how you…" She cleared her throat. "…sirs take it."

Her boss chuckled. "We'll get to that. First, please call me Owen. No need to be formal."

Then he gestured to Joseph, saying, "Will you stay for dinner, mate? I can ring up Thom and get him to take you home after we eat."

"I'd be happy to," Joseph said. "But don't bother Hannity on my account. My wife can pick me up later."

He moved into the kitchen and looked around, finding the kettle on the stove and bringing it to the sink to fill. Morgan followed him, pulling out the cups and sugar, and the little tin of loose tea leaves.

Joseph whispered, "Don't worry. I can do this. You probably have things to discuss with Hargreave, at the moment."

Morgan's face grew warm and she backed away. "Thanks."

"Anytime."

When she spun around, Owen beckoned her over again. "Mrs. Flynn, please forgive me for leaving you hanging. I wasn't expecting to go on that trip, and once we got up there…"

He scowled and readjusted his big frame in the chair, sighing, "We had a little more excitement than planned. I was, uh…yeah, so I…anyway, some bugger shot me in the shoulder, and I had to cool my heels in the infirmary for a bit."

Morgan had no idea what to say. She was horrified, for sure, and dying to know more—but it didn't feel particularly appropriate to pepper him with questions.

Somehow, being a game warden hadn't struck her as quite so perilous back when Dr. Bing had mentioned it to her. It had just seemed sort of…hot. She flushed again.

"I'm so sorry that happened," Morgan finally managed to say. "And I should apologize, too. I know I shouldn't have come early. It just seemed silly to hang around there doing nothing when I could be here working."

She looked around frantically, as if a way to make herself useful would pop up out of nowhere. Morgan needed to do something with her hands right away, because she clearly couldn't be trusted to keep her mouth shut, otherwise.

She was also painfully aware that she should be the one making tea right now—but she'd been relieved when Joseph offered. She didn't have a clue how to brew it when it didn't come wrapped in neat little bags. She ought to have stayed in the kitchen to watch how it was done.

"Anyway, I'll be home for a while now," Owen told her. "The doc said I need to heal up before I go traipsing around the bush again."

"Understandable." Morgan agreed.

Her eyes lit on the pile of gear near the door, and suddenly her job seemed clear. She reached for the top bag and said, "Why don't I bring your stuff into your room for you?"

Morgan tugged on the handle, then paused. What the hell did he have in there? Bricks? It was way too heavy to hoist easily, and she'd never make it into his room without totally embarrassing herself.

Owen coughed a little, attempting to cover a laugh. "That won't be necessary," he told her. "I can take care of it later."

She eyed him. "But your arm is hurt."

He shrugged, flexed it like a bodybuilder, then winced. "Other one works fine," he grinned.

Morgan stood there like an ass, trying not to stare at his muscles, and at a mortifying loss for words.

Owen eased back carefully in his chair, stretching his long legs out in front of him. "So, how has it gone here? Have you found everything you need so far?"

She released a breath. This, at least, was a safe topic. "Yes, thank you," she said. "Kisima was kind enough to show me around when they brought me over. Conrad taught me how to work the water. I've cleaned and dusted, and..." Morgan stopped at his amused expression.

"Listen. I'm really sorry I came when you said not to. I just thought..." She trailed off again.

She had no idea what she'd thought. She *hadn't* thought. She simply acted, plain and simple.

Owen studied her with green eyes that didn't miss a trick, but he didn't look angry, thank god. His eyes shifted to the kitchen, then back to her. He ran his hand through his thick brown hair, and a small smile played at his mouth.

"No worries," he said softly. "I'm just happy it all worked out."

Joseph came out of the kitchen bearing two steaming mugs, handed one to her, then placed the other on the desk next to

Owen. He went back to retrieve his own cup from the kitchen counter, then perched casually on the armrest of the couch, facing Hargreave.

Morgan stood stiffly in place, glad to have something to hold, but not sure what to do next. She had to remind herself that she was the help, here. She probably wasn't supposed to sit around socializing.

Both men lifted their cups and sipped, but neither of them spoke right away.

Morgan cleared her throat. "Will you be ready to eat soon? You must be hungry."

She sounded exactly like her grandma. If only she had the woman's cooking skills.

Joseph raised his eyebrows and looked to Owen. Her boss asked dubiously, "You know, I didn't even think to ask before. I didn't leave much in the pantry—have you had a chance to pick up anything at the market yet?"

"Actually yes," Morgan said. "Mr. Hannity brought me over there yesterday."

She stood a little straighter and took a long gulp of tea. That was an accomplishment, right? She'd shopped, exactly like a housekeeper was supposed to.

Morgan's gaze drifted over her boss as she waited for his reply. His powerful thighs kept drawing her attention, like bees to honey. She wrenched her eyes away, dismayed.

He didn't seem to notice. Owen only snorted, rolling his eyes at Joseph and drawling sarcastically, "What a surprise."

Morgan soldiered on, unsure if she'd done the right thing or not now. "I hope that was okay. I wrote down how much I spent, but I didn't buy much. I wasn't quite sure what you'd like. Or when you would be back."

Or if you'd be furious I was here. She wished she could sink into the floor. Her inexperience was probably becoming clearer to them by the minute.

Morgan took another large gulp of tea to prevent herself from blurting out any other incoherent nonsense.

Why did Owen make her so nervous? For one thing, he was bigger than she remembered, but he was also so ridiculously...virile. He looked like he was capable of just about anything, and she was about to be alone in this house with him for quite a while.

She trusted him, though. Implicitly. Another enigma.

Owen shifted uncomfortably in his chair, grimacing again. "I'm sure whatever you have will be fine," he said. "We'll go again tomorrow if need be."

Morgan frowned, listening to his tone. Did he sound disappointed? *Damn it.* The poor man had been expecting a decent meal, hadn't he? She was a total idiot.

Joseph asked him pointedly, "Will you be able to drive by then?"

Owen nodded at the man, a sly smile quirking up the corner of his mouth. "Probably." It was clearly bravado, and Joseph chuckled.

"If I can't, I'm sure our intrepid Mrs. Flynn can manage it."

"That's right," Morgan agreed, trying to sound as capable as he expected.

She stepped past the men and slipped into the kitchen, heading to the sink to rinse out her curiously empty cup. She'd only taken two sips. When had that happened?

If it were more private in here, she might be able to think without them watching her. Morgan rested a hand on one of the refilled canisters, hoping for inspiration.

The men chatted for a few minutes, and then Owen went to kneel next to his gear, searching in the packs while he called someone on his cell.

As she watched him out of the corner of her eye, he rose gingerly and headed into his room, oblivious to her presence. *Naturally.*

Joseph materialized next to her, asking kindly, "Can I assist?"

"Sure," Morgan chirped, relieved.

She slid the tin she was holding closer, pried it open and said, "I thought I'd make some rice." She watched his face, which remained impassive. "Or this, if you prefer."

She opened a second can and showed him the contents. She couldn't remember what Thom had called it, but she was pretty sure it got boiled.

Joseph glanced around, then reached for the second can, saying carefully, "Perhaps you can peel and chop that pumpkin before we do the *ugali?*"

Morgan nodded quickly, grabbing the small gourd from the counter. This evening was nothing like Halloween, though—unless one considered her barely-believable housekeeper costume.

Joseph continued, "Then we can cook it outside..." At this, he peered in the icebox and retrieved a package, "...with this chicken, if you'd like."

While Morgan chopped, he rinsed the meat, plated it, and carried it out to the patio. He laid wood in the fire pit and started a low flame, then set a metal rack over it to make a grill.

The rest of the dinner prep went the same way. Joseph outlined what Morgan would want to do next, then perfectly performed the role of humble assistant.

He was smooth, she'd give him that—and Morgan had never been so grateful for a kindness in her life.

Owen only interrupted the process once, bellowing at the top of his lungs from the bathroom, then marching grimly by with the madly wriggling lizard gripped in one hand.

Morgan ducked her head. "*Shoot.* I forgot about that guy."

Joseph grinned, then went to throw the front door wide for him.

When he returned, he pulled the plates and bowls down from the shelf for her, grabbed the canister and a jar of water, and went back out to the firepit.

Morgan washed the utensils and dishes they had used so far and stirred the fragrant curried stew they'd made from the grilled chicken and pumpkin cubes.

She was curious to see what Joseph was up to, though, so she took the plates and bowls and headed out to the patio. She found both the men there, Owen sitting on the sun-dappled deck at the table, and Joseph cooking small flat rounds of bread on the little improvised grill.

They'd been talking quietly, but they stopped when they noticed her.

"I think the stew is about ready. Should I bring it out?" she asked.

"Sure. Thanks," Owen said. He seemed relaxed and easygoing, with a dark bottle of beer near his elbow that Joseph must have brought out to him without her noticing.

He'd put his arm in a sling, but it didn't hide the bulky bandage under his shirt. For his sake, Morgan hoped his doctors had given him some painkillers, too. *Poor guy.*

She retrieved the pot from the kitchen and set it on the end of the table. Joseph handed her the plate piled with his rounds of bread, so Morgan put that next to the mush he called *ugali*. It looked like cream of wheat, to her.

She ladled out full servings for each of them, feeling downright housekeeperly as she did so. She had a moment of anxiety when she got to her own bowl, wondering if she should take hers inside—but then Owen patted the place next to his, and nudged the chair out with his foot.

Morgan sat down, looked at her napkin, and popped up again.

"Forgot the forks," she explained, blushing what had to be a flaming red.

As she turned to go, Joseph offered a round of bread to Owen, who promptly began using it to scoop up his stew. Joseph handed another to Morgan, smiling kindly.

"Your fork," Owen said gently, "Mrs. Flynn." When he said her name, the deep resonance of his voice made her shiver.

To make it go away, Morgan plopped back down, humiliated by her uncontrollable reaction to him, but also by the fact that she'd forgotten what the bread was used for. At least it reminded her to eat only with her right hand, another bit of dining etiquette she'd learned on Conrad's safari.

Around the lump in her throat, she told them, "I know I must seem like a complete joke, but I'll get the hang of this. I promise."

Hargreave looked at her, his eyes soft with understanding. "I'm not worried," he said.

With that, they fell silent, eating companionably. After a while, though, Morgan found herself blurting out, "If you want me to call you Owen, you should also call me Morgan."

He said, "Fair enough."

For some reason, that made her mouth run away with her sense. "Besides," she barreled on, "I'm not a missus anymore. Even when I was, I wasn't Mrs. Flynn."

Given the way both men froze and stared at her, that might have been too…informative. Morgan kept her eyes on Owen's remarkably seductive wrist as he served her more of the stew, so she wouldn't have to look him in the eye.

"Right," he said, and then, after a slight pause, "So…Flynn is your…maiden name?"

Her eyes flicked up to his face, but Owen was looking down at his bowl, digging into his food.

"Yup. I'm back to being a maiden, I guess. Almost as if Chip McGee never happened," she squeaked, then immediately wanted to hide her head under the table. *TMI, you nitwit.*

There was a long, awkward stretch of quiet.

At last, Joseph saved her once more, this time by deftly changing the subject. "So, Morgan—what brings you to this part of the world, anyway?"

She chewed carefully, considering what to say. Telling your new boss and his coworker that you were a total train wreck, seemed like…not quite the thing one should do.

July 16

It's strange that a man built like a lumberjack would remind me of a painting I once saw in a museum —but the sight of Owen's profile, bent low over his book in a spill of light, does just that.
It's like he's been spotlighted—like I'm supposed *to pay attention.*
And I do—to the sinews in his forearms, sheened in the heat. And to his neck, somehow both thick and graceful at once.
He doesn't move except to turn pages, but he seems at ease—more so than he has in days.
I hate to disturb him, but I know I will. So I hold my breath, and pause a moment longer in the shadows.
I shouldn't watch him so much—I know that, but I can't seem to look away. He's my boss, and devastatingly handsome, and a mystery—and far too fascinating for this woman's peace of mind.

Chapter Fifteen

MORGAN'S LOVELY HAZEL eyes had followed him around the cottage for days, always watching—and knowing it had made Owen jumpy, like his skin was suddenly too tight.

He wasn't sure why she had such an effect on him. She was pretty, that much was true, but also kind. She was smart and practical and had enough of a lock on the sexy nursemaid vibe, that Owen had had to cower in his room for the majority of his convalescence.

Okay, so maybe he did have a clue why she flustered him. But he didn't want to think about what might have happened if he hadn't hidden himself away. Clearly, he was far, far too aware of his housekeeper—perhaps it was some bizarre side effect of being shot.

Whatever it was, Morgan kept busting him looking right back at her, and he couldn't stop wondering how long she'd be staying in the country. They hadn't discussed it yet and, at the moment, that information seemed critical.

As usual, though, Owen had bigger things to worry about today. It was his first day back in the office, and stuff had piled up in his absence—but the medics had sternly instructed him to take it easy for a while.

Owen turned on the electric kettle, then tramped across the creaky floor to the window. He opened the blinds to let in light and fresh air, then slumped into his desk chair with a groan. He'd waited to come in until after lunch, but even that sad effort had worn him out.

Owen glanced around his office. It always struck him how unfamiliar everything looked when he'd been gone for a while. He could probably list the books on the shelves, his personal effects, and all the tools and supplies with his eyes closed—but when he went away for more than a day or two, they always seemed to lose the sense of being *his*. The familiar became foreign, strange, no longer imbued with his life force.

However, the phone would invariably ring or Owen would crack open a ledger, and when he next looked around, the contents of the room had become *his* possessions again.

For some reason, though, in the doldrums of *this* warm and hazy afternoon, that transformation wasn't happening. Something was nagging at him—but he couldn't figure out what it was.

Owen massaged his healing shoulder, stayed quiet and still, and waited.

A nesting bird or animal didn't seem right, and neither did a snake or lizard. Owen couldn't see or smell any signs of those.

He leaned back in his chair and let his eyes travel slowly around the room. They hitched here and there on certain items, then moved on, but gradually he realized that they kept returning to his bookshelves.

At first glance, there didn't appear to be anything wrong. However, if Owen had learned anything from his years in the field, it was how much quicker his subconscious picked up on anomalies in the landscape.

He hauled himself to his feet and walked carefully over to that side of the room, examining the casement, the books, the floor, and the wall behind. As Owen explored, he absently began straightening the book spines, lining them up in even rows at the edges of the shelves.

In the next moment, he wondered why that was necessary at all. The day before his trip, he'd had a chat with Kisima right here. Owen could see her dusting these very shelves and straightening these books, while he'd moved around his desk and gathered his things to go.

That visual key unlocked the rest—the way the bookshelves themselves had been moved slightly out of alignment with each other, and the fact that two of the bottom doors were swung shut, but not latched. The piles of ledgers and mail on his worktable were now slightly uneven, and when Owen shuffled through them, he discovered they were out of order, as well.

He looked around the room and saw the dried mud that his own boots had left on the floor, but he also noted bits of dirt in the corners he hadn't visited.

Owen went to stand behind his desk so he could study it carefully. One of the drawers wasn't fully closed—the sticky one, that required a special lift-and-slide move to close properly.

Not one of these details would have been the slightest bit unusual after even half a day's work from him. They were only odd now because Owen and Kisima had made a point of straightening up the place before his departure, and he hadn't accomplished anything today yet.

His office *should* have remained empty and locked the whole time he was gone. He'd kept the key with him—in the field and when he was recovering—but it was possible that other people might've gotten access in the confusion of the shooting and its aftermath.

Joseph Teleki, in particular. His instincts told him he could trust the man, but some of the dots still weren't lining up properly. Plus, when Owen contemplated how little he knew about the former scout—and how much he'd been at his mercy out there in the bush—he couldn't help but bristle a bit.

Joseph was skilled, however, and Owen's office had not been searched by a professional. That much was clear.

He ruled out poachers and their ilk—they might have an interest in the game reports he had on file, but they would've been attuned to small nuances, as he was, and would have known how to cover up their tracks.

Of course, Owen's spy could easily be someone much closer to him. Thom and Nigel had both been here, and both been acting strangely lately.

Whoever it was had gone through everything, and then done a crap job of hiding it—almost like they *wanted* him to know they'd been there. But why? And what were they looking for?

Fortunately, they'd stopped here and hadn't decided to take a spin around his cottage, too. Morgan had been out there in the *wop-wops* by herself for days. Anything could've happened, and Owen would never have known the difference.

He pushed that thought away, not liking the way it made his whole chest feel tight. Morgan had been fine on her own and was undoubtedly still fine.

In fact, she'd mentioned this morning that she was going to try her hand at making pizza for dinner. Someone in distress didn't come up with stuff like that.

Owen's mood shifted a little, thinking about what a nice change that meal would make if she pulled it off. He was looking forward to it, because the idea was just spontaneous and optimistic enough that it seemed...kind of fun.

When was the last time he'd had any of that?

In the front room, the kettle started whistling, so he went out to fix himself a cup of tea.

Maybe he was making too much out of this break-in business. Whoever it was had looked everywhere, taken nothing important, and made an effort to put things back where they belonged.

The hot topic was whether they'd gotten what they came for, but Owen wasn't going to solve that puzzle by standing around speculating.

If he let his brain chew on it in the background for a while, without trying to force the issue, something was bound to occur to him eventually. There had to be a logical reason for the snooping.

Owen grabbed his cup and walked back to his office, then sat down at his desk. He stared at the piles of field reports on his desk but pushed them aside and picked up his phone instead.

He wanted to check with Morgan, in case she needed him to pick up any special ingredients on his way home later.

Before the call could connect, the bell on the front door jingled and Kisima came bustling in, the fringe of her head wrap blowing in the breeze. When she noticed him sitting there, she startled, then put her hands on her hips and scowled.

"Oh, no you don't," she warned. "You are not supposed to be back yet."

"Why not?" he smirked, scanning her face.

It was possible Kisima already knew that his office had been searched. It was equally possible she knew who did it. If she did, however, she gave no sign of it.

Owen reminded himself that she was his friend, and he trusted her. He tried to resist the urge to rub at his shoulder, not wanting to give her more ammunition than she already had—but the damn thing had started throbbing the minute she'd looked at it.

"You were not supposed to return until tomorrow," she continued, "So now you're going to be underfoot while I try to clean up this mess."

Kisima gestured at the crumbles of dirt his boots—and other boots—had left around the room. "I work hard enough already, picking up after you men."

"That you do," Owen agreed, smiling at her. "You'd also empty that dustpan of yours right into my tea if I said otherwise, *Bibi*."

"Probably worse," she chided. "I'd warn you not to cross me, but you're already doing it."

She looked him over, impatience warring with concern on her face. "You're not indestructible, you know."

"I have recently been made aware of that fact."

Kisima snorted, then clapped rapidly at him, like he was a misbehaving goat. "Are you going to toss something else on the floor before you get out of here, or are you going to make me work around you?"

When Owen dipped his chin and raised his eyebrows at her, she lost all patience and yelled, "You should be home! Resting!"

Oh, well. That look had always worked on his mum. "Kisima, I appreciate your concern," he said, "Very much. But I'd like you to take the day off instead."

"I wish I could!" she cried, then clammed up like she'd said too much.

Owen debated with himself. If she was unhappy about losing the day's wage, he could find a way to make it up to her. He'd hate for her to have to to skip getting one of her magnificent hairstyles because of his paranoia.

"Of course, you can," Owen reassured her. "I promise you can come in an extra day next week, if you want."

"*Hapana*, that's not the problem. Joseph called me yesterday. He told me Mr. Cotton wanted me to come *today*. He said it was important."

"Is that so," Owen murmured.

That was odd, indeed. Nigel was a stickler for hierarchy, and if he thought the office needed to be cleaned, he wouldn't call Kisima directly—in Owen's absence, he would have had Thom make the call.

So, why contact Teleki to act as his secretary? Unless…Nigel and Joseph had more of a connection than anyone realized.

The evidence appeared to add up. At least twice now, Nigel had approached Joseph personally, despite the man's supposed retirement.

Owen was confident Cotton wasn't throwing him the work out of an abundance of goodwill—so what did Teleki have that Nigel wanted?

Added to all that was the notion that Nigel had urgently wanted the office sanitized before Owen's scheduled return. He had trouble believing it was because Nigel wanted to welcome him back in pristine style.

"Kisima," he asked, "did Joseph explain why they wanted you here today? Were they expecting visitors or something?"

"How am I supposed to know? You call me, and I come clean. Mr. Cotton calls, and I get here quicker. I'm not paid to be your social director."

Owen crossed his arms over his chest and sighed. Kisima eyed the dirt on the floor with pointed disdain.

Dissembling was not exactly her forte. If Owen had to guess, he'd say she truly didn't know what had happened here.

However, he did want another chance to look around before she scoured the place. If there were any clues left for him to find, they'd never survive her inimitable efforts.

He changed tacks. "Don't worry about the floor, *Bibi*. It's just a little dirt. I can take care of it." When she looked at him, he gave her a conspiratorial wink.

She softened her battle stance a tiny fraction, resting a hand on her hip just like his mother used to do. "Well, I'll say this for you—at least you managed to come back in one piece. Sort of."

"You would never have let me forget it, if I hadn't," Owen pointed out. Then he ducked his head and peeked up through his lashes, like one of her young sons.

Kisima snorted and gave up on the schoolmarm routine, laughing, "Honestly. With the way you people carry on out there, you're lucky this kind of thing doesn't happen more often. Frankly, I'm surprised no one got you sooner."

Owen shifted in his seat, automatically bracing his bum shoulder as he did so. Kisima's eyes tracked the gesture, and she frowned again.

Before she could launch a new scolding, he said, "Listen, go on home and spend some time with your boys." He stood up and came around the desk, backing her out the door as he spoke. "I've got this."

She looked dubious, but she still turned and took a few steps. "Mr. Cotton is going to fire me," she said.

"He won't. I promise. I will swear that you were here and did a wonderful job," Owen told her, herding her closer to the front door.

"And Joseph? You'll tell him, too?"

He didn't care how suspicious she was, as long as she stepped over that threshold. "Joseph, too," he assured her. "You have my word."

Kisima considered that, and apparently decided he was full of it. "*Bwana*, please," she begged, trying to duck around him. "Just let me go in and sweep up the mud."

"Kisima, I said I would do it, and I will. You go home and relax. Enjoy your family." He stepped back into the office and shooed her off and was a little amazed when she actually listened to him.

As he watched through the front window, Kisima shook her head and walked off. Once she'd turned the corner at the end of the block, he closed the blinds and locked the front door.

Then he swiftly combed through his office and the front room one more time, pausing at Nigel's door for a few minutes before deciding not to risk it.

Once he was satisfied that he'd seen all there was to see, he put his office to rights, swept the floors, dusted every surface, and wiped down the WC.

It wouldn't pass muster with Kisima, but it would definitely fool Nigel.

Before he left, Owen thought about grabbing a few files to work on at home, but ultimately decided against it. If he really wanted to cover for Kisima, it had to look as if he hadn't been in today. Besides, nothing was so important that it couldn't wait until tomorrow, anyway.

Outside, Owen hesitated at the door of his truck, then went back and double-checked the deadbolt on the office door. As far as he knew, only he and Nigel had that key, which presumably meant the place would be secure.

Maybe that was wishful thinking, but it would have to do for now. He was hardly going to camp out here like a guard dog, waiting for more trouble.

Then he slid gingerly behind the wheel and set off toward home. About halfway there, out of nowhere, his brain offered up a small, but tempting, morsel.

Morgan.

Who was *not*, as it turned out, a married woman.

Owen shook off that thought. It was an irrelevant detail. Unimportant, even.

He shouldn't imagine her standing in his kitchen, and he shouldn't think about her slim, tan legs, or the pleasant lilt of her voice.

By now, Morgan would probably be kneading the dough for her pizza. By the time Owen got home, the cottage would be filled with the aroma of a new and interesting dinner cooking.

Owen blinked away the enticing thought and tried to refocus before he got too entrenched. First thing tomorrow, he had to track down the lab and see if they'd found anything during their autopsies of the gazelles he'd had sent to them.

As much as it pained him, he couldn't afford any distractions from the Rathbone situation—especially when they came in the form of lovely, hazel-eyed housekeepers.

Chapter Sixteen

THERE WAS NO doubt about it. Morgan's pizza experiment had been a gratifying success last night.

True, it hadn't come out perfectly, and Owen hadn't made a big deal out of it—but Morgan hadn't expected him to. He had, however, returned from work early and hovered semi-patiently around the kitchen until dinner was ready, then happily polished off almost the entire pie. That had to count for something.

She was on the right track.

If she were smart, Morgan would be focusing on that victory today, and not on things she couldn't control. However, she'd slept badly last night, and woken up with a headache.

It had put her in a bit of a mood, and the weather wasn't helping. The oppressive humidity promised a storm before long, so after Owen left for work, Morgan cleaned up the kitchen and then sat out on the patio, hoping to catch a breeze off the lake before rain forced her back inside.

She'd brought a book, but it just sat in her lap unopened while she watched the clouds roll in. They were getting darker and heavier at their bases, swelling and roiling as low rumbles of thunder reverberated through the air.

The surface of the lake was scattered with short little waves and reflected the scuttling clouds like a sheet of liquid mercury. In the stiff breeze, the grasses and reeds along the shore bent and danced, and so did the loose pages of her journal.

Morgan hadn't been able to concentrate on writing in it, when her mind was swirling with too many thoughts of Owen, Ruth, and her old life back in Boston.

The whole safari thing was supposed to have been a way to reconnect Morgan to normalcy again, but it hadn't succeeded. Instead, Morgan felt even more cut off—as disconnected and alone as she'd ever been these last few years.

And she'd leaned into it, of course, by choosing to stay someplace that had almost no contact with the wider world instead of going home and facing her failures and sorrows.

Morgan pushed the hair off her forehead and scooted her chair closer to the edge of the patio, so she could prop her feet on the smooth bentwood railing. Owen had told her he'd built himself, and it was beautiful—a winding, twisting work of art.

Gusts of air tickled along her legs, and Morgan knew she should find all of this beautiful.

Most days, she did. Today, though, she was out of sorts.

It probably wasn't helping that she hadn't made many friends yet. But how was that supposed to happen? She never went anywhere. She never talked to anyone. And even if she did, it probably wouldn't alleviate her emotional isolation. People didn't open up to someone they barely knew.

A month ago, none of this would've mattered. She'd been so sure then that disconnecting was what she needed to absorb the pain of her miscarriage and divorce. Once she had Ruth's death to grieve, too, the self-quarantine seemed doubly necessary.

Morgan had thought that, in this small slice of the world, she'd be able to process it all—or at least return to functioning adequately.

She wasn't so sure that was happening yet, because even though she'd been looking, she still couldn't see the way forward.

For now, she'd have to continue immersing herself in mundane chores and the physical exertion of maintaining a stranger's home, and see where it went. Maybe it would be enough

If she could ever focus on anything other than the man of the house, that was. The one place she needed a disconnect was the one place she couldn't seem to manage it.

Sharing this cottage with Owen was intimate, but it was an artificial intimacy, and she wasn't sure it was helping her emotional recalibration.

They were companions, sort of. Sometimes Hargreave seemed as if he was on the verge of kicking back and breaking the ice—but he always pulled back before Morgan could get to know him better.

His reticence smarted a bit. Morgan didn't think of herself as particularly needy, but she wanted Owen to like her. She wanted to crack open his quiet reserve, and she wanted to know what he was thinking when he got that little wrinkle between his brows. She wanted him to tell her things about himself, and she wanted him to be equally curious about her.

It seemed unlikely, though. Even when he'd come home, injured and barely upright, he hadn't given much away.

Thinking back, she still couldn't believe how matter-of-fact both men had acted about the incident, leading Morgan to assume that getting shot at was something mundane—something that might happen at any time in the life of a game warden.

She'd tried to roll with it, but it had shocked and worried her. Owen hadn't tried to lessen that feeling. He'd only holed up in his room and turned down most of her offers of help as he recuperated.

Her lack of detachment was probably reason number one that she made her a lousy housekeeper, though. People who did this job all the time probably never gave the relationship component a second thought. Unlike Morgan, they wouldn't get emotionally invested in Owen and how he viewed them. They wouldn't want to be friends.

Morgan let out a huff of frustration and laid her book aside, anchoring her journal pages under it. Wasting time out here sulking wasn't going to give her any big breakthroughs. She needed to go back inside and find something to constructive to do.

She could rearrange something—alphabetize books, or line them up by size. Arrange tchotchkes by height or fruit by color. She could even organize Owen's sock drawer.

Morgan snorted. At first, she'd tried to leave as little of a footprint in this house as possible, keeping things exactly as they'd been at the moment she'd arrived. She'd tried to erase her presence from the living room, attempted to be invisible in the bathroom, and kept her own room pristine, in case Owen decided he cared.

After a while, though, her efforts began to feel ridiculous. For one thing, she was alone most of the time, puttering around with only the birds outside as her audience. Even when Owen had been home recovering, he'd kept mostly to his room.

What was more, neither Owen nor his friends remotely approached the degree of formality Morgan thought she was supposed to maintain. Thom had been as laid back as men came, Joseph had been warm and kind, and even Owen seemed a little taken aback if Morgan acted too starchy.

Besides, the total suppression of her presence and personality was stiflingly boring. Morgan had never been much good at smothering herself—her sister Meg could attest to that.

So, Morgan had stopped playing ghost housekeeper, and started inhabiting the place. She wasn't a slob, but she did start adding little embellishments here and there. A big, interesting leaf in a jar on the coffee table, an artfully arranged stack of books on a shelf, a vase of wildflowers in the kitchen.

Morgan like to watch Owen's face for the moment he noticed the liberties she was taking with his house and his possessions. It wasn't the most exciting hobby. His reaction was the same every time.

First, he'd note the flourish with calm detachment, and then he'd return to whatever he'd been doing before. That was it. Owen's brow might furrow or his expression flicker, but he never said a word. It was maddening.

Overhead, a streak of lightning arrowed over the lake, followed almost immediately by a crack of thunder so sharp it made her jump. Morgan grabbed her book and the pages of her journal and turned to look at the living room.

Few of her decorating diversions lasted. In the absence of any commentary form her boss, she always started to worry that Owen hated what she was doing. After it had gnawed at her for a few hours and he'd gone to bed, Morgan always ended up tiptoeing out of her room to reverse what she'd done.

Brave and unapologetic, she was not.

Her taciturn employer never said a word about that, either. Of course, he didn't—the man was impenetrable. He was perfectly amenable whenever Morgan asked for help or had a question, but that's where it ended. And the times when she caught glimpses of a wry and clever side to his personality were so few and far between, it felt as if she'd imagined them half the time.

Morgan shook her head and groaned at her foolishness. She needed to stop obsessing and stay in her lane. Clean the house, cook the meals, full stop. No more approval-seeking behavior—she had bigger issues to deal with.

She eyed the threatening clouds and sighed. She was tired and grouchy, and it was definitely looking like she was going to be cooped up in the house for the rest of the afternoon.

Instead of lounging around like she had nothing else to do, she ought to be trying to think of something good to make for dinner. But how on earth was she going to surpass homemade pizza on four hours of sleep and with a splitting headache? How was she supposed to toe that line between amusing herself and trying to please Owen right now?

There was being a good employee, and then there was whatever *this* was.

There was no ignoring his appeal. He was an extraordinarily attractive, with his height and strapping build, rugged features, and deep voice. His restraint, combined with their physical proximity, only added to her fascination.

Morgan was aware of him every moment he was under this roof, and she often had to remind herself that she was the employee here. But she had her place, and there was no way to develop a repartee with him without it being awkward and unprofessional.

Trying to bridge the gap was not part of her job description. Getting Owen to like her—that was even shakier ground. He was her boss, not some potential conquest.

All of a sudden, she was jolted out of her skin by a deafening clap of thunder right over her head. The hairs on her arms rose at the electric shimmer in the air and a moment later, fat drops of rain began to pelt her.

With an undignified yelp, Morgan clutched her things against her chest and hurried into the house. She pulled the French doors shut behind her, fumbled with the damp latches for a minute, then turned, breathless and soaked.

Before she could blink, a bear of a man came barreling through the front door with a fitting roar.

Morgan shrieked. The man yelled again. They faced off, trying to wipe the rain from their eyes and ready for battle. Only gradually did it dawn on Morgan that she was staring at her boss.

He had clearly realized who she was, too, because Owen smiled sheepishly and mumbled, "Oh, hey Morgan. Sorry to startle you."

When she only squeaked in response, he chuckled awkwardly. "Came home early, again. Obviously."

"I see that." Morgan staggered over to the coffee table and dropped her book and journal pages to the wood. "Are you, uh…are you home for the rest of the day?"

"Yeah, definitely. Doc wasn't joking when he said it'd take a while to get back on my feet."

His hair was wet and plastered to his skull. He raked his hands back through it and her eyes snagged on his biceps, bulging under his shirtsleeves.

Swallowing hard, she wrenched her gaze back to his face, her cheeks flaming. Thankfully, he didn't appear to have registered that she was checking him out. Instead, Owen was studying the storm sweeping across the patio behind her.

"Don't worry, you'll get there," she told him. "I'm sure it just takes time."

"Right," he agreed. "And at least I have dinner to look forward to."

Dinner. She hadn't figured out dinner yet. Morgan's eyes flew to the little clock on the shelf above the couch and she wanted to groan.

Could that be right? How had it gotten so late already?

"Right," she smiled. Weakly, though, because her head was pounding.

Naturally, he picked up on that. "Yeah, sorry I didn't give you more notice," he explained. "I was doing fine, until I wasn't."

Morgan rubbed her temples and tried to think. "Okay, uh…"

"Do you have what you need? Will we need to shop again soon?"

Owen moved to his desk and absently shuffled some things around. When she didn't answer right away, his smile faded, replaced by another expression Morgan couldn't quite unravel.

"Although maybe Thom's beaten me to it. Has he been by to take you to the market again?" He looked up and gazed at her steadily.

"No, he hasn't. Not since that first time," Morgan assured him. "And I will need to go soon, if that's all right." At least she had a better feel for what they'd need, now that she'd fed Owen for several days. That would take care of next week, but it wouldn't solve tonight's problem.

"Absolutely. We can go in the morning if the rain lets up," he agreed. "And if not, I can try to get what you need in town."

Maybe shopping with Owen would go better than her outing with his friend had—he certainly seemed like the kind of man who'd command respect.

Outside, the rain was pouring down in torrents and the thunder was rumbling. Morgan plucked at her damp clothes uncomfortably, and his eyes flickered down, tracking her movements.

They were stuck here together for the rest of the day, followed by a long stormy night. Alone in the house with no one but each other. That shouldn't feel as erotic as it did.

All the air promptly squeezed out of the room.

"Great." Morgan nodded a bit too fast. "I'll just change into some dry clothes, and then I'll get started on dinner." She snatched up her book and ducked into her room before Owen could reply. It wasn't the best exit, but at least she hadn't mentioned "slipping into something a bit more comfortable."

When she'd been stewing out back, she hadn't been able to think of a single thing to do. Now that Owen was back early, however, it seemed like there were a thousand tasks she should have accomplished.

Before she could tackle them, though, Morgan needed to nix the wet t-shirt contest and take something for her stupid headache. It was getting worse by the minute, and if she didn't knock it out now, it was bound to turn into a migraine.

If that happened, she could be laid up for days. What would Owen think of that?

His voice sounded right behind her, far closer than he'd been a moment ago because she hadn't remembered to close her door. "One more thing, sorry. I found this out front this morning. I assume it's yours?"

Pooled in his large, calloused palm was the little gold locket Meg had given Morgan for her college graduation.

"Oh," she breathed, "Thank you so much. I've been looking for that everywhere." She reached for it and he tipped it gently into her hand.

"The clasp is getting touchy," she explained. "I really shouldn't wear it anymore, but it's sentimental, I guess." She touched it carefully and was taken aback that the metal was still warm from his skin.

"Glad to be of service," he said softly, then backed out of her room.

Morgan swung the door closed, shucked her wet clothes and draped them on the chair to dry, then dug through her medical kit for ibuprofen.

Once she'd thrown on a dry outfit and come back out, Owen was standing near the couch with a vague frown on his face. She still had no idea what she was going to cook for the man and already had a feeling his presence was going to be more of a distraction than an inspiration.

"Everything okay?" she wondered.

"I couldn't find today's thing," he told her, gesturing around. "I give up. Where is it?"

Morgan stood there, blinking at him like a doofus and not sure what to say.

He cleared his throat, like it might jog her into a response.

She glanced around the room, feeling like she was missing something. "Today's thing?"

He nodded.

"I'm not sure what you mean," she confessed.

"You know—the thing you do every day. I can't find it," Owen explained.

He looked like an overgrown kid, shifting in his shoes like he'd done something wrong. Owen wouldn't meet her eye, and she wondered if she was staring at him like he had three heads—the same way she felt like he often looked at her. Maybe they weren't so different after all. Maybe he wasn't made of stone.

Maybe it was kind of adorable that they now had this game between them. For some odd reason, his nervousness made her feel like she was flying.

"I didn't get a chance to do it yet," Morgan told him, feeling her face flame anew.

She looked at the books in his hands, and then at the shelves on the wall. He'd apparently decided to rearrange his books while she'd been changing, into the exact pattern she'd come up with days ago, and then undone hours later.

She waved at the shelf like a gameshow hostess. "Besides, it looks like you beat me to it."

Owen nodded, relaxing a little. "Back on your game tomorrow, aye?" He folded his arms across his chest, trying to look commanding. "No slacking off, madam."

Morgan grinned. "I wouldn't dream of it," she assured him, then straightened from her doorframe, where she'd been leaning like this was no big whoop, and not a momentous shift in their relationship.

All at once, though, she saw the papers on the coffee table. The loose pages of her journal were just sitting there, out in plain sight. Where *anyone* could read them, including her boss.

The warmth suffusing her abruptly drained away, leaving her panicked and cold. Morgan hustled her ass over, bumping past him to snatch them up—a little too abruptly, if the expression on Owen's face was anything to go by.

"Did I leave these here?" Morgan squeaked, her voice high and fake. "Got to be worth another demerit, right? For unseemly clutter?"

She booked back into her room and quickly shut the papers in her night table drawer. Who even wrote something that personal on loose leaf paper, anyway? Had she lost her mind?

Owen hadn't moved when she came out again. He just stood there, rooted to the spot and staring as Morgan marched into the kitchen and began banging around. While she poked through the fridge and the cabinets, hoping for culinary inspiration, she started humming to herself, just to prove how unaffected she was.

He probably thought she was insane.

Owen called out, "Hey, Morgan?"

She stuck her head out of the kitchen, trying to look inquisitive and not horrified.

Why couldn't the blank sheets of paper have been the ones on top? Why did it have to be yesterday's entry—in which she'd waxed poetic about him?

"You feeling okay today?" he asked.

Oh, Christ. "Yeah. Sure. Just a bit of a headache, that's all."

Owen studied her, then nodded. "That makes sense. You don't look...I mean, you look..." He trailed off, perhaps realizing that it wasn't exactly sporting to finish a sentence in which you told a woman you barely knew that she looked like shit.

Morgan might have even felt sorry for him if she weren't so utterly desperate to get away from his penetrating gaze.

"I'm fine!" she chirped, then ducked back into the kitchen.

She didn't feel like humming anymore.

Out in the living room, Owen let out a loud breath and flopped onto the couch.

So much for détentes.

August 8

Tonight, in the orange glow of the lantern light, Owen read the same few pages over and over. Between the shadows of concentration on his face, and the way those broad shoulders hunched toward the book—like he could prevent the words from getting away—I knew I couldn't resist. I had to know what had transfixed him like that.

When he went to bed, I found the book, and brought it back to my room. I flipped through the pages near his bookmark, searching for the passage and suddenly…there it was. It had to be.

A man remembering the love of his youth—lingering over memories of her. The fragrance of her hair, near the nape of her neck. The softness of the skin that covered her hips. The curve of her stomach, the wings of her collarbones, the whole of her both eternally precious and lost to the vagaries of time.

How am I supposed to reconcile such an imposing man with the poignance of those words? With the romance of them?

I can't help but wonder: who was the one that made him revel in those words? And when?

As always, I am alone in my bed, here in the dark, and Owen is alone in his…mere feet apart in distance, but legions apart in understanding.

Chapter Seventeen

WHEN OWEN NEARLY trampled the small gold oval in the dirt beside his car that morning, he'd had no doubt whatsoever who it belonged to.

More than once, he'd been transfixed by its metallic sheen, nestled in the hollow of Morgan's throat—it shifted and caught the light every time she spoke or swallowed or turned her head.

So when he returned it to her tonight, he had to make a real effort not to stare at her neck, or lower, as he did so—a task made doubly difficult by the fact that Morgan's t-shirt was more than a little damp, and clinging to her breasts in a very distracting way.

Owen blurted out, "Glad to be of service," like a goddamned butler, and prayed Morgan wouldn't notice how completely bollocks he was at human interaction.

Instead of thanking him and heading to the kitchen to cook them dinner, though, Morgan simply stood there with the necklace dangling from one hand and the other hand jammed in the pocket of her cargo pants.

She said she needed to change, you dolt.

Owen was supposed to leave now. Right.

He backed out and started toward his room, but turned back before he got there. He'd intended to ask her why that locket—so clearly important to her—was empty.

When he'd picked it up earlier, he hadn't been able to resist peeking inside. Probably anyone would have done the same. If he'd been hoping for some insight into his housekeeper, however, Owen had been disappointed.

Maybe in the past it had once held a photo of her ex-husband, but if so, it was gone now and Morgan hadn't seen fit to replace it with anything else.

He wanted to know *why*.

That was not his business, though.

Luckily, she headed off his prying by promptly closing herself in her room so she could shed those tight, wet clothes in privacy—and he was *not* thinking about *that*, at all.

Okay yes, he was. But at least one of them had some restraint.

Owen needed to find some too, if he was going to save this situation. Warm and dry or drenched in unseasonable rain, his new housekeeper was too pretty, and smelled too damn good, for any guy's equanimity.

As he glanced around the living room, he realized he hadn't had a chance to take part in one of his favorite parts of the day, yet—looking for one of Morgan's daily flourishes. Once he'd realized what she was doing, he'd made a small hobby out of uncovering the little tweaks as soon as he walked through the front door. He looked forward to it.

He stood still and let the details of his surroundings wash over him, his senses reaching out for anything that felt different.

Nothing registered right away, but he knew he'd find it eventually. It had to be here somewhere.

Owen smiled to himself, liking the way Morgan's presence changed the feel of this place. Disconcerting allure aside, Morgan made the place warmer and more welcoming. He'd been right to hire her.

True, he could've gotten someone to come in only a few times a week, like he'd done every time before. Hell, he probably *should* have done that, because facts were facts, and a single guy living on his own didn't need a live-in housekeeper.

If Morgan hadn't figured that out, though, Owen wasn't going to fill her in. He liked having her around, so much so that it made him realize how lonely he'd been before her.

Which was a tad pathetic, wasn't it?

He altered course and grabbed his pack from beside the door, dropped it next to his desk, and sat in the chair to unzip it. He unloaded the files he'd brought home, thinking he might take a stab at some work tonight—but he didn't feel like combing through them anymore.

He'd put in another appearance at the office and made the required fuss over Kisima's supposed cleaning efforts, but Nigel and Thom had shooed him back out the door shortly after. He hadn't had time to do much more than shuffle few papers and make a call.

Unfortunately, that call had been to the forensics lab, and the tech had informed him that the suspicious Rathbone carcasses Owen and Teleki found had never made it to the facility.

Which was a problem. Forget about the loss of such valuable evidence—the simple truth was that Joseph had promised to get it done for him, and he hadn't.

Naturally, Nigel and Thom had pled ignorance, dismissing Owen's concern even as they ushered him out the door. As if those gazelles hadn't been their first real break in this bloody investigation.

The evidence was long gone now, though, and somewhere along the way, his vest and its contents had gone missing, too. Owen would have to start from scratch. If anyone would let him, that was.

He sighed. Sure, he still got tired easily, but part of that was because everyone kept treating him like an invalid. Honestly, his shoulder was getting better every day, and there wasn't a damn thing wrong with the rest of him.

Morgan was the only one who seemed to understand that. Most women he knew would've freaked out about an unscheduled gunshot wound, but his housekeeper had stayed remarkably calm when he'd told her about it.

Since then, she'd helped him when he needed it, and backed off when he didn't.

It was uncanny, but maybe she had brothers. Or maybe her ex had gotten holes put in him regularly, and Morgan was simply used to it. If the man had been stupid enough to lose a woman like her, it certainly seemed possible.

Owen took a couple of books out of his pack and went to replace them on the shelf above the couch. Either way, there was still no sign of her special touch today.

Where had she hidden it? When he turned to study the room again, he noticed several handwritten papers laying on the coffee table, right where she'd dropped her book before.

That wasn't like her. Most of the time, Morgan was meticulous about trying to erase any signs of her presence from the house.

Owen snorted. Like *that* was possible. Her essence hung in the air no matter how much she dusted and wiped and swept.

As if to underline that point, he heard Morgan humming softly to herself on the other side of the wall. Owen stared at those papers, then leaned down and quickly scanned the top page. When she didn't immediately spring from her room in a fury, he moved it aside and read more.

It took him way longer than it should have to realize he was looking at her diary, and it was describing…him.

It seemed impossible that she'd spend much time thinking about him, given what she'd been through. Morgan had told him she'd gone through a divorce even before that incident on Conrad's tour, and Owen could certainly extrapolate everything that might have entailed.

Plus, given the diffidence she usually displayed, he'd kind of assumed she was a little afraid of him—not intrigued, as her writing seemed to indicate. It was flattering, but some of her thoughts made him frown.

Morgan didn't need to spend a minute worrying about women from his past. They were all ancient history—not that he could actually tell her that.

His mind spun, trying to process it all. He wanted to read more—*all*—of it, but that seemed too risky. She could walk out and catch him at any moment.

Owen straightened up and his eyes strayed to the books arrayed on the shelves in front of him. He had no idea why she kept undoing her efforts to redecorate. So far, he'd liked everything she'd done, though he supposed it wouldn't have hurt to tell her so.

So, why hadn't he? Perhaps because it always felt like…if Owen lightened up too much, he might find himself propositioning the poor woman a breath later. He had to hold the line, he reflected, tough as that was. Morgan had been through enough without adding workplace harassment to the mix.

Still, rearranging stuff gave him a reason to continue standing here listening to her hum, so Owen began pulling the books down, attempting to recreate one of her previous displays.

He was only halfway done and already feeling ridiculous when Morgan emerged again.

She looked from him to the table and, naturally, spotted the problem immediately. Owen tried to divert her by asking about the mysterious "change of the day," but it didn't help much.

Morgan still inched closer, fussing around and making a show of straightening things that were already perfectly tidy, so she could gather up the papers and stash them under her arm.

Once she secured the contraband, she marched into her room, and disappeared the evidence with admirable speed.

Owen was still standing like a buffoon, holding his books and flummoxed as hell, when she came back out and stared him down.

He shrugged and smiled and pretended it was about the books. What else could he do? "It looks better this way," he told her.

Fortunately, Morgan smiled back, and even managed some friendly banter—but it was obvious she was antsy about leaving those diary pages laying around.

He did his best to set her at ease, and by the time she headed for the kitchen, Owen hoped he'd made things a little less awkward—at least, he did until he screwed it up again, asking why she looked ill.

It could've been worse, he supposed. He could've outlined her unusual pallor, or the dark circles under her eyes, in greater detail.

He hadn't, but the horrified expression that washed over her face told him he'd done plenty.

Morgan hid in the kitchen, and Owen flopped on the couch and groaned.

If his mother and sister could see him now, they would have no more questions about why he was still single. Owen was beginning to understand it a little better, himself.

SOMETHING HAD CHANGED in the days since Owen had been shot. He was damned if he could put his finger on it, but his previously orderly world seemed to have tilted on its axis. It felt like one of those weird waking dreams now, where he walked around the same environment and talked to the same individuals—but it all felt strangely wrong.

Maybe because the police hadn't found his shooter yet and neither had the Preserve scouts, and it was getting increasingly difficult to not suspect at least a few of his close acquaintances of dark deeds.

Not all of them, of course. Not his housekeeper. Morgan didn't make him feel paranoid, she made him feel…well, better to leave that one alone for now.

It was Thom who was the most concerning, anyway. He kept managing to visit Morgan when Owen wasn't around, which would be bad enough if his friend's usual level of flakiness hadn't taken a hard left into something else. Something that had nothing to do with cute women but was decidedly shifty.

Owen didn't know what to do about it. And, as he sat at his desk for the umpteenth day in a row, wishing he were anywhere but there, he realized that he didn't have answers for a lot of things.

What to do about Thom. Whether to trust Joseph. How to get along with Morgan for the foreseeable future, without grabbing her and asking if she was up for something really dirty.

Owen snorted and rubbed his hands over his skull. That was before he even touched on the Preserve's director, or how weird he'd been acting lately. Some of his illogical theories were simply beyond comprehension.

He got up and rounded his desk, then headed for the bathroom. If he splashed some cold water on his face, maybe he could get his brain to wake the hell up.

Almost as soon as he entered the little washroom at the back of the office, though, Thom called out, "Hey, mate. Gotta run out for a minute. Be back in ten, okay?"

"Got it," Owen said.

He washed his hands, splashed some less-than-cold water on his cheeks, and thought. This could be an opportunity to learn what Thom did when he made himself scarce—something that was happening with increasing regularity these days.

Owen glanced quickly around the washroom and weighed his options. Thom would expect him to come back out the way he'd come in, and shortly.

But what if Owen didn't? What if he followed the other man to see where he went?

His eyes fell on the back door, half blocked by a waist-high stack of uniform boxes. Taking a deep breath, Owen reached over, unlocked the door, and swung it wide.

The boxes weren't overly sturdy. He had to balance gingerly on the edges until he got high enough to clear them, but once he did Owen was able to jump over the rest, and into the shaded alley that ran behind the building.

He turned the lock on the inside of the knob and checked to make sure his keys were still in his pocket before he pulled the door shut.

Keeping to the shadow cast by the Preserve office's building, Owen moved quietly toward the street, but before he even got close, he spotted Thom crossing the gap between the buildings.

Owen crept closer and peeked out. Hannity was sticking close to the buildings, striding quickly down the sidewalk in the glaring sun. He would hit the grassy square in the middle of town next, and Owen hesitated, trying to decide what to do.

If Owen left the alley, he'd have no cover if he tried to follow. All the man would have to do is turn his head and he would spot him—and Owen did not have a good excuse locked and loaded for why he was creeping around like a cut-rate burglar.

At a sound behind him, he turned and spotted a mangy stray dog slinking into the alley at the other end, snuffling around the trash cans clustered down there. Owen kept an eye on it, in case it decided to come this way and check him out, too.

Around the corner, Thom's footsteps sped up. Owen poked his head out and saw that he'd turned left at the square and was rushing down Banyan Street, checking his watch like he was late for something.

Owen could try to use his distraction to dart across the road and hide himself in some bushes, but he wasn't fully recovered yet, and the movement was bound to attract someone's attention.

He'd have to stay here for now.

Owen ducked back into the shadow of the buildings and checked on the dog. The mutt lifted its head and watched him for a few seconds, sniffing the air curiously and panting, but it ultimately decided that the trash was a more enticing prospect.

With the canine nose-deep in refuse once more, Owen peeked around the corner again. Thom was smiling now, strolling up to an unfamiliar black car that slowed to a stop on the side of the road. He reached inside to shake someone's hand, but the glare on the windshield obscured the driver's face.

Owen watched him and felt the same lingering uneasiness he'd had for weeks. It seemed as if Thom was *feigning* his usual easygoing persona—all of the expected earmarks were still there, but his posture was wrong, his spine held taut in an unsettling way.

But what would make a man pretend to be himself? And how far could he go before he needed help?

Over near that shiny car, Thom glanced over his shoulder, then accepted a small packet from the driver and shoved it deep into the pocket of his khakis. He talked for another moment or two, but when a pair of women turned the corner and drew closer, he gave the car's occupants a wave and strolled further down Banyan.

The car pulled away from the verge and headed for the lane outside Owen's hiding spot. As it passed the alley, Owen got a good look at the driver.

He didn't recognize the man, though. He was young and dark-haired and far too polished to have been out here for long.

He did know the car's second passenger, however. And Nigel Cotton was looking pleased as punch, smiling at his companion and dipping his head to light a cigarette.

The car rolled down the block and stopped at the corner. He held his breath and waited to see what they'd do next, but when a wet nose pushed suddenly into his hand, he nearly jumped out of his skin and gave himself away.

Owen looked down into the hopeful eyes of the stray—painfully skinny but still giving him a wary wag or two—and sighed.

"Hey, little guy," he whispered, crouching down to give the scraggly thing a pat while he checked on Thom's position.

Hannity had cut into the square, where he was sprawled on a shady bench with his own cigarette. He was trying to look casual, but he was too antsy to pull it off.

He shifted restlessly on the bench as his eyes darted around. He called out a greeting to the two women making their way up the block with their shopping bags, then checked his watch again.

After they turned the corner, he got up, looked around, and mashed his half-finished cigarette under his boot. He stuck his hands in his pockets and started back toward the office.

Owen didn't have much time left. He hurried down the alley with the dog trotting at his heels and fumbled with his keys. The stray plopped down on its haunches, quiet as a mouse as it tilted its head to the side and watched Owen struggle with the corroded lock.

The back door stuck, and Owen strained to push it free without making an unholy racket. The door gave way with a bang at last, though, and the pup let out an eager bark of victory.

Owen shushed it, then turned his attention to climbing back inside. A few of the boxes tumbled over as he jumped into the room, loudly enough that he figured he'd better go with it.

He swore for effect, then gave one a kick. The door was still shut, and thankfully locked—because soon the knob started wiggling like someone was testing it.

Low voices were mumbling on the other side of the panel. Owen flushed the toilet, then quickly closed and locked the back door under cover of the rushing water and groaning pipes. At least the stray hadn't followed him in.

Owen kept muttering to himself and tossed another box aside, then ran the water in the sink for a moment, too. Feeling unutterably foolish, Owen restacked the boxes in a messy jumble, then banged out of the lavatory in what he hoped was a believable temper.

Thom and Nigel, as well as the stranger from the car, all stood there smiling oddly at him.

Hannity smirked, "Everything come out okay?"

It was clear Owen had no future as a spy, he thought bitterly, since his little farce had apparently deceived none of them.

"We've got to do something with those boxes," he scowled. "Whoever stacked them in there did a crap job. Fell all over me." He massaged his achy shoulder and tried to catch his breath.

Nigel cleared his throat. "Later. For now, I'd like you to meet Stephen Thorpe, my old friend Sir Mark's son."

Owen stepped forward and extended his hand. "Welcome," he said.

Thorpe waited a beat too long before limply grasping his palm. *Strike one*, thought Owen, quickly adding a mental *strike two* when he noted the almost feminine softness of the man's skin.

"He's like a nephew to me," Nigel explained, eyeing Thorpe fondly.

Owen slid his gaze to Thom, who rolled his eyes but remained uncharacteristically free of comment.

"To what do we owe the pleasure, Mr. Thorpe?" Owen asked, using his best country club delivery as he gestured to some chairs. That, at least, elicited a rough snort from Hannity.

Thorpe looked skyward, and drawled vaguely, "Oh, nothing dramatic. I've just come to see the sights, you know. Have a little…*safari adventure*."

Owen sized him up, trying to determine what was causing the visceral reaction he was having to the pommy bastard. He had a posh, cultured accent and he could probably feed a whole village with the price of his shoes, but that wasn't all of it.

He remarked, "Englishmen do seem to love those," even though he was fairly sure that wasn't the accent he was hearing. He couldn't pin down what it was, though. Something familiar, hovering just out of reach.

Stephen sniffed and smirked and didn't correct him. "We'll see," he said.

Before Owen could inquire what the hell that was supposed to mean, Thom piped up. "Nigel and Thorpe's old man had some grand times together at school. You've missed out on the stories, mate. So many stories."

He cut eyes at Owen, making it clear how felt about all the reminiscing that had apparently taken place in Owen's absence. The look was so over the top, however, that Owen wondered if Thom might be an even worse actor than he was.

Nigel tried to regain control of the conversation, announcing primly, "Stephen's already seen the Crater and the Escarpment, so we thought he ought to have a look at some of our special four-legged friends now."

Cotton spoke slowly, defining each syllable and watching his guest carefully like he was coaching the man.

Scratch that, Owen decided. Nigel was obviously the worst actor out of all of them—Thorpe could barely manage to feign interest, slight or otherwise.

Still, the man dutifully agreed, "I hear you have a spectacular herd of Rathbone gazelles here. Uncle Nigel assures me they're not to be missed." Then he beamed, like that fact was terribly amusing.

Owen bristled at his pompousness. Those gazelles happened to be the pride of his park, and they were dying in frightening numbers these days.

"Yeah well, you're out of luck there," he said. "Something's got it out for them, at the moment. I've closed that part of the Preserve to visitors."

"Well, that's very unfortunate," Stephen replied acidly. "No one told me it wasn't safe." He sounded like a carnival barker selling haunted house tickets, and Owen's teeth ground together.

"It isn't," Thom said. "Our man Hargreave managed to get himself shot the last time he was up there. Isn't that right, mate?"

Owen wondered at the tension simmering between Thom and Stephen. Based on that interlude outside, he'd assumed they were already pretty chummy—but now they were taking great pains to pantomime dislike. Why?

Nigel interjected, "Nonsense. It's all perfectly natural ecological cycles. The Rathbone herd is simply shifting away from our small corner of the country, like they've probably done a thousand times before. But Stephen really must have a peek at them before they're gone."

Cotton turned to Owen. "No harm in giving the lad a look at the little buggers before they take off altogether, hey?"

"Oh, is that all it is?" Owen asked drily. "We're not going with poison, anymore? Or poachers?"

Despite his folksy delivery, Owen was nonetheless astounded by this turn of events. Nigel had seen the photos, too, and knew how concerning the situation was.

If Thorpe were really as close a friend as Nigel claimed, then why keep the truth from him and potentially put him in harm's way?

Owen rolled his shoulder and looked over at Thom, who was intently examining a scuff on the toe of his boot, refusing to get further involved.

Stephen yawned and stood up, stretching lazily. "Well, Uncle? Shall we get cracking?"

Nigel fluttered about neurotically. "Of course. As you say."

"Mr. Hargreave. See you again soon, I'm sure."

Thom heaved himself out of his chair with a sigh. He stood back while Nigel and Stephen gathered their things, then shuffled out the front door after them.

Owen watched him go in surprise. "Where are you going?"

Thom looked over his shoulder with a small smile of resignation. "It seems I'm on chauffeur duty."

Owen blinked and stepped back, then watched them through the front window. Thom caught up, then Nigel hustled ahead to unlock the car. Thorpe and Thom sauntered side-by-side, chatting quietly. Thom's hand strayed into his pocket, where he'd stashed that packet earlier.

Owen guessed it could've been money. Could've been drugs, too, he supposed, but it would've been a lot of them. Neither possibility filled him with good cheer, that was for sure.

He was struck by how Thom's body language had shifted to mirror the other man's, though. Hannity did that sometimes—unconsciously imitating men who impressed him.

But if Thom was mimicking Stephen already, it meant the two knew each other more than incidentally. Had they spent time together while Owen was up in the Preserve, or when he was home convalescing? It seemed like the kind of thing Thom might've mentioned.

Something else was bothering Owen, too. Stephen Thorpe's demeanor—his snarkiness—felt all wrong for who he was supposed to be. Owen had met plenty of privileged young men who ranked themselves superior. He could recognize that type from a mile away.

But for a young man who was purportedly having a great adventure, Thorpe was a shade too scornful of his surroundings. Plus, if Nigel was truly his father's old friend, he certainly didn't hold him in high esteem.

And then there was his name. What was it about that name?

All at once, he remembered where he'd heard it before—hadn't Joseph told him someone named Stephen was sent by Nigel to hire him for that last trip up north?

That didn't make sense, though. Why would Cotton send a tourist out on Preserve business? A tourist with dark hair, as it happened, just like the mystery man the Temba brothers had described in their interview.

Owen felt like the puzzle pieces were scattered all over the table, but none of them fit together yet. And though all trails appeared to lead to Nigel, Owen had a hard time believing that the old fuss-budget could be up to much of anything devious.

His jaw clenched painfully, and his mind spun. He might not know what was afoot here, but he sure as hell intended to find out.

Chapter Eighteen

A FEW DAYS after Journalgate, as Morgan had begun to think of it, Thom stopped by the cottage unexpectedly, with no clear reason for being there.

Another unseasonable storm had blown through that morning, and the air was still fragrant with the smell of wet earth and vegetation. When Thom arrived, Morgan was in the yard, casually gathering up some of the branches and debris that the wind had thrown around earlier.

It seemed as good an excuse as any to stay out of his way, so instead of heading inside like she'd planned, she kept at it and prayed she wouldn't get bitten by something nasty in the process.

Thankfully, Owen had returned from a short daytrip into the Preserve—his first since getting shot—a few minutes before. He hadn't even had a chance to change his clothes when Thom pulled up.

Their visitor bounded into the house, full of enthusiasm, and even from her vantage on the lawn, Morgan could tell Thom had been expecting to catch her alone. Maybe Owen realized that too, or maybe he was simply tired—but either way, he didn't sound thrilled to see his friend.

After a while, though, he brought Thom outside and they settled on the chairs on the raised back patio. They lit a small fire in the metal pit at their feet, and the two men drank beers while they talked and watched the day start to fade.

They both looked determined to play out the friendly charade, but Morgan wished she could be somewhere else while it happened.

She glanced at them periodically, as she wandered around the yard. The men acted differently with each other than they did with her, and it was fascinating to watch—even if something seemed off between them.

Thom looked restless and reedy in his old t-shirt and jeans, with an avid, elfin face and a narrow frame that seemed even more boyish next to Owen's strapping chest and shoulders.

In contrast, Owen appeared solid and steady. His button-down was wrinkled and the sleeves were rolled up over his elbows, but the white linen still looked stark and perfect against his skin. He'd tucked his khakis into tall field boots and after the day spent in the bush, those boots were scuffed and muddy—but they still made his legs look long and strong.

The outfit made him stand out, but once it was combined with Owen's height and rugged face, the total effect became spectacular. He looked like a man from a different time—like a character in an old movie or a hero in a book.

Morgan looked away and tried to focus on the pair of egrets picking their way along the shoreline of the lake.

She appreciated that Thom had tried to look out for her in his own bumbling way, but she didn't kid herself. He teased her, but his jokes held a suggestive edge, and she knew she had to be careful or he'd get the wrong idea.

What was more, Morgan hadn't forgotten the conversation she'd heard between him and Carol Connelly. Whether he wanted to acknowledge it or not, Thom was spoken for.

Her boss, on the other hand, was not. Owen was an intriguing mystery, though, and one that Morgan increasingly wanted to unravel—but not because she was interested in him. She was only curious by nature.

She did live with the guy, after all.

She still had no idea why he thought he needed a housekeeper, however. He repeatedly urged her not to make a fuss over him, and he wasn't the least bit messy.

Not that she minded. Being around him every day had turned out to be…quite invigorating.

Morgan shook her head and pushed that thought away before it gained any traction. Instead, she moved closer, dropping her armload of twigs on the pile she'd started for the fire pit, then lingering for a minute so she could hear what Owen and Thom were talking about.

She could only catch bits and pieces of their conversation but realized almost immediately that they were talking about her. Morgan inched a little closer and pretended to restack the kindling.

Thom announced, "I'll tell you what, mate. She might not know her way around a market, but I've never seen her slacking off. She's always plugging away at some thing or another."

Owen snorted. "What's wrong with that? That's what I pay her for."

"At least she stopped asking me how you liked things," Thom chucked. "Probably realized there's no pleasing you, poor kid."

Morgan felt her cheeks go hot and ducked her head in embarrassment. Her made her sound so pathetic when he said it like that.

"I wouldn't say that. You probably just weren't any help," Owen countered.

Morgan couldn't decide what was going on between them. Thom was trying too hard to be buddy-buddy, and Owen was only pretending to be relaxed.

Maybe they'd had it out over something at work and didn't want to clear the air with her hovering around, but Morgan suspected Owen needed to rest, too. He was much better than he'd been, but he wasn't all the way healed yet.

As the conversation moved on to other topics, Morgan considered how to get Thom to move along, too. She was running out of reasons to be hanging around out here, and soon Owen would want some dinner.

She swiped at the hair sticking to her face and blew out a breath. It was more humid than she'd realized, and she was getting filthier by the minute. The gnats were coming out, and even though Morgan had defended this chore to Owen, saying she could use the exercise, it was time to cut the farce short.

Morgan decided to make one more foray across the grass, gathering a final armful of branches to add to the pile. By the time she returned to the side of the house, the conversation had returned to the subject of her—probably because she was the most interesting thing happening out here.

Clueless woman roams free in local man's garden. News at eleven.

On the patio above her, she heard Thom say, "What do you know about Morgan, anyway? Does she ever talk to you?"

"Not really," Owen told him. "She keeps to herself."

There was a long pause, and then Thom asked, "Ever tell you about that tour she was on?"

"Not a word."

"I bet it's because she's writing about it," Thom said.

Morgan flushed, still agonizing over those stupid pages she'd left on the coffee table. If Owen had read them, it would be an epic disaster.

Maybe he hadn't, though, because the next thing she knew he was asking curiously, "Why do you say that?"

"Educated guess. Why else would she have needed pencils and paper from the market?"

"To send letters to people," Owen assured him. "Why else?"

Morgan wanted to hug him. He sounded so confident. Thom would never suspect a thing.

"Perhaps you've heard of a little thing called email," Thom scoffed. "Has she ever asked you to mail a single thing for her?"

Or maybe not. He was on to her, after all.

Owen mused, "Okay. Well, maybe she's a poet. Or a…a fledgling Hemingway."

He sounded amused, though, and Morgan wondered whether that was because he knew for a fact that she wasn't, or because he already found her completely ridiculous.

She bent to drop her branches on the pile and felt something soft and muscular moving against her forearm. She gasped and jumped back.

What *was* it? Nothing leaped out at her, so Morgan kicked skittishly at the sticks, spreading them out a bit. All at once, she saw it—a thick black snake writhing in the crabgrass, probably four feet long and heading right for the house.

Morgan swallowed painfully. She did *not* want to meet up with this creature again in, say, her bedroom—or worse, the shower. But she also didn't want to call for help and broadcast the fact that she'd been standing here eavesdropping this whole time, either.

In desperation, she looked around for a long, thick branch so she could catch the fiend, then steeled herself to get closer to it.

Unfortunately, it had figured out that she was there, and had slithered around to face her. Heart hammering, Morgan sidled closer and tried to wedge the end of the branch under its midsection, wondering the whole time how poisonous it was, and whether she was a damn fool for provoking it.

The reptile slinked toward her, then clung obligingly to the branch when she jammed it under him like a spatula and lifted it in the air. It was surprisingly heavy as it lazily curled and redistributed itself, and the length of the branch only made it more awkward to carry.

Morgan tried not to think about how fast the snake could strike her face if it chose to and walked as quickly as she could toward the trees near the shore.

By the time she figured she'd gotten far enough away from the house, the creature had inched way too close to her hand for comfort. Morgan dispensed with finesse and tried to hurl the branch as far as she could into the thicket.

It didn't go far, landing no more than a few feet away with a quiet thud. Thankfully, the snake wasn't interested in revenge, though. Without a second look, it slithered into the undergrowth until it was out of sight.

Morgan backed away and tried to calm her pounding heart. When she was reasonably confident that she could hold it together without freaking out, she turned her back on the demon reptile and marched back to the house, sneaking looks over her shoulder the entire way in case it had a change of heart and decided to come after her.

It was hard to fight the urge to take off running, but she managed it. And since she'd clearly accomplished more than enough pointless yard work for the day, Morgan was quite, *quite* finished out here whether Owen and Thom were done talking about her or not.

She was tired and hungry, and a little bit dizzy from the adrenaline and terror coursing through her veins, but Morgan still set her jaw and faced that patio, knowing Owen and Thom had to have seen her and were undoubtedly laughing their asses off.

They were standing at the railing, watching her approach. Thom, of course, was grinning from ear to ear. Morgan didn't think her boss was—but she was too humiliated to look him in the eye, so she couldn't be sure.

As she trudged up to their level, her hands began to shake. Morgan knew better than to get distracted in the brush. She knew firsthand that bad things could happen if you did.

But she'd still ended up carrying around a big, scary snake not once, but twice.

Morgan winced at her stupidity. Then, because she apparently liked punishment, she reviewed the names of all the poisonous snakes she'd learned about on Conrad's safari. *Puff adders. Vipers. Boomslangs. Cobras.*

Oh, god. Cobras.

If Owen scolded her right now, she would probably burst out crying. So, Morgan pleaded with the universe to please, *please* not let him not say anything.

Naturally, Thom piped up first. "Making some new friends, sweetheart?"

Morgan rolled her eyes and turned toward Owen, looking somewhere left of his face. "I can get some dinner started if you like," she said, and hoped he wouldn't invite Thom to stay.

"Take your time," he replied, mercifully abstaining from embarrassing her any further. "I'm ready whenever you are."

Thom looked between them with a startled bark of laughter. "Do you two seriously talk to each other like this all of the time?"

Morgan shook her head and pushed past him.

Thom cried, "Aw, come on, Morgan! Give me a smile. I don't bite."

"Not in the mood, Thom," she muttered, and went into the house.

Owen followed her in, stopping her with a hand on her arm before she got very far. He dipped his head and murmured in her ear, "That bloke in the grass doesn't bite, either. I promise."

Morgan took a deep breath and let his calm authority steady her as he squeezed her arm. She nodded and resisted throwing herself at him—and tried not to think about the way his warm breath feathered over her ear and sent a shiver down her spine.

Owen nodded too, gave Morgan a little pat, then released her and stepped back.

She tried to look dignified as she closed herself in her room. Even if that snake never came back to murder her, she would probably have nightmares about it for weeks—maybe years—to come.

When she wasn't dreaming about Owen whispering in her ear, that was.

Morgan flopped onto the floor and groaned, then laid there wondering if she could pull off never going outside again. But then she heard voices, drifting in her open window so clearly, they may as well have been right next to her.

Were Owen and Thom talking about her again?

"I have to say, mate. She's made me a happy man," Thom announced.

"Whenever you sound that smug, it usually means I should worry," Owen fired back.

"Don't be jealous. I'm sure you're not the whole reason that girl of yours is starting to fancy me."

Morgan rolled over and sat up, frowning hard.

Owen asked, "What girl?" but Morgan had a sinking feeling she already knew.

"Your girl," Thom confirmed, "Morgan."

Her chest felt uncomfortably tight at the phrase. *His girl.* She let herself contemplate the idea for long, dangerous seconds—feeling Owen's steady gaze on her. His *hands* on her.

Outside, her boss laughed, "Don't be ridiculous."

"No, it's true," Thom said. "Did you see how happy she was to see me?"

"Morgan is very polite," Owen replied, beginning to sound annoyed. Who could blame him? His buddy was essentially claiming that the housekeeper had the hots for him.

"It's not politeness, mate. Your sweet little housekeeper wants to bang your bro."

Morgan cringed at Thom's gloating. She'd been nice to him, but nothing like he was claiming.

"Thomas, pull it together. Just because Morgan didn't punch you on sight, does not mean she wants to climb into bed with you. She needed a ride to the market that one time. That's all," Owen insisted.

Morgan really hoped her boss believed what he'd said, because that truly was it. She hadn't seen much of Thom, and she'd told Owen that.

"You're wrong," Thom argued. "I'm going to wear the little duck down with my wit and charm. She'll be mine in no time. You'll see."

Morgan stood and peeked out the window. A tall shrub blocked most of her view, but she could see Owen's leather boots, extended in front of him. When Thom leaned forward, she could see the edge of his face, too.

He had a weak chin. A weak…everything.

"I seriously doubt that," Owen grumbled. "Morgan is not your type."

"Oh, she's my type, all right," Thom retorted. "And when she's screaming my name, you're going to wish you moved on her first."

Morgan caught sight of his shoulder and then his elbow, and realized Thom must be crossing his arms over his chest, like a petulant child.

Her boss was quiet for a long time, and she wondered whether he was actually considering what his friend was saying about her. She couldn't defend herself, if he was. She wasn't even supposed to be listening.

But then Owen inquired softly, "I wonder, Thom, what Carol will think of her. After the way you left things last time, I've got to believe she'll have an opinion."

"Come on, man—why'd you have to say that? Can't I have fun for once?" Thom muttered. "It's not like they'll ever see each other, anyway."

"Why can't you have fun? Let's see. Maybe because you keep messing with my fucking housekeepers and I'd like to hang on to this one. Not to mention the fact that this particular woman has been through quite enough, without having to worry about your shenanigans in her life," Owen barked. "Does that clear it up for you?"

Morgan blinked, grateful for his defense, but also a little taken aback that this seemed to be an established pattern between them. How many housekeepers had Thom gone through, anyway?

"Well, someone is going to have to take her to the market," Thom sniveled. "And I'm no fool. I won't fight her off when she makes her move on me." He gripped the armrest of his chair, his knuckles white.

"She won't be making any moves," Owen fumed. "And besides, you won't have to drive her to the market again."

Morgan slid to the floor, leaning against the wall under the window. Why did it seem like there was more to this pissing match than it appeared?

"What? Why not?"

"Because I'll be doing it myself, now that the worst of the poaching season is over," Owen said.

"The worst part isn't over. Not by a long shot," Thom argued hotly. "There are still poachers everywhere."

Another long silence stretched out, and Morgan thought that was going to be the end of it. But then Thom's chair scraped on the patio and he cried, "God damn it, I should've known. The minute I said I was interested, you decided to take her for yourself, didn't you?"

Owen made a low, scornful sound. "She's not a possession," he pointed out. "I can't take her any more than you can."

Oh, but you could, a soft voice whispered in her brain. *Again and again.* Morgan wrapped her arms around her shins and dropped her forehead to her knees.

Thom echoed her thoughts painfully clearly. "You can, and I bet you're going to. You're going to steal Morgan from me, because you're a selfish prick and I won't be able to do a damn thing about it."

Thom's whine hung in the evening air and in that moment, it was hard to envision how the two men had become friends in the first place.

Was Owen blind to Thom's problems, or had he simply grown accustomed to them over the years? It was hard to say.

People changed, Morgan knew. Sometimes, it took a while to face what they'd become.

"For god's sake, Thom," Owen grumbled then. "Stop acting like a child. I'm not stealing Morgan, and neither are you. We are both going to respect her and leave her be, so she can do her job in peace." He sounded awfully confident of that, which was only a little bit humiliating.

Okay, maybe a lot humiliating.

"I should never have tipped you off," Thom countered, "but I thought I'd have more time to convince her. The trips to the market were my in."

"Too bad. If you were really as hung up on her as you say, you'd have come up with something better than just hoping for her gratitude."

"It's no use, anyway. I should've known you'd wreck everything, you jealous bastard."

Owen barked out a laugh that made Morgan flinch. "Jealous? You've got to be kidding me."

"I'm not. And if you had half a heart, you'd leave that girl for me."

August 16

When I came here, I was a creature made of tacks—with some points aiming outward, and some pointing in.
I've melted into something softer now, like a pool of wax. Impressionable enough to leave a fingerprint in when hot, but quickly turning cold again.
If anyone is going to write on this empty page, though, it will be Owen.

In his house, in his presence, my mind and body think too much about what that means.

The situation might be tenable, if not for my heart. It turns out that traitor was not dead, as I assumed, but only biding its time until a proper quarry presented himself.

Which means…I'm screwed.

Chapter Nineteen

OWEN HAD NO idea what made him say it. One minute, he was thinking that his friend was just begging for a bloody nose, and that he'd be more than happy to oblige him. He even gave his fist an experimental flex, out there on the patio.

But the very next minute, he blurted out, "Anyway, Morgan's not a girl. Girlish, maybe, but not…not a girl."

He tipped back his beer and waded even further into the weeds with, "Pretty sure she's been all grown up for years."

Almost instantly, he realized what a horrendous mistake he'd made, so Owen put down his beer and smoothed the wrinkles from his pants with steady hands, then scanned the tree line to find the wood owl he'd heard hooting there.

He acted as if he hadn't fucked up, and then some.

Thom slumped down at his words, his elbows and knees jutting out at awkward angles while he faced the water and sulked for a while. Eventually, he turned away from the darkening metallic sheen of the lake and stared hard at the side of Owen's face instead.

Owen didn't look. He just squinted straight ahead and tried to act preoccupied while he figured out how to extricate himself from the mess he'd created.

As Thom eyed him, he measured the size of the wavelets rippling across the lake and knew that engaging with Hannity at all had been akin to waving a red flag in front of a bull. However, once Owen admitted that his housekeeper was all woman, he'd basically declared war.

So be it, he thought brutally. Remind Thom who he was up against.

And so, acting like a hormonal teenage boy in a man's body, Owen folded his arms across his chest and flexed, just enough to make his point. Out of the corner of his eye, he noted Thom's gaze traveling over him, and felt a savage stab of triumph when his friend, at last, winced.

OWEN THOUGHT OF that the next day, when he told Morgan to come to him whenever she needed to go shopping. And he thought of it for a few more days while he waited—with more than a little anticipation—for her to do so.

It was ridiculous that something so ordinary would get him worked up like this, but Morgan seemed to have that effect on him. No way was he going to back down and let Thom have his way with her.

So, when she'd *finally* approached him yesterday and asked if they could go to the market this morning, Owen had been so pleased he'd taken the day off and planned to make an outing of it.

To that end, he arose by habit at the crack of dawn and shuffled groggily out of his room, fully expecting that he'd have plenty of time to work out what he wanted to do.

Owen soon discovered that not only was Morgan already up, however, she was also showered, dressed, and industriously piling some shopping bags near the front door.

The coffee was made, and a plate of eggs and toast was on the counter, apparently waiting for him. That was a surprise, to say the least.

His normal hours at the Preserve usually had Owen awake and out the door well before Morgan woke. Because of that, he'd never asked her to make him coffee, or breakfast.

"You seem to be getting an early start today," he mumbled.

Morgan jerked upright. "There you are," she smiled, and darted for the kitchen.

Her movements in there seemed louder than they probably were, but he was also used to spending this part of his day in utter silence. It was odd to have to make nice with someone—even her.

Morgan emerged with another little smile and put the plate of food on his desk for him, then handed Owen a steaming cup of coffee, pale with added cream.

He blinked down at it in confusion, trying to understand what had happened. It wasn't like his housekeeper to get details wrong. Didn't Morgan remember that he drank his coffee black? Christ, what if she'd put sugar in it, too?

"Thanks," Owen told her, then sat at his desk, set the cup aside, and picked up his fork.

Eventually it occurred to him—in a muzzy sort of way—that Morgan would have no way of knowing how he took his coffee, since she was never awake while he was drinking it. Furthermore, she'd undoubtedly made the obvious assumption, and prepared Owen's coffee the way he took his tea. It wasn't her fault she'd gotten it wrong.

He only wished he'd had a little more time to compose himself—maybe wake up a bit more—before he had to tell her that. Perhaps then he might've known how to head this off in the first place.

Since Morgan was hovering a little, he took an experimental sip of the java and lied, "This is good. Thanks."

A real charmer, this bloke. But Owen wasn't a morning person, and he wasn't used to having to face other human beings so early. It was discombobulating.

Almost as disconcerting as the fresh-scented fragrance wafting off Morgan every time she moved past him. She looked alive and bright and wholesome and pretty.

In contrast, he felt like a bear coming out of a nine-year hibernation.

Owen ran a hand through his hair and eyed Morgan's ponytail when she bustled toward her room. It was sleek and shiny and still a little damp on the ends.

He was surprised he hadn't heard her in the bathroom. Would it have been better—or worse—to wake op to the sound of her showering?

She turned in her doorway and put her hands on her hips. "So…when do you think you'll be ready to leave?"

Owen blinked. "Leave?"

"I figured you'd want to get going soon, since it's so far away," she said, shifting uncertainly.

"Sorry?"

"Don't you…don't you want to get there before it's too late? Won't they run out of stuff?"

Owen frowned and tried to process what she'd said. "Morgan, the market is only twenty minutes away. And—" he checked the clock on his desk, "—the vendors won't even set up for another hour or two."

She stared back at him, her mouth moving. No sound came out at first, but finally she said, "But…it took Thom and me forever to get there. He said everyone's stock was low because we got there so late."

Owen sighed and rubbed his eyes, not the least bit surprised. However, he definitely needed some caffeine, immediately, if he was going to have to explain it to her.

He stood and carried his mug into the kitchen, dumped the creamy brew down the sink, then rinsed out his mug and poured himself another. Morgan followed him and her watchful hazel eyes missed nothing.

"What did I say wrong?" she asked, turning a little pink as she watched him gulp down his new, blessedly unadulterated coffee.

Owen cleared his throat and tried to smile. "Nothing. However, we have a perfectly good market quite a bit closer than the one Thom must've taken you to."

"But why would he…?" she began, then stopped. Morgan opened her mouth to continue, and promptly closed it again as she tried to unpack this development.

"It appears that Thom enjoys your company," Owen explained weakly. "A lot."

Morgan flushed a sudden and vivid red, but "Oh," was all she said.

"I'm sorry," he told her. "I wish I'd been around to help more. Given you a proper orientation, and whatnot."

"No, it's my fault," Morgan laughed ruefully. "You asked me to wait for you to get back and I didn't. Anyway," she gestured toward her room, "I'm just going to go, uh…" She trailed off, looking pained.

Owen felt bad that he'd embarrassed her, but Morgan's door was already halfway closed before he could begin to apologize.

"I'll let you know when it's time to go," he called after her. "Thanks again for the breakfast."

Morgan told him, "Enjoy!" then closed herself inside.

THE MARKET OWEN took her to was organized by a businesswoman everyone called Miss Lenah.

She held the gathering weekly, weather-permitting, in a field next to her small general store, halfway between Victoriaville and the neighboring village.

Farmers and craftsmen came from all over the area to sell their wares, and Owen liked to think that he'd built up a good relationship with most of them over the years. Hopefully, that goodwill would extend to Morgan today.

When he pulled his truck up beside the road, things were just getting underway.

"Wow. So, you weren't kidding," Morgan said, eyeing the spread. "This is close."

Owen shrugged and smiled. He couldn't imagine where the hell Thom had dragged her—nowhere smart, if he had to guess.

They got out and he beckoned her over. "So, how much did Thom explain to you?"

"Nothing," she admitted. "Once we got there, he ditched me to go talk to people, and I basically got swarmed."

Owen winced. No wonder she looked nervous. At minimum Thom had been mean, but depending on where they'd been, he could very well have put her in danger, too.

"Okay, well…this place is different. Look—the market is set up like a department store. You see? Food on this side, and other stuff on that side. Up front is the produce," Owen gestured, "and towards the back corner is the meat and eggs and so on. Over there, you have housewares at the front, and handmade jewelry and clothes in the back."

His housekeeper blinked, looking surprised. "Oh. That's not so hard."

"From up here, you can see the pattern, right?"

"Yeah, I can. It makes a lot more sense than that other place."

"Good." Owen started down the hill, then reached back to help Morgan down, too. When she slipped her hand into his, he couldn't lie to himself—it gave him a jolt. A *thrill*.

At the bottom, he held on a moment longer, simply because it felt good. He couldn't read Morgan's expression once he let go, though.

She looked curious as she glanced around, but a little wary, too. She was also sticking close to his side, so Owen set his hand lightly on her back and steered her toward the first stall.

Her skin was warm through her thin t-shirt. The ends of her hair brushed his wrist. He tried to pull himself together.

"How do you want to tackle it?" he asked. "Would you like to explore a bit before it gets busy, or do you want me to introduce you around first?"

"Actually…I think I'd like to look around a little. If that's okay."

"Take your time," Owen said. "I'll take care of a few things, and we can meet back here when you're ready. I'll show you who my usual people are."

"Okay." She stood stock still, rooted to the spot.

"Sound good?"

"Yup." Still, she hesitated.

"Don't worry, you'll be safe here. And just to make sure, I'll keep an eye on you, too," Owen smiled.

As if he could avoid watching her, he thought ruefully.

She drew his eye like a moth to flame, whether Owen wanted her to or not. Her gray cargo pants hugged her hips and rear, and he could just catch the raised edges of her bra straps through the back of her shirt.

Morgan finally looked mollified, and she wandered slowly away, peering around her and smiling at the vendors as they unloaded their goods and stacked them on tables and blankets.

Her boots left a path of treaded prints through the dirt, like a trail he was supposed to follow. And her gleaming blond ponytail was as easy to pick out of the array of colorful fabrics and people as if she had a neon arrow following her around.

How many shades of blonde and brown streaked through that hair, exactly? Owen had studied it plenty, but he kept finding new ones. It seemed almost symbolic, like the way Morgan continued to surprise him when he didn't expect it.

He forced himself to move, heading in a slightly different direction and greeting a few people he knew. He tried to keep a discreet watch on his housekeeper without outright tailing her.

Morgan might have gone to that other market with Thom, but Hannity clearly hadn't taught her a thing. She still looked shy and completely clueless about how to proceed. She didn't barter, she didn't buy—she hardly interacted at all, actually.

Owen suspected Thom had used the long car ride to spend more time with her, but he could just as easily have been avoiding someone here.

Watching the way Morgan floundered now, Owen regretted inadvertently putting her in Thom's sights with his negligence.

He'd known that Morgan was only a tourist when he'd hired her, and he shouldn't have just thrown her in the pool and expected her to swim. He could've asked any number of reliable people to give her some pointers while he'd been away, and then maybe she wouldn't have felt the need to take matters into her own hands.

It wasn't like Owen to be so careless, but some days it felt as if his housekeeper had arrived on his doorstep plastered in warning labels and waving red flags.

She felt dangerous, in more ways than one, and Owen usually made a habit of avoiding that sort of thing.

As he tried to keep Morgan in his sights, he ended up jostling a young woman balancing a bucket of guavas on her head. She rolled her eyes and muttered something under her breath, then had to pull her child out of his path, too.

This was ridiculous. He ought to go help Morgan now, and he wanted to.

The problem was, Morgan hated when she couldn't figure things out on her own. It was like she expected herself to intuit how to do new stuff through a mysterious combination of her own perception and the odd comment from Owen here and there.

He had no idea if it was pride, mulishness, or both, but they'd never had a formal discussion of her duties or his expectations. He'd assumed Morgan would request clarification when she needed it, and figured he was doing her a favor by not overwhelming her all at once.

That had been lazy of him. He realized that now.

And perhaps her adamance about learning for herself meant that she was trying not to be the hapless American everyone assumed she was—that would be better, certainly, than her being afraid of him. She'd arrived in the wake of such unusual events, that he could hardly blame her, if she was.

He checked on her again and saw that she was already making her way back to their designated meeting spot, looking sheepish and a little defeated. Owen headed toward her immediately and debated how to show her the ropes without being too obvious about it.

If he got it wrong, Morgan would think he had no confidence in her. She'd hate that.

He had no idea why he cared.

Right on time, though, Owen's solution presented itself in the form of Nadra, striding into the market with her growing belly leading the way, and two of her children hanging on her hands.

Owen changed course and marched over to her, acutely aware that Morgan was probably watching his every move. He wanted to make it clear that his old housekeeper was an ally and a friend, however, so he smiled wide.

"Woman, please tell me that you didn't walk all the way here in your delicate condition," he teased. The little ones giggled.

"Oh, look, girls—such a *polite* gentleman we have here," she fired back, rolling her eyes at the kids and adjusting the vests of their little school uniforms.

To Owen, she proclaimed, "We *would* have enjoyed riding in your bumpy old chariot, kind sir." For his benefit alone, she added under her breath, "Had you thought to offer, that is."

Owen chuckled. "When you never accept, madam, the offers stop coming. I wish you'd reconsider now, though. It must take you twice as long to walk here as it would for me to come pick you up."

Nadra sighed dramatically. "I beg your pardon. It takes me four times as long, especially with these two." She narrowed her eyes at the children as they started to sidle away. "But we like to walk, don't we?" They returned to her side guiltily and nodded. "Besides, the exercise is good for me."

"You look well," Owen told her. "Are you feeling any better?"

"I'll feel better once he joins us on the outside," she said.

"He?"

"That's what *Bibi* says. We'll see."

Owen nodded, and glanced back at Morgan to make sure she was still all right.

"That's the new girl?" Nadra asked quietly, peeking around his shoulder at her.

"It is."

"She's quite pretty."

Owen glared at her. Nadra looked from him to Morgan, and back again. "Okay, then what's the problem? Does she not know what she's doing, or do you just miss me?"

"She's not bad in general. I just think she needs some help, here, that's all," he admitted.

"So, help her. What's wrong—are your legs broken? Or your brain?"

"No," he drawled, making a silly face at her daughters. "I didn't want to embarrass her." Surely Nadra could understand that. It wasn't like it *meant* anything, after all.

"Honestly, what a grown man like you needs a housekeeper for, I never will know," she carped. "It's…it's pure European arrogance, that's what it is!"

Despite her words, though, she shrugged and winked at Morgan, who smiled tentatively back.

"Technically, New Zealand is in Oceania," Owen pointed out. "And while I don't necessarily need a housekeeper, it is nice, and it makes things easier. But that's hardly important at the moment. Right now, I think Morgan could use some help, and isn't too keen on asking me for it."

"Why would she do that? It's not like you're her boss, or anything."

"Come on, Nadra. Be nice."

"Let me guess. Despite me being off your payroll, you want me to do your dirty work for you. In my—what did you call it? *Delicate condition?*"

"Take it as a compliment. It means you did a good job," he pleaded.

"Oh, really. Don't you think I had your whole helpless routine figured out from the start?"

Owen rubbed his hands over his face. "Come on, Nadra. *Please.* I'll take these two up to Miss Lenah's, if you'll show Morgan around. People will be extra nice to her if she's with you."

The kids, who'd been watching their mother and her former boss with rapt attention up till then, chimed in immediately, begging to go with him. Like their mother, the girls had Owen's number, all right.

Nadra sighed, but she capitulated. "All right, big man. Lead the way."

They wound through the stalls to where Morgan stood waiting, and she greeted them curiously, "Hey. I'm all set, if you want to get started."

"First, I'd like to introduce you to my former housekeeper, Nadra Mreme."

"Owen told me about you," Morgan smiled instantly, "It's nice to finally meet you."

"Mrs. Mreme has coerced me into babysitting her little knee-biters while she does her shopping," Owen explained, winking broadly at the children, who dissolved into giggles again.

Nadra leveled a flinty look at him for his blatant lie, but she went along with it. She turned to Morgan and said, "If you have time, maybe we can walk together. I can show you who has the best chicken, and you can help me carry a few things." She rested a hand on her belly and smiled hopefully.

Morgan took the bait eagerly. "Of course," she said, "I'm happy to help."

She glanced at Owen, so he asked, "You have everything you need?"

She nodded and patted the little bag she wore slung across her chest, where she'd tucked the money he'd given her earlier.

"Okay. Then I'll leave you ladies to your business. *We* will be at the Miss Lenah's if you need us." Nadra's children cheered and pulled at Owen's hands, trying to drag him away.

Morgan smiled at Nadra, who only huffed, "I can assure you that we will *not* need you."

The women turned and made their way to the first set of tables, with various melons piled in tall pyramids. Nadra immediately pointed out the ones Owen liked best, and Morgan deftly took the woman's basket from her, so she'd have her hands free.

The children pulled him up the hill to the Dar Es Salaam Café and Shop, which overlooked the market. The proprietor, Miss Lenah, must have been watching, because she quickly emerged in a fragrant swirl of scarves to whisk the kid inside for the bottles of cold cherry soda she knew they loved.

As Owen heard it, Lenah had come from Zanzibar to take over the shop years ago, when she'd inherited it from an elderly aunt. She'd started the weekly outdoor market soon after, as dignified up here on the hill as the scene below was boisterous.

Nadra, of course, had been the one to introduce Owen to her, and he'd liked the quiet woman immediately, though she spoke neither Swahili nor English. He hung back as she fussed over Nadra's daughters, staying out on the shady front porch so he could watch, in guilty fascination, as Nadra and Morgan moved around the market.

They looked happy as they chatted with each other. Morgan also looked about as relaxed as he'd ever seen her. It transformed her from simply pretty to outright breathtaking.

Owen felt a burst of pride that she lived with him. She also cooked for him, folded his laundry, and brought him tea before he went to sleep at night.

True, he paid her to do it, and it shouldn't give him such a territorial charge. It wasn't like Morgan was his wife. She wasn't even his girlfriend. She worked for him. That was all.

For the first time, Owen wondered if her current situation bothered her. As far as he could tell, Morgan was perfectly content living at the cottage. She never appeared to be bored, homesick, or lonely, even though she had to have left some kind of life behind to do so.

Perhaps that had been the plan. Maybe she'd had a crappy life in America. Or maybe her self-imposed isolation was her way of working through the grief of her friend's passing.

Still, it was unusual, wasn't it? Didn't she have family? Friends who missed her, or a career to return to? It seemed inconceivable that some lucky man, somewhere, hadn't laid claim to her.

But of course, one had, at some point. Not-a-missus Flynn had told him that much on their very first day together. Whoever, and wherever, "Chip" was, he had to be a sodding fool.

Owen shut down that dark thought with a scowl and forced himself to focus on the giggles of the children in the shop. It was a far sight better than obsessing over things that were none of his business.

As he watched Morgan and Nadra together, he was glad that his friend had shown up at the market that day, though. If Nadra approved of someone, it was nearly impossible to not get along with her, and Owen hoped she'd been able to assuage at least some of Morgan's nervousness.

At some point, Lenah left Nadra's children prattling happily on the stools at the small counter inside and stepped silently onto the porch next to him. She adjusted the scarf across her forehead, linked her arm through his, and watched the women weave through the market.

After a few minutes, she turned and studied Owen's face, then nodded slowly and patted his arm like she approved.

Owen raised his eyebrows at her. "What? What do you think you see?"

Lenah didn't say anything, of course—she simply smirked and turned back to the market. She pointed out some men gathering around a table near the base of the rise, then frowned as their exchange with the vendor got more heated.

Owen didn't recognize them. "You know those guys?" he asked.

Lenah shook her head and shrugged. Before Owen could go down and investigate, however, the vendor called a young man over who looked so much like him, he had to be his son. The son brought friends.

The strangers weren't pleased, but the tactic worked—soon, they turned and headed for a fancy black car, parked up by the road.

Owen watched them get in and roar away, but the incident made him uneasy. It was rare to see people he didn't recognize here. He didn't like it. He scanned the market spread out below him again, but fortunately things seemed to have returned to normal.

Morgan looked up just as his eyes found her, and she gave him a happy wave. The women left the market proper and began climbing the hill. Nadra was moving far more slowly now and Morgan was carrying most of what they'd bought together, so Owen started down to help.

He called over his shoulder, "All right girls, go help Mama," and in two seconds flat they were racing past him and down the stairs.

From the interior of the shop, Miss Lenah cried, "Wait!"

Owen froze, startled by her use of the English word, and her urgency, but when she emerged, she was only carrying an armful of baskets.

She shoved them at Owen, though, pointing at Morgan as she did so.

"*Hehe*," she stated firmly. "*Milulu*." Lenah tapped the baskets, and he looked closer.

Understanding dawned. The *Hehe* people were master craftsmen, weaving creations out of *milulu* grass that were admired throughout the region. People prized them for their combination of utility—they were sturdy and woven tightly enough to carry water—as well their beauty.

The set Miss Lenah was giving him was a particularly fine example of *Hehe* workmanship, and a quick glance at the market confirmed what Owen already suspected—no one down there was selling anything like this, which meant that Lenah had somehow procured these baskets on her own.

And now, she was offering them to him.

Once Lenah was satisfied that Owen had that information down, she gestured from the baskets to Morgan enough times that he'd have to have been a total dunce to not catch on.

"You think she should have these?" he asked her. "You're probably right."

Lenah preened, and it was uncharacteristic enough that he had to chuckle. "Alright, settle down. How much?"

She waved him off.

"Not even going to give me a clue, huh?" Lenah shook her head and smirked, and Owen examined her prize once more. The three baskets nested in each other, and had sturdy handles and a delicate, rust-colored pattern.

They weren't some junky tourist souvenir—they were truly beautiful works of art, and in pristine condition, too. Lenah occasionally carried such treasures in her shop, but to his knowledge, she'd never dictated who they should go to before.

She indicated Morgan again, who was still juggling her own shopping bags, along with Nadra's parcels. Clearly, Lenah thought his housekeeper needed better gear.

He did, too. Owen wanted Morgan to leave with these baskets badly enough that he wasn't the slightest bit interested in haggling. He came up with a price, added twenty percent, then announced it.

Lenah's eyes went wide, and she chuckled. He'd impressed her.

Owen grinned at the little woman and pulled out his wallet, extracting some TZs to cover the kids' drinks and the baskets, plus a little extra. She clucked her tongue and shook her head, but she accepted the money.

Her eyes shifted past his shoulder to the two women again, and she gave him a subtle lift of her chin that told him, unequivocally, to *pay attention.*

Owen focused on the conversation taking place behind him. Morgan greeted the girls and exclaimed happily when they told her about their treat. And then…Nadra asked her if she had any children of her own.

His entire body went stock still. He'd never even considered the possibility.

Chapter Twenty

WHEN NADRA ASKED if she had kids, Morgan didn't know what to say for a moment. Wasn't it obvious that she didn't? What kind of mother would she be, to stay in another country indefinitely, so far away from them?

But as she thought about it, she had to acknowledge that plenty of good mothers did exactly that, if they thought it was best for their children. Nadra didn't know Morgan at all, though—it would be easy for her to assume that she was selfish, instead of noble.

With a quick glance at Owen to make sure he was still occupied, she decided to tell Nadra the truth.

"I was pregnant once," she admitted, "But I lost the baby. And then I lost the father, too. So…no. No kids for me, yet."

Nadra's face went soft with sympathy. "I'm sorry. That's hard."

Morgan shrugged, but she couldn't summon a denial. It *had* been hard—the hardest thing in her life, at that point. But people endured harder things all the time, especially here. It seemed like poor form to make a big deal of it.

Nadra's adorable daughters were oblivious to their discussion, darting around their legs in a sugar-fueled game of tag. Morgan's heart ached with longing, but she forced a smile to her face and refused to let that old despair claim her.

The woman called Miss Lenah cleared her throat to get their attention, but when Morgan turned, she found Owen looking at her with an unreadable expression.

Had he heard what she'd said? Would he even care? It wasn't like Morgan had provided details—and there were a thousand variations of decision, accident, providence that could have led to a bad outcome. He would never have to decide if the miscarriage had been Morgan's fault or not.

Nadra looked back and forth between them curiously, but Owen looked away. She wondered if he'd be embarrassed to know such an intimate detail about her former life. Her *real* life, and the one to which she would eventually have to return.

Lenah nudged her boss and tapped the pile of baskets he was holding. Owen nodded and came down the porch steps, and by the time he reached them, Morgan had pulled herself together again. She even managed to smile when he attempted to relieve her of the various packages and bags she was carrying with one hand, then give her the baskets with the other.

Nadra smiled, too, and waved over Owen's shoulder. Miss Lenah was watching them intently. She pointed at the baskets and then at Morgan, impatient for Owen to explain.

He laughed and announced, "Morgan, Miss Lenah thought you should have these baskets. People around here use them a lot, but maybe I should ask if you even like them before I saddle you with them."

"I do. They're beautiful," she said, turning them in her hands so she could admire their intricate patterns.

Nadra added helpfully, "They're good for shopping, but you can also store stuff in them at home."

"Thank you," Morgan called to Miss Lenah, "I love them!"

The woman beamed, then simply waved and went back into her shop. Owen watched her go with a fond look and a shake of his head, then led them all to his truck.

MORGAN HAD DONE what she could to help Nadra, but the woman was obviously tired from all the walking they'd done. She refused Owen's offer of a ride, however, insisting that she and the girls would rather make their own way home.

As a compromise, the woman agreed to rest at Lenah's for a while before setting out, and allowed Owen to take her purchases, so that he and Morgan could drop them at her house on their way home.

Once everything had been arranged to her satisfaction in the bed of his truck, Nadra stood back, examined it, and lunged forward again.

"No, wait. Morgan, these are yours," she said, extracting a tightly wrapped bundle of cloth, and handing it to her. "You should keep that up front, so it doesn't get dirty."

Morgan quickly stuffed the material out of sight, under her new baskets in the passenger seat. Owen looked curious, but he didn't ask questions.

He was too busy listening to Nadra lament that her husband didn't know an eggplant from a papaya, her mother-in-law wasn't coming to help until after the birth, and the baby wasn't due for several more weeks. She promised to call if she needed anything before then, though, and with a little wave, she herded her daughters back in the direction of Miss Lenah's.

Owen seemed to be brooding a bit as he and Morgan got in his truck and pulled away, and in the silence, Morgan tortured herself about why he'd foisted her off on Nadra, instead of taking her around the market himself, like they'd planned.

Was he unhappy with the job she was doing? Did he hope Nadra would whip her into shape?

They drove for several minutes before Owen asked her, "So, how did it go? Did you and Nadra get along?"

Morgan couldn't decide what she was supposed to have gotten out of the meeting. She clutched the pretty baskets in her lap and closed her eyes against the breeze coming in the window.

"Yeah, we did. I liked her a lot," she told him. "Thanks for introducing me."

"She's a good person," Owen agreed, but then he cleared his throat and said, "You seemed a bit off at the end, though. I was worried that she'd said something to upset you."

Morgan panicked a little, then realized she could offer him a partial explanation that would make perfect sense. "No, she was fine. Sometimes old stuff, uh...jumps up and bites me unexpectedly, but I'm okay. I'm good." *Good enough, anyway.*

Morgan swallowed hard.

"Understood. And if you ever need anything…" her boss began.

Morgan cut him off. "Thanks," she said, "But you don't have to worry. I swear I'm okay."

"Alright," he shrugged. "Offer still stands. Whenever."

Then he spent the rest of the drive trying to diffuse the awkwardness that fell between them, pointing out interesting trees and plants and telling her all about the animals he oversaw in the Preserve.

Morgan let herself be lulled by the motion of the truck and his calm, deep voice, and tried to believe her bravado.

She was fine. She was okay. She didn't need a thing.

A FEW DAYS later, Thom showed up at the cottage again, slamming the door of his car and striding across the yard with an arm tucked behind his back.

Morgan waited on the porch, feeling uncomfortable. Overhearing that conversation on the porch had been bad enough, but ever since Owen told her that Thom probably took her to the wrong market on purpose, she'd been feeling humiliated by how easily the man had taken advantage of her.

Morgan wished Owen was here now, to keep Thom from doing it again. He wasn't, though—so she'd have to handle this herself.

Luckily, Thom was essentially harmless, if a bit of a pain in the ass. It wasn't his fault that she'd eavesdropped on him and Owen, either. Maybe it wasn't really fair to hold his unfiltered words against him.

Besides, his visit probably wouldn't last long. Owen was due home from work in the next couple of hours.

"Morgan, my girl, have I got a treat for you!" Thom called.

"It better not be a snake," Morgan warned.

"No, unfortunately this surprise is less exciting than your buddy. But I still think you'll appreciate it." His eyes were glittering in an unnerving way.

Overhead, a bank of black clouds rumbled with the threat of a big storm, so Morgan waved him inside.

"I'm not sure I like the look on your face," she muttered.

Thom grinned like a kid in candy store. "Come on! Don't be uptight. Let me show you what I brought."

"Just give me a minute."

Morgan moved around the cottage, securing shutters against the impending storm, while Thom hovered near Owen's desk, shifting impatiently.

Now that her boss had taken over the market trips, Morgan had assumed Thom wouldn't drop in for any more unscheduled visits, especially since he'd been warned off. She wondered what Owen would think of this—but suspected he wouldn't be pleased.

It felt like his friend was sneaking around behind his back. There was no doubt in her mind that Thom would enjoy it for that very reason.

Morgan should be calling him out for taking her to the wrong market, but he had just gotten there. Perhaps she should wait for a good opening before jumping on his case.

So, she asked him, "Can I get you anything?"

"Only a couple of glasses," Thom called over his shoulder.

Damn. He'd brought booze, hadn't he?

"This guy is something else," Morgan muttered.

Thom strolled through the living room before landing on one of the deep wooden deck chairs outside. He propped one foot on the extraordinary railing, with its thick, twisting branches and smooth, shining finish.

Morgan often marveled at the creativity and workmanship that had gone into such a labor of love. She would have loved to watch Owen make it, imagining his tanned shoulders and thick, strong arms flexing in the sun as his masterpiece took shape, rail by rail.

Reluctantly, she refocused on the man at hand.

Thom's leg was jumping with impatience. He was sitting in front of that beautiful view, and he looked like he was cooling his heels at a motor vehicle department.

Oh, well. Better get this over with. At least Owen had given his friend a talking to, and Thom wouldn't be angling for more than friendship from her anymore.

Morgan pulled down a glass from the shelf in the kitchen, then stood at the counter and debated for a moment. It wouldn't kill her to lighten up a *little* bit. So, she got a second glass for herself and headed outside.

She supposed Thom was cute enough in his way, but he had the distinct misfortune of having to follow Owen in her mind. In comparison to her boss, Thom just looked like a freshman year science geek.

Whereas Owen was all grown up—bigger, stronger, and rough around the edges. A shiver snaked down her spine.

Owen was a *man*, through and through, that much was clear. Morgan salivated a little, thinking of all the impossible possibilities.

She forced herself to go outside, where Thom was busily unwrapping the predictable brown paper bag.

"Even in Africa the bags are brown?" she laughed.

"Of course," he said. "And let me tell you—it wasn't easy, but I finally found a club that had it, and agreed to sell me a bottle."

"Had what?"

"This!" Thom exclaimed, triumphantly hoisting a bottle of tequila.

Morgan blinked. "Wow, Thom. That's…*wow.*" She frowned when he showed her the label. "And expensive."

"I know!" he cried, pleased with himself. "Remember when you were joking about drinking it in school? I thought it would be fun for you to have some here, since you're so far from home."

"We drank way cheaper stuff, Thom, but…that was nice of you," Morgan said.

She *had* told him and Owen about it, the night of the yard snake incident. Thom had overstayed his welcome and joined them for dinner. Morgan had been nervous, trying to deflect attention away from her stupidity and her eavesdropping, and trying to defuse the tension simmering between the men.

She'd told them some stories about college in Boston, but she'd hadn't made a big deal about the tequila. Maybe an offhand comment, nothing more. And they'd all told tales, hadn't they? Not just her?

Thom kissed the label, then unscrewed the cap and began pouring out the liquor.

Another crack of thunder rumbled overhead, so loud it made Morgan jump.

They were probably going to have to head inside soon, but she really didn't want to. Somehow, being stuck in there with Thom seemed even more inappropriate than this.

He grinned from ear to ear and handed her a glass. "Don't just sit there. Have some!"

Morgan paused. Something felt off about this. As she considered why that was, though, she realized it was probably only a knee-jerk reaction to having been so good—so *spartan*—for so long. She was clearly out of practice being normal.

A simple drink between adults was not anything out of the ordinary. It only felt strange because *she* was strange.

"Hold on," she said, jumping up and running into the kitchen. She returned with the salt. "We'll need some of this."

Thom tilted his head. "What for?"

Morgan mused, "Although, it probably won't matter without limes, too."

"Listen, I had a hard-enough time trying to get you this stuff," Thom complained. "How was I supposed to find limes out here, too? It's not even market day."

The sky boomed, and crack of lightning slivered over the horizon.

Thom added plaintively, "Plus, there's this storm."

Morgan waved him off. "It's okay, we'll just work around it. Now, what else could we use?"

"Instead of being all mysterious, tell me what it's for."

"Thom, you said yourself that you're basically a lush. How can you not know how to shoot tequila?"

"Sweetheart, I drink beer and the occasional scotch," he retorted, exasperated. "Fill me in."

"Fine," Morgan told him. "If you really want to do shots of tequila like a college kid, you have to lick some salt first, knock back the tequila, then bite a wedge of lime after."

Did she have a lemon in the kitchen, perhaps? That might work.

Thom snorted and announced, "Too much work," then took a long swig from his glass. His face immediately contorted. "*Ech.* Really? *This* is what you were raving about?"

"Well, I wouldn't call it raving. I…" Morgan broke off, took a small sip from her own glass, and frowned. "It does lose a little something out of context, I guess."

"You think?" He kept drinking, though.

"What did we know? We were just kids. After weeks of studying nonstop, cutting loose at someone's crappy apartment of the night was a big deal. A pressure valve, you know?"

"I get it," Thom said, looking her over. Maybe he thought she could use some release right now.

Morgan wasn't so sure he was wrong. She took another sip, and rambled on, "We were so broke, but we'd get all this terrible pizza, and it tasted so good. Although, that was probably because it hadn't come from the dorm cafeteria."

"I thought American kids only ate, like, hamburgers and french fries," he laughed.

"Oh, we ate those too. But pizza is the same back home. It's fast and cheap and tasty."

"Which apparently also made you thirsty," Thom commented, leaning forward to refill his glass.

"Yeah, apparently. We'd stuff our faces, and pull out the tequila, and you know how it goes—someone in the group always had a thing for someone else, so they'd want to do shots to help things along."

Morgan hesitated, trying to find a way to capture the memory. It seemed like that part of her life had happened eons ago.

"All you rich kids are too damn fancy," Thom griped. "Would a beer have killed you? How hard is that?"

"Oh, we drank beer, too, believe me. But tequila shots were fun. A level up, if you will." Morgan watched him top off her glass, and added, "Besides, who said we were rich?"

"Wasn't hard to figure out," he muttered.

However, despite being less-than-enchanted with Morgan's teenage social life, Thom was still gamely soldiering through his drink.

Morgan could feel the warmth seeping into her belly, and the lightness in her head, already. She tried to remember the last time she'd had anything alcoholic to drink. There'd been a glass of wine with her sister Meg, before she left on the trip, she thought vaguely.

Only that couldn't be right, could it? That had been…four months ago. *Jesus.* What was Morgan doing with her life?

The breeze kicked up, and Morgan and Thom leaned back in their chairs to enjoy it. The respite from the glaring sun and oppressive humidity of the morning was nice, even if it heralded incoming weather.

It almost felt cool out. Less hot, anyway.

The trees skirting the lake were so different from the oaks and maples at home. When they waved in the breeze, they looked like misshapen drawings in a children's book.

A clink sounded beside her. Morgan looked down and realized that Thom had poured more tequila in her glass. *Again.*

"Would you stop?" she protested. "I need to keep track of how much I'm drinking."

"Just trying to hide how much I'm having," he laughed.

Thom was clearly trying to get her drunk, but why? Did he think it would be funny, or did he want to get her in trouble with Owen? Or…was Thom after something more?

It was getting hard to focus. Morgan waved a bug away from her face, and the sudden movement made her head swim.

Crap. That hadn't taken long.

But…Thom wouldn't have slipped her something, would he have? He seemed so silly—it was hard to believe he was capable of something like that.

Still, there'd been that testy conversation with Owen, and she wasn't in Boston anymore. Maybe it was naive to believe that people were the same everywhere you went, just because they spoke your language.

Morgan blinked. She probably could've gotten roofied in Boston just as easily as here—if that was even what was going on. Maybe she was simply a lightweight, and Thom a heavy pourer.

She huffed and blurted out, "Oh, for god's sake. I'm drunk. Big deal."

Thom burst out laughing.

"This is pretty embarrassing," she announced, but her enunciation was not as clear as she'd hoped for. She seemed to be adding in extra letters and leaving out syllables.

"Why? You're a grown woman," Thom smiled, clinking glasses with her. "If you want to get drunk, then do it."

"I didn't *want* to get drunk. I think I just forgot how strong this stuff is."

Thom rolled his eyes, unimpressed. "Okay, doll. If you say so."

Morgan shifted in her seat, abruptly feeling uncomfortable. She wished she could reverse the tequila's effects, but the damage was already done. She'd probably continue getting drunker, even if she never lifted her glass again.

Even her lips felt numb.

Thom piped up suddenly. "Here's what I don't understand. Why did you call them body shots that last time? Is it because it feels like you've been shot?"

Morgan peered at him, trying to decide if he was serious. Thom looked pretty woozy himself, but she was hardly the best judge.

Her face felt hot, like she'd gotten a horrible sunburn. "These aren't body shots. In fact, these aren't shots at all," she explained, holding her tumbler up and eyeing it warily. The view of the lake refracted through the glass, wavy and gray.

"But what makes it a *body* shot?" he pressed, demonstrating a remarkably inconvenient tenacity, all of a sudden.

"Tequila. Just…different," Morgan grimaced.

Had she *really* joked about doing body shots in college—in front of her hot boss and his friend, no less—the last time they were all together? What even *was* that?

The memory was foggy, but she could almost see now how Thom had set her up. When they'd started bantering with each other, he'd made Morgan feel like a little kid, trying to keep up and prove how cool she was to the big boys.

But even if he'd goaded her, she'd still been ridiculously gullible and had handed him all he needed to corner her into her current predicament.

Thom's opinion of her should not have mattered one bit. Owen's either, for that matter.

"So? What are they, doll?" Thom waved his glass unsteadily at her.

"Shit," Morgan said. "You're really going to make me explain this, aren't you?"

Oh, look—the swearing had arrived.

That was a bad sign. Morgan always swore like a sailor when she'd had too much to drink.

She moved her glass farther away and sighed in defeat. When was Owen coming home, anyway?

"Of course, I'm going to make you. I found the booze. The least you could do is give me the full experience," Thom prodded. "I mean, did you pour them over your head or what?"

Like a dog with a bone. "No, Thom. In order to do a body shot, you need someone else. Ideally, someone you're attracted to."

Thom smiled and squinted comically, like he was trying to unravel it.

Morgan licked the taste of tequila from her lips and tilted her head. She could almost hear the sound of the shovel as she dug a deeper hole for herself.

Up above, the clouds were rolling closer over the lake, swelling and turning black at their hearts. If she and Thom didn't go inside soon, they were going to get drenched—but sitting on the couch with him seemed even worse. Spectacularly ill-advised, some might say.

"So…"

"*So*, someone puts the salt on their neck or their chest or whatever, and then they hold the lime in their mouth…"

He held up a hand. "How do you get the salt on your neck? Or off it, for that matter?"

Morgan blinked. "No, not your own neck," she sputtered, getting flustered.

"That sounds very scratchy. And I don't see how you're supposed to drink anything with a lime in your mouth," he argued.

She looked at him in exasperation, fairly sure he was messing with her. Sure enough, Thom's eyes were dancing, and his grin was wide. Once again, she'd fallen right into his trap.

That snake. He had her right where he wanted her.

"You are such a trouble-maker," she muttered ruefully.

Thom's expression changed slightly. He fell silent for a moment, studying her, then said softly, "Sweetheart, can't you feel it, too?"

Gingerly, he picked up her hand, like he was afraid of spooking her.

"What? The tequila? Because they can probably feel my buzz in Dodoma," Morgan snorted.

She tried to keep her tone light, but she hadn't missed the change in him. She jumped up from her chair and pulled on her hand, but Thom pulled back, tugging her onto his lap.

Before she could process that development, he'd brushed a lock of hair off her neck and poured a stream of tequila down it. Morgan's head was fuzzy and her heart was pounding, and she knew she had to stop this insanity before it went any farther.

But Thom gripped her arm tight as he sprinkled the salt on her neck, then set the shaker down on the ground next to his boots.

"Thom—"

"Hush," he told her.

Holding Morgan still, he leaned down to lick her neck just as she felt the first huge drops of rain pelt her. He leaned back and took a quick gulp of his drink, then pulled Morgan's mouth to his.

His kiss was deep, and almost painful in its urgency. Morgan pushed at his chest, but it didn't do much good. Thom had his arms locked around her, and he was stronger than he looked.

Everything had happened so fast, and she was off-balance and confused. Morgan didn't want this, not with him.

Thom knew that. He wouldn't force her. Would he?

It felt like he was forcing her. Morgan struggled against him a little more, trying to pull her mouth away, trying to stand. The clouds broke open with a crash.

Thom knew what he was doing and his desire for her was obvious. Maybe he thought if he held on long enough, she'd fall in line.

Morgan frantically shuffled through her options. They were all alone out here. By the time Owen got home to break this up, it might be too late.

Owen. He was the person Morgan wished she was with, but he was also the last person who would—*should*—want her in return.

Thom was pushing the straps of Morgan's top off her shoulders and groaning as he plastered her neck and her chest with hard, sloppy kisses.

"Thom, *stop.*"

He chuckled, like it was all a great big joke, but he held on.

Morgan couldn't seem to evade his tight grip or his wet lips, and she tried not to cry in frustration. This wasn't right, but she couldn't figure out how to get away.

He kissed her, and groped her, and it was as if she was watching him do it from somewhere else.

Like she wasn't even a party to it.

But—Morgan didn't *want* this. It wasn't *right.*

"Thom! Stop!" she cried, working her arms between them and pushing at him again.

He was getting clumsier in his enthusiasm, clearly enjoying the game.

"You want to tussle, doll?" he laughed. "I'll give you a tussle. But let's make it a horizontal one."

"No," Morgan insisted. "Let me go." She tried to swat his hands away so she could pull up her wet shirt.

Thom ignored her, pinning her hands behind her. "Come on, sweetheart," he murmured against her skin, his hair plastered to his scalp by the rain. "You know want to."

Morgan didn't feel fizzy and light anymore. She just felt ill.

"Thom!" she said, loud and scared. "What are you doing? I said *no*. I want you to stop!"

He pulled back far enough to peer into her face, his eyelashes in dark wet spikes, and his irritation radiating off him in waves.

Morgan pulled out the only gun she had. "Owen is due home any minute," she said. "What's he going to say when he sees you mauling me?"

Thom froze, his entire body going taut as wire. She was ready for the reaction, and wrenched herself backward, up and off his lap before he could catch her.

She looked wildly around for a weapon, one that wouldn't bring her closer to him again. He looked her up and down.

Finally, he sprawled back in his chair and sneered, "*Owen*. I know that bastard like I know my own name. He might talk trash, but there is no way he moved fast enough to get to you before me."

Morgan shook her head and backed away. "What are you…what are you talking about?"

But she knew, didn't she? She'd overheard them bickering over her—and she remembered every word. *If you had half a heart, you'd leave the girl to me.*

Thom picked up his glass and drained it, as if he had all the time in the world. "I'm talking about winning, Morgan. I'm talking about the underdog finally coming out on top." When he chuckled again, it was a mean, bitter sound. "Or in this case, just *coming*. While on top."

Morgan gulped. "You—you aren't going to do that. Not with me."

Scared tears pricked at her eyes, and her hair stuck to her face. She edged toward the back door.

"Of course, I am," he slurred, getting to his feet. "Hold on, there, dolly. Let me get the glasses." He turned around to look for them in the downpour.

What had she done? Morgan had known better than to give him an opening, and she should never have agreed to have a drink with him. She shouldn't be the least bit surprised that it had escalated like it had.

And now, Thom wasn't only not getting the message—he seemed fully prepared to assault her. Damn. *Damn.*

Morgan spun and burst into the house, running blindly. She slammed the door shut behind her and fumbled for the latch, but when Thom lumbered toward her, she reeled and rushed into the gloom...

...only to barrel right into a very large, very solid wall of male. A small shriek escaped her before she realized who it was.

Owen. Thank god.

Chapter Twenty-One

OWEN WAS DRIVING fast by the time he hit the lane that led to the cottage, so much so that his truck caught air on a few of the larger ruts.

He'd left the office later than he'd intended, however, and if Morgan was making dinner, he didn't want to be the reason it got ruined.

Plus, an ugly-looking storm was blowing in. He needed to do a perimeter check before it hit, to make sure nothing had been left out that shouldn't have been.

At least Owen wouldn't be walking into a dark and empty house this time—not like he had so many times before. His housekeeper would have the home fires burning, and the thought set off little flares of anticipation in his veins.

There was only one little flaw in his fantasy. No, make that two.

That nasty storm beat him home. And when Owen pulled up to the house in the driving rain, he saw Thom's car parked outside.

That could not be good.

He dashed from the truck to the porch and mopped off his face with the tail of his shirt, then quickly wiped his boots and stepped inside.

The cottage was dark. Empty. Not a peep coming from any corner of it. Owen's chest went tight. Where the hell was Thom? Or, for that matter, Morgan?

He took a few steps toward her room but stopped before he got there. Maybe he didn't want to know.

Owen didn't have long to agonize. All at once, Morgan flew through the back door, wet as an otter, and barreling right into him.

He wrapped his arms reflexively around her, steadying her while she gasped and trembled. She froze for a long second, but soon buried her face in his chest and hung on for dear life.

Morgan moaned a little, and Owen was pretty sure she whimpered, "Thank god."

He was surrounded by that heady scent that always followed her around and transfixed by her softness. He tightened his hold and noted that her body—so nice to look at—fit his perfectly.

Morgan was soaked, however. His shirt was already plastered to his chest between them.

"Hey, honey," he said softly. "I'm home."

Owen couldn't believe he was actually holding her, but now that he was, it was obvious how much he'd wanted to.

Morgan's arms were tight around his waist and when he spoke, she looked up at him with an expression of such gratitude and relief that before he knew it, he was dipping down and kissing her.

It was no polite little taste, either—Owen devoured her, hungry after denying even the existence of his attraction to her for weeks on end. Her mouth melted under his, salty and sweet, laying waste to all his careful restraint.

Owen bent to lift her against him, needing Morgan even closer, when he finally realized what she tasted like. *Tequila.* He could just catch its flavor, unmistakable on his tongue.

Which meant Morgan had been drinking. *Shit.*

Owen should not be doing this. Or at least...not right now.

He broke off the kiss as gently as he could and pulled back to study her face. Did she look drunk?

Her eyes were closed, but when they opened, she looked stunned.

Just then, something large crashed against the back door, making her jump. That's when Owen remembered how frantic her expression had been when she'd rushed in from the rain, and the fact that Thom's car was parked out front.

At a yell from the back patio, his head snapped up, and he spotted Thom standing out there in the rain, fumbling with the doorknob and juggling a bottle and a couple of glasses.

"Morgan!" he bellowed in frustration, "Come on, doll. Let me in."

Owen looked down into Morgan's face, saw the panic in her eyes, and he *knew.*

"Did he hurt you?" he asked.

She shook her head. "No, he…he tried to…but then I…and you…"

She swallowed and tightened her hold on him, hiding her face in his shirt once more. Owen would've liked to take a moment to enjoy it, but Thom managed to rattle the back door open and stumble inside.

The glasses he'd been holding were slippery with rain, and they slid from his arm and shattered all over the threshold.

"Fuck," Thom muttered.

Owen set Morgan gently aside, making sure she wouldn't falter before stalking back to confront his erstwhile friend. Thom swayed when he looked up, annoyed to see Owen standing in front of him, instead of Morgan.

"Oh, look," he said, "It's a boy scout."

Owen's temper slipped its leash. Without even thinking, he buried his fist in that ridiculous, court-jester face, watching with savage satisfaction as Thom dropped like a stone. Owen eyed him for a minute or two, making sure he was going to stay down before he turned back to Morgan.

She was watching him with round eyes and her mouth hanging open.

"Are you okay?" he asked. His voice sounded weird—gruff and rusty.

Morgan nodded, and looked from him to Thom and back again. "Holy shit. That was…you're kind of brutal, you know that?"

Owen went over to her but hesitated when she backed up a step. He wanted to recapture that feeling from before, to put his hands back on her, and his mouth, as well—and she had to know he would never hit *her*.

Except this was way worse than Morgan having had a few too many—this was her narrowly avoiding an assault. As if to emphasize that point, she wrapped her arms around herself and shivered. She looked wet and cold and miserable.

"Morgan, I am so sorry. I had no idea Thom would—"

"No, I'm sorry," she countered, edging back into her room. "I don't know how this happened. I didn't mean to make trouble."

Owen shook his head, trying to clear the blood thumping furiously beneath his temples. *Trouble?* He didn't care about trouble. He was so mad at Thom for so many reasons, that hitting him had almost been a relief.

He did care whether Morgan was okay, though. Well…about that and the fact that they'd finally *kissed*. He wanted to know how she felt about it. He wanted to do it again.

Although…probably some other time. When she wasn't, say, quaking in fear.

"Are you sure you're okay?" he managed to ask instead. "He really didn't touch you?"

She paused, long enough that his jaw began to hurt from clenching it closed. Eventually she murmured, "It's okay. He didn't get far," before her teeth started chattering.

Owen hated the sound of that. "Morgan, honey—you're soaked. Do you want to get some dry clothes on while I make you some tea?"

When her eyes darted to Thom, he added, "Don't worry. I'll take care of him."

She winced, probably because that bit had come out slightly sinister. Owen could admit that.

"Okay," Morgan whispered, hunching into herself as she backed into her room. The lock on her door made a loud click as she engaged it, and soon he heard the shower running.

Owen took a deep breath and looked around. He stepped over Thom, kicked aside a couple shards of glass, and securely latched the back doors. The rain was pounding on a squashed paper bag laying on the deck, and one of the chairs was on its side.

He turned back to the disgraceful lump out cold on his floor and contemplated him. Owen had been a fool to assume that Thom would leave Morgan alone, simply because he'd asked him to. If anything, their little spat about her had probably only encouraged the jackass.

If Morgan hadn't been here, Owen might have been tempted to leave Thom there to rot—but he'd told her he would take care of the man. And so, Owen dragged him over to the couch and laid him out and checked his vitals to make sure he was okay.

He hated keeping him in such close proximity to Morgan, but Owen also didn't want to leave her alone now that night was falling.

The best option seemed to be letting Thom sleep it off here, under Owen's watchful eye—then packing him off once he'd sobered up and the weather cleared.

If Thom knew what was good for him, he'd stay unconscious for a good long while, though. Owen's rage at the bastard still simmered and thrummed along his veins. If Thom woke now, he would only hit him again, and probably harder.

With effort, he drew back and forced himself to go in the kitchen to turn on the kettle. It wasn't until he paced back to the couch, that he noticed the bottle that had rolled under the table.

Owen bent to retrieve it. *Top-shelf tequila.* So, he'd been right.

He glanced from Thom to Morgan's room. Had Thom tried to get Morgan drunk on purpose? Or just gotten carried away?

Owen couldn't decide what this was. Thom might simply be grasping at a shiny new toy that he'd been denied, or this could be something more—something to do with the dying gazelles and Stephen Thorpe.

Unfortunately, Owen couldn't remember why—when he'd been decidedly troubled by Thom's fascination with his housekeeper—he hadn't said anything to her. He supposed he hadn't wanted to come across as proprietary and jealous.

He hadn't anticipated something like this, obviously.

Owen's heart knocked around in his chest as he thought about what might have happened if he'd been delayed even longer at the office or stopped on his way home.

How much of this had Thom planned out? How far had he *gotten*, exactly, before Owen arrived?

Questions on top of questions, and none of them were getting answered with Thom dead to the world and Morgan hiding in her room.

He walked to his desk and set the bottle down, then dropped heavily into his chair. He listened to Thom snoring loudly on the couch and wondered if he'd broken his nose. He hoped so. It would serve the man right.

Sounds were coming from Morgan's room, too. Owen wasn't positive, but it was possible she was crying her eyes out. Because of Thom, or because of him, though?

Likely both.

Owen clenched his fists on his knees and waited for the kettle to boil. He stared into the gathering gloom and listened to the storm raging outside, and realized what a complete caveman he'd been.

First, he'd rubbed Thom's nose in the fact that he couldn't have Morgan, and had apparently driven the man to try taking instead of asking. Then, Owen had punched him so hard in the face, he'd knocked him out—and thereby scared his housekeeper even worse than she'd been before.

Just to top things off, somewhere in there, Owen had found time to suck face with Morgan, directly after his supposed friend had attacked her.

He was an all-around stellar gent, it seemed.

Worst of all, however, was that Owen suddenly had a great big problem. Now that he'd kissed the lovely and elusive Morgan Flynn, he didn't have to guess what it would be like any longer.

He knew for certain, just like he knew that one taste of her would not be enough. It would *never* be enough.

He was going to have to win that woman and do it well enough that he'd get to keep her.

Which meant that if Thom so much as looked at her again? He was going to get a hell of a lot more than a punch in the teeth.

ONCE OWEN HAD delivered Morgan's tea and reassured her that he would be guarding her door all night, he parked himself in the armchair next to Thom and made himself comfortable.

He propped his feet on the coffee table and stared at the ceiling, listening to the sound of her light footsteps moving around her room. Owen let the memory of how she'd tasted—how she'd felt in his arms—grow roots in his mind.

Several feet from where he sat, Morgan was going to climb into that big canopy bed and tuck herself under the crisp white covers. She'd smell clean and fresh from her shower, with damp hair and warm skin. Owen could picture it perfectly.

As inviting as the image was, though, it killed him that she was probably really upset in there. She might need him. He *wanted* her to need him.

He also wanted her to *want* him.

Morgan was undoubtedly too busy figuring out how soon she could press charges, however. She hadn't wanted to call the police tonight, even though Owen had offered. Maybe she'd want to tomorrow. No matter what she decided to do, he'd help her.

Owen turned his attention to Thom and began thinking of all the ways he could make him pay for what he'd done. It was hardly as exciting as kissing the beautiful woman in the next room, but it would have to be enough to keep him warm tonight.

HE SAT IN that damn chair all night, watching Thom snore. Toward morning, the man started getting restless, tossing and turning and whining about poachers in his sleep. By then, Owen was tired, stiff, and pissed-off—and not in the mood to listen sniveling.

So, he kicked Thom in the thigh, hard enough to wake him up.

"What the *hell?*" Thom squawked, jerking awake.

"Wake up, asshole. I'm sick of looking at you. It's time for you to go."

Thom scrubbed at his face. "Am I still dreaming?"

Owen tried to keep his voice level, but it wasn't easy. "I guarantee you I am as real as the blood on your face. But honestly—*poachers everywhere*, Thom? Could you be any more dramatic?"

Thom mumbled something that sounded like, "There are."

"The season's almost done," Owen said, watching him carefully, "and we're bound to find out who's targeting the Rathbones soon."

It was a shot across Thom's bow, and they both knew it.

Thom was too out of it to not take the bait, though. His voice climbed unnaturally high and he insisted, "They *are* everywhere. You'll see."

"Oh, now you're a fortune teller, in addition to a date rapist? Spreading yourself a bit thin, aren't you?"

Thom blinked at him in confusion for a moment, before his face cleared. "I didn't—"

Owen growled, so he started over, "You don't know what you're talking about, mate. The worst is yet to come."

Owen had had quite enough of the Madame Zorba crap. He pointed at Thom and told him, "You bet it is. If you don't get the hell out of this house right this second, I will *end* you for what you did to Morgan last night."

He stood up, grabbed Thom's arm, and hauled him to his feet. "Don't let me ever see you here again. You hear me? You don't visit her. You don't call her. You don't even *think* Morgan's name. Am I clear?"

Thom hitched up his pants, felt in his pocket for his keys, and shuffled toward the door. He looked steady enough on his feet, so Owen probably didn't need to worry about his driving or following him home.

"Oh, you're clear, all right. But you don't know as much as you think," Thom muttered. "Remember that, big man."

Owen watched him go, then stood on the porch and listened to the sound of Thom's car driving away, until he couldn't hear it any longer—until the only sound he heard was the birds singing, and the occasional drip of rain from the eaves.

Around Victoriaville, and in some of the areas beyond, Thom had a reputation for being outgoing and funny. Maybe a little flaky, Owen knew. Maybe reckless, too—but that was mostly with his own safety.

For the first time, however, Owen stopped to really consider those things—to wonder what, exactly, those surface-level qualities might be papering over.

People could pretend to be a lot of things, he knew, but that didn't always reflect what was wriggling underneath the log.

Right now, Thom's whole persona felt like a put-on—a log that Owen might need to kick over soon. He wasn't so sure he'd like what he found underneath, however.

The truth was, he knew his own reasons for coming to Africa—but why, in all their years of friendship, had he never learned Thom's?

OWEN THOUGHT OF that the following day as he sat outside Charlie's, eating lunch. The café was crowded, but he'd been able to grab a table around the corner, in the shade cast by the building. He could only assume that was why no one noticed him during what happened next.

Halfway through his meal, Nigel roared past the square in his old Renault, and screeched to a halt in front of the Preserve office. He got out quickly and slammed his car door.

Thom held open the office's front door for the man, then leaned out to glance up and down the street before he ducked back inside.

Without really thinking about what he was doing, Owen gathered up the rest of his food and shoved it into the bag, then crossed the street—keeping carefully out of sight of the Preserve's front window as he did so.

He walked up the block a bit, paused next to the dress shop on the corner, then continued on to the alleyway behind. The sidewalk was empty, so he sidestepped into the narrow gap with no one the wiser.

Further down, Owen could hear Nigel's voice spilling out of his office window, ranting about something.

Owen walked quietly closer, then slouched against the wall.

Nigel bellowed, "Those goddamn bureaucrats at TANAPA—they're killing me with their bullshit! *Sign this. Prove that.* They're going to ruin the whole bloody operation."

There was a pause as the man struggled to catch his breath, then the sound of him dropping into his creaky wooden chair. "*Jesus*," he grumbled. "Where's Hargreave, again?"

Thom piped up, "Who the hell knows. He left about 45 minutes ago to clear his head. Whatever that means." His disdain came through loud and clear.

Just then, something cold and wet touched his hand. Owen looked down, and sure enough, there was that same stray dog as last time, sitting on its haunches and watching him with its avid little face tilted to one side. Its tail swished back and forth on the dirty concrete, grubby, but pleased.

In case the pup could read minds, Owen silently begged it to stay quiet, and not give him away.

Inside, Nigel was snorting at Thom's words. "Doesn't matter what it means, as long as he stays away from us." There was the sound of paper shuffling, and then Nigel said, "Listen—the Rathbone population reports I brought down weren't enough. They think we're just dealing with some kind of migratory cycle, or something."

Heavy footsteps crossed the room, and everything fell silent inside. The dog edged closer, slinking like a cat, to check out Owen's lunch. He lifted the bag well out of its reach, but when his weight shifted, the rocky dirt under his boots crunched softly.

Owen froze, holding his breath. In the old days, Thom would've heard that, and known it wasn't normal.

Inside, Nigel spat out, "Will you *please* stop hovering? Open the blinds, so you'll see him coming!"

A chair scraped on the floor, and then Thom asked hesitantly, "If those reports didn't do the trick, then…then we'll have to do more, right?"

"You're damn right we have to do more! Those idiots in Dodoma can drag their heels about one or two bloody herds, but our people aren't going to wait around forever for us to fix this."

"Do you think they'll find someone else?" Thom asked. "Besides us, I mean."

Nigel muttered, "Not if I have anything to say about it."

After a pause, Thom's footsteps crossed the room, and a moment later Owen caught the sound of the bathroom faucet from the next window over.

Nigel's shuffling gait cut across his office, too, and then his door slammed.

Apparently, the meeting had come to an end.

Owen straightened and crept out of the alley, back onto the sidewalk that ran along Banyan Street. With a little whine, the stray trotted after him.

At the corner, Owen called a greeting to Lauren, returning to her shop with a parcel balanced carefully on her head. After she passed, he squatted down to scratch the dog behind the ears.

It was skinny and definitely had fleas, but it seemed healthy enough. Still, it couldn't hurt to bring him by the vet one of these days. For now, he fed the pup some meat from his lunch, gave him a belly rub, and shooed him off.

Before he left for home later, Owen would have to remember to set out some water and a couple of old blankets near the Preserve's back door, so the little guy would have a decent place to crash.

With that decided, Owen strolled down the block, squared his shoulders, and banged into the office. He wouldn't say his head was clear, though—if anything, he had even more to worry about.

"Gentlemen," he said, by way of greeting.

Thom came out of the lavatory and headed for his desk, clapping Owen on the shoulder as he passed. "Got it all worked out now? Brain box nice and vacant, mate?"

Owen bristled, but he'd had all morning to get used to the fact that Thom was going to act like nothing had happened out at the cottage. He hated that the man would walk away from the incident with nothing more than a black eye and a split lip.

Morgan didn't want to press charges, though, and Owen wasn't going to force her.

As discreetly as he could, he kept an eye on Nigel's closed door, and sure enough, moments later, he heard the man slam down his phone receiver and swear, "Bloody *hell!*"

Cotton stomped out of his office, spotted Owen standing there, and stood fuming for a second before stalking back to lock the report he was holding in his desk. He came out of his office again, pulled the door shut and bolted it, and shoved the key ring into his pocket.

"If anyone needs me, call me on my mobile," Nigel muttered, then stormed out.

Owen arched a brow at Thom. "What's with him?"

Thom watched Nigel's Renault speed away. "If I had to guess, I'd say that Stephen is being a spoiled little shit again."

All trace of his former cheek was gone. Thom sorted papers on his desk and looked subdued.

"Well, that's no surprise. What's he want this time? A private tour of the museum?"

"Damned if I know. If it isn't one thing with him, it's another," He swiveled in his chair and started filing things.

Owen marveled at how Thom—normally loquacious to a fault— seemed to have suddenly mastered the art of not actually *saying* anything.

Maybe he'd always been that way. Maybe Owen was only noticing it now.

Regardless, he wanted to have a crack at whatever Nigel had locked in his desk, and Owen couldn't risk Thom knowing about it. Which meant, of course, that Thom had to go.

He looked over at him. The man seemed restless and as irritable as a wet cat. He ran his arm across his sweating brow and complained, "Man. It's hotter than hell today."

"It's not the heat, it's the humidity," Owen joked, out of habit. "Why don't you turn on the fan?"

"Because it's broken, *Boy Wonder*," Thom sneered.

Owen walked over to the switch on the wall, looked down, and saw the plug laying on the linoleum. "No, it's not. It's just unplugged. Kisima pulls it out sometimes when she's cleaning."

Thom ought to have remembered that. He only flushed and rolled his eyes, though. Owen switched on the fan, pushed a hand through his hair, and turned back.

"Listen," he said carefully, "the old man's obviously not coming back. Why don't you kick off for the day?"

Thom's head snapped up and he frowned. "Why? What are you going to do?"

"Not a lot. I'm wiped out. I only have a couple more things to look at, and then I'm going to leave, too. I want to take that stray that's hanging around out back to the vet before we get bad weather."

"Well, it's no surprise you're tired. You went running out of here like your ass was on fire, but people don't go on random walkabouts in the heat of the day for a reason. What the hell were you thinking?"

Owen tried to play it cool. If Thom suspected anything, he'd never leave. "I told you, mate. There was a horsefly in my office the size of a turkey vulture, and it was buzzing so loud I couldn't hear myself think."

He watched Thom carefully when he added, "Plus, this thing with the Rathbones is getting on my nerves. I'm ready for it to be over so Nigel will relax, for Chrissakes."

If Thom felt anything about that last part, he didn't show it. He only frowned at the front door, deep in thought. "You sure you don't mind if I go?" he asked after a while.

"I'm sure. Head home and have a pint," Owen urged. "Even with the fan, it's too hot to get much done, anyway." He cringed at how fake his voice sounded, but Thom didn't appear to notice.

"All right. But you should take off too."

"I will. Ten minutes more, at most."

With that, Thom shrugged, heaved himself to his feet, and ambled out. Owen watched him cross the street, get into his banged-up blue car, and pull away.

Once he was sure the man was gone for good, Owen closed the front door and locked it, then rushed to his desk and pulled his keys out of the top drawer. He flipped through them, looking for the one he wanted.

Finally, he found it—so Owen walked to Nigel's office and tried the bolt. Sure enough, it slid open.

He smiled in triumph. Naturally—bureaucracy being what it was—no one had ever bothered to change the locks.

He doubted Nigel even remembered that Owen had once occupied his office, years before Cotton had been transferred out here. He'd certainly never suspect that Owen had kept the key.

That wasn't Owen's problem, though. If Nigel wanted to keep things from him, he'd have to find a hidey hole a damn sight better than here in the office—and he'd do well to have a good reason for doing so, too.

Once inside, he made short work of the ineffectual lock on the desk drawer and extracted the report that Nigel had stashed there. He flipped through it quickly, noting the memos and reports that Nigel had signed off on, as well as the official responses with TANAPA's seal at the top of the letterhead.

Owen scowled. He'd never seen any of these.

Why would Cotton try to convince TANAPA there were no more Rathbones left in the Preserve? The park had only managed to secure a special charter and stay in private British hands during the country's transition to independence because of its carefully protected herd of the rare gazelles. Once they were gone, though, the Preserve looked a lot less unique.

Fortunately, those gazelles were still spread out over most of the northern quadrants of the Preserve. Owen reviewed the scouting reports routinely. Even considering the recent spate of "poaching," there ought to be plenty of stable families left come breeding season. Which meant, Nigel was definitely jumping the gun a bit.

Owen fumed. What was the man thinking? No Rathbones meant one very outdated special charter, and some very sketchy job security—for *all* of them.

He thought about Thom's words earlier, when he'd said, "*We'll have to do more.*" Nigel had been angry, but he'd agreed.

The thought had Owen shoving the report back in the desk, locking it up, and jogging to his own office. He flipped through his files, looking for the most recent scouting reports.

He'd filed them not two days ago—but they weren't there any longer. He stepped quickly into the front office, his heart thumping clumsily in his chest as he pulled open the drawers behind Thom's desk.

Owen pawed through the folders, but they were a total mess, jumbled and out of order. Yet another reason he wanted to wring Thom's neck. He'd been a disaster at office work from the beginning.

In the past, he'd made up for it with his abilities in the field, but now, Owen wasn't sure *what* the man was good at besides drinking and lying.

Even so, Owen eventually found the folders from the week he'd been shot and pulled them out. He realized immediately that something was wrong, and when he set them on Thom's desk and cracked them open, it was clear that everything inside had been ruined.

It looked like a dark liquid had been spilled all over the reports and photos, warping and staining them beyond recognition. They were already starting to fuse together with mold, too. Completely useless, in other words.

Owen returned the mess to the folders and re-filed them, then brushed the residue from Thom's desk.

As he stood there, considering whether the damage had been purposeful or not, he remembered how Nigel had slammed down his phone before he took off.

Owen dashed back to Nigel's desk, picked up the receiver, and hit the redial button. After an oddly large number of clicks, the line finally began ringing, and a posh Englishwoman answered, "Thorpe Industries, Sir Mark Thorpe's office. This is Sabrina. How may I assist you?"

Owen set the receiver back in its cradle and stared at it. Apparently, Nigel and his "dear friend" had had a bit of a dust up.

At the sound of a knock on the front door, however, he spun around, and frantically tried to come up with an explanation for what he was doing.

It wasn't Thom or Nigel standing out there, though—it was Joseph Teleki.

When he opened the door, the man leaned on the door frame, looking Owen over and smiling quizzically. "I was in town, so I thought I'd stop by and see how your shoulder is feeling," he said.

Owen felt his neck get hot. He let Teleki in, then went over to shut Nigel's door and lock it—and he checked the knob twice to make absolutely sure it had latched.

Then he turned and eyed his visitor. He'd bolted the front door earlier, so he was reasonably certain the man hadn't seen anything. So why did Joseph look like he knew what he'd been up to?

If Owen was going to continue digging around like a cut-rate private eye, he really needed to be more careful. And get a thicker skin.

"Shoulder's fine," he told the man. "Still aches sometimes, but nothing serious."

Teleki's eyes flickered to Nigel's door, so he added, "My phone's not working properly. I wanted to check on the old man's before he got back from Dodoma."

Joseph nodded, but his expression, as usual, was hard to read. Owen genuinely had no idea if he would he report back to Nigel about this little interlude.

He cursed under his breath and decided he'd better clear out before anything else went awry.

"Anyway, I was just closing up shop for the day. There's a stray hanging around out back. I'm going to bring it to the vet, but I can give you a lift home after, if you'd like."

Owen really hoped the vet took walk-ins—it looked like "one of these days" was *today*.

Joseph waved him off. "That's kind of you, but I have some things I still need to take care of before I head home." He started for the door, then turned to inquire, "How's Miss Morgan doing these days?"

Owen narrowed his eyes, but there was nothing in Teleki's tone or expression that suggested he knew about Thom's attack. He was only being polite.

"She's fine," Owen told him.

Rearranging his house. Communing with nature. Looking completely seductive no matter what time of day it was. Kissing like a goddess.

Owen wanted to groan at the sheer torture of it all.

Joseph nodded, but he studied Owen's face with eyes that saw far too much. "I'm glad to hear it," he said, "And listen—I don't want to keep you. We can catch up another time."

He gave Owen a little wave as he stepped outside and walked away.

Owen watched him go, then carefully examined the door jamb and the deadbolt for signs of forced entry. Of course, there weren't any.

Perhaps, the man would be on his way to Cotton the minute Owen left, but Owen didn't have time to worry about it. The vet closed in thirty minutes and he still had to collar that pup in the alley and convince the beast to take a ride in the truck with him.

Owen wiped his face on his sleeve and hoped to hell the little mutt wouldn't fight him. Thom had been right before. It *was* infernally hot in here.

As he headed for the back door, he tried to unravel what he'd learned this afternoon. Stephen Thorpe's father seemed to be in on whatever was happening around here, but Owen had no idea what to do with that information.

Owen stepped into the alley and looked around for the dog, but the mutt had seen him first, and was already trotting over eagerly. That was one task accomplished, at least.

But what was the use of snooping, he wondered, if it got you nowhere? Owen wasn't made for all this sneaking around. He made a lousy spy, but he couldn't give up now.

Chapter Twenty-Two

ONCE MORGAN HAD a chance to sleep off the tequila—and whatever else made it hit her like a ton of bricks—she felt ready for some introspection. And given the way everything had spiraled last night, she figured it was necessary.

She crawled out of bed in the faint light of approaching dawn, then stood near her bedroom door, listening to Thom snoring out on the couch.

In retrospect, Morgan could acknowledge that Thom had been giving her what Meg liked to call *David Eyes*—so named for the boy who'd sat next to her in Algebra, staring with an unsettling mix of longing and misery—for quite a while leading up to his failed seduction.

David's moony gazes were seared into Morgan's memory, so she certainly *should* have noticed Thom delivering them. Unfortunately, she'd been too busy giving Owen her own longing looks to pay much mind to Thom's.

Looks could only get you so far, though. They'd never worked for young David, and even Thom had given up on them. Morgan would undoubtedly have to, as well. If she wanted something, she would have to fight for it.

It made her wonder, though—what *did* she want? Was it Owen?

Morgan still couldn't believe the way he'd gone after Thom. He'd delivered that deadly blow with grace and precision, and without a second's hesitation. Owen simply stepped up to the plate and swung for the fences, knowing he wouldn't miss.

She leaned her shoulder against the wall and pictured Thom's boyish face, probably already purpling across the nose and eyes. Did he sleep like a man with a clear conscience, she wondered? Would he even recognize what he'd done wrong?

How far would things have progressed if Owen hadn't arrived? Morgan didn't know how hard she might have had to fight, or if Thom would have tried to force her. She didn't know how bad things might have gotten.

After it was over, Owen had offered to call the cops, but she'd been freaked out and confused, and hadn't wanted to make things worse. Morgan still wasn't sure she was thinking clearly.

In the light of day, she wasn't positive how much tequila she'd actually drunk, or how hard Thom had pushed—or even whether he really could have slipped her something extra when she wasn't looking.

She didn't want to think about it anymore. Her eyes felt gritty from crying herself to sleep, and her head ached. Maybe she'd be out of a job today.

Morgan was a fool, and in way over her head.

Last night, she'd stood under the shower until the warm water had run out, trying to wash away her crushing shame. She'd dressed in an old t-shirt and pajama bottoms and crawled into bed. Owen had brought her a cup of tea and vowed to protect her.

That was the kind of man he was—fierce and noble and kind.

Morgan had laid there and stared at her ceiling for hours, listening to her boss shift in his chair and mutter under his breath when Thom's snoring got too loud or he talked in his sleep.

Somehow, she'd managed to kiss both of them last night. The embarrassment from that alone was enough to make her want to crawl under her bed and hide for a week.

Unfortunately, Morgan didn't have that luxury. She needed water from the kitchen. She was desperate to purify herself, somehow—to eradicate any trace of that tequila, and the persistent feel of Thom's hands and mouth crawling over her skin.

She already wanted another scalding shower, but she was frozen in here, unnerved by Thom's presence out there on the couch, as well as her trepidation about how Owen would look at her later. About what he would *say*.

He'd been so apologetic last night when he'd explained to her that Thom had to stay. Thom hadn't been in any condition to drive, and Owen hadn't wanted to leave her alone in order to take him home himself.

She'd probably looked like she was about to have a breakdown, and maybe she still did. But then and now, she wished there'd been some way to get rid of the man without having him hauled off in handcuffs.

Giving up on the water, Morgan climbed back into bed, drank the cold remains of the tea on her nightstand, and listened to the sound of the rain against the back windows, now reduced to a steady drizzle.

She must have fallen asleep again, because the next thing she knew, it was much lighter outside, and much quieter in the next room.

When she tiptoed to her door and peeked out, she discovered that Thom and Owen were gone. The tequila bottle was standing on Owen's desk, though, and his boots were sitting by the front door.

Morgan leaned further out and could see that his bedroom door was closed now. It was peaceful and serene in the cottage, which meant Owen must have gone to sleep, and Thom had to be long gone.

She padded to the front window and peered out, confirming that Thom's car wasn't out there. In the kitchen, she poured herself a glass of water, grabbed a box of crackers, and retreated swiftly to her bedroom.

She locked her door behind her and sagged against it. "What have I done?" she whispered.

Her head was spinning as much as her thoughts, though, so Morgan sank to the floor and tried to unravel what had happened again.

Owen had clearly recognized that she needed protection and had immediately leapt into action, but at some point, he'd also discovered that bottle of tequila. Had Owen seen Thom groping her before she ran inside, too?

She drained the glass of water and nibbled on one of the crackers. Morgan couldn't begin to imagine what he'd think of her.

She knew what he would assume, however—especially considering her refusal to involve the police. Owen would think that she'd been drinking with his friend, that she'd led Thom on a bit, and then changed her mind once she heard her boss come home.

Morgan winced. And that was all before the part where she'd flung herself at him. There was no other word for it. She'd glommed onto Owen like grim death, and then…

Then, Morgan had gotten in the deep end with him, as well. Her boss had held her safe in his big strong arms and kissed the living daylights out of her. Owen had kissed her like it was his freaking job.

He'd kissed her like he cared—like Morgan meant the world to him.

She munched on another couple of crackers and considered it. She had never been kissed like that before, not once. Morgan was one hundred percent sure of that memory, at least.

Oh, god. Could she be any more unprofessional, right now? Her face burned with shame, and she felt a little sick to her stomach.

Actually—maybe a lot sick.

Morgan dropped the crackers and rushed to the bathroom, feeling like a complete fool. She hunched over the commode and vomited as quietly as she could, and prayed it was raining hard enough to drown out the sound.

She already felt ghastly, inside and out—if Owen had any clue what she was doing, she'd just feel ten times worse.

Right on cue, though, a soft knock came from the boss's side of things.

"You all right in there?" he called, his voice laced with concern.

If he was that worried about a simple hangover, Morgan couldn't imagine what he'd do if she told him she suspected Thom had slipped her something extra. This wasn't the best time to explain, however.

She choked out a weak, "I am now," then stood and frowned at herself in the mirror over the sink. She tried to detangle her hair for a minute, but it was a lost cause.

She hadn't heard his floor creak—Owen was still out there, waiting.

Morgan told him, "I'm sorry I woke you up. Do you mind if I take a quick shower? I'll go fast, and then the bathroom's all yours."

She felt bad using up the last of the hot water but figured it couldn't possibly make his impression of her worse. If he was going to despise her, she might as well be comfortable.

"Take your time," Owen said. There was a pause, and then he asked, "Are you sure you don't need anything?"

"All good," Morgan called, mortified beyond belief. "But thanks."

With that, she turned away from her reflection, unable to look herself in the eye for one more second. She waited until she heard Owen's footsteps cross his floor, then peeled off her pajamas and turned on the spray.

When she showered at night, the water in the cistern had usually been warmed by the sun all day. As she washed her hair and soaped up now, it was decidedly chilly—and she felt guilty that she'd wasted so much last night.

She…wasted that much every night, come to think of it. Owen had to have been shaving and bathing with ice-cold water every morning since she'd arrived, and he'd never said a word.

He was determined to be a gentleman, but as Morgan rushed through her freezing shower, she felt awful that he had to start every day like this. Yet another item for her growing list of infractions.

Luckily, Owen didn't look like he was suffering any ill effects from his daily ice baths. He was as gorgeous as ever, which she supposed made her lucky, too.

Although maybe *unlucky* was the better word. Why did it feel like she'd jumped from the frying pan into the fire, all of a sudden?

MORGAN ENDED UP having plenty of time to pull herself together, since Owen spent most of the day at his office. He returned home in plenty of time for dinner, acting a little more solicitous than usual, but otherwise treating her pretty normally.

There was no discussion about behaving unprofessionally or being fired. There was no mention of tequila and no talk whatsoever of the fact that she and Owen had shared that brief, searing kiss. Morgan was relieved.

Maybe he was going to pretend like it hadn't happened. It would be weird for a bit, she imagined, but it could work. After all, how long could she possibly nurse a one-sided crush?

Eventually it would get buried under embarrassment or fade away from neglect, right?

But as Morgan finished straightening up the kitchen for the night, she lingered over it, surreptitiously watching Owen read a book at his desk. Plopping down on one of the couches and cracking open a novel, too, would be a little too chummy, she supposed.

Even if there was nothing else she could possibly accomplish tonight, kicking back right in front of him seemed like rubbing his nose in her uselessness. The last thing Morgan needed right now was for him to realize how extraneous she was.

Once Owen figured out that he could easily take care of all this stuff himself—with a lot less drama—he'd pack her on her way, and Morgan could *not* go home yet. No way.

It was just that…his radio silence on *the incident* had her very confused about how she was supposed to act.

On the one hand, they were living together in close and isolated quarters, she was growing more attracted to him by the day, and they'd recently shared a very hot kiss that was probably etched into Morgan's brain for all eternity.

On the other hand, Owen was her boss, and—up until he'd taken a no doubt temporary leave of his senses—he had always treated her with a degree of reserve that ensured she was kept at arm's length. Morgan ought to respect that and try not to rock the boat.

She hung her dishcloth on the side of the sink and started for her room, but as she passed by Owen's desk, he suddenly stood and caught her hand.

"Morgan, wait," he murmured.

His fingers laced easily through hers, and she reveled for a moment in the way they fit together. For a fraction of a second, she let herself believe that he was going to pull her closer.

Just as quickly, however, Owen dropped her hand—perhaps remembering that bosses weren't supposed to do that kind of thing with their housekeepers. He took a deep breath and opened his mouth.

Here it comes, Morgan thought. *Here comes the end.*

Whatever he was going to say was cut off when a soft knock sounded at the front door, though. They both jumped a little.

Morgan headed over, asking him over her shoulder, "Were you expecting someone?"

Owen shook his head and held up a hand to stop her.

He tiptoed across the floor and peeked out the window, then called, "Who's there?"

"Joseph Teleki," the visitor said.

Morgan smiled and reached for the knob, but Owen shook his head again.

"Just a minute," he called.

Morgan had assumed Joseph was a friend, so she was confused about why Owen would act so worried right now— but something that worried a man like him couldn't be good.

She held her breath and waited for him to tell her what to do. Sure enough, Owen held up a finger, and leaned in close.

He whispered in her ear, "Don't let him in. Wait for me to get back."

Then he slipped across the living room and out the back door. Morgan stood still, heart skittering, and wondered what the hell she was supposed to do if he *didn't* come back.

Soon enough, Owen ducked back in the house, though, sitting casually at his desk, and giving her the go-ahead.

Morgan unlocked the front door and swung it wide, plastering a sheepish grin on her face. "Joseph, I am so sorry. I was cleaning up and had a few things blocking the door."

"No trouble at all," Joseph reassured her, stepping inside. "I hope this isn't a bad time?"

His eyes found Owen immediately, and his expression was bemused—almost as if he knew exactly what had just happened in here. Morgan bit her lip and looked between them.

Owen stood and sauntered over, but he gripped his shoulder like it was bothering him. Morgan frowned. As far as she knew, it was mostly healed now.

"No, of course not. You're always welcome," he said.

He guided Joseph to the couch, but then turned and gave her a conspiratorial wink behind the man's back.

Morgan swallowed hard at the charge that zipped down her spine. Good grief, was her boss *flirting* with her? She hadn't thought Owen had it in him.

Unfortunately, even in tiny doses, his charm was devastating. That could not be a good thing for her.

Owen quickly regained his senses. He massaged his shoulder again and inclined his head, telling Joseph, "Please. Have a seat."

Morgan was trying to follow his lead, but she had no idea what was transpiring here. She turned on another lamp in the corner, then waited for Joseph to sit.

From behind him, she mouthed, "Tea?" and Owen nodded.

Morgan came forward and smiled. "Would you like some tea?"

"No thank you," he smiled back. "I've just had dinner."

Then he folded his hands in his lap and waited patiently.

Morgan liked Joseph. She didn't want to him to be a bad guy. However, she also trusted Owen implicitly, and if he wasn't convinced, then she wouldn't let down her guard, either.

"Nothing for me," Owen told her, sitting across from their guest and looking at him expectantly.

Morgan hovered a moment, wondering if she should stay or leave. Joseph looked perfectly content to sit in silence all night, which could lead to an even weirder standoff than their last one.

Finally, though, Owen cleared his throat and inquired, "So, *rafiki yangu*, what can I do for you?"

Joseph hesitated before answering, glancing up at Morgan with a wary expression on his face. She'd obviously overstayed her welcome. Of course, she had.

She wasn't anyone's friend here. She was the *help*.

Morgan said quickly, "I'll give you guys some privacy," and backed toward her room.

Owen gave her a subtle little nod, then dropped his hand over the side of his chair and gestured for her to lock her door.

Morgan blinked. Why would he smile and call Joseph his friend, but then act like he was dangerous?

She did as Owen instructed, however, locking her door, and then—after sitting on the edge of her bed and considering for a minute—getting up and locking the bathroom door, too.

She looked around, latched her windows, and double-checked both doors again.

Morgan hating feeling so vulnerable, even with Owen nearby, presumably looking out for her. She needed something to take her mind off it, but she felt too jumpy to read, and there was no way she'd be able to sleep.

After debating for bit, she decided to pull out her photos from the safari. She'd taken wonderful pictures of the birds near Victoria Falls—maybe she could do drawings of some of them and send them home to Meg.

Morgan laid out her sketchbook and her pencils and flipped quickly past the snapshots with people in them. She definitely wasn't ready to see Ruth's smiling face, but she couldn't deal with that now.

She wouldn't worry about Owen, either. He might not trust Joseph, and Morgan might not understand why—but there was one thing she did know.

Her boss could handle himself, and then some.

September 19

Drunk and wet and in a compromising situation with his friend—that's how Owen found me. And yet I, in a show of remarkable overachievement given the time frame, found a way to kiss him, too.
I've managed to appall even myself with my total lack of restraint, so I can only imagine what my boss must think of me.

Was I distressed when he dropped Thom with lethal force, at the first hint that I wasn't willing?

Oh, no. I was thrilled.

By his feline grace. By his protectiveness. By his kiss. That kiss—

Tomorrow, maybe I will pretend that I was too drunk to know better, but I'll know it's a weak excuse.

I wanted him. I tried to bury it deep and refused to acknowledge it, but it sat there, biding its time. Like a snake in the woodpile, I never saw it coming.

And now look at me. I'm a caricature and, in all likelihood, a cautionary tale.

Chapter Twenty-Three

OWEN SULKED IN his office nearly the entire day, struggling to untangle the mess his life had become. He looked at the problem from every bloody angle, but he made no progress whatsoever unraveling things.

And who could blame him? After kicking Thom to the curb before it was even light out, he'd managed to catch a few hours of sleep—but he'd awoken to the sound of Morgan getting sick in the bathroom, and that was the end of that.

By the time he'd dressed and wandered out to the kitchen, his poor housekeeper had shaken off her upset stomach and was in the kitchen brewing coffee.

She'd looked vastly better than she had last night…until Owen had gone and ruined it, anyway. He hadn't been able to help himself, though. The sight of her in his kitchen, in her soft pajama bottoms and haphazard ponytail, had *done* something to him.

Before he'd realized what he was doing, he'd found himself standing way too close to Morgan, laying a hand on her bare arm as he reached across her for a mug. Like he had every right in the world to touch her.

She'd smelled so good, that he honestly couldn't help breathing that scent in. She'd definitely heard his inhale. How could she not? It was a monster, count-to-ten, lung-filler of an inhale. Problem number one.

That hadn't been the worst part, though. That had come when he said, "Hey, you. Feeling any better now?"

Morgan hadn't enjoyed the reminder that she'd had an audience while she was tossing her cookies, so she'd gone stiff as a board beneath his hand and her face and neck had flushed a vivid crimson.

She'd appeared to have a little trouble speaking for a minute, there. She hadn't said a word as she backed away, skirting around Owen with plenty of room to spare as she fled the kitchen.

Once free, she'd only managed a frantic, "Yes, thank you. Sorry I woke you. *Doyouneedanythingelsebeforeyouleaveforwork?*"

The part that had been implied, of course, was the *Oh, god, not you again. Please leave me alone.*

In the moment, Owen had been startled, but in retrospect her behavior was hardly surprising. What he'd feared had come to pass. His housekeeper despised him.

And why shouldn't she? He'd acted like a complete barbarian the night before. Not only had he left her vulnerable to a man who apparently couldn't be trusted to keep his dick in his pants, but then Owen had promptly molested her himself.

What's more, once he had her nice and flustered, he'd proceeded to punch Thom's lights out right in front of her. If he were Morgan, he'd run from himself too.

He felt awful for making her bolt again and had desperately wanted to apologize. He didn't want Morgan to hate working for him. It wasn't like she could go home at the end of each day—she had to live here with him. The sooner they were back to normal, the more manageable that would be for her.

Unfortunately, once she'd scurried into her room, she hadn't emerged again.

Which left Owen heading to work with his tail between his legs, and spending the day trying to figure out how to fix things. Perhaps he might have made some headway, too, if one thought hadn't kept nagging at him.

He was dead certain that Morgan had enjoyed that kiss of theirs. Owen had, as well. He couldn't get it out of his mind. The feel of her, the taste of her, the way she'd melted against him—he had a pretty good imagination, but even he couldn't have predicted how incendiary that would be.

So…was a man supposed to apologize for something that good? When he not only wasn't sorry, but wanted to do it again and again?

And all that, of course, was before he even touched on the issue of Thom. When the man finally strolled into the office just before lunch, Owen thought they might come to blows again.

Except Thom was exuding an odd, brittle cheerfulness that confused him. He didn't act defensive, or petulant, or even embarrassed—he just…laughed.

Like Owen was ridiculous. Like he knew something that Owen didn't.

It was damn peculiar. It left Owen nowhere to go, so he shook out his fist and retreated to his office—where he spent some time ruminating on what other damage he could do to that smirking, freckled skull.

Owen spent half the day like that, periodically scrubbing his hands over his face like it would force his brain into working order again. He consumed more than his share of weak, tepid tea, and for all he knew, maybe that was the joke.

Maybe Thom had poisoned Owen, along with Morgan. *That bastard.*

NOW THAT HE was home and sitting across from Joseph Teleki on his couch, Owen still couldn't find anything to laugh at.

He'd been searching for a moment to talk to Morgan ever since he'd gotten there, and right when he finally decided to bite the bullet before she disappeared into her room again, Teleki had shown up.

Unexpectedly. At night. With spectacularly bad timing. Why was the man here right now?

After the crap Thom had pulled, Owen would just as soon not have another man set foot in this house ever again. He hated that he'd made Morgan nervous with all his cloak-and-dagger bullshit, but he'd *had* to make sure Joseph was alone.

And now he had to find out what this was about, so he could get the guy out of here and finish what he'd started with Morgan.

Once she closed her door, Joseph said softly, "I hope you'll forgive me for dropping in like this, but I think it's time we talked. Frankly, too, so we can be sure we're on the same page."

"All right," Owen said, though he had no intention of expressing any of the doubts or suspicions *he* had.

"Listen, I would've come sooner, but given your relationship with Thom Hannity, we weren't sure if we could trust you," Joseph said.

"We?" Owen blinked and waited for his obviously overtaxed brain to catch up.

"Then, of course, we figured that your own guys probably wouldn't be shooting at you, and you didn't seem to know Stephen Thorpe from Adam."

"Stephen Thorpe? Nigel's buddy?" Owen couldn't seem to do more than repeat Joseph's words back to him, but it appeared to be sufficient to keep him talking.

He continued, "Yes, Stephen—the dark-haired man. Though it wasn't until I found you looking dodgy in the Preserve office the other day, that I knew for certain we were after the same goal."

Joseph stopped and smiled slightly.

Owen shook his head, still not getting it. "I'm sorry, mate—but what the hell are you saying?"

"Here. You should read through this, first." Joseph removed a sheaf of papers from his satchel and handed them over.

Owen glanced at the first page. "This is the report from our foray up north. I've read this."

"Not this copy. This one is...unabridged."

Owen sat back and stared at the man. He remembered how much more detailed Kisima's translation had been, compared to the transcript Joseph had provided him. This was basically an admission of what he'd done, but Owen wasn't sure how to take that.

He asked, "Why didn't you give this to me at the beginning?"

"Well, at that point we weren't sure how close you were to Thom and Stephen. There was still the possibility that you'd gotten shot in some kind of internecine spat." Joseph shrugged, like that wasn't a bonkers thing to say. "Page through to the end. You'll see some more information from Sully and Andrew there."

"The Temba brothers, right? Those scouts we met up there."

"Yes. They've run into Thom and Stephen—and some of their cohorts—more than once."

"Ah." Owen tried to steady his breathing as he scanned the pages. Once he finished, he looked up at Joseph, who spoke quickly.

"There's also this." The scout reached into the bag at his feet and withdrew a bloody piece of clothing, then handed it to Owen.

It was the vest he'd been wearing when he was shot. Owen had assumed the medics had lost it, since he'd been in and out of consciousness, and hadn't even realized it was gone until it was too late.

Owen immediately felt in the pocket, Joseph nodding along like he knew exactly what he was looking for. Remarkably, his evidence was still there—the bullet he'd found in that carcass at the poaching site.

Holding it up to the light to get a better look, Owen told Teleki, "I figured this was long gone."

"I know. I took the liberty of having it examined, though," Joseph replied. "I can get you a copy of the ballistics report, if you like."

Owen closed the spent ammunition in his fist and gazed over at him. Who *was* this man?

"I'm sorry—you can't keep the bullet. We need to hang on to it for a while." The man paused a moment, then said, "We use different calibers at TANAPA. That's how we knew it couldn't be one of ours."

His words hung in the air, explaining everything—and nothing.

Owen gaped at him. "You're…TANAPA?" What the hell was the Tanzania parks authority doing sending secret agents into the Preserve? It wasn't their M.O. *or* their jurisdiction.

Joseph nodded.

"The Tembas, too?"

He nodded again.

Owen contemplated this information, as the pieces began to fit together in his mind. "This goes a bit beyond park wardens and tourism, I'd have to think. Not exactly part of your mandate."

"You could say that," Joseph said, a little smile playing on his lips again. "But we do take threats to our natural resources pretty seriously. So, we created the tools to fight them."

"Teleki, exactly how many people does TANAPA have posing as scouts in my park?"

The man didn't speak, but his smile grew slightly wider.

Owen shook his head and tried a different tack. "Nigel knows about Thom and Stephen, doesn't he?"

Joseph said, "Let's just agree that he is not a rare gazelle's best friend. He's wary, too. It's been a challenge trying to get him to trust me."

"But I don't understand why—"

Joseph interjected, "Listen, Hargreave—we're pretty sure Thorpe is the key to this. When he showed up, we put someone in Dodoma on it, but I haven't heard anything back. I don't know if they've been able to trace who he really is yet."

Owen had thoughts about that. "Yeah, I wasn't really buying Cotton's story, either. Have you talked to Sir John in London? Might he know?"

"His family holds the charter to the Preserve, correct?" Joseph asked. "I believe Scotland Yard has asked to have a chat with him, but we don't believe he's involved with Thorpe."

Teleki settled back on the couch and eyed Owen carefully. "And before you ask—yes, the Arusha police know we're looking into this. That's why the investigation into your shooting seems like it's hit a roadblock."

Owen nodded and leafed through the pages again, focusing on some snapshots toward the end. "Can your agents get better photos than my scouts? Maybe I could help figure this out if I could get to a site before it degraded so much."

"They're trying. I'll let you know what we come up with."

The thought of all those dead gazelles saddened Owen. Killing such docile creatures was so senseless. Civilization and modernization were already encroaching on them from every side—and he was supposed to be the one looking out for them.

He said, "I want to help, obviously. What can I do?"

"Try to keep things business as usual, if you can. Follow up on each site, like you've been doing, but try to mislead Cotton and his associates about your conclusions," Joseph suggested. "If you don't let them know you're close, they probably won't come at you again."

"They *must* be suspicious," Owen told him. "They know I wouldn't let something like this go so easily."

"I know they're paranoid. Just don't take any more major risks until we know who we're dealing with. We only need you to buy us a little more time."

With that, Joseph seemed to feel he'd said enough. He held out his hand for the bullet, then dropped it in a plastic baggie and stuffed it into his satchel.

He rose, shook Owen's hand, and quietly let himself out.

Owen stared up at the beams crisscrossing his ceiling and tried to process what he'd been told. This was bigger than Thom acting strange, or Stephen seeming sketchy. This was something clandestine and dangerous, and somehow, he'd gotten put right in the middle of it.

UNFORTUNATELY, ANOTHER PERSON lived in his orbit—a very vulnerable woman, as it happened. Morgan had no idea what was going on, locked in her room and probably scared half to death. Owen needed to talk to her, but first he had to get rid of the damning papers Joseph had left him.

He gathered everything up and walked into his bedroom, then glanced around. It wouldn't do to keep them in here long-term—if anyone was inclined to come looking for them, it would be one of the first places they'd search.

For the time being, he shoved them in his bureau and resolved to come up with somewhere better later. When he could think clearly.

What the hell was he going to tell Morgan? In retrospect, Owen was a little embarrassed by his overreaction to Joseph's arrival, but he'd taken one look at the surprise on Morgan's face—at the undertone of worry—and he'd felt irrationally protective.

Now, he needed to smooth things over. He had to reassure her that it had all been a mistake—that she had nothing to fear from Joseph, Thom, or anyone else.

Owen went into the living room and knocked quietly on Morgan's door. In the off chance that she'd fallen asleep while he and Joseph talked, he didn't want to wake her. She probably hadn't slept well last night, either.

"Yes?" she asked, her voice muffled by the thick panel of wood.

"It's me," Owen told her. "Coast is clear, madam." Then, when Morgan cracked her door and peeked out, he smiled and added, "False alarm."

His housekeeper edged out and looked around, but she was no dummy. She turned on him suspiciously and demanded, "Is there something I should know? What's going on?"

Owen considered how much to tell her, and quickly decided that the less Morgan knew, the safer she'd be. "I'm sorry about before. Suffice it to say, things have been a bit fraught at work. Joseph just wanted to vent a little. I shouldn't have overreacted like I did."

"Uh-huh." Morgan didn't look convinced.

"Everything's fine," he said, then realized that would make her think exactly the opposite. Still, Owen couldn't help telling her, "Let me know if you see anything—or anyone—out of the ordinary, okay? To be on the safe side?"

Morgan's expression said the entire world was *out of the ordinary* at the moment, but she nodded along.

She asked, "Am I in danger out here?"

"No, of course not. Not that I know of." Owen hoped he sounded convincing, but it didn't seem likely.

He watched her fidget and was struck by how brave she'd been so far, soldiering past her friend's death and taking on a whole new life as she had. Given what an invulnerable front Morgan usually put up, this sudden case of nerves was fascinating to him.

Like a tiny window into her psyche, he wanted to crack it wide open. Owen felt another wave of protectiveness wash through him. Even now, Morgan was managing to keep herself under control. She wasn't the histrionic type, though.

"Would you like some tea before we turn in?" he asked, sounding for all the world like his mother.

Morgan nodded. "I would. But don't worry—I'll make it."

"Nah, I got this one. You can have next."

Morgan watched him with a quizzical frown as he trooped into the kitchen. Probably trying to decide if he was full of shit or not.

As Owen set the kettle on the stove, he castigated himself for his cozy tone. He doubted he'd be able to prevent it from happening again, however. Morgan had been doing some unholy things to his mental equilibrium from day one, but everything had been thrown into overdrive since he'd locked lips with her.

Owen kept forgetting that she *worked* for him and wasn't hanging around because she liked it here.

As he reached for the tea leaves, he paused. He liked being able to do something nice for her—he liked it just as much as he enjoyed Morgan caring for him.

Which sucked, actually.

Owen couldn't count on her being here forever. Eventually, she was going to return to her real life in America, and he'd be on his own again. What then?

He grabbed two cups from the shelf above his head and set them on the counter while he waited for the water to boil. He thought about Morgan, and the crap going on in the Preserve, and those papers Joseph had left him.

Morgan was not of this world, in any way at all. She knew nothing, and no one expected her to—which was helpful, come to think of it.

As casually as he could, Owen sauntered out of the kitchen and asked her, "Hey, sorry to intrude, but would you mind if I went into your room for a minute? I think I might have left something in that armoire before you got here. I was looking for it the other day, and I keep forgetting to ask you."

"Of course," Morgan replied, her brow wrinkling into a frown again. "Have at it. And, uh…just move my things aside if you need to."

Owen could see the wheels turning in her brain as she tried to decide what he might see in there. Her underpants, he supposed, or…maybe more of her writings. Either option would be an agreeable side benefit of his little incursion.

He straightened his spine and walked into her room, then made some noise with the creaky wooden doors of the armoire.

Out in the living room, Morgan put her feet up on the ottoman with a sigh, and called, "Sorry. It's kind of a mess."

"Didn't even notice," he called back.

Owen crept noiselessly into the bathroom and through the connecting doors to his room. He grabbed Joseph's papers and a few other items, then returned to Morgan's bedroom praying she'd stay put on that couch.

He opened the bottom drawer of the wardrobe to make some more noise and spotted several silky-looking items that— under almost any other circumstance—he would have liked to inspect a lot more closely. Now was not the time, though.

Reluctantly, Owen closed the drawer and turned, casting around for a good hiding spot. He settled on the mattress— back when it was new, he'd accidentally ripped the seam of the cover when he'd hoisted it onto the bedstead.

Keeping one eye on the door, he felt under the hanging covers for the gap he knew was there, then worked the packet into it. The mattress had to be too heavy for Morgan to lift when she made the bed, and she'd probably never have occasion to go under it. She'd never find his hiding place.

What was more, no one who'd guessed about the papers would ever think to look for them here. Owen had to keep it that way, too. In order for this charade to work, he couldn't let anyone discover what he knew.

With the packet secured, he turned and made some more noise with the armoire doors, then stood and pulled a few handkerchiefs and a small stone figurine from his pocket—just as Morgan stepped into her doorway.

"Tea's almost ready," she said, glancing around.

Owen lifted the items in his hands and smiled. "Success," he told her. He headed back to his room, Morgan looking at him strangely the whole way.

He shouldn't have been surprised. Morgan was sharp as a tack and very perceptive. Her lovely eyes had a way of boring right through him, so he'd have to be careful going forward.

On any number of fronts.

That didn't preclude him from saying what he had to say, however.

Once he'd tucked his things back into the drawer where they'd resided to begin with, he fetched his tea from the kitchen and went over to the couch. Morgan was just settling in with a book and her own mug.

"Mind if I join you for a minute?" he asked.

Her cheeks turned pink. "This is your house. I should be asking you that."

"Come on, you know I'm not like that."

"Do I?"

Owen felt his own face get hot, but this needed to be said. He cleared the boulder lodged in his throat, and told her, "Listen, we should talk."

Morgan released her breath in one big rush. "I am so glad you said that. I feel so bad about what happened yesterday, and I can assure you that it will never happen again."

She leaned forward to set her mug on the table and clasped her hands in her lap primly. "I don't..." She frowned a little, like the next part was confusing. "...I'm not a big drinker, and I don't know why that tequila hit me so hard."

Owen had his own theories about that, but rather than freak her out more than she already was, he said, "I am not worried about that part at all. What I wanted to tell you has more to do with what happened after that."

"You mean when you hit Thom."

"Uh…no. I mean when you and I…when I…"

Now he was the one wheezing. It was one little word—why was it suddenly so hard to say?

"Ohhhhh," Morgan gasped, and those pink cheekbones darkened into an angry-looking flush. "I am really, *really* sorry about that, too."

Was she? "I'm not," he blurted instantly, and then, when her whole face went slack with shock, he added, "But I don't want you to worry. I just wanted you to know that you have nothing to fear from me."

"I know that."

Owen tried to stay focused, but it was hard when those hazel eyes of hers kept hitching on his mouth. When he spoke up again, his voice came out a little strained.

"Anyway, I'm the one who should apologize. There's no excuse for what I did, and to be honest, I'm not exactly sure how it happened to begin with. I promise you, though, I won't lay a hand on you again."

"Oh. Okay." Morgan pitched forward suddenly and grabbed for her cup, then drank a big gulp that had to have burned her mouth. Her gaze took a long, lingering lap around his frame, from his arms to his thighs, then back up to his mouth. Her eyes watered a little, and she looked…

Well, shit. She almost looked disappointed. Which was probably why the next, totally unplanned words exited Owen's mouth.

He said, "Unless you want me to, that is."

With that completely insane declaration, he figured he'd better beat a speedy retreat before more gems spilled out of him, so he got to his feet, tried to smile like this was all totally normal, and took off for his bedroom.

Owen closed his door behind him and sagged against the wood. *Christ.* Now what was he going to do?

Chapter Twenty-Four

MORGAN WAS SURPRISED to see Owen looking so haggard when he returned from work the next day. But when he let himself in, he walked straight to his desk and dropped into his chair—then stared out the back windows for a full minute before he even acknowledged her.

Morgan hovered in the kitchen, and eventually he turned and gave her a weak smile. It seemed forced, but whether that was because of the bomb he'd dropped last night, or something else, remained to be seen.

"Everything okay?" she asked.

"Yeah. Fine." His entire demeanor said otherwise, though.

Morgan glanced around the kitchen. Offering him a beer or a cocktail was out—Owen rarely drank those and only if they were about to eat dinner. Dinner wasn't going to be ready for a while yet.

Instead, she decided to make him a cup of the peppermint tea he'd picked out on their last trip to the market. When he'd found it, he'd explained that it was great for destressing, so maybe it would help him now.

While Owen took a few files from his bag and glumly shuffled some papers around, Morgan boiled the water, measured out the tea leaves, and prepared his cup. She tucked a few cookies on the saucer, then set her offering down on the corner of his desk.

"Here," she told him, "You look like you could use this."

There were unfamiliar lines bracketing his mouth, but there wasn't much she could do about them if she didn't know why they were there.

She'd already turned away when Owen reached up and laid a hand on her arm, absently murmuring, "Thanks, love," as if it were the most natural thing in the world.

Morgan froze. He'd touched her the same way yesterday morning, when she'd been too tired and hungover to respond in kind. This time, her heart began pounding again, but at least she managed to smile and not run away like a coward.

Then one of the photos on Owen's desk caught her eye and cut off any response.

She pointed at it. "Hey, South Africa's most eligible bachelor, right?"

Owen jerked around and stared at her strangely. She'd definitely crossed a line—again.

"What did you say?" he demanded, tightening his fingers on her arm.

Morgan looked down at the other photos spread under the first, and gasped. "Whoa," she said, "You're working. I'm sorry I bothered you."

She forced her gaze away, staring at the wall behind him so she wouldn't have to look at the carnage in those pictures again.

"No, it's not that," Owen said, searching her face intensely. "But I do need you to repeat what you just said."

Morgan swallowed and looked down. "The man in that picture. Isn't he one of South Africa's wealthiest single men or something?"

"You *know* him?" Owen looked stunned.

He sorted through the photos, found an enlarged shot of the man's face, and held it up.

"This guy right here?"

"Well, no. I don't *know* him," Morgan hedged.

"But you've seen him before?"

"Not in person."

"Where?" he pressed.

His soft green eyes held a dangerous glint she'd never seen before, and Morgan wanted to wilt in the face of it.

"He was in the airline magazine, on the flight over here. It was just a silly article—" she stammered, "—something, uh, something about the continent's richest bachelors. We were joking about it, but I don't remember this one's name."

"But you're sure of the face? *Really* sure?"

Morgan nodded, examining the photo once more. "Yes. He stuck out, at the time. You know, *which one of these things is not like the other ones?*"

"And why was that?" Owen's expression was alert, boring into her unnervingly.

"To be honest, he was the only white guy on the list. It was unexpected, I guess. Like he was some kind of imposter."

Morgan bit her lip, wishing she didn't sound so painfully naive. "That sounds stupid. I mean, I know there must be perfectly nice white Africans, but…but once you've taken a history class or two, it's hard not to think of them as colonizing assholes."

The warmth of Owen's palm on her arm was incredibly distracting. This was not the best time to dwell on it, however— *or* on his promise to touch her if she asked him to.

Owen studied her, and Morgan felt about as foolish as she ever had. She glanced quickly down at the photos again and asked him, "Why do you have pictures of him, anyway?"

He responded with a question of his own. "Morgan, listen— this is really important. Do you remember *anything* else? Can you think of anything from that article besides him being rich and single?"

She thought back to that long, long flight, and the three of them joking semi-deliriously about the articles in the magazine. Morgan could see Ruth laughing, vibrant and wholly alive, and eyes welled up.

Ruth scoffed, "Sounds rough. Where would you even wear them all?"

Nina cooed back at her, "To bed, darling. Where else?"

Owen pulled Morgan back to the present with a gentle tone, "You still with me, love?"

She nodded and choked out, "Diamonds. His family's in diamond mining. The article said that guy had big plans to take over a chunk of the market from his competitors."

Owen must have taken her hands in his at some point. When he let them go again, Morgan missed them immediately.

He folded his arms across his broad chest and sat back abruptly.

"I'll be damned," he muttered, shaking his head at the photos spread across his blotter. "No wonder they came up empty in Britain."

Morgan gripped the corner of his desk, trying to steady herself. Between the unexpected sight of those grisly pictures, and all the emotions her memories had stirred up, she was reeling. "I don't understand what's going on. Did I say something wrong?"

Owen jumped like she'd startled him. "No." He tapped the photos and said, "No, love—you just solved a mystery. Someone thinks our little park is going to make him rich."

"Rich*er*." Morgan corrected, unable to help herself.

"Right," he agreed. "The problem is, some of our four-legged friends must be getting in his way."

"Did you take these?" she asked.

"No. I wish I knew who did, though."

"Where did you get them?"

"A friend," he shrugged.

Morgan watched as he sorted through the snapshots, stacking them and shifting them into a folder. But when Thom's face appeared on the top of the pile, she sucked in a breath.

"Wait." Her finger shook as she pointed. "Is that who I think it is?"

Owen looked pained, but he nodded.

Morgan pinched the bridge of her nose. She said, "I had no idea," but she was so mortified she could barely look at him.

He seemed to understand the direction of her thoughts, though, because his face instantly turned rueful. "Trust me, neither did I."

Owen gathered the rest of the files from his desk and carried them into his room. When he returned, he slung his bag across his chest, then knocked back the now-cold tea.

When he realized which one she'd given him, he smirked. "Did I look that bad?"

Morgan nodded. "Maybe even worse."

He let out a ghost of a laugh, then brough the cup into the kitchen. He looked anxious to leave, suddenly.

"Listen, I've got to go back out for a bit, but I won't be long. Dinner as usual, yeah?"

Morgan was relieved by the mundane question. Focusing on it gave her just enough emotional distance to hold herself together a little longer.

She'd been an even bigger idiot than she'd realized, and right now, she needed to *think*.

"Of course," she agreed. "But you don't have to rush. It'll keep."

"Even so, I'll be here," he said.

Owen strode to the door, but then stopped with his hand on the knob. "Morgan…I want to apologize for leaving you alone with Thom like I did. I didn't think he was dangerous. There's no excuse for it, but I can assure you—you won't have to worry about him any longer."

His voice sounded strained, but he hadn't turned around and she couldn't see his face.

"That's okay."

"No, it's not," he went on quietly, "But I promise he will never set foot in this house again." With that, he left, closing the door behind him.

Morgan gaped as the latch clicked into place. "But he's your friend," she protested, her words falling into empty air, "Isn't he?"

Owen was gone, though, leaving her alone with those ominous words and the image of his bloody photographs seared into her brain.

It was only later, after she'd skewered the last of the chicken for dinner, that her brain circled back to that loophole he'd opened for himself yesterday.

He'd lay a hand on her if she wanted him to, huh? That definitely merited further contemplation.

Unfortunately, Owen seemed to have some life-and-death things on his plate, at the moment. Morgan had to wonder if he'd even be around long enough to ask.

Would he need to make more trips into the Preserve now that he had those pictures? The idea knotted her stomach and made her chest feel tight. He'd been up there, after all, during her first days working for him.

Owen might have an imposing physical presence, exuding the rugged sort of capability that made her think he was more than up to a challenge—but a tendril of foreboding had slithered down her spine when she'd seen Thom's photo among all the others.

Owen's honorable instincts could easily be used against him. And if something happened to him, she could end up in trouble, too.

Perhaps that was only the residual effect of her run-in with Thom, though. A simple drink had spiraled out of control so quickly, it'd made her doubt herself—doubt whether she had what it took to exist here.

Right now, it felt a little like Owen was the only firewall standing between her and potential disaster.

Morgan finished mixing a marinade and poured it over the kebabs, then stuck them in the fridge. She went into her room and pulled out her luggage, searching for the State Department warnings she'd printed out before her trip, listing all the dangers and diseases she might encounter here.

Once she found them, Morgan spread the pages on the floor and scoured the paragraphs about lurking predators and strange bacteria—as if the exercise would somehow protect the man she worked for.

The man she was sort of falling for.

Shit. Morgan was definitely losing it. She crumpled up all those pointless printouts and shoved them in the trash.

When Owen came back for dinner, she could always ask him whether he was really in danger. He might not be. He'd been doing his job for a long time, and there couldn't be too many things left that would surprise him.

But could she believe him if he told her he was safe? Owen had more to worry about than wild animals and snakes now— he also had to worry about humans.

As far as Morgan was concerned, those were the scarier predators. He'd probably just laugh it off if she said anything about it, though. He wouldn't be wrong, either. She'd had more run-ins than he had—with both male and reptilian adversaries.

So, who was she really worried about? Him? Or herself? Because Morgan would be at the mercy of a hell of a lot without Owen's protection. She did trust him. It just didn't seem totally healthy that he'd become a base of security from which she didn't want to venture very far.

She was grateful he'd hired her, and that he never took advantage when it would be so easy for him to do so. She appreciated that Owen was decent to her every day, even though he had to view her as an oddity.

But without Owen acting as a buffer, Morgan suspected she couldn't cut it here. She'd have to go home.

She couldn't do that. Not yet. She had to toughen up.

With that, she got to her feet, dusted herself off, and marched into the kitchen to start cooking.

Resolving to buck up was all fine and well, she supposed, but...there was still the little issue of her lusting after her boss. In the face of the fire Owen had ignited with that one, all-consuming kiss, all thoughts of concern, gratitude, and admiration seemed totally inconsequential.

Morgan lit the pilot light in the oven and admitted that she'd never been kissed like *that* before. And to have had it done by a man of such heart-stopping prowess? She was lucky she'd retained any ability to function whatsoever.

In comparison to Thom's sloppy fumbling—*forget it*. There wasn't any comparison.

Remembering sent little shivers of awareness throughout her body. Morgan shoved the pan of skewered chicken in the oven and slammed the door a little too hard, like that was going to help snuff out her ridiculous fantasies.

Owen had said he wouldn't touch her again unless she wanted him to, but every moment they existed in this house together Morgan was going to wonder if he was waiting for it. *For her.*

She didn't know what, if anything, she was going to do about it—what she should do about it. The "shoulds," after all, were always the trickiest part.

October 14

Are endings always final, or do they sometimes lead to beginnings? When I think about Chip, it feels like our marriage happened to someone else, like something I read about in a book, or saw on TV. A lot of it has faded to a blur. Who was wrong, who picked up the dry cleaning, who hurt who, who bought the food...it's all running together, and I don't care anymore.

What stands out to me now is only the longing I used to feel—to be cherished, mostly. To matter to someone.

Maybe that was wishful thinking. Immature. Or maybe a different man would've known how to make me feel precious to him.

By the end, our marriage was empty. We were like automatons, going through the motions, like our parents before us.

Maybe it doesn't have to be that way, though. Maybe now that the proverbial door has been shut, another, unforeseen one, can open. When I lay in bed these days, the darkness is the perfect backdrop to the images of Owen that flood my mind.

Sometimes, I can hear his voice, so deep and real I can almost feel his breath against my ear, whispering sweet nothings that melt my iced-over soul.

Chapter Twenty-Five

AFTER DINNER, OWEN fled to the covered sleeping porch he'd added onto his bedroom a few years ago, in the hope that he could enjoy the relatively cool evening while also avoiding his housekeeper.

The small lantern he'd hung beside his hammock swayed slightly in the breeze, throwing shadows against the wood of the shower wall—the shower that let in light and air, but still gave privacy to the bather.

It was a design detail that he was deeply thankful for at the moment, because the shower was occupied by the very person he needed to keep clear of.

He couldn't think about that now, however. Owen was still trying to make sense of the strange turns his day had taken.

It had started out with Nigel bursting into the Preserve office, bellowing, *"Afternoon, gentlemen. I've got this week's reports for you to look over."*

He'd then instructed them to give the reports a good once-over since, *"The folks in Dodoma want a clear headcount on the remaining Rathbones, as soon as possible."*

"That ought to be easy," Thom had scoffed. *"Hardly any of the buggers left."*

Owen had tried not to react to that as he'd taken the files Nigel proffered. He'd asked, "*Any more poaching?*"

"*Our predator seems to have moved on,*" Nigel had tossed over his shoulder. Then he'd closed his door behind him.

Owen had flipped through the dodgy copies, and asked, "*Where are the originals?*" Thom had only shrugged.

So, he'd tried knocking on Nigel's door. He'd had to repeat his question through the wood.

Nigel had called, "*That's all they sent me.*"

Owen assumed Cotton had meant the field station heads—who, for some inexplicable reason, had all decided to send their half-assed reports directly to Nigel instead of Owen, as they normally did.

But Joseph had asked him to lay low—so, Owen had ignored every protesting bone in his body and accepted the explanation. That hadn't been the end of it, though.

As he'd sat there scratching his head, wondering how the entire Preserve had suddenly fallen into unmitigated serenity, his phone had rung. And while he talked, he'd noticed that Nigel's line was lit up as well.

When he finished his call, he'd hesitated for only a moment before carefully depressing the other button.

"*We can't be so bloody sloppy any longer,*" the man had hissed, and the line went dead.

Owen had immediately redialed the supplier, then nursed the conversation along when Nigel had stalked out of his office to glare at him.

He'd given Owen a cold look and growled, "*Having a little phone trouble, Hargreave?*"

"*Sorry about that, mate. Finger slipped.*"

Fortunately, reinforcements had arrived in the nick of time.

"*Teleki! Just the help we need,*" Nigel had said brightly. "*Thanks for coming in on such short notice. We've got to compile some headcounts quickly. Since you tagged along with Hargreave that last time, I thought you could assist.*"

Joseph had looked surprised, so Owen had gestured him into his office. He'd handed over the reports, ended his call and tried to get back to work.

Teleki had lingered by his desk, however.

"*Sorry, I think you gave me these by mistake,*" he'd said.

Joseph had returned to Thom's desk and started working, and Owen had looked down to find the handwritten note that read, *Two Days Ago.*

Owen shook his head and scrubbed his hands over his face, making the hammock creak and sway. He still couldn't get over those damn photos.

Turned out there was a big difference between wondering if your buddy was up to no good and knowing for certain.

The photos had been crystal clear and shot with a powerful lens. If Nigel Cotton was not a gazelle's best friend, as Joseph had indicated, then Stephen Thorpe and Thom Hannity were probably its worst enemies.

Blimey.

And so, Owen had slid that folder into the bag at his feet, slung the strap across his chest, and walked straight out of his office, closing the door behind him.

"*Listen, you blokes,*" he'd said, "*I'm knackered. Call me if you need help, all right?*"

He'd had to get home, so he could examine those photos properly. They told a very different tale than Nigel's bogus reports.

Owen knew he probably shouldn't have gone through everything with Morgan hovering around, delivering restorative cups of tea and little biscuits. If he hadn't, though, he might not have learned what he had—which was that Stephen Thorpe's trail was not going to originate in Britain.

No, the man they needed to investigate resided far closer to home and Owen's housekeeper was the one who'd solved the mystery. What were the odds?

Morgan had probably thought he was off his rocker, fleeing the coop like he had.

Owen had wanted to tell Teleki in person as soon as possible, so he'd driven straight over to deliver the news. Even though Joseph had refused to tell him where or how he'd gotten his hands on those photos, he'd been delighted at the breakthrough, so Owen had been in decent spirits when he returned home to enjoy the lovely meal Morgan had cooked him.

But after forty cozy minutes with her—in which he'd been able to envision a thousand such dinners—he'd finally had to plead exhaustion so he wouldn't be tempted to snuggle up next to her on the couch.

Instead, he'd found himself trying to read in the hammock while the sound of her taking a shower slowly drove him insane.

Things had been a awkward since the incident with Thom— and its aftermath. Owen had attempted to apologize, but he wasn't sure what else it would take to completely repair their relationship.

Scratch that. He knew.

He'd left the door to a thorough shagging wide open, hadn't he? He'd made sure Morgan knew he would only touch her again if she wanted it—naturally, he wasn't a savage—but he couldn't, for the life of him, understand what he'd been thinking when he'd blurted out that little caveat.

Owen clearly hadn't thought far enough ahead to realize that having that offer hanging between them would make him crazy. He'd just wanted to retain a tiny shred of hope that he might be allowed to kiss Morgan again someday.

To take that kiss ten steps further.

As he pondered the sound of that running shower, Owen uncrossed, then recrossed, his legs, and tried to focus on his book. He'd become hyperaware of Morgan's every move. He couldn't seem to stop watching her. *Studying* her.

It turned out that everything from her voice, to her shoe size, to the freckles on her nose was endlessly fascinating—which was inconvenient, to say the least. Morgan was reserved, and she didn't give up details about herself easily.

She'd also grown markedly more modest around him since they'd kissed, clumsily making efforts to keep her physical distance from him respectable, and her words and actions guarded.

Sadly, that was only proving to be inversely seductive. People weren't lying when they said absence made the heart grow fonder.

Owen pushed off the floor with his foot, launching the hammock into a lazy swing. He thought about darting in for a quick shower after Morgan was done, knowing the water would be plenty cold enough to douse some of his ardor.

The more he considered the idea, however, the more Owen realized that standing bare-assed amidst all the glaring evidence of her recent nakedness would only make matters worse.

And…he had apparently regressed into a teenager.

Owen groaned softly.

Before they'd kissed, he'd thought he wasn't seeing Morgan as a sensual being, though she was obviously attractive. He hadn't acknowledged that shiny fall of light brown hair, streaked and tipped with blonde, or her pretty, changeable eyes that were sometimes golden brown, sometimes sea green. He hadn't had thoughts about her legs, or her cute little derriere.

He'd been awfully smug about his professionalism too, damn it, considering how cozy this cottage was getting. Now that he'd tasted her, it was obvious what a raging delusion that had been.

Owen had been excruciatingly conscious of Morgan Flynn's every exquisite nuance, right from the beginning. Making out with her had only made it worse.

Were all those subtle splashes and drips coming from that shower being amplified, somehow?

Nadra had said he didn't need a housekeeper—that Owen was more lonely than untidy. It was utter nonsense, of course. Just Nadra pushing his buttons.

Still…*would* Morgan ever want him to touch her again? What would she feel like, without all those wet clothes getting in his way?

Owen's mind drifted, lulled by the sounds of the breeze and the water. He pictured Morgan stretched out in her bed, with her hair tousled and her limbs relaxed. He'd like to watch her fall asleep, he thought, to watch her eyes close and her expression grow peaceful.

It was silly of him. In truth, if Owen ever found himself in Morgan's bed, he wasn't going to let her sleep a wink.

The sudden clank of the shower spigot shutting off startled him out of his reverie. His head was frozen at a tilt, his ears straining for sound.

Owen looked down at his book. All this time, he'd pretended he was reading, but he hadn't even turned a page, and his arms and legs were nearly asleep from holding still for so long. *Pathetic.*

He straightened himself out and flipped back a few pages, trying to pick up the thread of the story.

When Owen heard Morgan's bedroom door close, he finally let out the breath he'd been holding and felt his muscles relax.

There were only two cures to this nonsense. He could get on with his whole "win her" plan so he could eventually, hopefully, shag the woman—or he could pack her back to the States.

At the moment, Owen couldn't decide which option would be his undoing.

THE FOLLOWING MORNING, Owen was back at the office, leafing through the bogus headcounts Thom and Joseph had put together after he'd left.

He didn't give it a lot of attention. Thanks to Joseph's little gift yesterday, Owen knew the numbers were meaningless.

He was too distracted by thoughts of Morgan, anyway, and the underhanded way Thom had conducted his attempted conquest of her.

The more Owen dwelled on it, however, the less he knew what to think. Had it simply been a matter of Thom grabbing for the shiny new toy in town—or had there been a darker motivation?

There was the problem of those files Owen had stashed in Morgan's room, after all. Now that he knew Thom was one of the people with an interest in their contents, he had to wonder if seducing Morgan had been Thom's effort to have a look around for them.

Thankfully, he'd never made it that far. And even though the papers hadn't ended up under Morgan's mattress until after Thom's shenanigans with the tequila, Owen and Thom had worked together for a very long time.

The guy knew the way his mind worked. Owen couldn't rule out the possibility that Thom had wanted to get into Morgan's bed so badly because he suspected Owen would use her cluelessness as a cover. He couldn't rule out Thom giving things another try.

And underestimating the man could be dangerous. Owen worried about how often Morgan would be alone at the cottage—but hoped that Thom had some sense left and realized that he'd already pushed Owen too far.

Morgan didn't want anything to do with Thom now that he'd tried to assault her, but that was only half the story. She didn't know about the way he picked up and discarded women so readily, and she probably had no idea about Thom's checkered history with Carol, either.

Owen leaned back in his chair, remembering how Christine's sister had returned to town around the same time Morgan had started bunking with the Twospeaks. The timing was interesting, since new drama always developed between Carol and Hannity whenever she lived within spitting distance of Victoriaville. Had her arrival somehow instigated Thom's encounter with Morgan, as well?

The entire line of thought made Owen's blood boil. There was something brewing between him and Morgan—something true. It had streaked through his veins like quicksilver the moment her body had melted against his.

But was he reading the situation correctly, or was he thinking with body parts best left out of the equation?

All of a sudden, Nigel appeared in his doorway, rapping his knuckles soundly on the wood.

Owen raised his eyebrows at the sudden intrusion. "Yeah?"

Cotton regarded him coldly. "I've got to make another run to Dodoma," he announced. "Are you finished with the headcounts yet?"

"Not quite. I—"

Nigel waved him off. "Forget it. I'll give them what we have so far."

Owen picked up the file and extended slowly.

Nigel stalked forward and snatched it from him. "I sent Hannity over to E Quad to check out the acacias that were cleared without the proper permits last week. Some idiot farmer, I expect. Thom said he'd probably get back late tomorrow."

"Okay."

Nigel studied him. "You know…if you need a hand before then, you could try ringing up that Teleki bloke again. No idea why the man retired. Hasn't missed a step, as far as I can tell."

Owen couldn't think of any reply that wouldn't convey his utter amusement at that statement, so he simply nodded and murmured, "Mmhm."

"Right. Off I go, then." With that, Nigel spun around, file in hand, and marched out of the office.

Owen listened to the retreating sound of the man's old Renault and thought about what he'd been told. If Thom was out of town, it might be a good time to have another look around his property.

Perhaps Thom had been careless and left something important laying around. If so, Owen was going to go find it.

HE COULD HEAR the racket behind Thom's bungalow almost as soon as he killed the engine, so Owen got out of his truck and walked slowly around the side of the house, following the sound.

When he reached the back yard, he couldn't say he was completely surprised to see Carol Connelly there, but her condition did give him pause. Dressed in a filthy tank top and cut-off khaki shorts that had to be Thom's cast-offs, Conrad's sister-in-law was grimy, sweaty, and wildly disheveled—not to mention cursing a blue streak.

She was also crouched over a tin tub full of suds on the ground, scrubbing what appeared to be old clothes. Why?

If Thom's old washing machine was on the fritz again, she could've gone to her sister's, or the Laundromat in town. It would've been a far sight simpler than whatever she was trying to do now.

Owen cleared his throat so he wouldn't startle her, but he ended up having to call out twice before she heard him over all of her grumbling.

At last, though, Carol sat back on her heels and looked up in annoyance, wiping the wet strands of hair off her face with a sopping forearm.

"What are you doing here?" she spat.

"Hey, Carol. Owen Hargreave," he said, walking over and holding out his hand. "Remember me? Thom's buddy?"

"If you say so." Carol got to her feet, wiped her hands on her shorts and shook his proffered hand. Then she looked him over and inquired frostily, "What do you want?"

He could hardly blame her for being pissed-off about her current pursuit, but it was hardly like he was to blame.

Owen glanced at the tub again. The murky water had an odd reddish-brown tint, but he couldn't think of place around here where the dirt was that color.

Strange.

Carol snapped her fingers in his face. "Hey! I asked you what you're doing here."

Owen shrugged and jammed his hands in his pockets, which only seemed to irritate her more. "I was out this way, so I thought I'd drop by for a pint with Thom," he said. "Is he around?"

Carol eyed him suspiciously. Maybe Thom had told her who'd given him that shiner.

She tossed up her hands and suddenly started raging, "You have got to be kidding me with that crap. First, that bastard brings me over to this shit hole because he can't take care of his own goddamn laundry, and then he takes off and leaves me here. And now, you show up and want a *beer*? It must be a hundred fucking degrees out here. If anyone's getting a beer, it's me, asshole."

Owen winced and looked away, his gaze landing on that weird tub water again. As he stared, he realized he could smell that awful rotting odor once more, even stronger than the last time.

Carol had stopped ranting and was staring at him expectantly.

He peered around the yard and into the surrounding trees. Owen said, "Hey, do you want me to have a look around real quick? I think Thom's got a dead animal out there somewhere."

He looked back at that tub. *Or possibly right here.*

Carol's eyes glittered dangerously. "Did you hear a word I just said?" She stepped between Owen and the tub and stabbed the air near his chest with her finger. "Do I look like a moron, to you? You probably know exactly where Thom is." She paused, then asked, "He probably put you up to this—sent you over here to smooth things over with me? Well, you can tell that fucker he better get his ass back here yesterday, if he knows what's good for him."

Owen sighed. If he hadn't already known that Thom was mixed up in some dirty dealing, Carol's attack might have been very convincing. Now, though, her tirade simply sounded rehearsed, like she was gauging his reaction to her performance with every word she said.

He figured he'd better play along, however, before she began wondering why he was there again. So, Owen smirked and raised his hands in submission, backing toward the side of the house.

"All right. You win. I'll tell him," he said, then turned and started walking fast, half-expecting that metal tub to sail through the air and brain him on his way out.

"*Assholes*," she muttered behind him. "Every one of them."

When Owen peeked over his shoulder, Carol had upended the tub and was standing there with her hands on her hips, contemplating the spreading stain.

That wasn't red dirt in the water. That was blood.

Even worse, Owen skirted the side of the bungalow, and heard two male voices approaching. Sure enough, once he rounded the corner, he saw Thom and Stephen Thorpe walking up the driveway.

Thom was clapping his hands together and brushing at his shirt and pants, trying to knock off the dirt clinging to him—but naturally, Stephen looked as haughty and pristine as ever.

The men noticed Owen's truck, then Owen himself, in quick succession. Old habits being what they were, Thom raised his hand to wave, then dropped it almost immediately.

Thorpe elbowed him and jerked his chin toward the house, then strolled over. Together, they watched Thom clomp up the steps and go inside without a word.

Stephen turned and smoothly launched into his spiel—as if he and Owen were old pals who understood each other.

"Bloke took it upon himself to show me around Arusha," he said. "Of course, he took time to get snockered straight off. So, there I was, trying to find my way around with a bloody drunk giving directions."

"You seem to have found your way, but lost the car," Owen commented.

"Nah. It's up the way a bit. As soon as we got close, Hannity jumped out. Said he'd rather walk the rest of the way than listen to me cry like a little bitch."

Owen stared at him. "Why not follow him with the car?"

"Right. And when the bugger went running off into the woods, how was I supposed to find my way back?" Stephen sniffed, like the pompous prick he was. "At least it wasn't too far."

"What were you crying about?" he asked. "And why is Thom so dirty?"

Stephen shrugged impatiently and swatted at a tsetse fly buzzing around his head. "Too many reasons to list."

"Bastard," Owen said, but left it open as to who he meant.

Evidently, Thom had neglected to mention how long he and Owen had known each other—because almost nothing of the tale rang true.

For starters, Owen could tell at a glance that Thom wasn't especially drunk, and certainly not snockered, as Thorpe was claiming.

Still, maybe he could learn a little more while he was here. He stuck his hands in his pockets and asked, "Can I give you a lift to your hotel?" It couldn't hurt to know where Thorpe was staying, for example.

"Not necessary," Stephen demurred. "I'll make my way back with Hannity's car. He can come get it later, or he can sod off, for all I care. I think I left my phone in it, anyway."

"Well, that's no problem. If you left the car up the lane, we'll pass it before we hit the main road. You can get your stuff on the way out."

"Wouldn't want to trouble you," Thorpe countered, growing more annoyed as Owen persisted.

He wasn't feeling nearly as chummy now, Owen noticed. *Excellent.*

"Nonsense. How are you going to find your way, otherwise?" And then, because he couldn't resist, he asked, "Where are you staying, anyway?"

"Really, I'll be all right from here," Stephen insisted. "I'm sure I'll recognize the right road now that I don't have to listen to a lush."

Oh well. It was worth a try.

Owen knew he shouldn't be antagonizing the man while he was out here alone, and no one knew where he was, but he couldn't help one last jab. "Awfully confident for a bloke who was just complaining about finding his way here to begin with."

Stephen's eyes narrowed. "I said I can handle it. Besides, shouldn't you be checking on your mate in there? A guy as drunk as he is could probably use a nanny."

With that, he spun on his heel and strode stiffly back up the drive.

Owen called after him, "Just out of curiosity, how is Thom supposed to come get his car when he's stranded out here?"

"You can bring him," Thorpe fired back.

Owen strolled to his truck and leaned against the side, waiting to hear the familiar mechanical agony of Thom's car coming to life in the distance. The sound never came, though. What he heard instead was the predictable ruckus of Thom and Carol arguing inside the house.

Owen was pretty sure he'd spent more time creeping around in the shadows this month than he had in his entire life before but decided he could give it one more go. He crept into the shade on the side of the house and found the bucket he'd left upended there a few weeks ago.

Owen balanced on top and peered in the window, to see Thom and Carol continuing their spat. Thom was tossing things from his pack into the steamer trunk that he used as a coffee table.

As Owen watched, he tossed in a couple of knives and a small saw, and three packets of cash that were the wrong size and color to be Tanzanian shillings.

Not exactly standard Preserve issue.

Carol bent over, trying to make Thom look her in the eyes. She grabbed his arm to get his attention, Thom shook her off, and Carol stumbled a few steps back to regain her balance.

When she did, she happened to look right at Owen.

"*You,*" she snarled.

Chapter Twenty-Six

ALMOST IMMEDIATELY, THOM registered Carol's surprise, and wheeled around in time to see Owen stepping off the bucket.

He came charging outside in a fury, roaring, "What the hell do you think you're doing?"

Now Owen was positive that Thom was sober—for as long as he'd known him, he'd never been an angry drunk.

But then Carol came out of the house, too, nervous. Apparently, they'd been too busy tossing around cash and weapons to notice that his truck was still parked out front.

Still, this was quickly becoming a sticky situation, and Owen would have to think fast. While he scrambled for an explanation, he reached into his pocket for his keys, in case he came up blank and had to make a break for it.

Instead of keys, however, he felt a small oval object and a delicate chain—Morgan's locket, which she was perpetually losing. Owen had found it on the way into work that morning, stuck in the passenger seat of his truck.

Just like that, though, he had his excuse.

Thom started down the porch steps with Carol glaring over his shoulder, and Owen tried his best to look apologetic.

"Look, mate—I'm sorry to lurk, but Morgan asked me to come by and check on…on Carol," he faltered. "I was going to take off, but then I heard all the shouting," he shrugged. "I didn't want to intrude if it was nothing, but I had to make sure she was okay."

Thom narrowed his eyes and barked, "She's fine."

Owen eyed Carol's filthy clothes as pointedly as he dared. "She doesn't look fine," he fired back.

Thom froze, and Carol glanced quickly at him before she said, "Oh, real nice. Thanks a lot."

Owen shook his head. He had no idea whether Morgan and Carol had interacted much, but he could make use of Carol's rocky history with Thom, and he could definitely leverage Christine's well-known displeasure about it.

He soldiered on, "Morgan said she ran into your sister at the market. It seems word's gotten around about Thom's…drinking, and Christine mentioned that she was worried about you. Morgan told me about it and asked if I would come check on you."

Thom looked at Carol, his expression uncertain.

She looked dubious. "If that's true, why didn't you say anything before?"

Owen noticed she hadn't disputed the basic facts. Besides, he had sisters—he knew very well what kind of information they shared with each other.

As long as Owen was careful not to over commit, he was probably on the right track.

"Carol, come on," he said. "You know how that went down. You didn't exactly come off as a woman about to be victimized. I figured Morgan and Christine were overreacting."

Thom was still studying her, and she shrugged a little.

Time to wrap this farce up. "Look guys, I didn't mean to aggravate whatever's going on between you, but when Thorpe said Thom was tanked, I thought I'd better stick around for a minute and make sure things didn't get out of hand."

Owen watched their reactions carefully. Thom looked confused and Carol suspicious, but neither of them was doing a very good job of keeping eye contact with the other. Not a whole lot of trust in each other, it seemed.

Carol had to have heard the stories about Thom's benders, like every other occupant of Victoriaville, because she didn't bat an eye when Owen mentioned him being drunk.

The wheels were turning in Thom's head, too, but Owen didn't want him to get too far. He needed Thom to forget that he was supposed to be on Preserve business in E Quad right now, and that Owen might have just witnessed the evidence of a crime.

So, Owen brought out the big gun, and aimed low.

"After what happened the other night, Morgan was pretty upset," he said pointedly. "She was afraid you might…well, you know."

Thom flushed crimson and looked away.

Carol walked down the last few steps and moved to Thom's side, but he wouldn't look at her, either. She'd clearly picked up on the elephant in the room, however, and didn't appreciate that it had another woman's name attached to it.

She put her arm around Thom's waist, and began, "Do you mean—"

Thom silenced her with a harsh slash of his hand. Owen could see the questions in their eyes, and the way they were each weighing his motives.

Without knowing what, exactly, he'd stumbled into the middle of, it was hard to know what to say next. Owen had never intervened in one of Thom's relationships before, but he was counting on the two of them seeing him as an irritating boy scout. He couldn't tell if they'd bought it, though.

If he'd made them believe that he truly thought Carol was in danger—or, better yet, that he thought Thom was screwing up badly enough that Owen had to save him from himself—then he'd be home free.

If he hadn't…he was screwed.

Owen waited, and let them struggle with what he'd said.

He hoped that he'd managed to plant enough seeds of uncertainty between them that he could get out of there in one piece. At least he didn't have Thorpe to worry about, too.

Eventually, Carol turned toward the house, pulling Thom with her. Hannity didn't look entirely ready to back down yet, but Owen kept looking him dead in the eye, and maintained his apologetic smile.

"Come on, mate," he said. "What was I supposed to think? After what you did with Morgan—"

Thom cut him off with a growl. "I told you I didn't hurt her," he said, then stalked up the stairs, Carol following close behind.

Owen booked for his truck and locked himself in. Thom stared at him through the front window as he pulled away, and he knew he had to get to Morgan.

The two of them had to talk to Christine Twospeak, and fast.

Carol could be calling her sister even now, but Owen doubted it. If he'd played this correctly, she and Thom would be diving deep into a discussion about the nature of Thom and Morgan's relationship first.

As HE SPED down the rutted lane that led away from Thom's bungalow, Owen was too deep in thought to really notice much. He only raced through the dappled sunshine, and never once thought to look for tire tracks or signs of where Thom and Stephen had abandoned that car.

He'd regret that later, but was relieved once he reached the main road, since he could drive faster on the pavement. It was a straight shot toward home, with only two shorter turns into the surrounding bush once he got closer to his property.

Owen knew the route like the back of his hand, so while he drove, he let his mind wrestle with how to spin this to Christine

Twospeak. He wasn't exactly sure how to approach her, and he had no idea if she would believe him over her own sister.

But Morgan could help in that regard. Owen hated to drag her into this mess, but he reasoned that at least some of the ensuing confusion could be attributed to her being new in town and relatively clueless.

In her defense, she'd had no idea what she was getting into with Thom. *He thought.*

For the briefest of instants, Owen considered the possibility that he'd somehow roped Morgan into his schemes, too—but just as quickly dismissed it.

There was no way. Morgan was a straight shooter. He'd bet his mother's life on it.

OWEN'S THOUGHTS WERE still on his housekeeper when he finally pulled up to the cottage, so he wasn't prepared to see another car already parked there. But sure enough, there was a small, dusty red coupe off to the side, tucked unobtrusively in the shade cast by the house.

Owen felt a shiver of apprehension across the back of his neck. He didn't recognize the vehicle, and he already had one problem he had to fix. He didn't have time for another right now.

Besides, barely anyone knew Morgan. Who would have descended on her in his absence?

He got out of his truck, crept onto the porch, and silently unlocked the front door. When he edged inside, he heard Morgan's soft voice drifting out of her bedroom. Owen heard the timbre of a man's voice soon after, but it was too quiet to make out who it belonged to.

Heart pounding, he stepped toward the doorway—but halfway there, a telltale mechanical click stopped him dead in his tracks.

Oh, shit. Only one thing on earth made that sound. Owen grabbed for his pistol and flew forward, coming to a screeching halt just over the threshold, his gun extended as he scanned the room.

In a quavering voice, Morgan said, "Owen, it's okay."

He blinked at her and dropped the muzzle, unfortunately aimed right at her nose.

"Are you all right?"

She nodded, her eyes wide and worried.

Beside her, Teleki cleared his throat and leaned forward, pulling Owen's attention to himself. "Stand down, my friend," he said. "Everything is fine."

Owen dropped his hands, letting the gun hang at his side as he gradually registered details. Joseph and Morgan were sitting side by side on the trunk at the end of her bed—close, but not *too* close.

His housekeeper was holding a handful of bullets in trembling hands, and Teleki had a handgun in his.

"What's going on?" Owen demanded. "Did something happen?"

Joseph was calm. "It occurred to me that Morgan should be able to protect herself if she's going to be out here alone so often. I thought it might make sense to show her how to point and shoot."

Owen weighed that statement, testing whether it felt truthful. Before he could get very far, however, Morgan explained, "As it turns out, I'm not exactly a natural."

Joseph kept his eyes on Owen, his gaze direct and pointed. "She's fine. She just needs practice."

"Teleki, maybe you and I need to talk," he retorted. "Why don't you come out here and sit with me for a minute."

Morgan looked relieved to be off the hot seat for the time being, and keen to get rid of the ammunition she was holding. Owen stepped forward and held out his hand, so she could pour the bullets into his palm and scrub her hands on her thighs.

Even a touch as simple as that one gave him a charge. Owen closed his fingers over the metal and absorbed the residual warmth from her skin.

"First things first," he announced, as Joseph checked the safety on his gun and got to his feet. "Is that your car out front?"

Teleki smiled faintly. "My wife's. She's visiting her sister down in Tabora for a couple of days, so I thought I'd bring it in for an oil change."

Owen nodded, then said, "Morgan I found your necklace in my truck on my way to work." He pulled it out of his pocket and handed it over.

"Go ahead and keep losing it," he told her. "That thing saved my hide and then some this afternoon."

Morgan examined it curiously before clasping it around her neck. "How so?"

"Not important. But just out of curiosity, when was the last time you saw Christine Twospeak?"

She had to think for a minute. "I'm not really sure. Not when we went to the market this week—maybe the time before that?"

"So…two weeks ago?"

"Give or take, yeah."

Owen took a deep breath and glanced at Joseph. "I don't suppose you discussed her sister Carol, by any chance?"

"I…no," Morgan frowned. "Not that I recall. Why?"

"It's complicated."

He'd been hoping the two women would've had more contact, or that Carol might've come up in conversation between them. As things stood, however, he had hardly anything to work with.

"Hargreave—what's going on?" Joseph wondered.

Owen sank into the carved wood chair next to Morgan's door and exhaled heavily. "So, I went out to Thom's place and ended up having a bit of a dust-up with him and Carol." He glanced at Morgan and winced. "I had to use you as an excuse when they caught me looking in the window."

Morgan's eyes went wide. Joseph just grinned.

"Not like *that*," Owen groaned. "They were arguing."

"Oh, that's much better," Teleki smirked, earning an eye roll in return.

"Let me guess," Morgan piped up, any trace of nervousness gone from her voice. "You need me to call Christine and fix it."

Owen shrugged and tried to smile.

"Okay, tell me *exactly* what you said."

"I told them you saw Christine at the market, and that she told you she was worried about her sister since Thom has been drinking a lot. I said you'd asked me to go check on Carol, to make sure she was all right."

Joseph just shook his head and chuckled.

"Sorry. I was in a tight spot," Owen added, embarrassed. It sounded even lamer when he explained it out loud.

Morgan was unnervingly intent, though. "Is that it? Was there anything else?"

"I implied that you were especially worried because of what happened between you and Thom."

"Really?" Morgan squawked, at the same time Joseph raised his eyebrows and demanded, "What happened between her and Thom?"

"Nothing," Morgan and Owen said together.

Morgan then gazed off into space for a few minutes, lost in thought. Suddenly, she stood up, took her mobile from the top of the bureau, and strode out to the living room, calling, "Okay. I think I can work with that."

Owen and Joseph looked at each other, then followed Morgan out. She was already talking fast, her faux distress apparent in her rush of words, and cracking voice.

"Christine, I'm sorry. I don't even know what Owen was thinking." She listened for a time, then added reasonably, "Well, I know. But remember when you told me about Carol and Thom that one time? I guess when Owen mentioned Thom's drinking last night, I put two and two together and…what? She did?"

Morgan mouthed, *"Carol already called her."*

"Christine, listen—I really apologize. Owen must have misunderstood when I told him I'd spoken to you."

She held her breath, listening hard, then sniffled a little, for good measure. Owen had to admit, it was all very convincing.

"Yeah, I assume so. I just thought that since they're such good friends, he'd…oh. I didn't realize," she murmured.

Joseph leaned closer and whispered, "This is quite a performance."

Owen agreed. "A little frightening, to be honest." He searched Morgan's face, but she wouldn't look at them.

When Morgan spoke again, her voice was abashed. "I guess I thought maybe Owen could help. It was dumb of me. I shouldn't have interfered."

As she listened to Christine's response, she began nodding, then gave them the "okay" sign.

"I'm sorry, too," she said contritely. "I certainly didn't expect him to go tearing out there like that. He must have been more worried than I thought."

As Morgan finished up her conversation, Owen led Joseph over to the couches. With a quick glance to make sure she couldn't hear him, he whispered, "There's something else. I ran into our friend Stephen Thorpe out there, as well."

Joseph looked startled. "You don't say. I just came across young Thorpe myself, today—on my way over here, as a matter of fact."

"Where?"

"Right where your driveway hits the main road. I stopped because I thought someone was broken down up there."

Owen stared at him. "You're kidding."

"No. I pulled over, but no one was in the car."

"Then where the hell was he?"

Morgan disconnected her call and joined them before he could answer.

She rolled her eyes and explained, "Christine probably thinks I'm an idiot, but you should be fine now."

"I owe you one," Owen said. "Believe me."

He turned to Joseph, who continued, "Anyway, when I got out to see if someone needed help, Thorpe came walking right out of the trees."

Morgan frowned and looked between them, but she didn't interrupt.

"What the hell was he doing in there?" Owen asked.

"That's what I wanted to know. He said his car died and he waited a while for someone to come along, but that he had to, uh, relieve himself."

Morgan snorted, and Joseph stopped to peer at her curiously. "Inside joke," she quickly explained, then inquired, "Who are we talking about, again?"

Joseph remained silent, so Owen told her, "Would you believe, South Africa's Most Eligible Felon?"

"He was here?" When Owen nodded, she turned to Joseph. "Is that why you wanted to teach me about guns, all of a sudden?"

Now it was Joseph's turn to shrug and nod. It was becoming a bit of a theme, Owen decided.

Morgan's frown had turned to consternation, though, so before she could launch into a further interrogation, Owen prodded Joseph with a steady, "So, what happened?"

"I made a show of checking the engine for him, but of course it started up just fine."

"Do you think he recognized you?"

"If he did, he didn't let on."

"Why would Thorpe come here, though?" Owen mused. "He knew I'd probably still be at Thom's."

Joseph shook his head, but his eyes shifted meaningfully to Morgan and back again. That prickle of apprehension tickled Owen's neck again.

"Incidentally, if you didn't decide to arm my housekeeper until you saw him, why were you coming here to begin with?" Owen thought to ask then.

Teleki shrugged casually. "I wasn't, as it turns out. I really was only passing by, but when I saw that car, I thought I'd better check on you two."

Owen considered that, and asked, "What kind of car was it, anyway?"

"Black Mercedes, very flashy."

Owen's brows knit together. "Are you sure?"

Joseph sniffed, "Hargreave, it looked like the president's car. I'm sure."

No wonder Stephen hadn't wanted Owen to take him to it, and no wonder Owen hadn't been able to hear it leave. The question was, where the heck had it been stashed?

He wracked his brain for any clues he might've missed during that whole encounter—for anything that might point to what Thom and Stephen had really been up to over there.

But Owen was pulled from his thoughts when Morgan suddenly squeaked, "Guys—am I safe here?"

Both of them hesitated, but Joseph was the one who actually managed to get some words out. "Of course," Teleki said. "Just remember what I taught you and practice with Owen. You'll be fine."

"Oh, real reassuring," she carped, then walked to the kitchen, where she began banging pots and pans and chopping things a little more strenuously than seemed necessary.

Owen and Joseph sat and fell into conversation, rehashing the events at Thom's house and dissecting how to best proceed. Clearly, they needed to get a closer look at the contents of Thom's steamer trunk, but neither could decide how to best accomplish that.

However, Joseph did connect a few of the details in Owen's story that he hadn't had time to sort through in his mind. "The bad smell, the muddy red water…I think you're right that Thom must have stashed parts of a carcass or two nearby," he confirmed. "You saw those photos."

"And on that note, Andrew and Sully sent me another message a few days ago. They think they've found a couple new sites, but they've already been swept. Maybe Hannity and Thorpe moved those Rathbones down here."

Owen agreed, "Could be. Carol's clothes were filthy and Thom was covered in dirt when he came up the driveway—he was brushing it off his hands and his pants before he noticed me."

"They could have been digging in the woods somewhere right around there," Joseph said, then paused. "Well, Hannity could've been, at least. I can't see Thorpe handling much of the dirty work, and he looked clean as could be when I met up with him."

Owen scowled into space, remembering. "I wonder where Thom's car was, though. I didn't pass it on my way in or when I left, and Thorpe wasn't driving it when you found him. There couldn't have been enough time for him to switch the cars out, either, unless he's staying somewhere close by."

Joseph hummed under his breath. "If they were using it to transport the Rathbones and drove off the road or the driveway with it, they might have left tire tracks in the bush. I'd need to be able to look around a bit to find them, though. Without Hannity there."

"How are we going to to get inside Thom's house, though? I don't want to risk getting caught there again," Owen said. "Once was plenty."

"Give me a little time," Joseph told him. "I'll come up with something."

In the kitchen, Morgan had gotten quieter, and the enticing cooking aromas were beginning to waft out into the living room.

Owen knew he'd have to reassure her somehow, later—though he wished he felt more confident about her security himself.

Having Stephen Thorpe skulking around the place was not a welcome development. And as much as Owen wanted to believe Morgan would not end up in anyone's crosshairs, he had to admit that none of them knew enough about what was going on to be entirely sure.

That, more than anything else, was what troubled him now.

Chapter Twenty-Seven

MORGAN STOOD IN the kitchen chopping up leftover chicken to put in a stew and trying not to eavesdrop on the guys in the living room.

It was a hard not to be curious, however, when the topic revolved around how to get into Thom's house for a look around without him knowing they'd been there.

Owen obviously couldn't get caught there again—not without exposing Morgan's call to Christine as a total farce. And Joseph, for whatever reason, wanted to maintain a low profile altogether.

Neither of them was coming up with any good ideas, though, and the more Morgan turned the idea over in her mind, the more she thought she *had*.

She'd never been a big fan of the *We Need to Talk* conversation before now—it had always felt condescending to lay out the reasons why a relationship wasn't going to work, and why the other person needed to get over it. That being said, she had a feeling it would fit this situation perfectly.

After all, Thom seemed to believe he had reason to expect something more than friendship from her—though Morgan suspected "more" constituted a casual friends-with-benefits arrangement rather than any actual relationship. Owen had dispensed with the man before anyone had a chance to resolve the particulars, thankfully.

But now that meant Morgan had the ability to spin Thom's delusion to their advantage. If she wanted, she could act like his attempted date rape had been a big misunderstanding. And she could bring the game to him, on his home turf.

She could be the one who got a look around his house, and no one—not even Thom—would suspect a darn thing. Morgan took a deep breath and exhaled slowly.

Did she really want to do that, though? If Owen hadn't returned when he had that night, things might have turned out far worse for her, and the thought of putting herself back in Thom's orbit—where he could potentially try his hand again— did not fill her with warm and fuzzy feelings.

She couldn't forget those photos on Owen's desk, however. Those poor little animals hadn't deserved that.

Morgan had to help.

She turned off the stove, and tentatively approached Owen and Joseph, still sitting with their heads together on the couches.

"Guys?" They stopped talking and looked up at her. "What if I did it?"

Owen looked perplexed. "Did what?"

Joseph, however, recognized what she meant immediately.

"What if I went to Thom's and looked around? You could tell me what to look for, I could try to take pictures, and at least I'd have a believable reason for being there."

Now it was Joseph's turn to look confused. Owen must not have told him what had happened. "You do?" he asked.

Before her boss panicked completely, Morgan rushed on, "I should probably set him straight, don't you think? At minimum, given his relationship with Carol?"

Owen announced, "I do not want you anywhere near that toad," so staunchly that her heart did a little flip in her chest. Morgan tried to ignore it. It didn't mean anything.

Joseph looked between them, blinking rapidly. "Wait. I'm not sure I understand. Have you been *dating* Thom Hannity?"

"In his mind," Owen muttered darkly.

Morgan cringed. "Not exactly," she explained, "but there was an uncomfortable incident."

Joseph sat back in shock, trying to absorb that tidbit.

She shifted on her feet, waiting for one of the men to say something and wondering if she'd overstepped once again. And the longer Morgan stood there suffering their scrutiny, the more she wished a big crater would open up and swallow her.

"Never mind," she said, after a while. "I just thought—"

Owen barked, "It's too dangerous. I don't like it."

"Nevertheless, it would probably work," Joseph mused.

"I wouldn't go alone," Morgan said quickly. "And I doubt Thom would try anything with you waiting right outside." She wasn't certain about that, however, and unfortunately neither of them rushed to agree with her.

"It's not necessarily Thom that I'm worried about," Owen commented eventually. "What if someone else happened to be there, too? Then what?"

His scowl was kind of ferocious, Morgan thought. It looked incongruously cute.

"Look, I'm not trying to be a hero here," she reasoned, "I just thought I could help."

She cleared her throat painfully. The idea had seemed solid in her mind, but once she'd said it out loud, it had turned mortifying. "Besides, maybe if I settle things civilly, face to face with him, Thom won't carry around a grudge about how that night shook out. And maybe he won't want to get even."

She'd been worrying about that ever since.

Owen looked like he wanted to pick up an armchair and hurl it through a window. "No offense, Morgan, but I don't like it. No—scratch that. I hate everything about it."

Joseph looked thoughtful, however. "I understand, but I'm not seeing a better option at the moment. I think we need to consider this."

WHICH WAS HOW, a few days later, the call was made, and Owen arranged to bring Morgan by Thom's bungalow—ostensibly at her insistence.

Owen would wait in the truck while she and Thom talked, and Joseph made vague references to keeping an extra set of eyes on them if he could.

Morgan still couldn't believe they'd agreed to it. Owen hadn't been thrilled with her suggestion, but he'd been even more dumbfounded by Joseph agreeing with it. To make him feel better, she'd repeatedly assured him that she wouldn't take any unnecessary risks, but her boss had insisted that the word "unnecessary" left entirely too much room for error.

He hadn't wanted Morgan to wade into a hornet's nest without adequate protection. So she'd made sure to point out that if Owen didn't count as "adequate," she didn't know what did.

Shockingly, that had done the trick. He'd folded faster than a lawn chair.

When the appointed day arrived, however, she had far less bravado coursing through her. Morgan only felt anxious to have the whole thing over and done with, and she got ready to go way too soon.

While she waited, she paced around the living room, trying to relax—but her breath was coming in short, shallow gasps and her chest felt like it was coiling in on itself.

Eventually, Owen couldn't take her fidgeting any longer, so he shooed her into his truck, and they set off. He seemed tense as he drove, so Morgan kept quiet, staring out the window at the passing bush and counting down the minutes.

It was felt hot and sticky outside, and steely clouds were beginning to gather at the edges of the horizon, heralding another evening storm. She hated this kind of weather. The oppressive humidity always gave her headache, and her current stress wasn't helping.

She wasn't going in cold, however. She knew what to do. Owen and Joseph had rehearsed her to death, so Morgan mentally reviewed everything they'd told her one last time.

She'd go in, say her lines, and come out, and the whole thing probably wouldn't take more than forty-five minutes. An hour, tops.

Piece of cake.

Unfortunately, when they arrived Thom's car wasn't parked outside—and Owen pointed it out immediately.

"I guess the bastard's not home yet," he groused. He leaned forward to pluck at his shirt, where it was sticking damply to his upper back.

Morgan folded her arms across her stomach and pressed against the ache that was starting up in there. "Is he late?"

"He said he had some things to do today, but that he would meet us here." He glanced at his watch. "We're fifteen minutes early, but Thom usually runs late."

Morgan scanned the front of the small bungalow, with its thatched roof and raised wooden porch, and then looked into the surrounding trees. She cracked open her window and sniffed the air.

"Where did you say that bad smell was coming from?" she whispered. "I don't smell anything."

Owen kept his hands low in his lap and gestured off to the side. "Maybe out there. It couldn't have been far—the odor was pretty strong both times I was here."

She took another look around, then opened her door. She couldn't sit still any longer.

"I'm going to see if it's locked," she declared, hopping down and quickly shutting her door before Owen could stop her. "If Thom gets here, tell him I had to use the bathroom."

"What?" Owen gaped at her. "No. That's not the plan."

Morgan shrugged and marched toward the house.

He leaned out his window and hissed, *"Morgan. Get back here."*

The sudden sound elicited a chorus of chattering from the little knot of black and white monkeys perched in the branches of a nearby tree. Morgan turned to Owen and held a finger to her lips, then smiled at the shaggy monkey faces following her progress.

She marched up the porch steps, knocked lightly, and then tested the door—like she was at her grandma's house, and not pretending to be some kind of secret agent.

It swung open easily, so she turned to Owen, shrugged again, and stepped inside.

As the door swung shut behind her, Morgan called out, "Thom?" but it was clear no one was home. The place was silent as a tomb.

Okay. Maybe that wasn't the best analogy.

Now that she'd gotten in here so easily, though, Morgan knew she couldn't screw this up. Owen and Joseph hadn't expected her to be in here unattended, so they hadn't coached her on what to do in this scenario.

She had to figure out how to *not* get caught with her hand in the proverbial cookie jar once Thom arrived. She also had to make sure she used his bathroom, in case Owen said something to Thom outside and Thom decided to cross-check their stories.

Morgan stood in the center of the room and looked around, trying to decide what her excuse would be if she was caught digging through the trunk. She went over and sat on it, testing its stability, and as she did so the pocket of her cargo pants snagged on the latch.

Why not, she thought. If Thom walked in on her, she could claim that her pants had gotten caught on the latch as she looked for his bathroom, and that it took some doing to extricate herself without tearing them. It was a thin excuse, but it would have to do.

Morgan still hadn't heard Thom's car pull up or Owen's voice greeting him. Figuring it was now or never, she felt along the trunk lid and lifted it carefully. As she peeked in, she kept her pant leg pressed against the side, for the sake of appearance.

Just as Owen had described, there were stacks of currency—not TZ's or American dollars, but a lot of whatever they were—and tools, along with a few knives. There was some wadded-up material, but it wasn't obvious what it was. It could've been anything from clothes to a tent.

Without getting in there and digging around, Morgan couldn't make out much else. She cursed under her breath, snapped as many photos as she dared with her phone, and lowered the lid. Then she bent and fussed with her pocket, just in case.

To complete her alibi, she had to find the bathroom—and while she was at it, she could take a look around in there, too. Morgan turned toward the shallow hall at the rear of the house. There were two closed doors, which presumably led to a bedroom and bathroom.

Before she took a step, though, she froze. Her scalp prickled and her heart lodged in her throat. There was a cough behind one of those doors. She was certain of it.

Was it Thom, spying on her? Or someone else?

Morgan's pulse kicked into high gear, but she had to stick to the plan—well, the new one, anyway. She was supposed to be in here using the bathroom, so that was what she had to do.

"Thom?" she called, trying to keep the tremor out of her voice.

She forced herself to step toward the door on the left, and gingerly tried the knob. It jiggled a little, but it was definitely locked.

"Damn," she muttered, quietly—but clear enough that someone on the other side could hear her.

Morgan looked toward the second door, but all at once her bravery gave out on her. Instead of trying that one, too, she backed across the creaking floorboards, her eyes on those two doors.

She felt behind her for the handle on the screen. "Owen?" she called loudly and, she hoped, innocently. "It's locked. I'm going to have to go out there."

She fumbled a little with the handle, scrabbling to open it while her heart skittered around like a panicked mouse. Morgan was terrified to turn her back on whoever was in that room, but she had no idea why—so far, it didn't seem like they intended to come out and confront her.

The hinge squeaked loud enough to wake the dead when she finally got it unstuck, and then she was back out on the porch, pressing herself against the weathered paint of the concrete wall.

She made herself walk down the porch steps toward Owen, holding his gaze and gesturing frantically, but it was obvious he had no clue what she was trying to tell him.

He frowned and started to get out of the truck, his expression grim. But then Thom's car swung into view around a bend in the drive, and they were out of time.

Morgan stopped on the bottom step and tried to calm her breathing. If that was Thom, then who was inside?

Owen stood beside his truck, eyes boring into her, as he weighed what to do. He hadn't shaved that morning, she noticed—his stubble looked almost red in the slanting afternoon sun, giving his square chin and the hard planes of his face a warm glow.

"Never mind," she said brightly. "Here he is now."

Thom pulled up alongside Owen's truck, peering into the passenger side and finding it empty. He scowled and tossed up his hands.

Owen didn't take the bait. He only nodded toward the house, where Morgan stood waiting on the porch. As he got out of his car, Thom grinned, wide and bright.

Still, he leaned toward Owen when he passed him and muttered, "No spying this time, all right mate?"

Owen smiled thinly, but his expression was murderous. "Don't fuck this up," he said. He stared daggers at Thom's back as the man passed Morgan and headed stiffly up the stairs.

She and Owen hadn't come to a clear agreement about how long she should stay inside. She'd wanted to play it by ear, but Owen hadn't wanted to leave her undefended for too long.

How long was that, though? Especially now that she knew someone else was in there?

Before she followed Thom, Morgan tried to send her boss a reassuring look. She couldn't catch his eye. Owen was too busy glaring into space, like he was willing himself not to charge after her.

He didn't know Morgan had already accomplished the hard part. They'd rehearsed the next part. She knew exactly what to say, and as long as the mystery person stayed behind door number one, it would all be over soon.

BY THE TIME Morgan delivered her lines and made her escape, the headache she'd awoken with had exploded into a full-blown migraine. She felt queasy and dizzy, and the perfectly normal degree of daylight outside might as well have been lasers drilling into her skull.

It had been harder than she'd expected to act normal with Thom. The whole time, she'd been waiting for him to attack her, or for his secret guest to burst out with mayhem in mind.

Fortunately, neither of those things had happened, so all Morgan had to do now was walk down the porch steps—moving slowly and naturally so she didn't spook anyone—then look over her shoulder and say goodbye.

She had to act as if she and Thom were parting as friends, when what she really wanted to do was run away from the faceless threats in that bungalow, and straight toward Owen and the safe haven he represented.

Somehow, Morgan made her way to the truck without dramatics but before she got in, she realized she had to pull off one last thing in order to solidify her performance. She almost couldn't believe she was going to try it, but events were progressing relatively smoothly so far. There was no reason not to.

Morgan drew even with Owen's window, awkwardly aware that Thom—and possibly someone else—was watching her.

"Get in," Owen murmured softly, "Let's get the hell out of here."

"In a minute. First, tell me about those blue flowers out there." She made a grand, sweeping gesture to indicate the ones she meant, scattered throughout the undergrowth in the thicket of trees, and very visible from the house.

Owen studied her, obviously wondering where she was going with this. "Those are violets. They're harmless," he said. "Didn't Thom let you use the loo?"

"He claimed it was out of order, but I think there might've been someone else in there. But listen—those violets aren't going to poison me or anything, right? If I pick them?"

Owen shook his head. "No. They're just violets. There could be snakes, though. Be careful." He smirked a little when he said it, but then he registered the rest of what Morgan had told him. "Wait—what do you mean, someone else is in there?"

Morgan spun and headed into the trees. "Be right back," she called.

She chose the largest trunk she could find in the copse, positioned herself behind it, and crouched for a couple of minutes like she was peeing. Then she picked out a haphazard route back to the truck, bending occasionally to pick herself a bouquet of tiny indigo blooms—while also scanning the ground for anything that might have given off a rotten smell.

Morgan chanced a quick peek at the bungalow, but Thom hadn't gone inside. Instead, he was gripping the porch railing and staring intently at her.

After a while, he turned to Owen with glittering eyes and barked, "What the fuck is she doing?"

Owen didn't miss a beat. "Said she had to take a leak."

"And the flowers?"

"Nadra told her she could make dye from them. She probably wants to try it." He shrugged and shifted to watch Morgan, too. He had to have a pretty good idea of what she was looking for out there, but his patient expression never wavered.

To keep the act going, Morgan beamed at him and yelled, "These are going to be perfect! Look how blue they are!"

She hoped Thom wouldn't suddenly decide to act on his consternation, though. The last thing she needed was for him to stomp out there and try to pat her down—as gross as she felt, she was liable to barf on his shoes.

Fortunately, he only stayed a few moments longer before shaking his head, giving Owen a perfunctory wave goodbye, and going inside.

Morgan dallied a little longer, meandering among the trees, trying to look like she was finicky about the flowers she picked, so she could cover more area. The violets were delicate and not very easy to pick, and there were prickly vines trailing everywhere amongst them. The rotting smell had strong out here, too—nearly unbearable, actually. How had she missed it before?

She knew her time was running out, but even with that odor to guide her, she was coming up empty. There was so much undergrowth that she doubted she would know if she were standing right on top of tire tracks or freshly dug earth.

The mosquitoes were eating her alive, and her arms and neck itched like crazy. She felt like crap, too. Morgan gave up.

She was tromping around some exposed tree roots so she could make a beeline to Owen's truck, when a crack underfoot caught her attention.

There weren't any blooms here, so Morgan dropped a handful of what she'd gathered as an excuse to bend down and investigate. For good measure, she untied and retied both her boots.

And that's when she saw it—thin and startlingly white against the loose, loamy earth.

Yes. Owen and Joseph were going to be so excited.

INSIDE THE HOUSE, Thom clenched his fists deep in his pockets while he continued watching Morgan messing around in the bush through his living room window. She was alarmingly close to where he and Stephen had buried some Rathbone parts a while back, but he tried not to worry.

There'd been a lot of rain lately. Any trace of footprints or digging would've been washed clean away. The underbrush would've rebounded and then some. And even if that weren't the case, Morgan would have no idea what she was seeing, anyway.

Behind him, the bedroom door clicked and the gentleman who'd been in there, biding his time, walked slowly up and stood behind Thom's shoulder.

"I find it very interesting that you and my son said you had everything under control," he mused. And then, after watching their visitor in silence for a time, the man snapped, "Well? What does she know?"

Thom shook his head. "Nothing. There's no way Morgan knows a thing."

When he turned to check, Sir Mark didn't look convinced, though—probably because Thom himself wasn't convinced. He reached out to grip the windowsill, but glanced down when he felt a bite in his palm. His knuckles looked chalk white against the splintery wood.

"Son, anything is possible. You, of all people, should know that."

They watched Morgan as she finally emerged from the trees, displaying her bouquet to Owen with a sheepish grin and a little curtsy. Owen gestured her into the truck, and they pulled away. Thom exhaled in a great gust.

The look she'd leveled on Hargreave made it eminently clear what had gone wrong between them. Thom had made his move, but as usual he'd been too late. Morgan was a class act, though, coming over here to break it to him gently like she had.

"Fucking broads," Thorpe scoffed coldly. "That one might think she's cute, but she's a bit of a tease. Isn't she."

It didn't seem to be a question, so Thom didn't bother answering. And soon, his visitor walked back to the laptop he'd set up on the writing desk in the bedroom—either oblivious or uncaring of all the bristling Thom was doing.

Not like that would matter. Thom was in way too deep for it to matter now.

Chapter Twenty-Eight

MORGAN DIDN'T SAY much once she got in the truck and they pulled away. Owen tried to give her some space and stifled the urge to immediately interrogate her, because pretty much the second they were out of sight of Thom's she began to look sort of peaked.

After a while, she closed her eyes, dropped her forehead into her hand and pressed her mouth into a grim line. With every bump in the road, she curled further into herself.

Owen was beginning to worry. Once he heard a soft groan from her, he gave up and asked, "What's going on, love? You all right?"

"I need you to pull over," Morgan suddenly pleaded. "*Now.*"

He veered onto the shoulder and threw the truck in park, and she barely had time to stumble out and onto her knees before she began vomiting into the weeds. Owen pulled some bottled water from the pack behind his seat, then got out and squatted next to her.

He managed not to smooth the damp hair from her forehead—which seemed a shade too intimate—but he did lay a tentative hand on her back. Morgan's body was shaking, but her ponytail felt smooth and sleek under his palm.

"Okay, sweetheart. It's okay," he murmured.

When she only grunted, he asked her, "Do you think Thom might have slipped you something again?"

The thought was concerning. Without knowing what she'd been given, he wouldn't know how to counteract it.

Though maybe he wouldn't have to—there couldn't be much left in her system at this point.

Owen allowed himself the smallest stroke along her hair, but since it was only for comfort—nothing else, damn it—he ignored the impulse to twine it around his fingers. God, he wanted to, though.

"No," she croaked as she sat back on her heels. "He couldn't have. I didn't eat or drink anything while I was there. This is just a migraine."

"Bit sudden, no?"

Her color was wan, especially for the muggy weather. She looked miserable.

"I felt a little off this morning," she admitted, "but I didn't want to say anything. I knew you wouldn't let me come if I told you."

"You're right about that," Owen agreed, handing her the water. "But it's done now." Another stroke along that quivering back, and then, out of the corner of his eye, he caught movement in the grass.

"Uh…why don't you come sit in the truck," he said quickly, taking her arm and hauling her to her feet. "You'll be more comfortable up there."

"I don't think I'm ready to drive yet," she mumbled.

Owen helped her into the passenger side and checked to make sure the snake hadn't come any closer. The distinctive grey and black pattern of the puff adder had turned aside, though, slithering deeper into the bush a stone's throw from the verge. He breathed a sigh of relief.

"Take your time," he said, rounding the hood. "Whenever you're ready, we'll go home, and you can lay down."

Morgan nodded as he slipped behind the wheel, and he gave her another gentle pat. He cranked up the truck's temperamental A/C and once she gave him the go-ahead, they set off again.

She nodded off quickly, slumped boneless against her door for most of the drive, even with all the jostling. Once they got home, Morgan made a beeline for her room, pausing only briefly next to his desk to pull something from her pocket and set it on the blotter.

Owen stepped into the kitchen to trash the wilted violets he'd grabbed from the truck, then rethought it. He placed them on the kitchen counter, instead. *Dye from violets*, his ass. Where had he even come up with that nonsense?

Leaving the flowers for the moment, he paced over to his desk, curious about what she'd left him. When Owen's eyes fell on the object, though, he inhaled sharply.

Christ—it was a *bone*. Two pieces of a gazelle's delicate radius, to be exact, probably snapped in half by one of Morgan's sturdy hiking boots. The break looked fresh, but otherwise it hadn't degraded much.

He moved the pieces together to make a whole, and nodded, smiling to himself. He hadn't wanted to go along with Morgan's hare-brained scheme, but so help him, it might have actually *worked*. It was possible he was looking at some of the first solid evidence they'd managed to get so far.

A soft knock at the back door startled him, and it took a moment to discern Joseph's backlit form in the deepening shadows of evening. Once he realized who it was, however, Owen quickly let the man inside, then brought him over to the desk.

"I came by to see how it went," Joseph explained. "What was she doing out in the trees? We didn't ask her to do that."

"Tell me about it," Owen laughed. "And that's not even the half of it."

Joseph looked around. "Where is she?"

"We'll have to wait to hear the whole story, I'm afraid. Morgan's down for the count at the moment."

When the other man frowned, he told him, "She said it's a migraine. Unrelated, hopefully."

"Ah."

"Regardless, it turns out that my housekeeper is quite the sleuth, and a pretty incredible actress, to boot." Owen gestured at the bone on his desk. "Look at this. What do you think?"

Joseph smiled a little and nodded, just as Owen had. "Well, I'll be damned."

They looked at each other and laughed. *Got him.*

Just then, Morgan cracked her door and peeked out. She'd changed her clothes, Owen saw, and the hair around her face was damp, like she'd just washed her face. She still looked like death warmed over, though, and she didn't come out to stand with them.

She only asked in a small voice, "Did I find what you needed? Is it a Rathbone?"

Owen could've kissed her in that moment, visitor be damned. "Yeah, sweetheart, you sure did," he said.

She sagged in relief, then cocked her head like she was listening to the chirping of the insects and birds coming through the back door. "Good. That's good."

"Can you tell us more about what happened?" Joseph asked.

"Only if you feel up to it," Owen said.

"There was a sound," she began, and launched into her story.

MORGAN ONLY TALKED to Owen and Joseph for a little while before she begged off to go lay down again. That was okay, though—she'd already sent them her photos and told them everything they needed to know.

Before Teleki slipped out the back to leave, he'd seemed truly optimistic for the first time in weeks.

Who would have guessed that the person least suited to the task—on paper, at least—would be the one to garner them such solid information? Owen only wished Morgan had been able to enjoy her success a bit more.

She'd spent most of the night feeling ill, instead, seeming incapable of much more than laying still or staggering into the bathroom to retch or refresh the washcloth she kept on her forehead.

Owen didn't have any experience with migraines himself, so the longer it dragged on, the more worried he got. If Morgan needed help, he had a duty to get it for her—particularly since he'd done such a piss-poor job of getting her situated here or shielding her from Thom's peccadilloes.

And so, sometime during the night, he got out of bed and waylaid her in the bathroom. "Morgan, how can I help you?"

"Don't worry," she told him blearily. "I'll come out of it eventually."

"Eventually?" he balked, not liking the defeat in her voice. "What does that mean?"

She shrugged. "A few hours, if I'm lucky. A couple days, if I'm not."

That pronouncement—and her total resignation as she made it—knocked him back a step. "Should I be taking you to a hospital right now?"

"Not necessary," she murmured as she shuffled into her room and crawled back under the covers. "I'm used to it. Usually, I have a prescription, but I haven't found anyone who can fill it yet."

"I wish you'd told me that sooner. Who do you think could do it?"

"A clinic with a neurologist on staff might work," she told him. "But I don't think Victoriaville has one."

Hence, her current predicament. Owen would need to find her someplace in Arusha—which he couldn't do until the morning, when things opened up and he could make some calls.

He sighed and backed off. "I'll look into it," he said, then left her to rest.

Owen grabbed his phone and went out to the living room, so he could piece together a plan of action. A while later, Morgan stopped all the up and down and her room went quiet. He hoped that was a good sign.

But as the silence stretched on and on, he began to wonder. Maybe it was a *bad* sign. Maybe his housekeeper was unconscious in there. Maybe she'd had some kind of catastrophic neurological incident.

He had to check on her.

Owen padded over and knocked softly on Morgan's door, but there was no answer. Undoubtedly, that was because she was asleep, and not dead. He was probably being ridiculous.

Although…as her employer, didn't he have a moral obligation to look after her welfare? It probably wouldn't be too much of an invasion to simply crack her door a bit and peek in.

As quietly as he could, Owen turned the knob and stuck his head in the gap, but with the blinds closed, her room was too dim to see much. Owen couldn't even make out whether she was in there or not.

It didn't help that the deep covers on Morgan's bed—more suited to the climate of his former home in Christchurch than that of Victoriaville—were so rumpled. They completely obscured any hint of her petite frame in that big canopy bed.

Owen held his breath and listened for the sound of her breathing. *Nothing.*

He stepped back, closed the door, and reassessed.

If he opened the bathroom door instead, he'd have a better chance of seeing her face, especially if he turned on one of the washroom lights.

To his relief, that door was unlocked, too—probably because she'd needed to come in and out so often.

He'd guessed right, as well. Owen could see her much better from this angle. She was laying on her side, her face relaxed in the weak light, her chest rising and falling in slow, steady breaths.

His eyes traced her, committing the peaceful sight to memory. The thin strap of her top had slipped off her shoulder. It made Owen want to go over there—to do *what* exactly, he wasn't sure.

His feet took action before he could think better of it, and before he even realized what he was doing, his fingers were trailing feather-light along the line of that drooping white strap, and right across the ridge of Morgan's collarbone.

She sighed softly. Owen jerked his hand back and swallowed hard.

Christ. What was he doing?

Her skin was even silkier than he'd imagined, dewy and warm. He should not have touched her, though—it felt creepy and weird without her knowing or agreeing to it.

Owen backed swiftly through the bathroom door, and promptly stumbled over a towel that had fallen to the floor. He caught himself, but when he tried to pull the door shut the floorboard creaked so loudly it may as well have been a Rottweiler alerting her to intruders.

Morgan inhaled in a large gasp, but shockingly didn't wake up. She only rolled over and snuggled deeper under the duvet.

"*Lala salama,*" Owen whispered, watching her a moment longer. *Sleep well.*

There wasn't a chance in hell he was going to be able to do the same. So, he dressed and gathered his things as quietly as he could, left her a note on the counter, and decided to drive into town.

He clearly couldn't be trusted to stay in the house with her right now. The woman was sick, and all Owen itched to do was return to that room, join her in that bed, and explore more of Morgan's skin. More of her softness.

Instead, he wrapped his fingers around his keys, let himself out of the cottage, and locked the door safely behind him.

OWEN HOPED TO run into Conrad Twospeak at Charlie's, the café across from the Preserve office. The safari guide frequently popped in there when he was between tours, and for a while now, Owen had been meaning to ask him if he'd seen anything out of the ordinary since that incident with Morgan's group.

Teleki had assured him that TANAPA had reached out to the wardens of the surrounding parks, in case Nigel, Thom, and Thorpe were covering a wider area than the Preserve, or even crossing north into Kenya.

However, since Conrad often ran tourists into Arusha National Park, as well as the Mount Meru Forest Reserve, he had eyes on the ground closer to home.

Owen reckoned the man would have heard if there'd been trouble in either of those areas. And knowing how widespread this issue was, might help them determine the severity of what they were dealing with.

Was it only the Rathbones being targeted? Or were other species, in other areas, being killed, too?

Based on what Morgan had told them, and what Joseph's people had since learned about the Thorpe family, they'd decided this whole thing *had* to be about diamonds.

It was common knowledge that there were pockets of them scattered all over the region, and the location of the Mwadui mine, in particular, was hardly news to anyone.

The problem was, it appeared the Thorpes believed there could be a cache within the Preserve—one of the last remaining sanctuaries of the Rathbone gazelles. It couldn't be a big vein, if that was true, and it didn't seem terribly practical of them to focus on one small pocket of stones when they were trying to challenge the industry behemoths that dominated the market.

It begged the question—what did the Thorpes think they knew?

Whatever it was, Owen's Rathbone herd presented an obstacle, and Owen had a duty to stop this insanity, so he and

Teleki and the rest of the TANAPA blokes could save the animals that remained.

Speaking of which, Joseph continued to insist that he couldn't risk his connection to TANAPA being discovered yet, or even the nature of his association with Owen. Until they had a better understanding of what the Thorpes were after and the resources they were bringing to bear, he thought their best chance to subvert them was to play dumb and lay low, hoping the men would show their cards.

After all, besides Nigel and Thom, they still didn't know who else might be helping the Thorpes. There was no way the outsiders would attempt this alone, though—to pull it off, they'd need local muscle in their pockets, as well.

If anyone knew who those turncoats were, however, they were keeping it to themselves.

With so many uncertainties, Owen didn't know how long he and Joseph's men could protect the remaining Rathbones, or if it would be enough to get some answers.

To that end, he wished he could get a look at wherever Stephen was staying. A wanker like that was too in love with his own cleverness to take adequate precautions, so he'd undoubtedly leave something instructive laying around—Owen only had to figure out where to look.

Of course, then he had to be able to recognize the evidence when he found it. Diamonds and mining were not his strong points. He could get in there and have something staring him right in the face and be totally oblivious.

Hell, maybe he'd already seen something important, and didn't even know it.

The thought drove him bloody insane, but what was done, was done—there was no fixing it now. Still, he couldn't sit around on his hands and do *nothing*. He had to educate himself, and fast.

Owen would have to hit up the library in Arusha and see if they had archives on the subject, when he went to see about Morgan's prescription.

First, though, Owen had to glean whatever information he could from Conrad Twospeak. He drove by the stand of fig trees on the edge of town, then made a left at the square and was encouraged to note Conrad's truck—with its distinctive game viewing platform bolted to the roof—parked by a curb.

However, once Owen left his own truck in front of the Preserve office and looked in the window of the café, the guide was not among the early breakfast patrons. Owen lingered outside and looked up and down the street, pondering where the man might have gone.

Thankfully, he didn't have to wait long to figure it out. In moments, Conrad banged out of the electronics repair shop across the street, laughing and juggling an armful of field radios.

He chuckled harder once he spotted Owen. "Well, well. I was looking forward to seeing you."

Owen jogged over to walk beside Twospeak as the man made his way back to his truck.

"Why's that?" he asked, though he could certainly guess.

"Because I cannot *wait* to hear the story behind Morgan's last call to Christine," the man said.

Owen cleared his throat. "Ah. Yeah, that's a good one." There wasn't a whole lot else he could add, but luckily, it didn't appear to be necessary.

"I'd buy you a cup of coffee," Conrad chuckled, loading the radios into the back, "but I'm running behind this morning. Next time, though, yeah?"

"Sure thing. But listen, mate—mind if I ask you a quick question before you head out?"

"Not at all." Conrad opened his door and stuffed his burly frame behind the wheel.

"We've been having some poaching trouble up in the northern quadrants of the Preserve. Just wondering if you've seen anything odd on the tours lately."

Owen tried to make his voice as casual as he could, like it was no big deal. No need to get rumors started, if he could help it.

"Nah, can't say that I have," Conrad replied, but he seemed distracted. He fiddled with his keyring longer than he probably needed to before finding the one he wanted and sliding it into the ignition. "Besides that one gal who offed herself, it's been pretty quiet for months now."

He started his truck and revved the engine. Owen was a little surprised by his callousness and his impatience, though he supposed the guide *had* said he was in a rush.

He stepped back. "Good to hear." Conrad nodded and gave him a little wave out the window as he started to pull away.

"Stay safe out there," Owen called.

"Always. You do the same." With that, the man drove away, kicking up a cloud of reddish dust in his wake.

Owen checked his watch. With that task complete, he still had plenty of time to stop in at Charlie's for a bite. Morgan probably wasn't even awake yet—she wouldn't mind.

After he ate, he could run into the office and pick up a few files and leave a message for Thom or Nigel that he was going to work from home today. That way, if Morgan still needed to see a doctor when he got home, he'd be able to take her right away.

Owen might be overreacting, but his cottage *was* pretty remote. It was safer to err on the side of caution with this kind of thing. Morgan hadn't been in the country terribly long, and she might not realize how many serious illnesses could start out with a headache and nausea. He'd rather she didn't succumb to any of them on his watch.

Owen tried not to think of that as he settled at a table and ordered himself a plate of fried *vitumbua* and sliced fruit, and mug of hot spiced chai to wash the little muffins down.

As usual, the food was good—but Owen felt antsy, sitting there alone. He kept thinking about Morgan, dwarfed by that big bed. He kept wondering how she was doing.

He wolfed down his food so he could get home faster and find out, then got up and paid at the counter, instead of waiting for the server to come by with his check.

The feel of Morgan's skin under his fingertips was haunting him, and when his brain wandered into even more intimate territory by combining the ghost of that sensation with the memory of their kiss, Owen knew it was time for a distraction.

He hightailed it across the street, to the locked and dark Preserve office. Owen let himself in, drafted a short note and taped it prominently to his office door, then gathered some work to bring home.

He took another cursory look around, then checked the time as he locked up again.

It was well past the opening hour. Where was everyone?

THAT THOUGHT DIDN'T gain a lot of traction, once Owen was on his way home again. He took the road too fast, thinking Morgan might be up by now, and might need his help.

When he stepped into the cottage a little while later, though, his housekeeper was sitting up in bed, placidly sewing in the patch of sun slanting through her window.

She looked far better than she had last night. It seemed she not only hadn't needed him, but she also hadn't missed him in the least.

That was completely fine, of course. Owen was relieved she was okay. He simply felt a tiny bit…superfluous.

"Hey. Feeling better?" he asked, hovering on the threshold of her room and gripping the doorframe. He tried to push down his strange restlessness, but it encountered far too much desire on the way down.

"I am. I'm still a little weak, though," Then she flushed, as if she was embarrassed that he'd found her lounging in bed. Combined with her tousled hair, those pink cheeks had the unfortunate effect of making her look like she'd spent her night doing far more enticing things.

She told him in a rush, "I'm sorry I haven't gotten much done yet. I'm doing that mending you had, though, and once I can get some more food down, I promise I'll be up and around again."

Owen rolled his eyes. God forbid her industriousness be waylaid by human weakness.

Morgan beckoned him over and handed him a neatly folded pile of clothes that she'd fixed up for him. "There," she said. "That's most of it."

Owen had to admit he was relieved. Now he wouldn't have to break in any new clothes or attempt the repairs himself.

He might be handy with a lot of things, but tiny needles weren't one of them. Usually, that left him walking around in soft clothes with tears sometimes. It hadn't mattered, before now—not until Morgan had shown up, anyway.

And apparently, his housekeeper had taken exception to the look, too, because she'd fished this stuff out of the laundry without him even asking, and had taken matters into her own hands.

"I appreciate that. Really," he told her, "But you should be resting. All this other stuff can wait."

Owen's gaze drifted over her bent head, tanned shoulders, and long, slim arms. He was surprised, just the tiniest bit, that Morgan was good at this kind of thing.

It didn't exactly fit the stereotype he'd always believed about American girls, he supposed. It was too…old-fashioned, maybe.

Anyway, it was a damn good thing his mum couldn't witness this cozy little scene, though—she, for one, would be ecstatic.

Morgan waved him off. "It's okay. At least I don't feel like I've wasted the entire day."

Then she gestured to a couple of shirts and some pants still piled beside her. "I meant to tell you, I couldn't fix these. The rips are fraying, and it would take a lot of material to close the holes. I don't think they'd hang properly with such big patches."

She fingered the sleeve of one of the shirts as she spoke, and Owen stared, transfixed by her nimble, feminine fingers.

"That's all right," he managed to croak out. "I can order some more of those when I place the uniform order for the scouts next month."

Morgan spread the material of the shirt, *his* shirt, across her lap. She was sitting cross-legged under the covers, and the material drooped down in the hollow between her knees.

He blinked.

Owen could not, under any circumstances think about any hollows between any pretty knees.

"Just throw them out," he told her. He dragged his gaze back up to her face with considerable effort. "They're not in good enough condition to donate."

"Actually, I thought I'd hang on to them, if that's okay," Morgan replied, still looking down and arranging the folds thoughtfully. "I might be able to use the material for something else one of these days."

"Whatever you think." Owen studied her face, but it was almost as if she was avoiding eye contact. "Are you ready to eat something? Or can I bring you some tea?"

Morgan hesitated, long enough that he felt his face get warm. "Sorry," he said. "I'm hovering. I should leave you alone so you can rest."

It was the last thing he wanted to do. Owen would much rather stay and investigate those hands and those blushes more thoroughly—preferably all over that big bed.

Because that was what a woman recovering from a migraine would want from her boss. *Christ*, what was his problem?

"I think I will try a little snack," she said, "But you're probably right—I do need some more sleep after that. I'm sorry I'm being so much trouble."

"Don't be silly. It's no trouble at all. Whatever else needs to be done can wait, or I can do it. Now, what would you like to eat?"

Morgan gestured to a little bowl of sesame crackers he hadn't noticed on her nightstand and smiled. "I'm all set."

"Okay. If you need anything, just yell. I took the rest of the day off, so I'll be here."

"Thank you," she said, and at last she met his eyes as he backed away.

He could get used to the sweet look she gave him. Very easily.

Owen forced his feet into motion and wandered into the kitchen to fix himself some tea, even though he'd only eaten an hour ago. He measured out enough for two, in case Morgan heard the kettle and changed her mind.

Some time later, when he hadn't heard a peep from her, Owen strolled past her room like he was going to look for a book on the shelves. Reading wouldn't be the worst idea, actually—if he took a book out to the patio for a while, maybe his brain would settle down enough to get some work done.

Except when he passed, Owen couldn't help glancing in Morgan's door, still half open like he'd left it. She was still awake and arranging pieces of material across her lap—colorful mud cloth she must have gotten at the market, and scraps of his old clothes, too. She crunched on her crackers and frowned intently, like she was trying to figure something out.

He wanted to know what it was. It looked like she was sewing something new—a shirt, perhaps, or a dress? Some other patchwork piece of clothing that was going to end up next to her warm, bare skin?

Owen's mouth went dry. Apparently, he was going to be nursing this little obsession of his for the foreseeable future. Because his life wasn't complicated enough.

When he fled back to the kitchen, something shifted underfoot, and Owen was dismayed to find the chain of Morgan's hapless locket under his boot yet again. Luckily, it didn't seem to have sustained any damage, though how it remained so indestructible, he couldn't fathom.

Owen popped it open as he'd done last time and wondered once more at its empty interior.

The wilted violets from Thom's place were still sitting in a little pile on the counter, and without stopping to think about what he was doing, he plucked a few petals from their stems and tucked them carefully inside the small gold case.

Owen latched it shut and dropped the necklace into his shirt pocket. Later, he'd leave it in Morgan's room for her.

He wondered how long it would take for her to discover that he'd filled it, or what she'd conclude.

November 22

I felt utterly transparent when I told Owen I couldn't fix his clothes, but he didn't seem to notice. I wasn't lying, but I also didn't want to part with those soft, worn shirts. It's like they're imbued with some essential, comforting maleness that Chip's dry-cleaned button-downs never had.

When I realized how well they matched the cloth I bought at the market, it was a surprise, but a happy one.

It solved my holiday dilemma, anyway. I don't know if they celebrate Christmas here in the same way we do (Thanksgiving came and went without a single comment), but it seems like the perfect opportunity to express my gratitude for all Owen has done for me. I have a plan for his gift now, but it's an ambitious one.

I'm going to need Miss Lenah's help.

Chapter Twenty-Nine

MORGAN GOT HER chance to visit Lenah's shop a few weeks later, when Owen invited her to tag along on one of his drives into town. He said he had some work to do in the Preserve office first but promised they could stop by the store on their way home.

She'd only taken a cursory look around the interior of Lenah's on their last expedition to the market, when they'd gone in to grab a snack at the food counter. In the time since the woman had given her those gorgeous handmade baskets, Owen had told her that Lenah often stocked all kinds of other household items, too.

Morgan hoped to find some frames today, for the handful of sketches she'd done as Christmas gifts—but she was also remembering the distinctive quilted and embroidered vest that the store's proprietor had been wearing the last time they'd seen her.

It had to have been handmade, and Morgan was banking on Lenah being able to answer a few questions about its construction, though the shopkeeper's spotty English made that a bit of a long shot.

However, she didn't want to share that tidbit with Owen, in case he suddenly decided to get nosy about why she cared. As far as she could tell, her Christmas gift for him was still a surprise, and she wanted to keep it that way.

A good present was the least she could do to repay him, after he'd taken two days off work to coddle her when she'd had that stupid migraine. Morgan still felt a little guilty about that.

But when they got to his office and it became clear how much he had to do, she just felt worse for pulling him away again. So while she waited, Morgan stepped out and called Nadra, to see if she wanted to go with her instead.

Owen's former housekeeper seemed eager to join her, so Morgan went back inside and knocked on his door.

His head snapped up instantly. "Everything okay?"

"Yup. I just wanted to let you know that Nadra is coming over. She said she'd come to Lenah's with me, so you don't have to."

Owen frowned a little. "Are you sure? I really don't mind."

"I know. But this way you can finish what you need to do without worrying about me."

Morgan already felt like she was underfoot. Every time she fidgeted, it seemed to distract him.

She knew the feeling.

"Okay, but take the truck," he said, tossing her his keys. "Nadra can show you the way there."

"Thanks." Morgan gave him a wave and wandered across the street to wait at the café.

Through the big plate glass window, she watched him pace around the office, then make stilted-looking small talk with Thom when he came in. Kisima arrived, too, setting her bag in a corner and bustling around, sweeping and straightening up.

Thom studiously avoided looking in Morgan's direction, but Owen kept a suspicious eye on him, anyway. Thankfully, Thom appeared to be behaving. Her boss was likely to strangle him, otherwise.

Owen was also taking periodic laps past the front door, where he'd pause and casually glance over to check on her. Every time he did it, Morgan tried not to laugh. No one looking at that physique would ever guess what a grandma he was on the inside.

Kisima was stealing frequent peeks across the street as she cleaned, as well. She'd warmed to Morgan considerably once Morgan and Nadra had become friendly. Morgan could easily see why Owen thought so highly of the two of them.

She was just about to run over and see if Kisima needed anything at Lenah's, when she caught sight of Nadra, making her slow progress up the street. The woman was free of children for the moment—external ones, at least—which probably explained why she'd been so keen to come along.

Kisima came to the door, shook her head with a little smile and called, "If she holds onto that baby any longer, he's going to be too big for her to deliver."

"He?" Morgan called back. "Does everyone think it's a boy now?" Nadra was certainly convinced, but as far as Morgan knew, that was only maternal speculation.

"Sometimes you just know," Kisima shrugged, smiling wider.

Nadra dropped heavily into the chair opposite Morgan, out of breath but still cheerful. "I only need to rest for a minute," she announced, "and then we can get going. I don't want to waste my big escape by sitting here all day."

"Take your time," Morgan laughed. "I've got the boss's car keys, now. We get to drive the big rig."

Nadra groaned and snatched up one of the sweating water glasses on the table, drinking it down.

Owen joined Kisima at the office door and looked over. "Why do I have the sinking feeling one of us is going to end up delivering that child?"

"Hell, you may as well. Probably yours anyway," Thom sneered from his desk.

Nadra only made a face at Morgan, but Owen and Kisima instantly turned on him. "She's *married*," Owen retorted, clearly affronted.

Kisima rolled her eyes and muttered, "Talk about the pot calling the kettle black."

Owen looked at Kisima. "Why don't you go with Morgan and Nadra? You can always finish up here later, if you want. Or even tomorrow," he offered.

Morgan yelled, "We won't be long!"

Kisima grinned, tossed her duster at Owen, and grabbed her bag. Soon, she and Morgan got Nadra on her feet and began helping her toward Owen's truck.

Owen turned to go back into the office, apparently satisfied that Morgan was in good hands, when all of them were stopped in their tracks by the Preserve's director, rounding the corner and breathing like an angry bull.

"Christ and damnation. All of this running back and forth is going to be the death of me," the man bellowed testily.

"How was Dodoma?" Owen inquired.

"Dar, this time," Cotton corrected, "And it was bloody awful, as usual."

Morgan knew there were government offices in both Dodoma and Dar es Salaam these days, so she had no idea why it seemed to matter which place he'd been. It obviously did, though, because Owen's face went dark as a storm cloud when his boss answered him.

The man wasn't done ranting, though. He sputtered, "I swear on my mother's grave, if one more of those mangy street urchins wails *mzungu* at me the next time I'm there, I'm going to wring its scrawny little neck and feed it to the hyenas."

Nadra mumbled something under her breath as she clung to Morgan's arm. The rest of the street seemed to hold its collective breath, as the men's words carried through the still air.

Kisima turned away from the scene on the sidewalk and quietly urged Nadra, "Ignore him, *mama*. There's no reasoning with stupid. Now let's hoist you into this truck."

Cotton mopped at his red face with a handkerchief and complained, "How many shillings am I supposed to throw away, exactly, before they leave me alone?"

Thom called out, "None."

The man craned his head to see around Owen's broad shoulders. "What did you say?"

"If you give them anything, mate, they assume you have more."

"I tossed them everything I had!" Cotton roared.

Morgan swallowed thickly and tried not to stare. She was hardly an expert on begging kids, but even she could tell that they were being awfully callous about it.

Kisima and Nadra clearly knew it, too. Tucked in the cab of Owen's truck, they had their heads together and were whispering grimly. Morgan knew she ought to get in, too. She shouldn't be eavesdropping like this.

From inside the Preserve office, she heard Thom drawl, "It wasn't enough. It's never going to be enough. So why bother? You're only driving yourself mad."

Owen met Morgan's eyes across the sidewalk and looked vastly uncomfortable. He held her gaze, but he was addressing his boss when he said, "If you're concerned about your shillings doing some good, you could try sending a check to St. Luke's, instead. Maybe change things up a bit."

Nigel glared at him for a full minute before hoisting his briefcase and pushing past him into the office. At top volume, he demanded, "Where's the girl? She's supposed to be in today."

"I asked Kisima to go out and help Nadra for a bit. She'll be back later," Owen replied, cool as a cucumber.

"Or tomorrow," Thom chimed in.

"How is it possible that your maid has not whelped yet?" Cotton cried irritably.

Inside the truck, Kisima whispered, "Morgan? Let's go. It only gets worse the longer he talks."

"I'm sorry," Morgan murmured back. "I'm coming. I just—"

Owen's deep voice carried out to the street. "Nadra's not due till the end of next month," he explained. "Though I'm pretty sure she's as ready as anyone to get things moving."

"Then what the hell is she doing trotting around town every other day? Shouldn't she be staying home? Or parking herself at the clinic to wait it out?"

"*I'll show him where he can park himself*," Nadra grumbled dangerously.

Thom piped up, "You know, I've been wondering that myself." His voice sounded sly. "Could she be meeting a studly Kiwi *inamorato?* What do you think, Hargreave?"

Owen's voice was frosty. "You can't possibly be serious."

"Morgan!" Kisima hissed. "We'd better go before Nadra gets back out of this truck and kills someone."

"Right. Okay," she agreed and turned to the door, fumbling Owen's keys and dropping them in the dirt.

Nigel announced, "Incidentally, our boy Stephen might be stopping by today. Try to be proper, civilized blokes for once in your lives, would you?" Then a door slammed.

Owen came out again, walking over to join them at his truck. "Why are you lot still here?"

Nadra smirked. "Forget it. You can't come with us," she said. "There's no room for you."

"It's my truck!"

"Not for the next two hours, it isn't."

"I suppose you'll be after my wallet, next," he complained, then bumped his shoulder against Morgan's.

The two women in the truck raised their eyebrows and stared at her, and she felt her face flush crimson.

"Now there's a good idea," Kisima said.

Owen grinned and glanced at Morgan, but movement across the street had caught her eye. She jerked her chin, and he turned just in time to see Stephen Thorpe striding into the Preserve office.

"Victoriaville's Most Valuable Villain?" she murmured.

"I'd better run," he said, "Try not to wreck the old girl, okay ladies?" He patted her on the back, then trotted across the street. Morgan slid behind the wheel.

Stuck in the middle seat, Nadra groaned wearily. "I'm not sure if he meant me or this blasted truck."

Morgan had to readjust everything from the position of her seat to the mirrors, given the difference in her and Owen's size, but eventually she was ready to go.

"Nonsense," she told the woman beside her. "This heap is clearly way older than you are. Now, assuming I can figure out how to drive it, which way do we go?"

OWEN HAD MADE sure that Morgan brought her phone with her that morning, and she was glad she had it now. Once she'd gotten used to how big his truck was, it hadn't given her any trouble, but she'd be happy to have a way to get in touch with its owner if it decided to turn finicky on their way back to town.

Plus, if Nadra went into labor early—not completely out of the realm of possibility, given the way she was shuffling around—Morgan could easily call in reinforcements—if she even had cell service out here, that was.

She pulled her phone out to see if she had any bars and suddenly, it began ringing.

"Already?" Kisima laughed, looking over her shoulder as she headed up Lenah's steps. "We just got here."

"*Bwana* misses her," Nadra chuckled. "The sorry fool."

"What?" Morgan protested, though it came out more like a squeak. "No, that's—"

Kisima stabbed a finger at the phone. "Better answer before he starts worrying."

Morgan answered quickly. "Hi! Everything okay?"

Nadra snorted.

"Yeah," Owen said. "Just checking to make sure you got there all right."

"So far, so good," she sang. Too cheerfully, too, based on Kisima and Nadra's wry expressions.

"Listen, I'm sorry to do this to you," Owen continued, "But could I talk to Nadra for a minute?"

"Sure. Hang on." Morgan put the call on speaker and Nadra leaned in.

"Yes, boss?" she drawled. "Though I no longer work for you and you have a new, perfectly capable housekeeper standing right here next to me."

He sighed. "This is different. I need a favor."

Morgan cocked her head. He couldn't ask her for favors? All kinds of favors?

Scratch that. Probably safer if he didn't.

"You still owe me for the last one," Nadra balked.

"It's important," Owen mumbled.

"It always is."

He seemed to take that as permission to proceed, because he blurted out quickly, "Listen, while you're there, can you and Kisima ask around about this Thorpe character for me? I need to find out if he's staying around here somewhere. Somewhere close."

Nadra reared back and stared at Kisima, then said hesitantly, "Okay…"

"Nadra," he warned. "Be discreet."

"*Bwana*, I am the very soul of discretion."

He exhaled, loud and clear. "Just…stick to folks you know and trust, alright? I'm not sure who he's dealing with, and I don't want you two getting into trouble."

You two, he'd said. As if Morgan wasn't standing right there.

Nadra shook her head at the phone. "Is this appropriate work for a woman in my condition?" she joked. "Besides, half the time you won't even let us walk home by ourselves. Now you want us to be your spies?

"Nadra, please."

"Okay, fine. We'll see what we can do, but it's not exactly in the holiday spirit, you know."

There was a beat of silence, and then Owen's deep voice murmured, "Trust me, I know."

Nadra clapped her hands and motioned to Morgan. "I assume you want Morgan, now?" she asked.

They heard Owen's desk chair creak, but he didn't say a word. Nadra and Kisima burst into laughter, and Morgan looked around for a rock she could go hide under. Preferably forever.

"I meant do you want to talk to her?" Nadra giggled. "Obviously."

He coughed and stammered out, "*No.* No, I, uh…I'll talk to her when you get back. Thank you."

Nadra laughed again. "I'll bet," she said, then tapped the screen to end the call.

Both women rounded on Morgan the instant the line went dead. She blinked at the avid looks on their faces.

Nadra fingered the long tails of her headscarf and hummed thoughtfully.

"What?" Morgan asked.

Kisima linked an arm through hers and steered her toward Miss Lenah's front door.

"So, Morgan," she said, "tell us how the job's been going. Do you like your new boss?"

Chapter Thirty

WHEN OWEN WENT back inside, Thom had dropped the chastened act, twisting his face into a comically sad expression as he jerked his chin at Nigel's closed door.

He said, "No room in the pow-wow for us, I'm afraid."

Owen could hear their voices in there, but he couldn't make out what Nigel and Thorpe were saying.

So, he decided to ply Thom for information. He didn't expect to get much, but it couldn't hurt to try.

Owen dropped into one of the old wooden chairs across from Thom's desk and asked, "Where's that kid staying anyway? With Nigel? Or somewhere else?"

Thom whistled, low and long. "That lad's been all over, but posh all the way, I hear."

"What do you mean?"

"I don't know. When he first got here, he was talking about some place called Jao Camp down in Botswana. I looked it up online. Some American architectural magazine did a big spread on it. Real high society, mate. No joke."

"Huh." Owen leaned back and examined his fingernails. "He can't be that far away now, can he?"

"No. Last I heard, young Thorpe was camped out at the Royal Livingstone," Thom said.

"You're kidding." Owen's head popped up. "I could see for a night or two, maybe, but—"

Thom shrugged. "I told you, not a pound left unspent."

Owen shook his head and looked out the window. Most of the folks lingering at the tables outside Charlie's had begun to disperse. The sun was beating down on an empty patio and a few birds looking for crumbs.

"Still," he mused, "the Livingstone is a bit far off. Couldn't the bloke find somewhere closer? Like the Coffee Lodge—I hear that's nice."

Nigel's door popped open, and the men strolled out. Thom clammed up right on schedule and pretended to be engrossed in his paperwork.

Nigel took in the sight of Owen sprawled in that chair, however, and sniffed, "Not enough to do, lads? I'm happy to dole out more work if you need it. It'll be like my own little Christmas gift to you."

Owen ignored the jibe and stood, proffering his hand to Stephen. "Mr. Thorpe, nice to see you again."

Thorpe squeezed his hand too tightly, naturally, and his tone was as sarcastic as ever. "Careful of your mate, there, Hargreave. I hear he's a bit of a troublemaker."

Thom gave the obligatory fake chuckle, and Owen smiled thinly. Stephen released his grip to clap him on the shoulder and pointed at Thom as he backed after Nigel's retreating form.

"Keeping my eye on you," he joked.

Nigel called, "I'll be back after tea. Make sure the maid finishes up today if she expects to keep working here. This is a real office. Not someplace she gets to come and go as she pleases."

"Such a festive holiday spirit," Thom chided. "Much more of that and people will think you've gone soft."

Owen waved him off, then stood at the door and watched the men get into a sleek black Mercedes and drive away.

What was his next move? Thorpe *had* to have a base closer to Victoriaville and the Preserve than the Royal Livingstone. He'd been popping up everywhere, and Owen didn't have time to drive up to Zambia and sniff around.

If he put out some feelers around here, he might be able to flush out where Thorpe had stashed himself. There were only so many places a rich foreigner could lay low without being noticed.

What was more, Thom had to know more than he was letting on. Owen was positive that all the nonsense about magazines and posh digs was just an effort to redirect him. But how could he get the man to talk?

Frustrated, he went into his office and checked the time, wondering if Morgan and the other ladies had made it to Lenah's yet. As he thought about the market—and the amount of information that got exchanged there along with the goods— he realized it could be the perfect low-key place to get the word out about what he needed to know.

He got up and told Thom, "Have to make a few calls," then closed his door and called Morgan.

With any luck, Nadra or Kisima might be able to accomplish what he and Joseph hadn't yet.

He was so hot and bothered by the idea, that when the conversation veered in an unexpected direction, it completely blindsided him. It also put some massively inconvenient ideas in Nadra and Kisima's heads that he was going to have to disabuse them of later.

Forget about him—he wished they hadn't embarrassed Morgan like that. On Christmas Eve, no less.

Christmas Eve. Owen rarely celebrated the holiday anymore, since he was usually out at the cottage alone and it seemed kind of pathetic to make a big deal for no one. Should he be doing something this year, though?

Probably not, he decided. Just because he was nursing a crush the size of Pegasus Bay on his housekeeper, didn't mean he should make things more awkward. It'd probably only make her uncomfortable, anyway—like he was trying to play house with her or something.

He put it out of his mind and refocused on the matter at hand. After some deliberation, he dialed up the Twospeaks next. Conrad often worked visits to the property into his tours, and while he probably wouldn't be home now, it was possible Christine might know the name of someone up at the Royal Livingstone he could call for information.

Before anyone could pick up, however, he changed his mind and ended the call. Owen couldn't risk Carol overhearing—or being told outright—of his plans. She'd no doubt pass that information on to Thom without a second thought.

The more he considered it, the more convinced Owen became that asking around in person was the only way to get more information. He'd have to wait and see if Nadra and Kisima came up with anything before he went haring off to Zambia.

Thom knocked on his door, and Owen realized how odd it must have looked for him to be closed in here for so long. Almost Nigel-esque.

He called out, "Just a minute," and quickly cracked the windows behind him so he didn't look like a total shut-in. By the time he reached the door to open it, Thom had already tried the handle and found it locked.

Owen rattled the knob a bit before he swung things open. "Sorry. I must've caught the lock by accident when I shut the door."

Thom eyed him suspiciously. "I was going to mail these requisitions at the post office, and then head home. You want me to drop you off at Lenah's on the way? You can buy me a last-minute gift while you're there."

"I'll pass," Owen snorted. There were about a hundred reasons why he shouldn't get into a car alone with the man.

"Come on. You don't want to be here any more than I do."

"And when Cotton returns to find the fort undefended later?"

Thom snorted again. "You know as well as I do, he'll have more scotch than tea and won't be back until tomorrow—if we're lucky."

Owen had to chuckle. He wasn't wrong.

Thom said, "If you make sure Kisima finishes up before Nigel gets in on Monday, we'll all be fine."

"You have this down to a science, don't you?"

"Trust me mate, the old man is easy. You're a lot harder to get around than him."

All at once, Thom seemed to realize what he'd just said. His cheeks turned ruddy and his eyes darted away.

Owen blew out a breath and made the decision. "Alright, let's go. I'd hate for Nadra to have that baby in my truck without me."

Being alone with Thom on a rural road might not be the safest endeavor, but Owen wasn't completely without resources.

He had size and skill at his disposal, and he had the contents of his pack. As he casually slung the strap of it across his chest, he followed the lanky man outside. He didn't enjoy the thought of having to use any of the more lethal items in the bag, but Thom had been unpredictable lately. If the man had a sudden shift in mood, Owen would be prepared.

Despite his concerns, nothing much happened. Owen texted Morgan that he was on his way, Thom chatted about Carol and some of the scouts, and then they debated whether to switch supply companies.

Before he knew it, Thom was pulling up beside Lenah's and dropping him off.

He watched as Thom's car puttered off, then breathed a sigh of relief. *So far, so good.*

It was a simple matter to find the women, since it wasn't a regular market day. They were as conspicuous as could be, congregated on Miss Lenah's porch and chatting happily.

Morgan juggled a large, awkward bundle while Kisima balanced a basket on one shoulder, but they both helped Nadra down the steep wooden steps when they spotted him.

Owen relieved Morgan of her parcel when she turned to say goodbye to Miss Lenah, then glanced around quickly, unable to contain his curiosity. Under his breath, he whispered to Nadra and Kisima, "Did you have any luck?"

Nadra rolled her eyes. "Oh Lord. Now he's a secret agent."

Kisima chuckled along with her friend, but still shook her head. "No, Mr. Bond. We didn't solve your problem. Today, anyway."

Owen scowled, already regretting involving them. They were never going to let him live this down.

Except then Kisima murmured, "It's okay, *bwana*. Don't give up hope yet. It'll work. You just have to give it time."

Morgan returned and looked between them. "Give what time?"

Before Nadra could rope her into the mockery, Owen blurted, "*Anyway*, we closed up shop for the day. Morgan and I will drive you ladies home. Kisima, you can finish up at the office Monday morning. Just…"

"Do it before Mr. Cotton comes in, right?" she finished for him.

"Yeah. Right," he laughed.

"Mr. Thom's big idea, yes?"

He arched a brow at her. "Done this before, have you?"

"Certainly not." She marched ahead, leading Owen and the others to his truck.

"Regardless," Nadra announced, trailing behind, "I'll walk. There isn't enough room for all of us."

"Nonsense. Morgan and I can ride in the back," Kisima retorted. At her friend's stormy expression, she added, "You can walk home from my place if you insist—but no farther, *mama*."

Right on cue, Nadra gasped and her hand flew to the side of her belly. "*Oh*."

"Nadra? Are you okay?" Morgan asked her.

Owen held open the passenger door, and waved Nadra in.

"It's just a twinge," she protested.

"Woman, we understand that you don't need help, and you feel fine, and everything is dandy—but would you *please* get in the truck," he groaned. "You have nothing to prove to any of us."

She sighed heavily, but she allowed him to help her up into the cab. Owen waited while she tucked the colorful folds of her dress around her legs, then carefully shut the door.

Kisima stood there shaking her head, like she didn't know what to do with the woman, either. "It's a wonder she even let you hire someone else," she muttered.

"Believe me, I'm aware," he said.

Owen went to the back and lowered the tailgate, then helped Kisima and Morgan climb in. He handed their parcels up after them.

"Are you two sure you'll be okay back here?"

Kisima rolled her eyes and tightened the knot of her headscarf. "Just drive the opposite of how you normally do, and we should be fine," she said.

Nadra twisted around and snapped, "Oh, like that's going to work. Have you met this man?"

All of their ribbing was worth it, however, because then Morgan slapped a hand over her mouth to stifle a laugh. Her pretty hazel eyes sparkled, fine blonde strands of hair framed her face, and her cheeks turned pink with mirth.

She looked lighter and happier than he'd ever seen her. The effect was…incandescent.

Owen swallowed the lump in his throat and got behind the wheel, then had to take a minute to let his heart settle down into a regular rhythm again. Finally, though, he had enough presence of mind to start the truck and pull away, and he tried hard to take it slow like they'd asked.

The four of them rumbled along in tired silence, the wrappings of their various packages flapping in the wind. Morgan and Kisima held things steady the best they could, while also trying to brace themselves against the sides of his truck.

Owen attempted to avoid the ruts, but he was distracted, too. He wished Morgan was up front with him so they could talk, and he kept checking on her in the rearview mirror, to see how she was doing. It was impossible to tell if she was curious about the new patch of passing countryside—the wind kept her hair in her face, so he couldn't see her expression.

Before too long, however, he dropped Kisima and Nadra at Kisima's tidy house, with its potted plants grouped around the door, and big red bows decorating the front windows.

Nadra waved off his offer to take her the rest of the way home, so Owen turned the truck around and headed back toward the cottage, with Morgan safely ensconced up front.

"They're a lot of fun," she told him happily. "I really appreciate you introducing me."

"I'm glad you all get along," he said, taking his eyes off the road long enough to peek at her putting her hair up with brisk and efficient movements. "They've been good to me over the years."

Morgan tilted her head and studied him, and her direct gaze felt like a brand against his skin. "They care about you," she murmured.

"The feeling's mutual."

When she rearranged herself in her seat, he glanced over again, this time noticing the length of her thigh and the bare skin of her arm, both of them only inches away from his—so close he could touch them.

Owen was not allowed to touch her, though, and especially not after he'd kissed her. Morgan needed him to employ her, not harass her. *Priorities.*

Except…there was still that little loophole he'd floated—the one Morgan had not brought up again. Would she ever? Waiting to find out was turning out to be excruciating, and bringing her home to his cozy, empty house abruptly seemed a little too fraught.

Owen blurted out, "You know, I think we pass by Joseph's house on our way home. Would you mind if we stopped by for a minute?"

"Of course not!" Morgan yelped, then winced.

Owen smiled. Her voice had been a tad too loud, but the question was, why? She might be overcompensating, acting extra agreeable because she was annoyed and didn't want to say so, but it could also be because he was the most maladroit male on the planet—around her, anyway—and she didn't know what to do with him.

She liked Joseph fine, however, and Teleki liked her. This little detour would be alright, and by the time it was over, Owen would once more be perfectly capable of coexisting with his housekeeper without turning lewd on her.

"Follow my lead," he told her. "We won't stay long."

"You can count on me," Morgan announced cheerfully.

Chur. Owen liked the sound of that, far, far too much.

AFTER A FEW more miles and a couple more turns, they pulled up to the Teleki home. There were no holiday decorations on display here, and almost immediately a tall woman leaned out of the front door and motioned for them to drive around back.

Once Owen had parked, Teleki stepped from a small outbuilding and beckoned them inside. Morgan frowned as he disappeared.

"Why does it seem like he was expecting us? I thought this was a pop-in."

"So did I," Owen told her.

He got out of the truck, walked around to hold Morgan's door for her, then led her to the barn. She followed him, but slowly.

"Should I maybe wait in the truck?" she wondered. "Or go to the house and introduce myself?"

Owen stopped and waited for her to catch up. "I'd feel better having you in sight. Let's see what this is about, first."

Morgan nodded, but she looked tentative. "Was that Joseph's wife back there?"

"I think so."

They reached the pint-sized structure and stepped inside, finding themselves in a warm space, crisscrossed with streaks of sunlight shining through chinks in the walls. Owen guessed the Telekis probably stabled their goats here.

It was a relief to be in the shade after the glaring sun at Lenah's. The hay smelled sweet, and the quiet buzzing of an insect near the door reverberated through the space with a low, friendly hum. Still, it was a strange place to receive visitors.

"Welcome to my humble abode," Teleki smiled.

"It's cute," Morgan told him, chipper as ever. "I love it."

Joseph looked pleased. "I saw you pull in," he said, "That's why I came out here. I thought we could use the privacy."

"Actually, I don't have a lot to report," Owen told him. "But we were driving by and I thought I ought to check in."

"I'm glad you did." Then Joseph glanced at Morgan, a question in his eyes.

She turned and spotted a carved wooden milking stool near one of the stalls and went to perch on it, shifting her body away from them.

"Don't mind me," she murmured mildly. "I'll catch up on email while you talk."

It wasn't perfect, but Owen wasn't worried about her overhearing them. His housekeeper was reliable—she wouldn't spread around whatever they said.

Once Morgan had pulled out her phone and started tapping away, Joseph began, "We haven't had much luck finding Thorpe's base of operations."

"Me either," Owen admitted. "I asked Kisima and Nadra to poke around at Lenah's, but if anyone's seen anything, they haven't said."

Teleki nodded thoughtfully. "It's a good idea, though. Let's give it a few days and see what happens."

Owen glanced at Morgan. She looked protected in her little alcove, like the complicated outside world was very far off. He could imagine her curling up on the hay with him, taking a nap while he watched over her and kept her safe.

He could almost see them like that, not here in this little goat barn, but home in Christchurch—in a sheep stable made of field stone, whiling away a hot afternoon doing everything but sleeping.

That was a fantasy for another day, however. Outside these walls, the world seethed with expectancy. They were all waiting—to discover where Thorpe and his men were lurking, of course, and also what their end game was going to be.

But Owen also balanced on the edge of something else. At some point, Morgan would tell him she had to leave for America. She might not have a husband, but for all he knew, there could be someone else. Someone who was waiting for her.

If he was kind, he would encourage her to leave now, before this mess with Thorpe blew up into something more dangerous than it already was. Morgan was open and kind. She didn't deserve to be in anyone's crosshairs, simply because she happened to have taken a job with Owen.

It didn't help that Morgan possessed a kind of restlessness, a need to go out and meet her fears, rather than to sit at home waiting for them to descend on her. That day at Thom's had taught him that much.

It troubled him. Humans could be so much more frightening than any animal. A beast had an agenda, certainly, but it was a simple one—survival. Kill or be killed.

The calculated cruelty of man was something else entirely, and he feared what might be coming.

Joseph seemed to pick up on his thoughts. "Are you worried about her?" he asked softly.

"A little. I can't be with her every moment. I'm not sure how to protect her."

As if she'd heard them, Morgan turned suddenly, shifting her shoes in the scattered hay. She looked them over, then stood and approached.

"What's up?" Joseph asked.

"I was just wondering—do you know where this Stephen guy hangs out?"

Joseph looked to Owen, but he was equally stumped. "What do you mean?"

"I mean, does he hang out at bars in Arusha, or nightclubs, or…what?"

He and Teleki had been down this road before with her. They scowled in unison and demanded, "*Why?*"

"Well, I've been thinking. Maybe…maybe I could go and like, flirt with him. You know, see if I could get him to take me to his hotel." Morgan faltered, eyeing their expressions. "Or I could get him to tell me, then take you back there so you could look around, instead…" She trailed off weakly, turning red.

"Have you gone mad? Meeting Thom was one thing," Owen pointed out, "And I didn't like that, aye? What you're suggesting now is a whole other level of crazy."

Morgan blinked, looking nearly as baffled that she'd said what she had as they were. "Okay, maybe that idea wasn't the best, but I would like to help. Why is it okay for Kisima and Nadra, but not me?"

Owen stared at her, momentarily speechless.

Joseph broke into a grin, chuckling warmly—like she was adorable, instead of off her rocker.

"Miss Morgan, that's very kind of you, but it's too dangerous," he said. "Kisima and Nadra know the people here. They know who they can trust, and who they should avoid."

"What are you, an adrenaline junkie now?" Owen wondered, regaining his wits. "You have a little success at Thom's and now you want to take down the villain himself? Through seduction, no less?"

Despite himself, his lips quirked up at the thought, and his heart stuttered a little in his chest.

For some reason he felt the need to add, "Not that I don't think you could do it, but seriously."

Embarrassed tears sprang into Morgan's eyes, though, and he immediately wished he could take it back.

She said, "I'm not, I swear—I just hate feeling useless. I thought I could help. I thought…I thought if your usual methods weren't working, maybe something unusual would."

Owen didn't like the considering look in Joseph's eye, so he answered quickly, before the man could suggest anything nuts.

"That may be," he told her, "But we're not using you as bait, that's for sure." And then, because he was apparently a horse's ass, he added, "Hell, if we did you'd probably be bedridden for a month afterward."

Morgan glared at him. Rightfully so—that had been a low blow.

Joseph kept shaking his head at her and smiling. His eyes were soft, though, like this lunacy was still charming him.

"Thorpe would undoubtedly take you up to the Livingstone, anyway," he told her. "I'm sure he'd want to show off to a…" he hesitated slightly, but finished with, "…to an American girl."

Owen doubted that was what he'd originally meant to say. Still, he agreed, "That's probably true. The pommy bastard."

Morgan still looked upset, however, so he rested a hand on her arm and told her, "Listen love, I really appreciate the offer but I cannot agree to put you in harm's way again. Okay? Thom's place was enough."

He said it as emphatically as he dared, searching her eyes for some sign that she understood. Owen squeezed her arm a little willed her to hear his thoughts.

I care. I care. I care.

"Don't worry," Joseph reassured her, breaking the moment. "Thorpe can't hide forever. We'll find him before long, and then we'll figure out how to stop him."

Morgan turned back to Owen, but a sudden sound out in the yard made him shove her behind him, where he could shield her from whatever was coming. He stared at the flimsy little door and listened intently.

Joseph had gone on alert, too, cocking his head and slipping to peer out of a crack between the slats of the wall.

Owen went to peek over his shoulder. Morgan stayed quiet, but she was probably wondering if they'd gone mad. The noise they'd heard had been so faint, she might not have even noticed it.

Joseph glided to her side a moment before soft tapping sounded at the door. Joseph didn't move a muscle, and as the seconds passed, Owen began to doubt his instincts. Perhaps it had been one of the goats moving around outside, or a family member.

But then they heard the tapping again, louder this time and accompanied by a small cough.

Owen knew that cough. He looked quickly at Joseph, who nodded and moved silently to the door, his hand resting on a large knife holstered at his belt. He opened things up, and helped the man who stood there inside.

One more quick glance around the yard, and the barn door was shut again.

Kisima's brother was even more feeble than the last time Owen had seen him. As Morgan watched with wide eyes, Owen took the man's arm and helped him to the stool she'd been sitting on before.

Tumelo moved stiffly, like an old man, but in truth, he and Owen were relatively close in age. He'd gotten horrifically gaunt, with new sores on his face and arms. Even in the heat, he wore the woolen hat his sister had knitted him.

He hunched on the stool and worked to catch his breath.

There was no telling how far Tumelo had walked to get there, but he'd obviously tired himself out. Joseph and Owen did their best to get him settled and to make him comfortable.

The barn door opened again, but this time Joseph's wife marched in, handed a chipped enamel cup of water to their guest, and turned to leave without a word. Joseph squeezed her shoulder as she passed, and then they waited.

Finally, Tumelo spoke, in his deep, gravelly bass. "Heard some talk. You looking for a stranger? A white man?"

Joseph nodded, so Owen added carefully, "Not just any man. One man in particular."

Tumelo held up a shaking hand. "I know the one," he croaked.

Chapter Thirty-One

NO ONE SPOKE while the man took a long drink of water. Then, as if he'd only just noticed her presence, his eyes fell on Morgan. His level gaze was uncomfortable.

She was still glued to the wall, afraid to move a muscle, but when she shifted clumsily, the man's eyes slid back to Owen. He raised his eyebrows, questioning her presence.

"My new housekeeper," Owen said, but that was all.

Whoever the new arrival was, he accepted the explanation and turned to study her again. As he stared, Morgan took in how painfully thin he was, and the lesions on his arms. He was obviously ill, and she could tell he was measuring her reaction to it.

Morgan had no idea what to do, so she waved and said, "Hi."

Which was dumb. Maybe she should've left, after all.

But the man nodded at her, cleared his throat and shifted back toward Joseph and Owen.

"Heard talk about your man. Up at the Royal Livingstone," he said, watching them.

Joseph reached down to accept the empty cup the man proffered. He told him, "No, that's not why you're here."

Owen's tone was likewise flat. "It's also not true."

The man smirked a little and nodded, seeming to enjoy the back and forth. As the moments dragged on, Morgan wondered if he'd say anything else.

Finally, though, he spoke up. "There is another place," he admitted. He looked Morgan up and down once more, then added, "North of here, a few kilometers off the Arusha road."

Owen's eyes met Joseph's in question, but Joseph only shook his head. "I don't know the place you mean," Owen said.

"My sister knows it well."

Joseph straightened up in surprise. "Does she?"

The visitor explained, "Kisima worked there…when she was a girl. When it was…more respectable." His breathing grew labored, like all the talking was wearing him out.

Recognition dawned on Owen's face. "Ah," he murmured, "The Shadey Inn, aye?"

Their informant nodded. "The old man's often there, as well. Brings that Twospeak girl."

Owen opened his mouth to speak but seemed to be at a loss for words. Both he and Joseph were staring at the guy in shock.

"Not the…guide's wife," he clarified. "The…wild one. Wife's…sister."

Regaining his voice, Owen asked incredulously, "I'm sorry—Carol Connelly and Nigel *Cotton*?"

The mystery man shook his head in exasperation. "Not him. The father of the one you seek. Poncy old sot." He tried to rise, but it was clearly difficult for him.

Owen sprang forward and gently helped him to his feet, then supported him as he shuffled toward the door. Joseph dug in his pocket, but his body blocked Morgan's view of whatever he handed over.

Money, she guessed, in exchange for the information.

"Why are you doing this?" Owen asked, but it sounded gentle, not accusatory.

The man was tall, but he hunched his shoulders at the question. "I…appreciate what you've done. For my sister.

I…have not been good to Kisima. She deserves…better. Besides. I'm as good as dead…anyway. What have I got…to lose?"

The visitor let himself out, grumbling, "Happy Christmas," before stalking into the bright sunshine of the yard.

"Wait—can I drive you somewhere?" Owen called.

Morgan couldn't hear the response, but whatever it was, it made her boss sigh. He stood watching the man for a long time before turning back.

While Joseph toyed with the handle of that cup, Owen demanded, "Thorpe's *father* is here, too? How did this get by us?"

Joseph shrugged and gazed at the floor unhappily. "We have more work to do."

"You're telling me. I've got to think Kisima didn't expect her own brother to be the one that came to us."

"And yet…I'm not terribly surprised, either."

Owen raked a hand through his hair and Morgan tried not to stare at the way his biceps bunched and strained under his sleeve. This was not the time.

"How did he even know we were here?" he wondered.

Joseph shrugged. "How does Tumelo know any of the things he seems to?"

"Should I go after him? He's not going to make it very far like that."

"You heard what he said. Leave him be," Joseph told him.

Owen frowned, but he backed off. Then, after a couple of beats, he announced, "I think I need to process this for a bit. I should get Morgan home, too."

Joseph smiled kindly at her. "That was a bit more excitement than I expected, that's for sure." To Owen, he added, "I'll let you know as soon as I talk to my people. We need to plan what comes next."

"I'll be waiting."

Owen gestured to the door and set his hand on the small of Morgan's back, and the warmth of his palm radiated through her limbs like bolts of electricity.

She took a few unsteady steps and said, "Bye, Joseph," but her voice cracked a little.

Joseph smiled again, though he didn't make fun of her. "Goodbye, Miss Morgan. Be safe."

She and Owen walked across the scrubby grass to the truck. The man named Tumelo was nowhere to be found. The woman in the house was watching them again, though, half-hidden by the back door. Morgan waved, but it was impossible to tell if the woman waved back.

Once they were inside the truck and on their way, she asked, "Did I hear correctly? That was Kisima's brother?"

Owen glanced at her. "Tumelo. Yes."

She struggled with how to phrase what she wanted to ask. "Is he, uh…" *Recovering? Dying?* "What is…"

Owen saved her with one succinct sentence, "He has AIDS. Poor guy's wife passed from it, too, just last year."

Morgan winced, but Owen's thoughts were elsewhere. "I'll be damned if I can figure out how Thorpe kept things so quiet. The Shadey Inn is not that far from Victoriaville. I should have thought of it sooner."

There was an easy explanation for that. "Money, that's how," Morgan told him. "Who did he pay off? Follow the cash and the whole thing comes apart, I'd imagine."

"*Bloody hell*," he muttered. "Straight from the movies, but you're probably right."

Morgan didn't dare say more. Owen was stewing, but whether he was unhappy with Tumelo or her—or what he'd learned about Stephen Thorpe—wasn't clear.

She tried a different tack. "By the way, was that Joseph's wife who came into the barn?"

Owen eyed her curiously, his expression softer now. "Yes. I haven't seen her in quite a while. Almost didn't recognize her."

"Not the outgoing type, is she?"

"She has her moments," Owen smiled, then returned his attention to the road.

She could hardly blame him for his reticence. He undoubtedly had a lot to think about right now. Morgan stopped trying to make conversation and stared out the window for the rest of the ride home, her mind drifting from thought to thought.

She tried to unravel the afternoon's events, but her brain didn't seem to want to stray from the visceral pull of the man beside her.

Owen was a study in contradictions. On the one hand, he was strong and brave and protective. Masculine through and through.

But on the other, he could be sensitive and caring. Whenever he talked about those little gazelles, his affection and concern were palpable. He was a natural with Nadra's kids and had been gentle and considerate with Kisima's sick brother.

Morgan appreciated the way Owen treated everyone with an equal degree of respect, no matter their color or social status. His innate decency toward other human beings stood in stark contrast to the way his boss Nigel had acted on that sidewalk earlier, and to her ex-husband's demeanor, too.

When looked at separately, each of Owen's attributes glittered like singular gems, but taken together, they crystallized into something larger—and perilously deep. Morgan could feel something bigger than attraction for a man like him.

With time, she could love him. And not just a little bit, either—Morgan could feel the sort of thing for Owen that she had always hoped for in her first marriage, but never had. An all-encompassing, soul-deep connection that lasted a lifetime.

At least, she could if he weren't her boss, and they didn't live on opposite sides of the globe most of the time. Still…not every relationship started with forever. Most began on far more accessible terrain.

And so, by the time they'd pulled up in front of the cottage, Morgan had made a decision of sorts. She might never meet a man like Owen again, and regret could cast a long, long shadow. She'd had enough of that feeling to last a lifetime.

Besides, Owen had already provided her with an opening all those weeks ago in the kitchen. If Morgan wanted a physical relationship with him, all she had to do was ask.

She steeled herself to do the one thing he likely did not expect. It might not be the smartest idea, and it might have big consequences, but it was time to admit that she wanted it more than anything else.

It was time, as they said, to take the bull by the horns.

WHEN OWEN PUT the truck in park, they both sat there looking through the windshield for a moment before Morgan took a breath, unbuckled her seatbelt, and turned toward him.

Owen glanced at her quickly and said, "Listen, I know you must have questions and that you want to help, but I want to keep you out of harm's way. I'd never forgive myself if something happened to you, even inadvertently."

He was taking this conversation way off track. Morgan needed to bring it back to where she wanted it, and fast—otherwise it could be weeks before she worked up her nerve again.

"Owen, forget all that. Right now, I want you to kiss me," she blurted out, and the noticeable quaver in her voice made her whole face go hot.

He froze with his hand on his door handle, clearly wondering if he'd heard her correctly. "I'm sorry. Can you repeat that, please?"

Morgan stammered, "You said…you wouldn't touch me again unless I asked you to. So, this is me. Asking you. To, uh…to touch me. If you want." She swallowed painfully while Owen gaped at her.

He thought she was delirious. That much was obvious.

Morgan glanced away and tried to decide if she ought to make a run for the house. "I'm sorry. I should not have said that. Forget I said that. I just thought I'd…"

Unfortunately, Owen had already hopped out of the truck and was stalking around the front of it, so he didn't hear her retraction. When he got to her side, he yanked open her door—presumably so he could toss her in the lake and fire her for harassment.

In no particular order.

Owen reached in and pulled Morgan's knees around so she was facing him. She couldn't bear to look at him, so she fixed her eyes on her hands instead, gripping each other in her lap. The painful flush heating her cheeks moved lower and made her neck prickle with mortification.

Had she been so awkward back when she'd first begun dating in her teens? It seemed impossible that she'd regressed that far, and yet…here she was. Smack in the middle of Dorkville.

Owen didn't immediately evict her from the Land Rover, however. Instead, he rested his hands on the sides of her legs, and caressed her calf muscles through the light material of her cargo pants.

"Morgan, you don't have to do this," he said grimly. "If I made you think you had to, or…or you feel obligated for some reason, then that's not okay. And that's on me. I don't expect anything like this from you."

"I know that. It's just—"

He barreled on, "If I make you uncomfortable, I can find you another position, if you want. Somewhere nice and safe. Or I could even help you get back home, maybe. We could—"

Morgan commanded herself to look Owen in the eye, even though she was fighting back horrifying, embarrassed tears. His flurry of words died in his throat.

"You don't have to do any of that," she said, her voice sounding oddly flat. "And don't worry—I won't ask you again. You…don't want to, obviously, so…" Morgan stammered, aghast at her own ineptitude. "Or maybe it's…I mean, maybe you already have someone else you like?"

Why hadn't she considered that possibility before now?

Owen cupped her face gently in his large, warm hands. "Morgan, no. There's no one else. You don't understand. I *do* want to touch you—to kiss you—very much. *Too* much. But you're a vulnerable woman, and you're under my care…you're in my employ."

She blinked. "Wait, you—"

"The problem I have, is that you are *so*…" Owen shook his head and ran a thumb across her bottom lip. "To be honest, Morgan, kissing you is all I ever think about. It's all I want."

His eyes searched hers, and then—impossibly—he leaned in to softly touch his lips to hers.

Morgan couldn't help it. She gasped. Owen immediately dropped his hands from her face and started to back away.

Before he could get far, she wound her arms around his neck and pulled him close, then crushed her mouth to his. In an instant he was opening hungrily to her, then just as quickly pulling away to grip her around the waist, lift her out of his truck, and set her on the ground.

Owen swung the door shut and quickly scanned the area, then grabbed Morgan's hand and towed her up the steps of the cottage. While he unlocked the front door, she slid her hands around his waist and rested her cheek against his back, and had to smile when he fumbled a bit before he could get things opened up.

She wasn't the only one with a case of the nerves. And that glimpse of his discombobulation settled her, making him seem far less intimidating.

Owen turned in Morgan's hold and backed inside, pulling her along with him as he peered over her shoulder another time, then shut the door and relocked it soundly.

"The last thing we need is for Stephen or Thom to show up," he chuckled, low and dark as molasses. "Or bloody Teleki."

"He does tend to turn up at strange times," she smiled back. "At least he's nice."

They stood there looking at each other for a long, laden minute. Owen seemed to feel honor-bound to give her one last out, but his jaw was tense with the effort.

"Morgan are you sure about this?" he asked. "Once we cross this line, there's no undoing it."

She closed the inches between them and cut him off with a finger pressed to his lips. "I won't want to undo it."

"Is this really happening? Or did Tumelo brain me and leave me unconscious on his way out of Joseph's goat barn?"

"This is really happening."

"Not that I'm in any hurry to wake up if it isn't, mind you. This is by far the best fantasy I've had about you, yet."

"Yet?" Morgan laughed.

When she ran her hands up Owen's chest, he pulled her in tight. And when Morgan tilted her face up to his, going up on her toes for a kiss, Owen lifted her up so she could reach.

She grinned at how easy that was for him, then locked her legs around his waist and kissed him with her eyes wide open, to watch his reaction.

Against her lips, Owen let out a breath like he'd been holding it and turned to lean Morgan back against the front door. She tilted her hips against him, trying to get closer, and it felt as if that little motion broke something wide open inside of him.

Owen might have been holding back all this time, but he was hard as steel for her now, and he wasn't shy about letting her know it. He ground himself against her core while he devoured her mouth, and his lips were soft and hot on hers.

With a low sound, he dropped urgent kisses along her jaw, down her neck, and across the top of her shoulder. When Owen bent and nipped at her earlobe, Morgan let out a whimper that she was sure she'd never made before.

He chuckled, hot against her ear. "I want to hear *that* again," he said. "Let's see if I can make you do it."

He gripped Morgan under her thighs and lifted her away from the door. "Your room or mine?" she asked him.

"Mine. Yours should stay yours, in case you regret this later." His steps faltered a little when he said it.

"I won't regret it," she assured him. "Will you?"

"Hell no. Having this with you is worth any price—any penalty—I can imagine." And yet, he still paused at the threshold of his room and waited.

"Please," Morgan whispered against his mouth.

She tightened her legs around him and that was all it took. Owen stepped all the way in, kicked the door shut behind them, and sat her on the side of his tall four poster bed. She whipped her t-shirt up and over her head before he could rethink things, and Owen stopped in his tracks at the sight of her breasts framed by her lacy baby-blue bra.

"Never, in all my guilty fantasies, did I imagine you had a confection like that under your clothes," he said.

"Surprise," she smiled.

The look on his face was almost feral. "I'd better find out if there's a matching pair of panties beneath these utilitarian pants of yours," he announced, and attacked the fastenings at her waist.

Morgan's laugh sounded breathy and sexy in her ears, which was both new and sort of strange. Still, she obliged Owen by lifting her hips off the bed so he could strip off her pants along with her shoes, and then scooted farther back on the mattress.

Owen leaned on his hands and dropped one light kiss on each of her knees, and looked her up and down.

"They match," she informed him.

"I see that," he said. "But you should know, seeing these legs in my bed could be the death of me."

His gaze raked over her, traveling up the curve of her stomach to the swell of her breasts. Morgan leaned back on her elbows, and Owen's eyes snagged on her collarbones. With one gentle fingertip, he traced the angle they made across the top of her chest, then touched the small gold oval of her locket where it rested in the hollow of her throat.

"You're beautiful," he murmured. "So beautiful, it paralyzes me."

He hesitated, and Morgan waited to see what he would do.

At last, he seemed to come to a decision. Owen told her, "Take down your hair," and his voice was even deeper than usual.

Morgan reached up to pull the elastic free, and he watched in fascination as her hair fell over her shoulders and down her back.

"Like this?" she asked, then felt a wash of satisfaction when he nodded.

"My pillows are going to smell like you."

"Maybe for days," she smiled.

"I'll wallow in that later. For now, I have you to savor."

Owen knelt on the bed with his knees outside hers, trailing his fingers up Morgan's legs and across the lace trim on her panties. He tore his eyes away to glance at her face, and she bit her lip, abruptly shy at the scrutiny.

"You're staring," she said. Her breath was sawing in and out of her lungs and her heart was beating erratically.

Owen looked back down, braced himself on his elbows, and dropped open-mouthed kisses across her stomach. "I don't want to miss anything," he murmured.

When he pushed up on his hands and ran his tongue lightly along the edge of her bra, Morgan let out a shuddering breath. He looked like it was an effort for him to go slowly—like he was trying not to scare her off.

"I won't break," she told him.

"I'm so much bigger than you are. I don't want to hurt you."

"You won't, Owen. I know you won't."

He nodded, but she wasn't sure he believed her. After a long pause, however, he grasped one of her bra straps in his teeth and dragged it off her shoulder. Morgan thought she might have squeaked out another high sound as he tasted the skin he'd uncovered, but it was impossible to be sure over the blood roaring in her ears.

She wove her fingers through Owen's hair, and tried to pull him away. He resisted only a little before he let her roll him onto his back. Morgan straddled his hips and attempted to glare at him.

It couldn't have been very convincing, given the way his green eyes twinkled at her. "Morgan," he laughed. "What are you up to?"

She shushed him. "You still have your *boots* on," she informed him, and looked pointedly over her shoulder, to where his feet dangled off the side of the bed.

Owen blinked up at her in confusion. "Do I?"

"Yes."

"Does that matter?"

"*Yes.*"

He couldn't seem to come up with a suitable response in the face of all the skin he was eyeing hungrily, but he did attempt to look contrite. Unfortunately, it looked more like a pained grimace stretched across his face.

"Let me help," Morgan said. She maneuvered herself around and leaned over to untie Owen's boots, and smiled at the dark grunt he made.

His fingers gripped her hips. "I should not take you like this," he growled unsteadily. "Not…not the first time, anyway." His hands smoothed over her skin, marking where her waist dipped in and hips flared out, and when he cupped her rear it felt like a brand.

Morgan knew what he was seeing. Between the ends of her hair and the waistband of her panties, the top part of her tattoo would be peeking out—and sure enough, Owen was soon pulling down the elastic so he could see the entire design.

"Whoa. Is that a griffin?"

"Yes."

Morgan loved the detailed work of art on her lower back, especially the way the red and white filigreed wings spread out wide from her tailbone. She and Meg had agonized for days over the design before she'd finally gotten brave enough to have it inked permanently.

"Very pretty," he murmured.

Morgan dropped his boots one by one to the floor, then pulled off his socks before she turned herself around again. She smiled down at him. "Thank you."

"Not as gorgeous as you, though," he said. "You're like a vision."

Morgan batted her eyes and went to work on his belt buckle, then on the buttons of his fly. She tugged Owen's worn t-shirt up his chest, and waited for him to sit up, so she could pull it off him.

She couldn't help humming a bit at the sight and feel of all those muscles rippling in his chest and shoulders and arms, and Owen took advantage of her distraction to reach around her back and deftly release the clasp of her bra.

He tossed the scrap of lace and silk triumphantly to the side, and Morgan wriggled closer for a deep, hungry kiss. She reeled at the sensation of all his warm velvet skin against hers, and when Owen stroked his hands down her back to squeeze her bottom tight against him, she sighed with happiness.

He was spectacularly hard, and clearly as eager to move things along as she was. Morgan drank in his enticingly masculine scent and the feel of him under her hands, while Owen inched her panties down her hips, then helped her out of them.

He chuckled a little unsteadily. "I'd say I feel like a teenager again, but I don't think my imagination was ever this good."

"Flatterer," she retorted. She knew she'd never imagined a man like him, even after she'd discovered the wonders of book boyfriends.

There was still way too much material between them, though, so Morgan yanked at Owen's pants, and somehow managed to get them—along with his boxers—down his thighs. His erection sprang free between them, and Morgan looked down at it curiously.

Nope. Not disappointed. Not even a little bit.

Owen bucked and kicked at his pants, struggling to get them off without dislodging Morgan from his lap. But once they dropped to the floor, he held still under her perusal, letting her eyes track slowly across his stomach and arms.

She lingered over his chest and then on his shoulders, until finally her gaze hitched on his mouth. Owen's muscles twitched and trembled, like he was a barely-tamed animal, dying to be let off his leash.

Morgan felt his soft exhale against her cheeks, and her eyes flew up to lock with his. She froze at the look he wore. She'd never seen such stark desire—it was carved into every plane of his face, and it sent a thrill of awareness through her.

"Not flattery," he growled, "You're hotter than the Sahara at high noon right now."

Morgan had been called cute before, and sweet. She'd never had a man tell her she was hot, but the truth of it was truly etched—however implausibly—across Owen's face. She believed him, and it made her feel powerful and free.

Was there a flicker of something else in his expression, too, a hint of something softer underneath all the rest? Morgan didn't dare look at it too closely. She also couldn't let herself hope for it, or want it.

She couldn't let Owen see what she really felt about him.

Especially not now, when only a few kisses and caresses had her heart tumbling into a panic-inducing free-fall.

A diversion was definitely in order, and Morgan knew exactly how to create it.

She reached between them, grasped the incontrovertible evidence of Owen's desire in both hands—and stroked.

Chapter Thirty-Two

OWEN GROANED WHEN Morgan took hold of him—what man in his right mind wouldn't? But at least he was rewarded by her sharp and sudden intake of breath.

Oh, she was affected by him, all right. Maybe as much as he was by her. He allowed himself a tiny measure of smugness about it, but with the way Morgan was stroking her fists up and down his length, it was hard to hold onto it for long.

Owen squeezed his eyes shut and tried to concentrate on anything other than the way her hands felt against him. No use having this whole thing over before it even got off the ground.

"*Owen*," Morgan called softly, drawing out the first syllable of his name like a siren call.

He forced his eyes open and was stunned all over again by her tantalizing curves.

"Am I hurting you?" she asked. He might've laughed if she didn't actually look concerned.

He took her hands and moved them gently away. "No, sweetheart. Just the opposite." Morgan bit her lip and tried to reach for him again, so he pressed her hands down into the mattress.

He said, "If you keep that up, though, this will be over sooner rather than later, and I want it to last."

His voice sounded thick and husky in his throat. Owen gripped her hands and braced himself, and the muscles in his chest and arms felt as taut as a lion's, ready to pounce. He waited to see what she would do.

"I see," Morgan murmured, gazing shyly at his shoulder instead of meeting his eyes. Soon, he understood why. "Um…I don't suppose you have anything? Any protection, I mean?" She peeked at his face and looked mortified, even though it was the right thing to ask. Suave, she was not.

Clearly, that little detail hadn't crossed her mind when she'd decided to proposition him. Trust Morgan to only realize it now, and Owen to be charmed beyond belief by that.

He smirked at her and gestured with his chin. "Night table drawer," he told her. "Want me to get it?"

Morgan was already shifting off him, though, and crawling for the goods—and giving Owen an excellent view of her derriere in the process. He tried to scrape his chin off the mattress while she slid the drawer open and found the box stashed inside.

It took her exactly two seconds to realize that it was sealed up tight, shrink-wrapped in the same plastic he'd bought it in. Owen rearranged himself beside her, propped some pillows behind his back, and readied for the inevitable snark heading his way.

Morgan shook the box at him. "Brand new?" she inquired archly.

"Yes, actually," he replied, and only a little sheepishly. "As it turns out, I haven't needed them for a while." *Since you arrived.*

Morgan watched his face, and Owen fought to keep from blushing. He did not want to explain why he'd decided to buy condoms, now. So, he asked her, "Do you want some help?"

Her eyes flickered down to the box in her hands, and she shook her head. Morgan made short work of the wrapping, retrieved one of the foil packets, and scooted back over to him.

She tore it open, reached out, and hesitated. Her hands were shaking.

"Here," Owen murmured, and guided her hands to his cock. He helped her put the condom on and tried not to hiss at the sensation. He didn't think he'd ever been this hard in his life.

Morgan threw a leg over his hips and straddled him again, and he took a moment to cup those perfect breasts in his palms, thumbing her nipples and watching the way it made her eyes flutter closed and her head fall back.

She felt so good pressed up against him, but right now, he was longing for a different angle.

In seconds, he had her flat on her back. Morgan looked mystified at how she'd ended up there so suddenly. Owen grinned down at her, and planted a firm, lingering kiss on her luscious mouth.

"Did I mention I wrestled as a lad?" he inquired, like they were making idle conversation over tea.

"No," Morgan squeaked, breathless and sexy as hell. "I think I missed that detail."

She moved her hands lightly up his sides and Owen's smile disappeared as fast as it'd arrived. He dipped his head and kissed her again, long and deep. Her taste—*damn*, her taste.

"Morgan," he said against her lips, "I want you."

She twinkled up at him, as if he'd pleased her. "Your accent is getting stronger."

"Probably because there's too much talking and not enough shagging," he pointed out. He pressed his hips against hers. "I want you now, love."

The words slid into a bit of a growl, but it must have worked for her because she pressed her hands against his back and hooked her legs around his thighs in invitation.

"Are you sure?" he asked, one last time.

"Very, very sure."

Owen glided once, and then twice, against her cleft, and then he couldn't wait any longer—he drove into her with one urgent thrust, and had to hold still for a minute so he could absorb the delectable heat and pressure of her body.

Morgan made a little sound, but it sounded like it'd come from far away. The blood was streaking through his veins like liquid fire. Owen kept himself buried deep inside her and leaned his forehead against hers.

"God," he choked out, trying not to tremble. The sudden rush of emotion was a surprise.

Morgan's fingers tightened on him, but she seemed utterly incapable of forming words. Owen scanned her face, and it was clear as day she knew. This was unreal. It was *extraordinary*.

Finally, Owen let himself move, and with that motion the world narrowed like a camera lens, shrinking around them to pinpoint focus. There was only this bed and their two bodies.

When he stretched down to taste the skin at the side of her neck, Morgan smelled amazing, fresh and feminine. And she felt amazing, too—everything from her long, lithe legs, to her soft curves, to her velvet skin.

She shifted and flexed with an athletic grace that took his breath away, matching his every move like they'd been made for this—made for each other.

Owen tried to draw it out, to make it last. But before he knew it, Morgan was coming, her body pulsing around his cock and a low, keening sound crossing her lips that was so inexpressibly sexy , it tossed him right off the cliff himself.

So help him, he groaned too, rusty and deep in his throat, and then had to brace himself to keep from crushing her. He rolled to his side before his arms could give out and pulled Morgan along with him.

"Mine," he murmured, nuzzling into her silky hair. "Be mine." He ran his fingertips along the side of her breast and could feel her heart pounding in her chest.

"Owen," she laughed, like he wasn't totally serious.

He demanded, "Say it again."

"What?"

"My name," he told her, "Say it again. I love how it sounds in your little American accent." He drew her arm across his waist, feeling the languid pull of sleep rolling toward him but not wanting to let her go.

"Owen," she smiled, "*Owen*. Could you not be so cute? It just makes me love—" she choked off abruptly, like she had something stuck in her throat.

When she stayed silent, he raised his head a fraction to peer at her face. "What do you love?" It was deliciously warm and cozy with her in his bed. It was everything he'd thought it might be, and so much more.

"I love the way you say my name, too," she replied smoothly, and her limbs relaxed against him.

Owen gazed at her quietly, contemplating the wonder of that. Finally, though, he gathered Morgan closer against his chest, rested his chin on the top of her head, and let his breathing slow until he'd lulled her asleep.

He loved more than her voice, he thought. How could he not? She was impossible to resist, especially like this. He had no idea what to do about it, however, or whether Morgan felt the same.

He had plenty of time to figure it out, though. Soothed by her softness in his arms, and the steady beat of her heart against his chest, Owen drifted into sleep, as well.

There'd be time enough for big decisions. *Tomorrow*.

THE NEXT MORNING, Owen woke slowly. Any coolness from the night before had long since dissipated, and his room felt stuffy and close—which meant it must be late.

Exactly how late it was remained to be seen. He'd been having more difficulty than usual getting up these days, but whether that was because he wanted to avoid the hassles that had been eating up his days, or because his brain had been saddling him with some oddly vivid dreams while it grappled with the Rathbone situation seemed immaterial.

Owen only knew he hated feeling so inept, and his subconscious was clearly struggling mightily with it. Of course, that wasn't all that he was wrestling with. There was also the problem of his housekeeper.

He jolted suddenly, remembering. *Morgan.* Had they really been together last night? In the light of day, it seemed impossible to believe, but his heart stuttered as image after image flooded his memory banks.

It had been incredible between them—better than he could ever have imagined. No way was it a dream. Just to be sure, though, Owen rolled over and pressed his face into the other pillow, and the fresh and clean scent of Morgan's hair flooded his nose.

That was good. However, it also appeared that he was a bloody blockhead and had overslept, since Morgan's side of the bed was decidedly devoid of her. And without her face to read, he had no idea what he'd be facing today.

Would she feel as ebullient as he did, or was she already regretting what they'd done? Owen didn't *think* he'd been terrible, but he'd also been so wrapped up in the sheer glory of it that he couldn't be sure.

Only one way to find out. He stretched and rose, then opened the shutters on his bedroom windows. There was no breeze, and the air stayed muggy and oppressive. He could use a shower, but he didn't want to wait even that long to lay eyes on Morgan.

As he tossed on an old t-shirt and some shorts, Owen thought he caught the scent of coffee brewing. Of course, he did. That woman was a goddess.

He ambled into the main room, and immediately spotted her on the back patio, leaning on the railing with a mug in her hand, gazing out across the glassy water of the lake. She was like a vision, standing there, and he tried to commit the sight to memory.

But it was hot out here, too, so Owen reached up to tug on the cord of the ceiling fan outside the kitchen. Morgan must have caught the motion out of the corner of her eye, because she turned immediately.

She smiled and sang out a chipper, "Hey! Good morning."

"Morning," he called.

As he stepped past his desk to join her outside, Owen noticed absently that the book he'd been reading had been moved on his desk. He trailed his fingers over the cover and wondered if Morgan had already managed to dust that morning.

It wasn't the first thing he would have done after what they'd shared, but what did he know? Still, she didn't usually rearrange his stuff when she cleaned, and it made him curious. Owen paused and let his mind return to the story, trying to remember where he'd left off.

He cracked the cover and let the pages shuffle open to his bookmark. Owen paged back, conscious of Morgan's eyes on him the whole time. Had she been peeking at his book, trying to get a bead on him before she took him to bed?

He glanced at phrases here and there and tried to see the storyline through her eyes. He tried to envision what she would've thought, knowing he was reading a love story like this one, night after night, so close to her.

And as he did it, clarity slowly dawned. Owen understood what had been vexing him about this cottage lately. He knew exactly what the unidentified nettle was, that had always seemed to be right at the edge of his consciousness, irritating and just out of reach.

He saw clearly all of the small steps they'd taken, linking together to lead them here. He'd never stood a chance. Loving Morgan was as inevitable as the world turning on its axis.

Owen hadn't liked how it felt to roll over and find her gone this morning, but if he wanted to keep her in his bed and in his heart, he was going to have to tell her how he felt. And maybe, just maybe, this book was the way to do it.

He glanced up at Morgan, still standing on the patio and smiling uncertainly back at him. Like the flower petals he'd already hidden in her locket, he could send her a message with his book.

Somehow. He had to figure out a way soon, though, because there was no way he was going to risk losing her. How long had he been in love with his housekeeper, anyway? And…would she grow to love him back?

He looked away from the book and something in the corner caught his eye. The dinner table against the wall had been set with the beginnings of a lovely-looking breakfast, with red and white flowers nodding in a vase at the center.

Morgan had also decorated a potted plant on the coffee table with small red bows and white paper snowflakes. Next to it lay a bulky package wrapped in tissue paper, a big red ribbon tied clumsily around it.

Owen wandered closer, taking it all in. Morgan came in the house, grabbed the steaming cup of coffee sitting next to his plate, and handed it to him. Then she stood beside him and looked at the plant, too.

"Merry Christmas," she said shyly.

He could feel the flush that worked its way up his neck. "My god, I'm such an ass," he told her. "I can't believe I forgot what day it is." He wrapped his arms around her waist and dropped a kiss on the top of her head. "Happy Christmas, love."

Morgan didn't sound angry. She seemed apologetic. "I hope you don't mind. I wasn't quite sure how to handle it since you never said anything. But it's my favorite holiday, so it seemed like a shame not to acknowledge it." Her hands felt tentative on his back.

"Of course, I don't mind. But you must think I'm obtuse for not realizing," he lamented. "Though, in my defense, I did have one or two other things on my mind yesterday."

He pressed a kiss to her lips, and immediately wanted to get lost in them again. Unfortunately, Owen also couldn't seem to take his eyes off that large, lumpy parcel on the table. Naturally, Morgan noticed immediately.

"It's for you," she said nervously, her cheeks turning pink.

She pulled back and crossed her arms over her stomach, and he blinked at the vulnerability coming off her in waves. "I have some things for other people, too," she continued, "Mainly little thank-you gifts, but if it's convenient maybe you could help me deliver them later."

"Whatever you need. I'm happy to help."

"I didn't want to make a big deal out of it. But everyone was so kind to me after Ruth…well, you know," she choked out, looking away. "I wanted to let them know how much it meant, even though I was a virtual stranger."

Her hand shook a little when she reached out and set it on the back of the chair. She was babbling a little, too, and Owen tilted his head, trying to understand what was going on.

Morgan spun away, went to retrieve the gift, and brought it to him.

"I think they felt very badly for you," he said, sitting at the table and smiling at how carefully she'd arranged everything. "Morgan, this looks terrific."

She set the big present gingerly in his lap. "Thank you."

He gripped the gift a little too tightly, and two of his fingers poked through the fragile tissue paper. He winced and looked up at her, hoping she hadn't noticed.

"Go ahead," she urged him, "Open it." Morgan slid into the seat next to him and shook off her memories. "I hope you like it."

Owen tore into the paper curiously, and instantly recognized the fabrics when he smoothed them across his lap. The remains of his old clothes had been combined with the fabrics she'd bought at the market, and there seemed to be a pattern to how they were sewn together.

Beyond that, though, Owen was baffled. "Thank you. I, uh—" He had no clue what else to say. "It's…"

What *was* it? A tablecloth? A technicolor dream coat?

"I know it's not quite the right season," Morgan rushed to explain, "But I didn't realize how long it would take to do by hand. My grandma taught me on a sewing machine."

"I see." *He didn't.*

"Miss Lenah ended up finishing it for me on her machine yesterday," she told him. "So it would be ready in time." She watched his face for a reaction, and Owen knew he couldn't keep sitting there like a log for much longer.

He wasn't effusive by nature—something she had to have realized by now—but was that even the proper reaction to…whatever he was holding?

Morgan looked crushed by his lack of reaction, though. She'd clearly put a lot of work into her gift, and was no doubt wondering if he hated it.

He had to think of something convincing to say. He was embarrassing himself *and* her—and that was before he even considered what he had to give her.

"I'm sorry. It's probably too big. I just…I thought you could use it when the weather cooled off," she said, her voice cracking. "I thought it would be a nice memento."

Owen was taken aback by her welling eyes and reached for her arm. "No, love—I'm sorry. I'm acting rude and ungrateful. It's just that I don't, uh…" Guilt seared across his cheeks like a bad sunburn. "Bugger it, I don't quite know what this *is*."

Morgan wiped at her eyes and lit up with a watery smile. She took the bundle from his lap and marched into his room. "Come here," she called.

Next to the bed, she shook out the armload of fabric and spread it across the rumpled duvet. Owen swallowed back a catch in his throat at the thought of exactly how it had gotten so rumpled and focused on what he could see *much* more clearly now.

"Look—it's a quilt," she said softly, gazing down at it. "I made it for you." She looked proud of the job she'd done, and he couldn't blame her.

Owen stepped closer and marveled at what Morgan had created. With bits of his old shirts and pants, and the new cloth from the market, she'd managed to piece together an exquisite savannah landscape at the center of a large circle, with colorful alternating stripes radiating out from the top like the rays of the sun.

Below the circle, varying rectangles of khaki and olive green stacked like bricks to the bottom hem of the quilt, evoking dirt and grass, moss and rock. Owen touched the rows of even stitches lightly, and when he did, he noticed several tiny birds and animals delicately embroidered onto the grass and trees of the central design.

It was a work of art, without question—one that had sprung from Morgan's incomparable heart and mind and hands. *For him.*

Owen was fascinated that she'd managed to accomplish something so extraordinary right under his nose. He'd been watching her all the time, but he'd never suspected a thing.

"It's beautiful," he breathed. "How on earth did you manage it?"

Morgan shrugged happily. "I had time to work on it at night, and like I said, Miss Lenah helped me finish it off. Do you really like it?" Her eyes were lit up like a kid's on…well, on Christmas morning.

Owen's eyes snagged on her mouth, where Morgan was nervously gnawing on her bottom lip. She wouldn't have nearly as much free time in the evenings as she used to, he thought. Not if he had any say in it.

"I love it, sweetheart. It's incredibly thoughtful and I don't think I've ever seen anything quite like it."

"I don't think I have either," she replied, relief stark in her voice now. "I kind of winged it." She backed out of his room and went to gather up the torn paper on the table.

"I'm going to finish cooking," she called out, "Are you hungry?"

"Famished," he said, mind spinning. "Need any help?"

"Nope. I'm all set."

Owen cast one more look at Morgan's lovely gift and sighed. He wasn't a total dunce. He hadn't forgotten Christmas *entirely*, even if it he'd put it out of his mind rather handily.

The fact that he'd been able to, underlined how long he'd been alone, far from family and childhood friends, and without a woman of his own. Too damn long, it seemed.

Between Tumelo's revelation and Morgan coming on to him yesterday evening, he'd lost track entirely of what day it was. And now, Morgan's kindness had him feeling like a fool.

Owen kept one eye on her in the kitchen, while he went to his desk and removed the envelope from the drawer. He could tell by the way Morgan was holding herself that she still felt nervous—perhaps about her present, or perhaps about what had happened between them last night. It was hard to tell.

If not for her, Christmas might have passed unnoticed and yet here he was, with nothing special to give her in return. Owen wanted to groan. He fingered the edge of the envelope and grew even more anxious about its contents.

A week ago, it had seemed generous—a lavish gesture that Morgan could interpret however she wanted. Today, however, so much had changed, and it no longer felt right.

In fact, it felt horribly *wrong*. But how could he have known that he would awake on Christmas morning, not only having spent the night with his housekeeper in his arms, but also having realized that he'd fallen in love with her?

Owen would definitely have found her a special gift if he *had* known, something to make clear how he felt about her. But now the die was cast, and almost anything he could go and get her would only come across as a lame afterthought.

Now, he was about to hand Morgan a check that would do nothing to assuage her worries and might even ruin everything growing between them. As Owen stood there, agonizing over what to do, she beckoned him to the table.

"Come and eat," she said, looking sexy as sin in her soft little shorts.

Morgan put a plate of food in front of him, then sat next to him and smoothed back the hair sticking to her forehead in the humidity. She fussed with her napkin and was about to lift a forkful of eggs to her mouth, when Owen put a hand out to stop her.

"Listen, Morgan—I have nothing to give you that compares to that blanket. But I...I meant for you to have this." He set the envelope next to her plate. "After last night, though, it just seems insulting." He grimaced as she reached for it, a question in her lovely hazel eyes.

"Oh. Well, thank you. But I didn't expect anything," she said, which only made him feel worse. She should have.

Owen pushed her plate back. He took Morgan's hand and turned it palm up, tracing the lines there carefully with his fingertip. "I'd like the opportunity to get you something better. Maybe for Boxing Day?" He cocked an eyebrow at her, and she laughed. "But you've earned this bonus, at least."

She looked curious, so he let her go long enough for her to lift the envelope and slide a finger under the flap. Morgan burst out laughing when she took out the check that he'd written her.

"My goodness," she murmured, eyeing him slyly. "So generous. Was I that good?"

"God, yes," he blurted stupidly, "That good and more. So good, in fact, that I don't reckon you could really set a price on..." Owen coughed and readjusted himself when he registered her face. He reached for his plate again. "You were joking, of course. As was I."

Morgan giggled, cradling that damn check in her hands thoughtfully for a moment before holding it out to him. "Owen, I can't accept this, anyway. It's too much. And you don't need to feel obligated to give me something just because I gave you that quilt. I did it because it made me happy, not to get something in return."

Owen was admittedly happy for the excuse to touch her again. He closed Morgan's fingers back over the bonus and gently pushed her hand back. "It's not because I feel obligated," he insisted, "I wanted you to have it. You deserve it as my housekeeper. But as my…as my…" He faltered, unsure what to call her now.

She raised her eyebrows at him, a sweet little smile curving her mouth up at the corners.

"I still want to give you something else," he finished lamely. Owen wanted Morgan to have a piece of Africa to keep with her, and a piece of himself to carry everywhere she ended up going. "I want to get you something special."

She smiled wider as she contemplated the food in front of her. "You gave me a lot last night," she said, then immediately bit her lip like she'd surprised herself.

"Happy to oblige," Owen chuckled, leaning over to kiss her soundly. "And I assure you there's more where that came from. The proverbial gift that keeps on giving."

"Joy to the world," she murmured, and stuck some toast in her mouth.

He suddenly had a very good idea of how the rest of their day was going to go, and his heart felt light at the thought. They were sitting here *flirting*, for crying out loud. It felt odd, but also wonderful.

Owen watched Morgan's flushed face as she ate and turned over in his mind what sort of present he might get her. Nothing seemed good enough, but he'd keep his eyes open, and maybe he'd know it when he saw it.

In the meantime, there was that book on his desk. It was one of his favorites, and he'd read it several times. It didn't take long to decide on which passage he'd leave it open to next. He only wondered how he would know if and when she'd read it.

December 25

And the award for Least Professional Housekeeper goes to...Yours Truly.
Apparently playing Nancy Drew with my boss was not enough—I had to add "with benefits" to my job title, too. I know ought to be ashamed of myself, but I can't quite bring myself to do it.
Sleeping with Owen was a revelation. It was spectacular. <u>He</u> was spectacular.
I can't even hate him for handing me a damn check the morning after, because he was so ridiculous and adorable about it.
We had ourselves a merry little Christmas, but I have no idea what is going to happen next.
Owen is an extraordinary man, and I don't know why he'd want someone as damaged as me. Eventually he's going to see that, too.

Chapter Thirty-Three

THE DAYS AFTER Christmas had felt like an idyll, running together into a blur of happiness that made Morgan feel like she was floating instead of plodding. It was a nice change of pace.

For weeks, Owen's troubles at the Preserve had seemed far away. Morgan had gotten to wake up to his handsome face every morning and drift off to sleep sated and content in his arms each night.

In between, she'd found herself anticipating his every smile or touch—afraid she had imagined them all but flushing with bone-deep contentment when they kept happening.

Owen kept a small piece of paper folded in his shirt pocket, and periodically his hand would drift to it. This morning, in fact, he'd presented it to a shopkeeper while Morgan had browsed around the store and pretended not to notice.

He'd been handed a small box, then gave her some shaky excuse so he could spirit it out of the store and into the pack stashed in the truck. Given the secrecy, Morgan suspected it might be something for her, but there was no time to find out for sure.

They weren't in town for fun today. They had a job to do.

That tip Kisima's brother had passed along had eventually panned out, and after a lot of careful planning, Joseph and Owen were finally ready to make a move on the Thorpes' secret location.

They'd even relented and assigned Morgan a small part to play. She'd had to wheedle and beg, and when that hadn't worked, employ some dirty tricks in her new-and-approved arsenal—emphasis on *dirty*.

But she'd won. So, if all went according to plan today, Kisima and her cousin Charlotte would search the Thorpes' rooms, the Temba brothers would bring anything they found to Owen and Joseph to photograph, and then Morgan would return the stuff so the ladies could replace it with no one the wiser.

It wasn't the best plan in the universe, but it was all they had. If it worked, however, they could gain much-needed insight into what Thom, Owen's boss Nigel, and the Thorpes were trying to accomplish by killing all those little gazelles.

And if they got lucky, Joseph and Owen might even learn who was helping the men, so they could avoid tipping them off while TANAPA figured out how to catch them.

While Morgan and Owen waited for the others to fulfill their tasks, they tried to act as if they were enjoying a simple day trip to Arusha. It gave them an alibi and a bit of distance from the real action, so after visiting a few shops that morning, they were now sitting in his truck in the scrub-grass parking lot of a busy café, making a production out of eating grilled rock lobster wrapped in naan.

Mount Meru rose into the sky not too far away, and the banana palms bordering the lot swayed in the breeze, their leaves a glossy emerald green.

It would've been easy to pretend they were on some marvelous, romantic date—if not for the TANAPA agent tucked under an old sheet on the floor behind their seats.

Poor Joseph was probably suffering under there in the heat, but he'd been determined to ride with them in case anything happened during the two handoffs—and equally determined to keep his presence a secret.

Joseph had a stash of water in his fort, along with snacks he'd brought from home. He'd stayed quiet for the most part, not complaining like she would've in his position.

Morgan had ordered him an extra lunch in the café anyway, and now, as casually as she could, she dropped it between the seats and passed him the paper tray filled with fried slices of banana and chunks of lobster wrapped in paper.

"Chin up, mate," Owen murmured. "Shouldn't be too much longer, I reckon."

Morgan had been privy to many of the men's discussions, but she still didn't know all the details of what was happening today. Maybe she never would.

Even though she wasn't sure what they were waiting for, she asked quietly, "So, the Thorpes are staying at some motel, right?"

"The Shadey Inn," Owen said softly.

It felt ridiculous to act so furtive, but they'd rolled down the windows to catch the breeze and none of them wanted to be overheard by the people cutting through the corner lot on their way to the café's front steps.

Since they couldn't put names and faces to all of the players in this game, they had no idea if they'd been followed or staked out. Joseph kept reminding them of that.

Still, Morgan had to laugh at Owen's words.

"What?" Owen's lips quirked up, but he looked confused.

"Don't you think it's a funny name?" she wondered.

Owen took another bite of his sandwich, chewed thoughtfully for a beat or two, then shook his head.

From under his sheet, Joseph whispered, "I don't understand, either."

Morgan rolled her eyes. "Where I'm from, *shady* means sketchy. Like something is disreputable or suspect."

Owen's smirk broke into a grin. "That's appropriate."

"Right?" Morgan laughed. "I told you."

"I hope they had the other meaning in mind when they named the inn," Joseph muttered.

There was some rustling, and then he complained, "I should've asked you to get chips. They'd be good with this."

"I had some," she told him, "Hang on, I think there's a few more." She sorted through the paper bag at her feet, then slid a box of them to their stowaway—but not before popping one more in her mouth.

Owen arched a brow at her, then mused, "If anything, I think it was wishful thinking. There can't be more than one or two small trees near the place. I doubt they make much shade."

Morgan shook her head and polished off her sandwich, then fished in the bag in case any stray fries had been left behind. She peeked around the parking lot, then murmured, "How much longer should we wait?"

"We don't want to draw attention by lingering too long," Owen told her. "Once we're done eating, we should move on to the next location."

"You know where to go?" Joseph asked.

"I'd have to be braindead not to." They'd reviewed the details over and over, to be sure no one made any mistakes.

"If we're not exactly sure what we're waiting for," Morgan wondered, "then how will we know when it happens?"

"Trust me," Joseph commented softly, "You'll know it when you see it." His hand emerged from under the sheet, sliding the remnants of his lunch toward Morgan's shoes.

Owen watched her stuff the trash into the bag and checked his watch. "Alright, I think we've played out this spot. Let's wrap it up."

He gathered their assorted napkins, bottles, and bags, and got out of the truck. As he ambled toward the big rusty trash can at the corner of the café, he carefully eyed the other patrons lingering around.

Morgan bent to scratch her ankle and whispered to Joseph, "Still doing okay?"

Whatever he answered was drowned out by the sound of a motorbike roaring into the grassy lot, though. Morgan watched as its rider, a man in a tan jumpsuit, went inside the café and emerged shortly after with a bag of food.

On his way back to his bike, the man pulled another bag from his jumpsuit and dropped it in the trash can where Owen was lingering. He was so engrossed by what was on his phone, he didn't even seem to notice the newcomer, and Morgan wondered if he'd gotten a text about the motel search.

The motorbike rider tore off as loudly as he'd arrived, balancing his food between his knees and leaning into the sharp turn out of the lot. He made such a commotion, Owen had to whistle sharply, to get her attention again.

When she looked back, he was holding the bag with the remains of their lunch high, pointing at it with peculiar emphasis. Morgan couldn't quite grasp what he was trying to tell her.

"I can't hear you over that motorcycle," she called, but he only squinted at her in confusion.

She held up her hands and shook her head.

Someone in the lot had turned on a radio, and between the music, the traffic, and the spirited lunchtime crowd, it was impossible to make out what Owen was getting at.

"What's going on?" Joseph hissed from below.

"Umm—" Morgan stalled, as Owen started toward the truck. "I'm not quite sure yet."

When he got closer, Owen held out one of the lunch bags. "Didn't you want to save these bananas, love?" he asked. "I think you gave them to me by mistake."

Morgan blinked at him in bewilderment. She hadn't eaten any bananas.

Owen jiggled the bag at her, though, so she took it and set it in her lap. It was quite a bit cleaner and markedly heavier than anything he'd walked away with.

"Thanks," she muttered, peering inside.

There *was* a fresh order of fried bananas right on top, steaming hot and dusted with sugar. She popped one in her mouth and chewed it slowly, wondering how he'd gotten it without her noticing.

"Okay, next stop," Owen announced, getting behind the wheel and putting the truck in gear.

When Morgan's hand drifted into the bag again, she encountered stiff cardboard instead of dessert. She let out a very undignified squeak and glanced at Owen quickly.

"Maybe you should share some of that with our ghost friend," he instructed. He brushed some sugar from her chin, then smirked and licked his fingers.

Morgan pulled out the treat, then put the bag on the floor between the seats, watching as Joseph's hand slid a battered accordion file free. He sat upright under the cover of his sheet.

Over the sound of the wind coming in the windows, she could hear him shuffling papers and taking picture after picture with his phone camera.

"Who was it?" Joseph asked, speaking louder now that they'd pulled into the flow of traffic on the busy road.

"Andrew," Owen called, "Dressed like a janitor."

Morgan sat back, impressed by how smooth the handoff had been. She hadn't even realized what was taking place. But if the Temba brothers were down here in Arusha, that meant…

"Wait," she said. "They didn't leave Kisima and Charlotte by themselves, did they?"

Owen rounded a corner and drove past the Barclays tower, tourists milling around its base, snapping photos as always. He picked up a road heading north and hit the gas.

"Don't worry," he told her, "There are other people working there. Besides, I don't think Thorpe's ever looked twice at her in the office."

"She said she was going to get new braids. Just in case," Joseph interjected.

Despite her concern, Morgan grinned at Owen. Kisima did love to try out new looks whenever her old style began to bore her.

Morgan caught at her own windswept mess, and futilely tried to smooth it back into some semblance of order. She wasn't half as put together as Kisima, but Owen seemed to like her hair, at least. He was eyeing it now the same way he had when he'd wrapped his fist in it a few nights ago.

Not now, she chastised herself, her cheeks turning hot. *This is important.*

They rode out of town and into the bush, eventually pulling off the road and up to a small rural store. They'd been here before—it wasn't far from the inn where the rest of their motley "team" was gathered. Owen took some money from his wallet and handed it to her, and Morgan steeled herself for her own little role in this play.

Joseph told her, "Take your time," and Owen gave her a warm wink. She slipped the money into her pocket, then set her hand on her door.

However, she paused when Owen murmured to Joseph, "So, what have we got?"

Owen was examining his fingernails like he was simply bored, but she could tell by the way his knee was bobbing up and down that he was anything but.

"It's just as I suspected," Joseph whispered back. "They have a bunch of surveys, but they're fifty years old."

"From the Brits?" Owen wondered.

"Yeah, looks like it. Only problem is, after independence, the government conducted several more surveys in your area, and all of them were more thorough than these. They proved once and for all that none of the little pockets marked on these maps have enough diamonds to merit a mine—just low-grade scraps scattered here and there."

"So why use the old surveys?" Owen asked irritably. "That's a stupid mistake."

He glanced at Morgan and gave her a little nod. "Time to go, love."

As they'd planned, she got out of the truck and headed inside the shop, then wandered aimlessly around for a minute or two, randomly grabbing drinks and snacks off the shelves. Once she thought she'd taken up enough time, she set everything on the counter, and waited to see what the man behind it would say.

If he completed the transaction and told her to have a good day, they still had plenty of time to peruse the documents some more. But if he told her she didn't have enough money, it was going to be a signal that the heat was on at the inn, and the documents had to be returned as soon as possible.

The cashier disconnected his call, dropped his phone in his pocket, and looked her dead in the eye.

"You need more money," he said grimly. "A lot more."

Morgan left the stuff on the counter and darted for the truck, heart pounding. Owen pivoted in his seat as she approached the passenger window.

She could hear Joseph explaining, "After 1964 or so, people like the Thorpes wouldn't have had access to the new surveys without connections in the new government. Maybe these maps were all they could get their hands on. It's possible they don't know more surveys were done."

Owen grunted in agreement, then asked her, "What's up?"

"I forgot my bag!" she exclaimed, loud enough that the small knot of men loitering near the side of the building could hear her.

Owen bent to pick it up and hand it to her, but Morgan had one more line to deliver. "And I need more money," she added, holding his gaze. "A lot more."

He swore under his breath. In the bright sunlight, his eyes glowed an almost luminous gold, the startling green of them melting into something closer to bronze. He looked like a lion, all of a sudden.

"Two more minutes," Joseph whispered.

Owen looked toward the front of the store, where the cashier was standing with his hands on his hips. Without the counter blocking their view, they could see that his short-sleeved shirt was untucked, and his khaki pants were frayed at the hems. His battered sandals seemed too big for his feet, too, like he'd dug the outfit out of someone else's bag of cast-offs.

"Sully's out of uniform and looking testy," Owen told Joseph. "I don't think you have two minutes."

"Sorry!" Morgan called, trying to sound cheerful. "I'll be right there!"

He scowled at them, to all appearances the epitome of a shopkeeper pushed beyond the bounds of patience. Morgan had never met the Temba brothers, but to her, the performance was entirely believable.

She turned back to Owen, mentally begging him to hurry while he pretended to dig in his truck's console for cash. Owen picked up on her nervousness right away, of course, and didn't appear any happier than Morgan was to be cutting it close.

"*Joseph*," he warned. He moved to rummage through his glove compartment, stalling some more.

He murmured to Morgan, "Hang tight, love. Almost there."

At last, Joseph announced, "That's it. I've got all of it now." His hand snaked out from under the sheet. Owen grabbed the file and slipped it into Morgan's shopping bag, then handed her everything through the window.

"Thanks." She followed Sully back in the store, where it only took him a minute to ring her up and exchange the file for the groceries. A second after that, Morgan was back in the truck and trying to make herself breathe again.

"We're done," Owen told her, dropping his hand to her knee and giving it a squeeze. "Now we go home and wait."

"Did I do okay?"

"More than okay. If the Thorpes have anyone watching us, there's no way they saw through you. You were terrific," he said.

Morgan exhaled. "I was nervous. I didn't expect Sully to rush me."

"I know. But I'll make it up to you later, I promise." He glanced at her quickly as he put the truck in reverse. "Remember those gifts, I promised you? When we get home, I'm going to give them to you, and then we're going to talk."

"Oh really?" That sounded kind of serious.

On the floor, Joseph cleared his throat, reminding them of his presence.

Morgan rearranged the bag at her feet, and Owen asked, "What'd you get, anyway?"

"Beer and snacks," she laughed. "With the way people drop in on us all of the time, I figured we could use them."

Before he could come up with a retort, a woman approaching the store in a pale green maid's uniform caught his eye. Owen slammed on the brakes and watched her march inside.

After she'd come back out and driven off, he chuckled and reached down to poke at Joseph. "Now Patty's a cleaning woman?"

From under the sheet, Joseph let out a muffled snort. "I told you Kisima would be fine."

Morgan frowned. "I thought her name was Patricia. Does she prefer to be called Patty?"

Owen pulled onto the road. Once they were out of sight of the store, Joseph flipped the sheet off and sat up between the seats. "No, she does not," he said. "If Hargreave ever called her that to her face, he would not escape unscathed."

"For the record, I have an aunt named Patty," Owen protested hotly. "And I love her."

"Well, my wife hates that nickname. She says it makes her sound like a hamburger."

Morgan smiled. "I'd like to meet her properly sometime."

Joseph nodded. "Once this whole thing is over, we'll arrange something."

"I'll look forward to it."

Owen glanced at her. "I wish I had more things for you to look forward to. I'll have to work on that."

Morgan shrugged. Like so much between them, it would have to wait.

"Hargreave," Joseph said, "There's something I haven't told you yet." His tone was grim.

Morgan cracked open a bottle of cola and took a sip, then frowned down at the label. The brand was a common one in the U.S., but it didn't taste quite the same.

Owen snagged the bottle from her and took a long drink, then prompted Joseph, "What is it?"

"It looks like Cotton's applying for a change in status—he's saying there are no more Rathbones left in the Preserve."

Owen was silent for beat, and then he sighed. "What does he want? As if I can't guess."

"To allow mining in B and C Quadrants. Shocking, right?" Despite his wry tone, there wasn't even a hint of amusement in Joseph's expression.

Owen looked equally bleak. He clearly tried to be a responsible steward of the small portion of Tanzania that had been entrusted to him, but he'd confided to her that he wasn't sure how much longer the Preserve could continue functioning as a private park, or whether it even ought to. She wondered whether he was thinking of that, now.

Owen pulled into a derelict-looking fuel station and told them, "Sorry, guys. The mileage on this thing stinks. I'm going to gas up. If that's okay."

Once he got out, Morgan asked Joseph, "Shouldn't TANAPA have known about that filing? It seems like the different agencies would share information like that."

"That's a very good question," Joseph replied. "And one I intend to find an answer to."

WHEN THEY ARRIVED back at the cottage, Owen angled his truck in a deep patch of shade out front. He left his door slightly ajar when he hopped out—giving Joseph a discreet and sheltered exit from the truck in case anyone was watching.

Morgan followed Owen inside, as if nothing at all unusual had gone on that day. He dropped his pack in his room, and she went into the kitchen to unload the bag of groceries.

As he leaned his shoulder against the door jamb and watched her, she felt reflexively for her necklace. The last thing they needed was for her to have lost it somewhere they'd been today, but despite all the times the clasp had slipped open, the thing was still where it should be.

Smiling a sexy, secret little smile, Owen told her, "I'm going to make sure we got everything out of the truck. Be right back," then slipped out the front door again.

Morgan had found the petals he'd left in the locket a few days ago, but she hadn't mentioned it yet. Maybe she'd wait and see what their big talk was about before she did.

She put the beer and cola in the fridge and wandered over to the window to see what he was up to.

He stood beside the truck, patting his pockets like he'd forgotten something. Owen reached in and fished around between the seats, no doubt making sure that Joseph had managed to slip out successfully.

Soon, he straightened and slammed the door shut, then messed around with something in the truck bed for a bit before he returned inside.

He met her eyes as soon as he crossed the threshold and gave her a barely perceptible nod. *Success.*

Joseph was free, but would he come inside to talk or find his own way home? They hadn't worked out that detail beforehand.

Morgan felt grubby and hot after driving around and pretending to sightsee for most of the day.

"I feel gross," she said. "I think I'm going to go change."

"Do what you must with your clothes," Owen smiled, "but leave the rest of you as is. I'm growing quite fond, if you must know."

She gave him a quick peck, then went into the bathroom to splash some water on her face. What she really wanted was a shower, but passed on it for the time being, in case Joseph decided to stop in.

Instead, she replaced her t-shirt and cargo pants with a fresh tank top and loose gauzy skirt that felt comfortable and cool in the humidity.

When she emerged again, Owen was just sinking into his desk chair. He leaned back and let his eyes drift from her hair to her toes, and back again, and leaving a trail of fire in their wake.

"Do you want tea?" she asked him.

"Only if you're going to make it for yourself."

He shifted to stare out at the lake, glittering like a mirror beyond the back windows. The water looked glassy against all the bright green vegetation ringing it, and the black and white patches of ibises stalking in the shallows.

Morgan turned to the kettle, and he murmured, "Why would they launch an undertaking like this on the basis of such poor information? So many Rathbones have been killed. For what? Money? It will take us years to undo the damage to the herd."

"Maybe the harm is reversible," she said. "There are probably a lot of agencies that could help, too."

Suddenly, a loud thump sounded in the bathroom. Owen shot to his feet. It'd sounded like something heavy landing on the shower floor. Morgan stood frozen in the kitchen, an empty teacup gripped in her hand.

Joseph's face appeared at Owen's bedroom door almost instantly. "Sorry—it's just me," he smiled. "Didn't mean to spook you."

Morgan let out the breath she was holding and poured Owen his tea. She didn't seat the cup on its saucer properly, though, so when she tried to set it down, it sloshed down her leg. With a sigh, she handed Joseph the cup she'd set aside for herself, then walked to the back of the house to close the shutters.

Once the main room was safe from prying eyes, Joseph followed Owen to the couches. They looked up at Morgan expectantly, like she was supposed to sit, too.

"Give me one second," she said, heading for the kitchen. "I just need to grab another mug." *And try to clean off the second set of clothes I've trashed today.*

In the living room, Owen said, "I'm glad you stayed. Do you think the brothers will come by, too?"

"It's possible. They might have more information for us."

Owen asked him, "I wonder why they needed everything back so fast. I figured we'd have to hurry, but that seemed especially quick."

Morgan went back over and sat in the armchair next to them, tucking one ankle behind the other and cradling her cup in her palms. "Something must have happened at the inn, don't you think?"

Owen was staring at her ankles a little too intently. She cleared her throat and gave him a look, so he'd knock it off.

Joseph looked thoughtful. "Perhaps. But I think they would have found a way to let us know if it was very serious."

Once Kisima had confirmed where the Thorpes were, the plan to search their rooms had developed quickly. Kisima and the Temba brothers had enjoyed the promise of skullduggery more than they probably should have, and it was now clear that

Owen and Joseph were worried the group had taken things too far.

Morgan realized that she felt too restless to sit there and wait calmly for news that might not come tonight. So she jumped up and carried her cup into her bedroom, then set it on the night table. She got the teapot from the kitchen and brought it out to the men, setting it on the coffee table where they could reach it.

"Won't you stay?" Joseph asked, looking perplexed. "I'm sure it won't be long before we hear something."

"I need to take care of a couple things," she said, hoping she wasn't offending him. "Just give a holler when you guys have news."

It seemed to placate him, because he smiled quickly. "We will."

When Morgan glanced at Owen, though, he was frowning, like he was trying to figure out what she was up to. He tried to cover it with a smile too, however, so Morgan resolved to explain herself later, when they were alone.

Alone. Her heart still gave a little flip when she thought about it, and she wondered how long that could last. At some point, she'd have to get used to the swooping butterflies Owen set off every time his lips touched her skin.

Preferably before she had to go home again.

She shut her door and sat on the big mahogany bed, its gauzy mosquito netting drifting down from the canopy like something out of a dream. Morgan sipped her tea and gazed fondly at the little landscape painting she'd bought at the market one day, now propped against the mirror on her dresser.

Something about it—the mood, perhaps, or the hazy lighting—captured the animals and countryside she'd seen on her safari far better than her own photos probably did.

Memories of the trip swamped her, and Morgan set her cup down and knelt beside the bed, sliding her largest duffle bag out from under it.

She unzipped the top and dug around in its dark recesses, finally finding the travel journal she kept during the expedition. Leafing through it, she was amazed by the things they'd been lucky enough to see.

Morgan studied her careful notations in the margins of the pages, marking where photos had been taken and which roll of film they were on. When she went through the book and tallied them up, she realized that she must have used a dozen or more rolls of film. Hundreds of photographs, sitting undeveloped in a bag under her bed, and she'd never thought once about them.

Somewhere, thousands of miles from here, she possessed a brand-new digital camera, undoubtedly still in its box. Morgan vaguely remembered deciding that it was "too nice" to bring on the trip. She hadn't wanted it to break or get lost or stolen.

Instead, she'd brought her father's bulky old film camera, with its long-range lens in a separate case. It was heavy as a workhorse, but her dad had sworn it would be just as dependable.

She rooted through the bag again, finding all the canisters of film so she could sort them into neat rows on her night table.

Fourteen rolls of film, altogether. At least she'd labeled them well.

Morgan gazed at the little black tubes thoughtfully and decided that tomorrow she'd ask Owen where she could get them processed. She wanted to see each of the steps she'd taken to get here, but wondered if any of them would stand out as significant.

It already felt as if the last two years had happened to someone else. Morgan didn't feel like the same person anymore, and that was probably a good thing.

A sudden burst of laughter from an unknown voice in the other room jolted her out of her reverie. Morgan hadn't noticed the arrival of new guests, what with all the self-reflection she was doing, but it was clearly time to head back out there.

Maybe this person had come bearing the information they'd all been waiting for. She should go see.

Morgan left the travel journal on top of her bed and tried to slide her duffle bag back under it. She kept meeting resistance, though, so she got down low and peered into the dusty gloom, trying to figure out what could be in the way.

There was some kind of packet, worked up into the slats on the underside of the bedframe. It must have shifted when she pulled her luggage out before, because now one corner hung down enough to block her bag from going back in.

Curious about what it could be, Morgan flattened herself against the floor and slid halfway under the bed, then picked at it with her fingertips until she'd pulled it all the way free.

She sat back on her heels and opened the file, and immediately recognized those grisly photos Owen had accidentally shown her. They were all there—Thom, Stephen, and every poor gazelle—stacked on top of handwritten reports and other, more official-looking papers. Whatever this was, it was important, and no one was supposed to know it was here.

Morgan put the packet back together and tried to replace it, but quickly realized it wasn't going back in the way it'd come out. The mattress was far too heavy for her to lift from below, and if she tried to do it from above, the file would end up too close to the edge for secrecy.

Owen had to have been the one to hide it here, but she had no clue how he'd accomplished it. Brute strength, probably. She couldn't ask him for a repeat performance, however—not until the other people visiting the cottage had left.

So, Morgan stood up and cast around her room for a new, secure location. Her first two ideas turned out to be unworkable, but she finally found the perfect spot. After she stowed the file, she stood and dusted off her hands, satisfied that it was safe for now. Later, she'd have to remember to tell Owen where it was, so he wouldn't worry if he noticed it was missing.

With that accomplished, she picked up her cup and peeked out her door, looking for who had arrived. The man she saw looked young and fit and seemed relaxed as he joked with Joseph and Owen. He must have heard her door open, however, because he turned immediately toward her with a grin.

Morgan's mouth dropped open when she registered his face. There, on the couch, was the motor-biking janitor from the café earlier, now wearing a striped golf shirt and pressed khaki pants like he was a real estate agent, instead of a covert poacher-hunting agent.

They all chuckled when she edged into the room and stopped, rooted next to the arm of the sofa where Owen sat.

"Perfect timing," he said. "I'd like to introduce Andrew Temba. You are not going to believe what he's been telling us."

Chapter Thirty-Four

OWEN WATCHED MORGAN'S expression transform from wary to intrigued as she realized who was sitting across from him.

"It's nice to finally meet you," she said, stepping forward to shake Andrew's hand.

Owen had learned the hard way that the scout had a startlingly strong grip, but Morgan didn't even blink—she simply held on, her palm dwarfed by the scout's as he gave it a few hearty pumps.

"Likewise," he smiled back. "I must say, my brother and I have heard a lot about you." His English had taken on a cultured, faintly British cadence for the first time in Owen's short acquaintance with the young man.

Owen glanced at Joseph and was met with a knowing look in return. *The pretty girl effect*—what a surprise.

Morgan looked faintly alarmed, however. "How concerned should I be right now?" she asked.

Owen rolled his eyes and patted the couch next to him. "Not at all," he told her. "After today, I'm guessing you won't be the most interesting thing in town anymore."

She parked herself primly beside him. "That sounds promising."

Once she was settled, Joseph leaned forward. "Andrew just told us about Kisima's exploits at the inn. It's quite the tale."

"Is she okay?"

"Oh, she's right as rain," Temba explained. "We all stopped for a drink before Patricia brought her home."

Morgan's eyes were shining with interest. Owen couldn't resist picking up the story. "She probably needed it. She and Charlotte had a little excitement when Stephen came back to the room too soon."

"*No,*" she breathed.

"Bugger went straight for his files, too," Andrew laughed. "Except, as you've probably guessed, the ladies hadn't had a chance to put them back yet."

Morgan's eyes went wide. "What did he do?"

"Well, it sounds like he caught Charlotte on her way out. He made her wait while he looked around, and when he discovered that his stuff was missing, he marched her straight to the inn's office."

While the scout polished off his tea, Joseph took up the narrative again, "Kisima was waiting for Charlotte in the laundry room, and she saw it happen. She called Sully and told him they needed the papers back immediately, then went back to Thorpe's room and acted like she was cleaning the bathroom."

Andrew cut in again, telling Joseph, "You guys got to Sully just in time. When Patricia brought the files back, Stephen and the manager were putting Charlotte through a holy inquisition in the breezeway. They didn't even realize Kisima was in the bathroom."

Morgan looked a bit dazed, and Owen could hardly blame her. "But... did they get the files back where they belonged?" she wondered.

"Shockingly, yes. Patricia passed the files to Kisima through the bathroom window," he said. "She wheeled her cleaning cart out of the bathroom, leaned behind it to set the brake, and slipped the file behind the dresser."

"No one *saw*?" Morgan demanded.

"Apparently not," Temba shrugged. "They said Thorpe was having a full-blown tantrum, pacing around and threatening everyone. The manager was trying so hard to calm him down, it took Kisima a few tries before she could get their attention." Andrew looked smug, no doubt relishing Thorpe's panic as much as the rest of them.

Owen hadn't heard this part of the story, though. "Is that where they found the file this morning?"

"Apparently it was taped to the back of the mirror above the dresser," Andrew clarified. "Kisima thought it might look like it'd slipped to the floor on its own. Quick thinking, if you ask me."

Joseph agreed, "She's very clever. I'd hire her in a heartbeat if she was the least bit interested."

Temba nodded. "Anyway, once Thorpe stopped to take a breath, Kisima grabbed the manager, insisted that they hadn't taken a thing, and demanded that he describe what had supposedly been stolen. The poor guy was a wreck, but he got Stephen to admit where the file was supposed to be. After that, the manager found the file all by himself. It couldn't have been more perfect."

"*Whoa*," Morgan breathed, gaping at the scout along with Owen and Joseph.

"Thorpe has definitely gotten on the guy's bad side already." Andrew grinned when Joseph snorted, then went on, "The man hustled the ladies out of there and never stopped to ask Kisima and Charlotte who the bloody hell they were—or why they were dressed as chambermaids at his inn—until they were safely tucked in Patricia's car and about to leave."

Temba collapsed into laughter, while the rest of them sat there stunned. It had been a close call, but somehow it had worked. Owen and the TANAPA guys owed Kisima and her cousin, and then some.

There was one small loose end, however. "Were they able to get anything from Sir Mark's room?" Owen asked.

Andrew shook his head. "Sorry, no. There wasn't time."

Something brushed against the edge of Owen's hand just then, tentative and light as goose down. He glanced down to see Morgan's fingers grazing his, hidden from the view of the others by a fold of her gauzy skirt.

He met her eyes and nodded as reassuringly as he could. *It's okay*, he tried to tell her. *All's well that ends well.*

If only he could believe it himself.

THE NEXT MORNING, Nigel strolled into Owen's office with a look of disgust. Dispensing with civility, he snapped, "Hannity's gotten himself into a fix again. You need to run up and fetch him."

Owen sized him up.

The Preserve's director was rumpled, and his usual dye job was starting to grow out. There was at least a half inch of startlingly white hair sprouting from his scalp, contrasting starkly with the rest of the tepid brown strands.

For a man as vain as Nigel, the lapse seemed like a neon warning flare. Owen's boss was coming apart. Why?

The peculiar request he'd made was setting off alarms as well, pricking along Owen's nerves like a thorny rash. Cotton had been keeping Thom busy—and away from Owen—for a while now. Sending Owen to bail him out was something he would've done in their pre-Thorpe days.

"Terrific. Where is he?" Owen sighed, with what he hoped was convincing resignation.

Nigel checked a slip of paper in his hand. "F Quad. Not too far." He turned to go.

"Wait—what happened? Is he at an outpost, or what?"

"The field station called down a few minutes ago. Sounds like he had a row with a scout or something."

Owen groaned.

"Kid's lucky no one shot him in the arse," Nigel muttered. "But you'll get him, yeah?"

"Yeah. I'll get him," he said.

Nigel made it across the threshold before turning around again. "I…won't be here when you get back," he said slowly. "I've got to…wrap up a few things with TANAPA. About that whole Rathbone business we had."

"Had?" An ominous chill shivered through him. "What do you mean, 'had'?"

Nigel hardly bothered to feign regret. "Lost the last of them a few days ago," he said. "Awful business, that. Never could understand it."

Owen stared at him, speechless.

Nigel took another step, then paused yet again. "I hope that while I'm gone, your little cleaning wench doesn't make off with any of my papers. I'm not nearly as understanding as others." With that, Cotton gave him a hard look, then strode to his own office and shut himself firmly inside.

Owen was, in a word, dumbfounded. How had Nigel discovered Kisima's involvement, and why was Owen more worried about Morgan, right now, instead of the possibility of a mole in the investigation team, or the supposed extinction of the gazelles?

He wasn't in the habit of ignoring his instincts, however, so a sliver of foreboding crept down his spine.

He checked his watch and considered how to cover all the bases in this game. F Quadrant wasn't too far away, but if it took a while to iron out Thom's mess, it was possible he'd have to crash at the field station tonight. Since that would leave Morgan alone and undefended, he decided he'd better line up someone to check on her later. Just in case.

Joseph was the obvious choice, but with Nigel still hanging around, it seemed best not to call him from the office. If need be, Owen could always drive by Teleki's place on his way to get Thom.

As a backup, however, he dialed the Twospeaks' home. If Cotton overheard, so much the better—at least he'd be on notice that the cottage wasn't empty, and Morgan wasn't on her own out there.

God. The thought was enough to freeze the blood in his veins. Owen prayed he was overreacting.

A feminine voice crackled over the line. "Hello?"

"Hey, Christine. It's Owen Hargreave."

"Hi! I've been meaning to stop by one of these days to thank Morgan for her wonderful gifts."

"I'm sure she'd love to see you," he said. "And actually, that's why I'm calling. Is Conrad in town?"

"Yes and no. His tour ended yesterday, but he's out doing some restocking right now. What do you need?"

"I was hoping you two could look in on Morgan later. I've got to run up to the Preserve unexpectedly, and I'm not sure if I'll have to stay the night."

Christine laughed a little. "Surely she can handle one night to herself."

"Of course, she can. It's just…it's a long story, but I'd feel a lot better if you guys could do it," Owen fumbled.

Christine hesitated, but at last she agreed, "Okay, then. We'll pop over after dinner, if that's okay. I'll tell Conrad when he gets back."

"Thanks, love. I really appreciate it."

"Owen…is Morgan doing all right out there?"

"Oh, she's fine. No worries," he assured her. "She'll be glad for the visit, that's all."

Owen was already congratulating himself for his efficiency when the woman threw a wrench in the works. "Well, even if

Conrad can't make it, I can always go with Thom and Carol," she said. Like that was helpful.

Immediately, Owen realized his mistake. His heart sank. Christine clearly had no idea that Thom was being detained up in the Preserve, and Owen had been so distracted by Nigel's odd behavior, that he'd forgotten all about her sister's connection to Thom—and to Sir Mark.

Bugger. Owen had stepped in it, and then some.

"I don't suppose Thom's there now?" he inquired, in what he hoped was a friendly tone. If Christine said yes, at least he wouldn't have to haul up to F Quad.

"No, neither of them are—but I think they're planning to get together tonight. That's what Carol said, anyway."

"Great," he said, feeling sick. "If anything changes, I'll let you know, aye?"

"Sounds good," Christine chirped, and hung up.

Owen set the receiver carefully in its cradle. A grim thought had begun to gnaw at him. What if, by trying to safeguard Morgan, he'd let his enemies know how important she was to him? What if trying to protect her had painted a target on her back?

Tramping after Thom felt more wrong by the minute. Since he had no idea what he was walking into, he couldn't bring Morgan up there with him. He had to go, though.

Owen checked his watch again. There wasn't enough time to drive Morgan out to Nadra's or Kisima's if he really wanted to make it back sometime tonight—and he'd have to get on the road soon.

Owen didn't want to alarm her for no reason, but he rang Morgan's phone anyway. She sounded unconcerned when he told her that he'd probably be home late—if at all—and to be sure to lock up after the Twospeaks left.

Owen reasoned that she still had the gun Joseph had left her—but if push came to shove, would she remember how to use it?

He rose and began to gather his things, but he couldn't shake the feeling that Morgan was a sitting duck out at the cottage. He tried to brush it off as paranoia, or evidence of his deepening feelings for her, but the gooseflesh prickling across his shoulder blades wouldn't subside.

He consoled himself with the thought that Teleki would know what to do. Between the TANAPA agent and Conrad, Morgan would undoubtedly be protected until his return.

He couldn't stall any longer. With one final look at Nigel's door, Owen hoisted his pack and stalked out.

The weather had been oddly dry for weeks and on the way to Joseph's, Owen drove so fast that he raised heaps of dust. He had to keep the windows down so he wouldn't swelter in the stifling humidity, and by the time he pulled up to the Teleki spread, he could feel the grit that had settled in the creases of his eyes and elbows. He could only imagine how disreputable he must look.

Owen needn't have worried, however. The moment he slowed in the drive, Patricia came out of the house, shaking her head.

"He's not here," she called, like she'd been expecting him and was none too pleased that he'd arrived on schedule.

She waved Owen away with absolutely no ceremony, then marched back into the house. He hadn't even come to a full stop, before she'd gotten rid of him.

Owen accelerated again, turning his truck around and making for the highway that would carry him to F Quad. He couldn't stop wondering what in the world he'd gotten into, though.

Patricia had been reserved before, but never outright unpleasant. Her strange behavior seemed like yet another bad omen, so he gunned the engine and pushed the truck faster.

Owen dialed Joseph, just in case. Predictably, the call went straight to voice mail, so he left a message, and then tossed his phone aside. He had to concentrate on getting to Thom as quickly as possible, anyway.

Owen couldn't fathom what the bloke had gotten himself into this time. Nigel had mentioned a row with a scout and that the field station had phoned, rather than Thom himself—but how much of that could he believe?

In the old days, Owen would have assumed that this was about drinking, gambling, or a woman—or some unfortunate combination of all three. These were different times, though. F Quad might be far from the bulk of the Rathbone killings, but he couldn't be sure this dust-up was unrelated.

Assuming there'd been a dust-up at all.

Owen drove northwest from Joseph's for close to an hour, eventually cutting into the Preserve through a checkpoint near the bottom corner of the park. The afternoon sun was glaring through his windshield, and he was glad for the relief of the tree cover along the little-used path.

Owen plowed doggedly ahead, finally pulling up to the field station after three separate stops to hack at the encroaching bush.

He shut off his engine and sat there, breathing deeply and trying to calm himself for whatever awaited him within.

Once he felt like he had a decent chance of keeping his cool, Owen got out of the truck, attempted to brush the dust off his face and arms, and stepped up to the porch.

All was in order out here—the low thatched roof in good repair, the little yard tidy and the undergrowth cut back. Two well-maintained vehicles sat off to the side, parked in the shade of a *mpingo* tree. The personal cars of the scouts, he surmised, eyeing them. As far as he knew, neither of them belonged to Thom.

Owen trudged up the three shallow steps and went inside. The screen door swung shut behind him, and he immediately found himself in the middle of a brawl. While he waited to be acknowledged, he tried to pick up the thread of the argument.

The head scout glanced at him, nodding briefly in recognition before continuing his tirade. Finally, Owen picked out enough of the Swahili to interject.

He entered the fray with, "There's a problem with Mr. Hannity, aye? I've come to take him off your hands."

The room instantly fell silent and all eyes turned to him. Owen counted three assistant scouts in addition to the head scout on duty but didn't see Thom. As quickly as they'd stopped talking, everyone began speaking at once again.

The head scout cut them off with a piercing whistle and a slash of his hand. He gave his assistants a severe look, then switched into English.

"We do have a problem, Mr. Hargreave, but not the one you came here for," he intoned stiffly. "It seems Mr. Hannity decided to take his leave a bit prematurely."

Owen's mouth dropped open. "Excuse me?"

"Apparently, these gentlemen were unable to keep him restrained until your arrival." He cast them another withering look.

"*Jesus*." Owen pinched the bridge of his nose. "Is he on foot?"

As a unit, the assistant scouts looked away, each of them guiltily studying a different corner of the room.

The head scout scowled at them. "No, he is not. It appears that Mr. Hannity liberated my car for his escape."

Owen blinked. "You're joking, aye?" The thunderous look on the man's face was answer enough, however, so he asked, "Did you see which way he went, by any chance?"

This time, one of the junior scouts raised a hand. "I did. He took the goat path, there. It heads south, and eventually meets up with the Arusha road."

Owen was already out the door and heading for his truck. "What kind of car is he driving?" He listened to the particulars as he got behind the wheel, then finally thought to ask, "Incidentally, what did you bring him in for to begin with?"

The head scout sighed wearily and gestured to two of the men. "Someone called in a tip. They found him burying some gazelle bones, and we knew you'd want to talk to him."

"We looked, but there was no carcass nearby," an assistant chimed in. "We thought maybe he brought them from somewhere else."

Another added, "Wouldn't tell us where he'd gotten them, though. If we'd had more time, we could've found out. Bring him back when you find him."

Owen's shoulders slumped. He'd prayed it wouldn't be this. "Did you bring any of the bones up here with you?"

"No."

Owen told the head scout, "Cordon off where he was digging and place a couple of guards. Don't let anyone near it until you hear from me directly."

With that, he started his truck and tore down the narrow track, mind spinning. As he left the field station behind, Owen tried to divine where Thom might be headed, and whether he had a snowball's chance in hell of catching up with him before the bastard did something stupid.

He thought once more of Nigel, disheveled and coming apart at the seams. He thought about Patricia's rudeness and Morgan, too—alone at home, with no one around for miles.

Something was very wrong here. Owen was certain he'd been set up, but whose hands was he playing into?

Chapter Thirty-Five

MORGAN FINGERED THE necklace of tiny bluish-purple beads she'd been wearing since last night, and remembered Owen's strong, warm fingers fastening it around her neck once everyone had left.

"Tanzanite," he'd said, "So you'll always remember me." As if she could possibly forget.

He'd touched the gems lightly, then kissed the back of her neck, and Morgan had been lost.

Later, Owen had given her a sweet little hippo figurine, too, that he said had been carved by his grandfather on his honeymoon. Morgan had felt a little guilty about accepting it, but Owen had insisted. There'd been a whole explanation about the inviolable nature of Christmas gifts—which, in retrospect, had been total nonsense.

Morgan smiled as she finished folding the clothes she'd taken down from the line, and stepped from her room. Owen had called a while ago to tell her that he wouldn't be home until late, and that Conrad and Christine were planning to stop by later.

She knew she ought to eat something, and maybe make Owen a plate for when he got back, but the thought of eating dinner alone had her dragging her heels. It was so much better when he was around. Owen had a way of filling the entire cottage with his warmth.

Still, a snack wouldn't hurt. Morgan was halfway to the kitchen when she heard the first creak. It was so faint that she paused for a moment, thinking maybe she'd made it herself. In that second, however, she heard another floorboard. That one was loud and directly outside the front door—and clearly made by an individual much heavier than she was.

Morgan froze. The hairs on her neck stood on end and her chest felt tight. For a split second, she wondered why she was so sure it wasn't Owen.

Then front door crashed open and three men surged into the house, brandishing guns and shouting in Swahili.

The first of them ducked immediately into the kitchen and systematically began tearing it apart. The second entered Owen's bedroom, where Morgan could hear him doing the same. The last intruder pulled Owen's desk over on its side, then pushed savagely past her to get to the living area. He began sweeping the various artifacts off the shelves, letting them smash on the floor.

No one could have missed her standing there, but they also hadn't acknowledged her yet—so Morgan backed toward her room and the gun she had stashed there. Her lungs felt like they wanted to curl in on themselves, and she fought to swallow the distorted, fearful sound trying to escape her lips.

Morgan didn't want to get trapped in her room, but the men could also cut her off easily if she tried to make a break for the front or back doors. However, if Owen's bathroom door was still closed, there was a chance she could grab the pistol, then climb on the stool and get out through the shower.

She frantically tried to picture the outside of the house. If Morgan hurried, she might be able to hide in the trees before they noticed she was gone. And soon, the Twospeaks would arrive and scare the men off.

Her heart pounded painfully in her chest. What if they didn't leave, though? What if Christine and Conrad got hurt by accident?

Morgan forced her feet into motion again, hurrying around the foot of the bed. She didn't want to think about what those brutal, unknown men might have planned for her, but she had to get to that gun under her mattress.

It sounded like they were destroying everything they touched in the other rooms. Morgan's hands were shaking and her vision seemed oddly unfocused, even though random things jumped out at her with hyper-definition.

Her shoe, on its side near the nightstand. The lampshade, off-kilter. Owen's folded t-shirts in a neat stack on the chair.

Morgan took one step, then another, and another. But before she got any farther, the man in Owen's bedroom came barreling through the bathroom, followed almost immediately by another coming through her bedroom door.

She was cornered—hemmed in by the wall on one side, the bed on the other, and the night table behind her. Morgan put out a hand to steady herself and felt the little hippopotamus Owen had given her.

It was solid and heavy, so she grabbed it, thinking any weapon was better than none. Then she wrapped her arms across her stomach and waited to see what they would do.

The men alternated between shouting at her in Swahili— none of which she could understand—and tearing apart her room. They yanked clothes out of her armoire and pulled the drawers from her bureau. They kicked her chair on its side and ripped the covers off her bed.

They seemed to switch languages when they called to their companion, who had moved on from the kitchen to the contents of Owen's desk, searching through the papers and office supplies until they were scattered all over the floor.

Morgan had no clue what they were demanding, so she just kept shaking her head at them. They grew more agitated. They crowded closer and the room swam. One of them grabbed her arm and yanked her away from the nightstand.

He pulled out that drawer, too, sending lip balm and condoms skating across the wood floor, then shoved the mattress askew with his hip and discovered Joseph's pistol. The third man came in and tossed him the rifle from Owen's room.

He threatened her with a gun in each hand—turning nearly purple with rage when she repeated, "I don't understand you. I don't know what you want," again and again.

He wasn't in charge, apparently. When that man stepped closer to her, the other two instantly drifted back. Morgan searched his face, looking for some shred of conscience—his features were severe, though, and twisted into a hateful expression.

Before she could say another word, he slapped her hard across the face, the sound cracking through the room like a shot. As Morgan blinked back the stars dancing across her vision, he grabbed her cheeks, keeping her from falling with fingers that dug into her skin.

The man stared into her eyes and dragged his hands down her face, then slid them further along the sides of her neck. He dug back under her hair and knotted his fists there.

He focused intently on her, each gesture calculated and measured for effect. When he stepped forward, crowding her up against the night table, Morgan's skin crawled with fear.

Her assailant stared at her mouth, then let his gaze drift pointedly down to her breasts. His hands tightened in her hair. Morgan felt a wave of nausea slither through her.

It felt like her consciousness had come unmoored from her corporeal body, floating up and over her shoulder to perch, disembodied, near the ceiling—like it had decided that what was coming next could not be endured within her physical frame.

Morgan watched herself and the men from above, at the same time she saw things from her usual vantage point—and the duality of it alarmed her. She didn't dare close her eyes, though it meant that cruel face would be seared into her memory for eternity.

The other two were still yelling incoherently, but Morgan could feel the stone hippo digging into her palm. She weighed whether cracking it against her attacker's skull would get her anywhere, but it was like he could read her thoughts on her face.

All at once, his hands released her hair and tightened around her throat. He let her gasp for a second or two, then yanked Morgan out of her corner. She stumbled, coughing, toward the bedroom door—but he was right there next to her, gripping her arm and dragging her into the main room.

The man's fingers dug into her skin. She tried to swallow, but her throat wouldn't work right, and she couldn't think of a single self-defense tactic. Morgan needed to *think*, but her brain felt sluggish and disjointed.

Abruptly, the men stopped shouting, a trio of bulls staring at her like they were waiting for her to say something. In the peculiar quiet, she heard another car outside. A door slammed. Feet crunched across the gravel. Someone else was here.

Morgan looked from face to face, desperately trying to figure out their intentions, but she didn't like what she saw. She edged back, her bare feet scraping on the broken pieces of pottery and glass scattered underfoot. They followed her, flanking her and not allowing her to put any distance between them.

Morgan shook her head, frustrated tears welling in her eyes. "I told you—I can't understand you. I don't know what you want."

A glimmer of an idea had crept in, however, like a cold wash through her veins. Maybe Morgan did know. There *was* something important hidden here. Could they tell?

Possibly. The putative leader cocked his arm and punched her in the face so hard that the room exploded in a burst of red. Her body sailed backward, but the fall seemed to last forever.

Morgan hit the floor with a bone-jarring shock, and the man's boot was there, grinding her cheek into the shards on the floor. He spoke without yelling this time, but his tone was so ugly, it sounded even worse.

"You know…what we look. Where…are… paper?" he asked in slow, halting English. With every word, his boot pressed harder.

Morgan coiled her body into a ball as best as she could, feeling the tears in her eyes and the blood on her face. The other two were still close by—she could feel them, too.

Slow steps rang out on the porch. The boot left her face, but only to prod her onto her back. Her attacker leaned in, peering at her neck, then ripped her locket right off her. Morgan gasped at the searing pain, but he ignored it. He only stepped back to examine his prize and slip it quietly into his pocket.

A tremor of expectation hung heavy in the air, and Morgan wondered if he was deciding his next move. She didn't want to wait for it, not with the front door so tantalizingly close. She forced down her pain and pushed herself to her hands and knees, getting ready to make a run for it.

Fresh air blew across her cheeks like a benediction, and new footsteps tapped slowly across the floor. The three pairs of boots flanking her hadn't moved. Morgan didn't dare move, either. She sank lower to the floor and braced herself.

The person stopped nearby but stayed out of her line of vision. When Morgan tried to peek at him, one of the men nudged her roughly with his boot.

A few curt words were exchanged in Swahili, and then more in that other language.

At last, the new arrival said to her, "Dabbling in things you do not understand comes at a price, Mrs. Flynn." The man's speech was accented, but unlike the others it had a posh, sophisticated cadence to it.

"The next time you visit a new country," he continued, "Perhaps trouble yourself to learn the language. I think you'll find it comes in handy on occasion."

Morgan was shocked that he knew who she was, but it solidified her suspicion that this was no random home invasion.

Those impeccable leather dress shoes shifted closer. "You do know, if your man has anything hidden here, we will not stop until we've found it. We will discover what he knows, and we will destroy him for interfering," the man boasted. "I shall let you be now, so you can tell him that."

He turned and walked out the door. Morgan craned her neck, squinting through her swollen eyes to get a look at him, but she could only catch a glimpse of his immaculate white linen blazer before he descended the porch steps.

One of the original three followed him out, pulling a cell phone from his pocket to answer a call. "No. Nothing…yet," she heard him say, in that same hesitant English.

Two goons remained. The first kicked her in the side, and when she toppled over, in the leg. The last stomped viciously on her forearm, sending a shock of agony streaking through her. Morgan's mouth gaped wide, but she couldn't even summon a scream. She could only shrink into herself and wait for the next blow.

Mercifully, it never came. Instead, the men marched past her and out the door. She heard the gravel of the driveway crunch under their feet, their vehicle doors close, and the engine noises fade as their cars pulled away.

She stayed where she was for a long time, watching the shadows among the ceiling beams get deeper and deeper, until eventually they swallowed the room. The usual twilight sounds of insects, birds, and frogs seemed muffled. Morgan could feel her pulse, thumping in her skull and her arm like the beat of a drum.

She knew she should stand up and call someone, but every inch of her body hurt. There was a vague fear taking root, too, warning her that someone could have stayed behind—and was just waiting for her to move before they sprung.

The front door creaked on its hinges in the breeze.

She cracked one eye, but the other one seemed to be swollen shut. Morgan squinted around her narrow field of sight, taking in what she could in the scant light from the rising moon. Nearby was the narrow wall that separated her bedroom door from Owen's.

A short expanse of parquet floor lay between her and Owen's room. No unusual sounds came in the windows, or through the door. Morgan couldn't even hear her own breathing, but soon realized that was because she was holding her breath.

She let it out in a rush and winced at the sudden, white-hot pain in her ribs. Each shallow breath was an agony and seemed impossibly loud. Every one of her senses felt brittle with terror.

She wouldn't know if she was truly alone unless she moved. She couldn't get help, unless she summoned it. She had to try.

There was a rumpled mound on the floor, several feet away near the foot of Owen's bed. She couldn't tell what it was but if she could get to it, she could hide behind it, under his big mahogany four-poster. If any of those men circled back before Owen returned, they might assume she was gone.

Against the grain of the floorboards, a small splash of color revealed what she was seeing. Morgan rolled painfully to her knees and dragged herself toward it, her teeth beginning to chatter like it was February in Boston. It felt like it took her forever, but when her fingers finally made contact with the soft material, she pulled it around her shaking frame with a ragged groan.

She clutched the stone hippo in her fist. Morgan was too tired to find her phone, but she had just enough energy to wedge most of her body under Owen's bed.

She tried to stay awake—to wait for Owen and the Twospeaks so she could warn them of the danger. The pain was too much, though. Morgan couldn't hold off the soft darkness creeping in at the edges of her vision and she had only one thought before she gave in to it.

Was Owen okay, or did they find him, too?

Chapter Thirty-Six

OWEN SPED OBSTINATELY down the road to Arusha for a full twenty minutes before he finally admitted to himself that he was never going to catch up to Thom.

The man had too much of a head start, for one thing. For another, Owen couldn't imagine where he might be headed and wandering aimlessly would not be an efficient use of his time.

What was more, he still had a bad feeling about all of this. There was no denying something was very wrong, but Owen still had no clue what it was. However, the fact that his mind kept snagging on the thought of Morgan out at the cottage by herself was not a good sign.

And so, at the next crossroads Owen turned the wheel left and cut back toward home. If, by some chance, Thom still intended to meet up with Carol tonight, then Owen needed to get to Morgan before they did. No telling what might happen, otherwise.

He didn't *think* Thom would try anything dodgy with Carol and Christine there, but the man had not exactly been playing by the rules lately. Plus, Carol herself was a bit of a wild card, and they still had no idea how far she'd gotten pulled into the

Thorpes' schemes. Juggling Thom and Sir Mark wasn't a mark in her favor, though.

As Owen flew along the cracked ribbon of asphalt, winding through the lush greenery that lay between the southern edge of the Preserve and home, the drive still seemed interminable. The rising urgency he was feeling only made it worse.

If he wasn't holding his breath, then he was breathing too fast—in quick, shallow gasps that brought in nothing but heavy air tinged with the scent of loam. He shouldn't have been conscious of his breathing at all, given the circumstances, but Owen couldn't seem to force it into any regularity, even with concentrated effort.

He grabbed his phone off the passenger seat and tried to call her, and when Morgan didn't pick up anxiety was a living thing, clutching his heart in its talons. He forced his old truck to go faster.

Why was he so sure that she wasn't okay?

At long last, though, Owen reached the meandering dirt drive that led to his cottage. He turned into it with relief but was almost instantly confronted with a shining black Mercedes, roaring out of the darkness, right for him. Owen jerked the wheel to the side in the nick of time, plowing the passenger side into the high bushes clumped on the verge.

The car streaked by in seconds, but Owen still marked the driver—none other than Stephen Thorpe, smirking behind the wheel with a nattily dressed, older version of himself riding shotgun in a white linen jacket and fedora.

Sir Mark, no doubt. Stephen snapped off a sardonic salute as he passed, and the smugness of the gesture turned Owen's blood to ice water. They hadn't even tried to hide their identity—didn't even care that he'd seen them.

"*Fuck*," Owen hissed. He worked the truck back onto level ground, then gave it some *jandal*, pressing the accelerator to the bloody floor.

At the house, he nearly collided with the back of Conrad Twospeak's truck—another unwelcome surprise. Conrad and Christine were getting out, like they'd only arrived themselves.

"Who the hell was that?" Conrad asked. "Bastards nearly took us out when they burst out of the trees back there."

Owen didn't bother answering, but the guide was quick, assessing Owen's panic as he sprang toward the front door and refocusing quickly. Twospeak scanned the front yard, tucked his wife behind him, and fell into line.

"What's wrong?" Christine called. "I thought you weren't coming back until later."

Owen eyed his front door, yawning open and showing only disconcerting darkness within. He hesitated on the threshold. "Did you two open this?"

Conrad came up the steps cautiously. "No. We only got here a minute before you."

Owen swung the door wide and stepped inside. "Morgan? Where are you, love?"

Even in the gloom, he could tell the house had been trashed. When Morgan didn't answer him, his pulse thundered louder in his ears.

Behind him, one of the Twospeaks fetched a flashlight and now they pointed it into the house. Christine gasped, "Holy crap. What happened?"

Owen edged forward, scanning the room with practiced eyes and ears, looking for signs of life. He tried to edit out the Twospeaks, moving awkwardly around, but helpful details were still in distressingly short supply.

Christine stumbled, cracking something under foot. "Sorry! I can't see where I'm going," she whispered. When she shifted, it sounded like more broken shards were nudged aside.

"I think the power's out," Conrad said, flicking the wall switch up and down. "I'll go get a couple lanterns from my truck."

"Be careful," Christine told him.

Owen held still and tried not to lose his mind. "Morgan? Are you here?"

Nothing. Not a word. He swallowed back the sour taste creeping up his throat and prayed those arseholes hadn't just spirited her out of here, right under his nose.

Christine murmured, "She's got to be here somewhere. Give her a minute. Maybe she hid from them."

Conrad returned and handed over the lanterns. At the entrance to the kitchen, he held his high, illuminating the wreckage within. "Not in here," he announced.

Owen's heart felt like a frantic, wild thing in his chest. He directed his own light into the corners of the main room, seeing plenty of destruction but no pretty housekeeper.

While Owen considered Morgan's doorway with crawling dread, Christine took her lantern into his bedroom. She let out a sudden squeak, so he rushed to her side.

"God, she scared the daylights out of me," she gasped, crouching down. "I thought it was just a blanket."

Owen searched the floor, finding Morgan wrapped in the quilt she'd given him, and wedged under the footboard of his bed. He fell to his knees beside her head, but even with all the commotion, she didn't move a muscle.

Christine reached out to take her wrist, like she was going to feel for a pulse, but Morgan curled tighter into the blanket with a guttural moan. Owen let out a breath. *Alive.*

Christine tugged gently on the edge of the quilt, saying softly, "Morgan, honey, it's Christine. Are you okay?"

Morgan's eyelids flickered, but that was it. Owen sent Conrad a desperate look.

"We need to get her out of there," the guide said. "But I don't want to make it worse if she's hurt."

Owen glued his eyes to Morgan's face, searching for signs of…anything, really. Christine tried to stroke her back, but she recoiled immediately, grunting in protest.

She was in pain.

Damn it. They'd hurt her.

Owen reached out and gently touched her shoulder. "What do you say, love? You want me to get you out of there? You'll be more comfortable in bed, aye?"

Morgan blinked again. It sort of sounded like she croaked, "Okay," but he couldn't be sure. Her grip stayed tight on the edge of the quilt, and she didn't budge.

"I can ring up the medic I use on my tours," Conrad offered, "if you'd rather not use one of the Preserve's people."

Owen weighed his options. "Actually…see if you can reach Joseph Teleki." He handed his phone to him. "He's in my contacts. If you get him, tell him what's happened and ask him to send the doctor who treated me when I was shot," he said.

It seemed like the easiest way to let Joseph know what was going on, without raising any inconvenient questions. He glanced around at the mess and added, "I had her number in my desk, but god only knows where it is now."

Christine looked from her husband to Owen. "So, you're going to move her?" she asked.

He wasn't sure it was a good idea, but he nodded.

"Which bed are you going to put her in? I'll put it back together for you."

"Mine is closer," he said, "but she'll probably want to be in her own space." He hated the idea as much as he hated the sight of Morgan's bruised and swollen face, but this wasn't the time for him to get all territorial and start raising eyebrows.

"Okay, give me a couple of minutes. Don't lift her until I tell you," Christine instructed. She picked her way through the bathroom and disappeared into Morgan's room, holding her lantern high so she wouldn't trip again.

"Never mess with the boss," Conrad chuckled in her wake.

"Don't intend to," Owen murmured. Christine had to have weathered a crisis or two, in her marriage to Conrad. She'd be handy to have around while Owen unraveled what to do next.

There was no telling how Morgan had managed to squeeze herself under the bed like that.

"I can't reach Teleki," Conrad announced after a minute or two. "Do you remember the doctor's name? Maybe I know her."

"Amelia something. I can't remember." Owen leaned to the side and tried to get a better look at the bottom half of Morgan's body. Was she on her side or her stomach under there? It was hard to tell but would make a big difference when he tried to slide her out.

"Maybe we ought to go with your guy for now," he murmured. "The sooner someone looks her over, the better."

"Agreed," Conrad said, gazing down at her. He hesitated, then added, "And I wouldn't worry—he can be discreet when the need arises."

Owen looked up sharply at that, but Conrad only tossed him his phone and put his own to his ear, wandering casually into the other room.

For the moment, Owen and Morgan were alone. He leaned down and gently brushed the hair back from her forehead, then kissed her lightly. The skin around her eyes was turning dark, and one of them had swollen shut entirely.

There was an array of small cuts and scratches across her cheek, and thin, angry red lines on both sides of her neck. Morgan was still wearing the tanzanite necklace he'd given her for Christmas, but her locket was nowhere in sight.

Owen swallowed painfully, trying to balance his savage need to go out and avenge this catastrophe with the opposing need to stay and take care of her.

"Hey sweetheart," he whispered into her ear, "Can you hear me?" He waited, smoothing his hand along her skull until she murmured something.

Owen tried again. "I have to get you out of there, love. I'm going to pull you toward me, then lift you up for a minute, so I can put you in your bed."

"*No*," Morgan whimpered, scrunching her eyes even tighter shut and shaking her head. "Hurts." After a moment of consideration, she tacked on, "Happy you're here."

At least, that's what he thought she said. That last part had been faint and mostly garbled and was probably wishful thinking on his part. Pathetic of him, to cling to it at a time like this.

"Listen, love, there's a doctor on the way. They're going to take a look and see what's wrong," Owen told her. He worked his hands under her shoulders. "Can you tell if anything's broken?"

Morgan didn't respond to that.

"Sweetheart, the floor's starting to get cold." He let her go and stroked her hair again, since it seemed to be the only part of her that wasn't battered. "I need you to help me out a little bit. Roll on your back and get ready. I'm going to tug you out, but I'll try to be careful. Okay?"

Suddenly, Morgan's good eye popped open and gazed at him. Between her ravaged features and fearful expression, Owen's heart clenched painfully in his chest. *Oh, god.*

"Hi, Beautiful," he smiled softly. "You ready?"

Morgan stretched her hand out and painfully gripped his forearm, oblivious to both his questions and his endearments.

"They didn't get them," she whispered urgently, demanding his full attention.

Owen's smile faded. "Get what?"

"Papers. I hid them," she insisted. "Better than you."

"What papers?" He examined her face, baffled. Had she hit her head? Was she even lucid?

Her voice sounded steady and sure, however. "That file you put under my bed. I found it. I moved it," she said, tightening her grip. "They didn't find it."

"*Jesus*," he whispered, knocked back on his heels with shock. Was that what this was about?

"Owen? Is that okay?"

"Yeah, love, it's okay. You did good. Real good. Thank you."

She exhaled and released him, then seemed to gather herself for a bit before she let go of the quilt and gingerly readjusted until she was flat on her back. Even in the lantern light, her face looked pale.

"How we doin' in there, Christine?" he called out.

"Done. Are you ready?"

"Yeah. We need to get this over with. Right now." Owen hooked his hands under Morgan's arms and braced himself, then pulled her out from under the bed as quickly and smoothly as he could.

Morgan started crying. "They didn't see it," she wept, tears spilling across her cheeks. "I moved it. They kept yelling at me, but I didn't tell them anything."

"Okay, darling. There's a good girl," he said, sliding his arms gingerly under her shoulders and hips and lifting her carefully.

When he stood, she let out a sharp cry when her weight shifted against him. Owen winced, but Morgan's warm, welcome scent surrounded him, unchanged by her injuries and as seductive as ever. A sharp flare of desire arrowed through him, utterly out of place, but inescapable.

"Off we go," he told her. He wanted to bury his face in her hair and never come up for air.

When he started walking, Morgan let out another, smaller whimper, then fainted clear away. Her arm dropped awkwardly out to the side, and there was a loud clatter as something rolled from her palm and hit the floor.

Looking down, Owen recognized the little hippo statue he'd given her for Christmas, pale gray and gleaming near his foot. He couldn't reach it, not now. Morgan was drooping against his chest, completely unaware that she'd lost it.

Why did she have it, though?

Owen would have to wait for the answers he needed. He maneuvered out of his bedroom door, sliding his feet along the floor so he wouldn't slip on the papers and shards of pottery strewn everywhere. It took forever to go ten feet.

By the time he'd worked his way to the side of her bed where Christine stood waiting, Morgan's eyes were open again. She stared at him in confusion. "Where—?"

"Here we are," Owen said, "Here's your bed." He tried to lay her down as gently as possible.

"Your eyes are always so green," she murmured, frowning. "Why can't I see them?"

Even like this, he was taken with her. "It's too dark." He smiled, but she flinched when he let her go.

"Too many pillows?" Christine asked briskly.

"Yes," Morgan said through clenched teeth.

Christine shouldered Owen aside so she could rearrange pillows and straighten out the bedding. She removed Morgan's new necklace and laid it carefully on the nightstand. Owen eyed those vicious red streaks on her neck and wondered if her locket had made them.

Morgan's hands were fluttering around at her sides, feeling the pockets of her shorts and the mattress near her hips. He went to retrieve the hippo, then carefully slipped it into Morgan's hand when Christine turned away. She gave him a grateful look as she wrapped it in her fist and hid it under a corner of the blanket.

Once as she had it back, she started to relax. Owen fetched the quilt for her, too, but beyond that, he was at a loss.

"Can I make you some tea?" he asked.

"No thanks," she murmured, watching Christine remove her sandals.

"How about a sling for that arm?" Morgan had it tucked up against her body and was favoring it pretty heavily.

"I'm okay, Owen. Really."

He looked to Christine for help. The medic might not arrive for hours. He had to do something for Morgan *now*, or his head was liable to explode.

Conrad took his arm and pulled, leading him away. "Christine's got her. Why don't we take some photos of this mess, and then you can tell me why you aren't calling the police right now."

Owen retreated reluctantly. He wanted to be the one with Morgan, but as Christine dabbed at her face with a wet towel, trying to clean away some of the dried blood, he realized he couldn't just stand there and watch.

The Twospeaks were bound to get ideas, and Owen had no idea whether Morgan wanted to tell other people about their change in relationship status yet. He had no idea how far her feelings extended at all, come to think of it.

Next to him, Conrad was efficiently taking pictures from every angle he could manage, then texting them to Owen bit by bit. Owen walked around and took several shots of his own, then looked for anything that might answer the standard who, what, where, and why.

It was useless without the lamps. He attempted to right his overturned desk in a fit of frustration but needed help to do even that. Conrad swooped in and grasped the other end, and they set it gently on its legs.

Owen tested it carefully. "Seems to be sound."

Conrad studied him, his broad face cut into severe lines in the flickering lantern light. "I took a look at the generator," he said. "There wasn't too much damage—only a couple of snipped wires. I tried to splice them. Want to see if it worked?"

Owen picked his way to the kitchen and was rewarded with a bright splash of light when he flipped the switch—and a more depressing view of the destruction around him.

"The medic wasn't far from here," Twospeak told him. "He shouldn't be too much longer."

"That's good," Owen replied, nodding. "Thanks."

The guide waited another moment, then cleared his throat. "Hargreave, might I ask what the hell is going on here? You asked us to check on Morgan—but then you showed up at the same time we did. If you expected trouble, why did you leave her alone in the first place?" Each accusatory word hit with the sting of a razor-sharp claw.

Owen flexed his fingers and exhaled carefully, debating how much to reveal.

"I'm a little—no, a lot—surprised that you aren't phoning the police to report a break-in and an assault right now. I'm wondering why you don't seem particularly shocked."

Owen had a sudden thought and met the other man's stare. "Wait—did Thom come by to see Carol today?"

"What does that have to do with anything?"

"Just tell me. Thom was supposed to see Carol this evening. Did he?"

Conrad narrowed his eyes, looking him over. "How did you know that?"

"Christine mentioned it this morning when I called." Owen tried to keep his voice casual, but it was hard. "Did he ever show?"

"Yeah. He stopped by for her, but she'd already left," Twospeak said, looking away.

"When?"

"Maybe five thirty or so. But what does that—"

Owen cut off the man's question. "Do you know where Carol went?"

"No. I got home after she left. Christine only told me that a friend had picked her up, but she didn't know who it was."

Owen's mind was jumping ahead now, lurching into agility and making connections once more. "Did Christine tell you what Thom did when she told him Carol was gone?"

"She said he tore off with the devil himself at his heels, but if you don't mind me saying, he's always been a bit of an odd duck," Conrad said. He gathered some papers from the floor, glanced at them briefly, and set them on the desk.

"That's it?" Owen pressed.

"Yeah. He looked surprised, then took off." Twospeak scratched his head and looked around. "We try not to get involved, you know? Those two mix about as well as oil and water. God only knows what she sees in him."

From the next room, Morgan suddenly cried out, "Don't touch that!"

Owen and Conrad rushed to her door, where Christine was standing with her hands up—like someone had pulled a gun on her.

"I don't know what I did," she exclaimed. "I was just trying to straighten up a bit while she rested." Keeping one eye on Morgan, she bent down and reached for a drawer on the ground. Clothes spilled from the top of it and were trampled across the planks of the floor nearby.

"Please don't," Morgan begged. She turned that over-bright hazel eye on him. "Owen," she implored, "She *can't*."

"All right," he said calmly, like he was talking down a cornered beast. "Shall I do it? It will be much easier for the medic to move around if we've cleared a path for him."

He felt like snapping and growling at Christine for upsetting her. Owen was aching to climb into that big bed with Morgan and fight off any and all threats that dared come near.

Christine nudged the drawer toward him with her foot, blinking at Morgan like she'd gone around the bend. Morgan simply stared at Owen as he bent down, grasped the sides of the drawer, and turned to the armoire next to him.

It wasn't until he placed a hand on the bottom to feed it into its tracks, that he understood the problem. Morgan had said she'd moved his secret file, and Owen had just discovered where. She must have fed it under the rails on the bottom of the drawer, the clever woman.

He slid the drawer into the armoire carefully, then did the same with the other one. Morgan relaxed into her pillow with a sigh.

Somehow, those drawers had both landed top-up when they'd been pulled from their cabinet—dumb luck if ever he'd seen it. Owen was only happy they'd been constructed from such heavy wood.

"Isn't that better?" he asked her. "Let's pick up the others now, aye?"

She nodded. "Thanks."

Behind him, Christine whispered, "What was that all about?"

Just then, a vehicle pulled onto the gravel out front, saving Owen from having to answer. The Twospeaks stepped out of the room to greet the medic, and he hurried to Morgan's side.

"Anything else?" he whispered, knitting his fingers with hers.

Morgan's good eye had closed, and her chest rose and fell in shallow, even breaths. She'd fallen out again.

Voices came through the front door, and Owen looked around one more time. Whoever had tossed the place had gone about it very sloppily. It couldn't have been professionals.

Which made him wonder—had the search for incriminating evidence been the focus of this sortie, or the attack on Morgan?

He couldn't help but remember her friend had died in the bush, only months ago. Owen felt chilled to the bone as he weighed whether that was important or not.

Still, someone was going to pay for this. Even if he had to deliver the bill, himself.

Chapter Thirty-Seven

MORGAN SPENT THE following days in a gray haze of pain. Her thoughts drifted, but often seemed to beat with a one-word refrain, like a pulse. Hurt. Hurt. Hurt. Hurt.

Owen was a steady presence at her bedside, and only Kisima and Christine's visits could convince him to eat and shower and rest.

Information was in short supply. As far as she knew, Owen had managed only a brief conversation with Joseph, but hadn't heard from the man since. It was concerning, but not as much as Owen's caged tiger routine, or his insistence that she keep Joseph's gun close, just in case.

The tense blanket of expectation that hung over the cottage had been lightened only once, the afternoon before, when Kisima shared the news that Nadra had finally brought a healthy, ten-pound bruiser of a baby boy into the world.

The family had named him Godwin, and the pictures were predictably adorable. Morgan felt encouraged by how easy it had been to look at his tiny, scrunched face—and not immediately think of her own loss. She was healing, in more ways than one, and it gave her hope.

Unfortunately, those good feelings didn't last long.

Christine Twospeak had stopped by soon after, bringing a basket of fresh produce from the market, her sister Carol, and Thom Hannity.

There'd been a tense standoff at the door, and Morgan had worried that Owen and Thom might come to blows. The sisters didn't know what Thom had tried to do to her, though, and Owen was too much of a gentleman to start a brawl in front of them, even when he was cross-eyed with fury.

He'd admitted the visitors, then blocked every effort Thom made to get closer to her for the entire ten minutes he'd permitted them to stay.

Morgan's skin still crawled when she thought about the way Thom had sounded, full of oily solicitude even from across the room. It'd been a show designed for his girlfriend and her sister, no doubt—but it had also felt like a pointed jab at Owen.

Morgan had tried to stay civil while they'd all chatted with her, but Thom's watery blue eyes had glittered as he took in the sight of the bruises on her face and the cast on her arm. It had thoroughly creeped her out.

She'd had to search out Owen's gaze over and over to remind herself that he was there, an impenetrable wall between her and harm. Thom, keen-eyed as a cat, had noticed, of course. If he'd been holding on to any lingering hope that he still had a chance with her—or that Morgan wasn't holding his near-date rape against him—the chilly reception surely buried it once and for all.

When Owen had reached the end of his tether and shooed them all out, Thom had looked different than when he'd arrived. Diminished, somehow.

They had no proof that he'd been involved in the attack, but after he'd left Morgan couldn't help but wonder. With Owen's explanation of where he'd been in the hours before he'd come home that awful night ringing in her ears, she'd known in her soul that redemption was going to be elusive for Thom.

The threat of that last, mysterious man still banged around in her skull, looming over her day and night. Owen swore he'd be careful, but the sense that they didn't have much time hung in the air like acrid smoke.

Someone had to do something. *Fast.*

WHEN CONRAD'S MEDIC arrived some time later to assess her progress, Morgan sent Owen out to the living room in the hope that he might catch a short catnap on the couch while she and the doctor talked.

Morgan knew he had to be exhausted. He occasionally dozed off in the chair beside her bed, but as far as she could tell he hadn't slept in a real bed for over a week.

Thankfully, her idea seemed to have worked. She only heard him pacing the floor for a moment or two before he flopped onto the sofa with a huff, and then fell silent. She'd never met someone who could drop off as quickly as he could.

Owen a light sleeper, however.

And he must have heard the medic packing up his case, because just as the man was preparing to leave, Owen staggered into the room, looking groggy and disoriented and blocking the way.

The medic—a compact, tidy man with an excellent bedside manner—waited patiently while Owen adjusted to consciousness.

He scratched at his stubble, then asked, "How's she coming along, Doc?"

"Very well," the man told him. "Ms. Flynn's ribs are going to bother her for a while yet, but they seem to be healing well. I want to keep the cast on her arm, though. Just to be on the safe side."

He'd already reviewed all this with Morgan, but if she'd learned anything about Owen during her recovery, it was that he was a nervous nelly hiding in tough guy clothing. He always asked for all the details from the doctor, then wanted them again from her.

Owen's eyes skittered over her face, and he looked a little apologetic when he wondered, "What about her eye?"

Morgan knew what he was thinking. Every time she looked in the mirror, she was a little taken aback by the bruises on her face, too. She looked like she'd gone ten rounds with a very competent boxer.

"Well, the swelling's obviously gone down quite a bit, so that helps. Even though it still hurts, I don't think any of her orbital bones were broken."

The medic looked at her quickly, then turned back to Owen. "I could tell for sure with a CT," he added tentatively, then rushed ahead when Owen stayed quiet, "I could take x-rays of her arm, too, and her ribs. Just to be sure, you understand—not because I'm truly worried. I could check if there are hairline fractures, or…or…" He trailed off when he registered Owen's stormy expression.

"Is any of that necessary to her well-being?"

"No. But I run a clinic down in Arusha," the doctor tried. "I could do it all myself. To assure Ms. Flynn's total safety and privacy."

The medic had tried to convince Morgan of the same thing minutes earlier—but she, too, had turned him down. She and Owen had agonized over the decision to have her treated at home instead of in a hospital, but given how little they knew right now, caution still seemed to be the best course of action.

Owen shook his head, as emphatic as she had been. "I'm sorry. We can't risk it. We still don't know who was involved. They could follow us down there."

When the medic opened his mouth to argue, Owen forestalled him by adding, "Until we *do* know who did this, bringing Morgan to your clinic—or any clinic—is a bad idea. We'd be noticed, and there would be talk. It's safer if we limit how many people know about what happened and how she's doing."

Owen checked her face, confirming they were still in agreement on that point, so she gave him a small smile and a thumbs up.

The medic frowned in thought. "If I may," he said, "It occurs to me that if more people knew, they might be persuaded to help you. They could assist in finding the thugs who did this, through channels you aren't even aware of."

His round spectacles glinted dangerously, reflecting the sunlight streaming in the back windows. His voice carried a hint of British inflection, as well as a note of disapproval. "Speaking of which," he inquired, "have the authorities made any progress?"

"My understanding is that they are following up on every lead," Owen replied obliquely.

Morgan fought back a smile. He obviously saw no need to elaborate on which authorities he meant.

That was undoubtedly because the medic had grown increasingly suspicious. From the beginning, he'd expected to give the police a thorough report on Morgan's injuries, and when he hadn't been called upon to do so, began to ask more and more pointed questions.

But all Owen and Morgan knew was what Joseph had furtively told them over the phone a few nights back: *no police.* Whatever that meant.

He'd warned them that making Morgan's condition known at a clinic—with its paperwork and reporting requirements— could get awkward. People would wonder what was really going on.

They might even start to wonder about Owen himself, and he wouldn't be able to disabuse them of whatever they came up with—not without jeopardizing TANAPA's secret investigation into the Thorpes.

When the medic glanced at her and frowned, Morgan stared at Owen, silently willing him to distract him before he started up again.

He seemed to understand. "Listen, can Morgan start moving around a bit more? If she feels up to it, maybe even leave the house?"

She thought she knew what he was getting at. They hadn't decided whether to move her somewhere else, but Owen definitely liked the idea. Morgan didn't want to go, however. Even though, the cottage felt scary sometimes, having to be apart from Owen sounded even worse.

"I'd say so," the doctor agreed. "A change of scenery and some fresh air will do her good. Just don't overdo it and be prepared for her to get tired quickly." If he had other opinions about the way they were going about this, the medic chose to keep them to himself. He only tacked on, "Remember, no heavy lifting."

"Aye, aye," Morgan smiled.

Owen steered the man out of her room, and toward the front door. "Thanks again for checking on her."

"As I said, it's no trouble. I'll stop by next week to see how she's coming along. But if anything changes for the worse before then, be sure to call me right away."

"Will do." As he'd done on all of the man's other visits, Owen discreetly handed him an envelope and murmured, "Thanks for your discretion."

"My pleasure," he said. "*Kwaheri*, Hargreave. Goodbye."

Owen locked up behind him, then came straight back. She patted the mattress beside her. "Come sit with me," she said.

He was careful as ever not to jostle her too much, grabbing her hand and twining his fingers through hers. "Well? What do you think?"

"I think you hired me to look after you, not the other way around," Morgan told him.

"How about we look after each other for the time being." He looked somber, though.

Morgan told him, "I'm happy things are looking up, and I don't want you to worry about those scans he mentioned. I'm sure I don't need them. I feel way better already."

Owen didn't look convinced. "I hate to see you like this. You look so small in this stupid bed. I'm afraid I'm going to hurt you if I touch you."

Morgan leaned her head against his shoulder. "You aren't going to hurt me. Besides, I want you here—I *like* you here."

He leaned over and kissed the crown of her head, and his old T-shirt was soft under her cheek. Morgan soaked up the warmth of his body, and something about the comfort of it, coupled with the peace of being alone with him, reminded her of that afternoon in Joseph's barn.

In the days since her attack, they'd repeatedly gone over what they knew about the Thorpes and their actions—but one small detail kept nagging at her, refusing to fit neatly into the narrative.

"Hey, can I ask you something?" Morgan wondered.

"Of course." Owen draped his arm behind her head and toyed with a strand of her hair. He was always telling her how good it smelled—even now, when she wore it up most of the time.

"One thing I haven't been able to figure out is why Tumelo helped you when he did. He said it was because of Kisima, but was it really? For some reason that didn't quite sound like the full story to me."

Owen knit his brows and glanced at her, surprised by her words. "Yeah, I don't think that was all of it, either. It probably had more to do with the money we slipped him. He probably knew we'd do that."

"Can he work? He seemed awfully frail."

"I'm sure he could do something, but unfortunately, not too many folks here would hire him anymore. People can be uninformed, and superstitious about illnesses. And Tumelo would never leave Kisima behind."

"Does he have kids?"

"No, and thank heaven for small mercies. When his wife died, it changed him—even more than falling ill himself did."

Morgan sighed, her sorrow for a man she didn't know feeling raw and too close to the surface. "Heartbreak can do that to you."

Owen studied her face, from the fading bruises around her eyes, to the cuts healing on her lip and chin. "You actually care about him, don't you?"

Morgan shrugged. "It sounds a little melodramatic, I guess, but I'm no stranger to hurt. I wouldn't wish it on anyone, whether I know them or not."

He digested that for a minute but didn't try to dig deeper. He knew a little bit about her divorce, but she hadn't told him about the baby yet. She would, though. Someday.

Eventually, he said, "Kisima didn't like her sister-in-law. She was distraught when Tumelo married her, and even more so when the woman didn't give up her wild ways right away. When the woman got sick and infected Tumelo, I thought Kisima was going to murder her for sure."

"That's sad."

Owen looked away. "It really is."

"I'm sorry," she said, squeezing his hand. "I'm being nosy. It's none of my business." When he didn't immediately reply, though, she started to worry. "Did I overstep?"

"No, of course not. Why do you ask?"

"You seem upset," she admitted.

"No, it's not that." Owen blew out a long breath. "It's just…I think sometimes about how Tumelo must feel. First his wife steps out on him, then she contracts a deadly disease, and gives it to him. He's dying a little more every time I see him."

"Poor Tumelo."

"Morgan, there are so many Tumelos in this country—on this continent, really."

"That doesn't make it less sad."

"I don't mean to sound callous. But it gets overwhelming, trying to properly mourn every person you have to say goodbye to. You start to get a little numb, after a while."

"I imagine so." Morgan gazed out her window sadly, but Owen cupped her cheek, gently urging her to look at him again.

"Kisima told me her brother still adored his wife, right up until the end. Can you believe that? And he still couldn't save her."

Morgan teared up, waiting for him to get out the rest of what he wanted to say.

"And here I am, looking at the state of your precious face," he growled, "and I'm nearly incoherent with the need to maul something. I hate that you're suffering and, just like Tumelo, I am powerless to make it better. I want to soothe you the only way I know how, but I can't—not without being a caveman, anyway."

"Owen, you are helping. You're doing so much—you've been wonderful."

He stared at her, his eyes soft and full of something she was afraid to name. Then he shook his head and the moment passed. "I don't want you to worry about me," he said, stroking her hair. "You just focus on getting better."

"Okay."

He turned again and looked her over. "So...the doctor cleared you to move around more. What do you think? You want to try a quick trip to the market today?" His voice sounded too bright, the forced optimism coming across as brittle, rather than cheerful.

Trepidation washed over her, and Morgan felt her body turn to stone. "Why?"

A host of expressions moved across Owen's face. "We need a few things. I'd go by myself, but I…" He swallowed and looked away. "I can't leave you here on your own."

He didn't say the rest of the words aloud, but Morgan could hear them loud and clear, anyway. *I already did that once and look what happened.*

"I understand," she said, and meant it. The poor man had been beating himself up over something that wasn't even his fault for a week now.

"It'll be okay. We'll keep it short and take it easy," he said gently. "And when we get home, I'll fix you a nice dinner."

"Owen…what if someone's there?" Her voice cracked, which was humiliating, but thankfully he knew exactly which *someones* she was referring to.

"I'd bet good money they won't show their faces around here anytime soon. Besides, no one will try anything if I'm with you. I might not be tougher, but I'm a way bigger opponent," he smiled.

Morgan snorted. He meant well, but she was tired of hearing how brave he thought she'd been.

"I hear your friends have been asking for you—Miss Lenah, especially," he tried. "Kisima told her you were under the weather."

Morgan pressed her lips together, trying to imagine walking around like it was no big deal. She could probably cover up most of her bruises with a hat and makeup, but she wouldn't be able to hide how stiffly she was still moving—or how panicked she might feel.

"Owen…what if they got to Joseph? What if he can't call because he's—"

"If something had happened, we would have heard about it," he interjected.

But would they have? Morgan had to wonder if he was reassuring himself, or her.

"Well…" she hummed, "I guess I have to get back on the horse at some point." Even she could hear how weak it sounded. "Just promise me you'll walk slow."

"I promise," he smiled back, squeezing her hand. "I'll even drive slowly."

"I'll believe that when I see it."

Owen helped her out of bed, then helped her change out of pajamas and into real clothes. Morgan tried to focus on something pleasant, instead of the fear.

They were going to stroll through the market, arm-in-arm like a real couple—like normal people, with normal problems. People would smile, and the sun would shine.

Nothing was going to happen, despite what her hammering pulse was telling her.

THE RIDE WAS torturous, inescapably bumpy despite Owen keeping his promise to drive slowly. When they finally reached the market and he helped Morgan down from the truck, she had to knit her arm through his immediately, to keep from sagging to the ground.

She was already exhausted, and the place was packed. Morgan clung to Owen's side, and tried not to let her terror show.

The air was thick with the smell of food and animals and sweating humans. Morgan swayed a little on her feet, and Owen gathered her closer, trying to shelter her with his body.

A woman chattering into her cell phone shoved past them, wearing an "I love London" t-shirt and bright, mismatched prints on her headscarf and skirt. After her came a knot of young boys, chasing each other and laughing as they darted this way and that.

Owen was scanning the crowd, searching the faces for any possible threats. It wasn't quite the romantic foray she'd imagined earlier, but Morgan still marveled at his protectiveness.

It might not be a declaration of eternal love, but it still warmed her from the inside out. He was the rarest of men, and for now, he was hers.

Another person bumped into her from behind, and Morgan winced at the arrow of pain that shot through her ribs. The market crowd shifted and swirled around them, her heartrate kicked up, and a bead of sweat trickled down her back. The sea of faces was overwhelming. She was one step away from burying her face in Owen's chest like a baby.

He stood strong as a pillar at her side. Morgan gripped his shirt and felt his taut stomach beneath the linen. She turned into his side and breathed deeply, letting his familiar scent comfort her.

"Doing okay?" he asked softly.

Morgan nodded, even though they both knew it was a lie. It was probably inappropriate for her to cling to him like this in public, but she couldn't bring herself to care. She was a hairsbreadth away from a meltdown, it felt like ages since Owen had touched her with anything more than hesitant affection.

She missed him.

He held her close and helped her to a less busy spot, then chuckled when a man called out to them. "We're in luck," he murmured. "Your buddy Malaak just spotted us. Let's start with him, aye?"

Morgan focused on where he was pointing, looking for the friendly man who'd sold her the material for Owen's quilt, along with a cute sundress and a couple of skirts she hadn't had a chance to wear yet. When she spotted Malaak's happy grin, it felt like a lifeline.

"Okay. That's not far," she said, determined. "I can do this." She stepped toward Malaak's stall, bolts of fabric and stacks of clothing arranged across it in a rainbow of inviting, saturated color.

"We can chat for a minute while we get our bearings," Owen began. "Then we can walk around the back to hit the food stalls. I think it's too busy today to cut straight across."

"What do we need, anyway?"

Owen didn't answer her. He was too busy dissecting the scene unfolding in front of them, his keen eyes weighing every detail.

Malaak had turned to help a woman who'd approached him, but the transaction erupted into angry shouts almost immediately. The woman stood her ground, but she was cowering a little in the face of Malaak's fury.

Morgan and Owen glanced at each other, then hurried the last few feet. "What happened?" she gasped, trying to catch her breath.

Malaak turned to Owen and unleashed a stream of angry Swahili, gesturing at the woman. She tried to defend herself but mostly just stood there, one hand curled protectively over her neck. Curious shoppers were beginning to stop and stare, with barely disguised looks of distrust.

Owen listened intently while Malaak kept pointing. More people were gathering around. The woman was trying to keep her chin up, but it was clear she was shaken.

"Owen?" Morgan asked again. "What's happening?"

"I'm sorry." He glanced from her, to Malaak, to the woman. "As far as I can tell, he's accusing her of theft. He's using slang I haven't heard before, though. I'm not positive."

"What does he think she stole?"

"It sounds like…maybe a necklace?"

Suddenly, Malaak reached across his table and yanked the woman's hand from her neck. Owen's eyes went wide.

"Oh my god," Morgan exclaimed, "That looks like *my* necklace." She looked to Owen for confirmation. "Is that my locket?"

That necklace had been ripped from her neck during the attack. She thought she'd never see it again. How had it ended up here, on this stranger?

"Where did she get it?" Owen thundered, visibly struggling to stay calm.

Malaak switched into English, his voice heavy with scorn. "She *says* her husband gave it to her." Then he switched back to Swahili to let loose another blistering tirade.

He reached for the poor woman's neck, but she covered the locket again and stepped back, bumping into several of the more aggressive spectators. They jostled her forward, then stood with their arms crossed over their chests, scowling as they waited.

"Who's your husband?" Owen asked. He gestured for the woman to hand over Morgan's locket, and when she shook her head, he nearly roared, "*Who is this woman's husband?*"

The crowd around them started chattering, suggesting names.

Malaak launched a final volley of angry words at the woman, and her eyes welled with tears. She looked at the faces around her, and then finally at Morgan. When she did, Morgan took off her hat, so she could see the bruises that surely had to be obvious in the bright sun.

The woman flinched, and at last, she whispered a name.

"Chagga," Malaak repeated, "She's Christian Chagga's wife."

Some of the bystanders nearest to the woman nudged her and muttered in her ear. After one last look, she lifted her chin and unclasped the locket, dropping it into Owen's waiting hand.

She muttered something under her breath as she stared off in space. Then she turned and—when the crowd didn't part to let her through—pushed her way out. Owen handed the locket to Morgan, and the onlookers began to drift away.

Malaak explained, "She said she didn't know where he got it."

"Pawn shop, maybe," Owen said, his expression stony as he watched Morgan.

She'd been so sad to lose Meg's gift, and in such a horrible way, but now that she was holding it again, it seemed dangerous and strange.

Reflexively, she clicked the locket open, then squinted at its altered contents. Inside, there were no more secret flower petals, but there was a tiny photograph. When she realized who it was, a strangled noise forced its way out of her throat, and she dropped the thing in the dust like it'd stung her.

"What is it?" Owen exclaimed, "What's wrong?"

He bent down to reach for the glint of gold in the dirt, and Morgan stumbled back, so he didn't make her look again.

Owen wouldn't think she was so brave, now. She couldn't even face that one little picture—not when the ringleader of her assault was grinning back at her like this was the best joke he'd ever seen.

January 15

The numbness I feel now is different than the fog I was wrapped in when I came here. I broke free of that cocoon, but I am so deep in this darkness, I don't know how I'll find my way out—even with Owen to lead me.
I got complacent. Amidst the bliss of learning Owen, I let myself forget how much I didn't know.
One thing I do know is this—somewhere, somehow, I fell in love with him. I didn't mean to. My heart makes me a liability—a burden and a weapon to be wielded against him.
I can't let him know.
Even though it's obvious he cares for me, too. I don't know if that's because I have his heart, though, or because this is all temporary. I don't know so many things.
Someday, Owen will move on, and I will have to go home.
Except…home has never seemed so far away. How will I survive that journey?

Chapter Thirty-Eight

AFTER THE ONLOOKERS dispersed and the hubbub died down, Owen and Malaak hustled Morgan up the hill to Miss Lenah's store, where the woman had promptly installed her on a soft chair brought out from the back and stuck a cold glass of juice in her hand.

The drink and the rest revived Morgan quite a bit, but the revelation that Christian Chagga—and undoubtedly some of his buddies—were probably the Thorpes' local henchman left them both too shaken to return to the scene of the attack right away.

Instead, Owen suggested powering on to Victoriaville, where he could take care of some routine tasks that he'd neglected at the office in the last week, and Morgan could rest some more.

If she was still anxious after that, they could always grab dinner at the café across the street. Owen didn't plan much farther than that. Surely, Morgan would be fine by then?

The hits kept coming, though. When they parked in front of the office and stepped up to the door, it was standing wide open. Kisima perched nervously on a chair just inside, with a cleaning rag gripped in her fist like a weapon.

When she spotted them, she leapt up and cried, "*Bwana!* Thank god you're here."

"We weren't planning to stay long." He checked his watch, and added, "It's also late. What are you still doing here?"

Rather abruptly, she seemed to realize that he wasn't alone. "And Morgan, too. Look how pale you are. Are you feeling all right?"

"I'm okay, but I need to sit down," Morgan said, sinking into one of the old wooden chairs in front of Thom's desk with a groan. "Too much excitement at the market today."

Owen eyed her wan face with concern. "The chair in my office is a lot more comfortable, and it's probably cooler in there, too. Why don't you head in there and I'll join you in a minute?"

Morgan nodded, but before she went, she fished the bottle of pain pills the medic had left her from her bag. "Is there some water I can take these with?"

Kisima pointed her toward the washroom. "There's bottled water in the big cabinet," she instructed. "Maybe splash some cool water on your face, too."

Once Morgan closed herself inside, Kisima rushed over to him. "Where has everyone been?" she hissed, glancing back to make sure the washroom door was still shut. "I've come in on all my regular days, but I haven't seen a soul all week."

That was a surprise. "They didn't tell you anything?"

"Not a word." Her eyes searched his. "What's going on?"

Morgan shuffled slowly out of the washroom, holding her side and moving stiffly. Owen hurried to unlock his door for her, then settled her in his chair.

She sank back and closed her eyes. "I'm really tired," she mumbled.

"I know. And those meds are going to knock you out soon," Owen said, stroking a careful hand down her back.

"Yeah." Her words already seemed blurred around the edges. "Sorry."

"It's okay. None of this day is going according to plan. You just rest for a bit. I'll take care of my stuff as fast as I can, and then we'll get you home so you can lie down." He frowned, watching how her eyes drifted closed for longer and longer intervals.

"Maybe you should go sack out in the truck. You could put the seat all the way back, at least." And then he wouldn't need to move her when it was time to leave.

Morgan shook her head, looking bleary. "I'm fine. Don't worry."

Owen nodded and backed away, pulling the door most of the way shut so he and Kisima wouldn't wake her if she fell asleep.

In the main room, he whispered, "I can understand Nigel not coming in, but I'm surprised Thom hasn't been here. He came by the house with Carol the other day, but he didn't mention that he'd been ducking work."

"Like he would show his face here after what they did to Morgan," Kisima scowled. "I know he was mixed up in it. I'd beat him senseless with my broom."

Owen chuckled, but she didn't even crack a smile. "Anyway, that's why I'm so glad you're here now," she explained. "I didn't want to worry Morgan, but…there's a situation."

"What kind of situation?"

Her hands gripped that rag a little tighter and suddenly, Kisima seemed a lot less anxious to talk. "Well…Charlotte called a few minutes ago."

"Charlotte." His brain felt sluggish, thoughts of Morgan and Chagga jockeying for position and screwing with his focus.

"My *cousin*," Kisima prodded, exasperated. "The one who works at the Shadey Inn. You remember."

"Yes. Sorry." He ran a hand over his face. What was wrong with him?

"Listen, *Bwana*. I know it's a bad time, but you need to drive there right away," she told him.

Owen snorted. "Kisima, I can't go now." He gestured toward his office. "You saw Morgan. I've got to get her home."

Kisima was already shaking her head, adamant. "I'll stay with her. You go, and go *now*. Charlotte will keep a look out, but you need to get there before anyone else does."

Owen tensed all over at her tone. "Why?"

She winced and passed a shaking hand over her eyes. "It's…she said it's Mr. Hannity. She saw him in Stephen Thorpe's room. Charlotte said you have to hurry."

Owen considered what she was telling him. If Thom was getting into mischief at the inn and Owen caught him doing it, that could be exactly the kind of breakthrough they'd all been hoping for. Coupled with the information he now had about Chagga, TANAPA's case against the Thorpes could be strengthened immeasurably.

He glanced toward his office, wondering if leaving was the right thing to do—and was stunned to see Morgan leaning on the door jamb, looking apprehensive but not quite as groggy as she'd seemed moments ago.

"Please don't make me get back in the truck yet," she said, "I don't think I can do it." Her voice cracked a little, twisting his heart into knots.

Kisima said gently, "*Bwana* has to go, Morgan, but you don't. You can stay here."

"You're going to leave me here alone?" He could tell she was on the verge of panicking. Her breathing was beginning to speed up and her knuckles were white where she clung to the door frame.

"Not alone. Kisima will stay with you. You'll be safe here," Owen reassured her, but she looked doubtful. She also looked ready to collapse. "Go sit back down, love. I'm going to get something from my truck, and I'll be right back." Morgan swayed on her feet, and Kisima rushed over to bolster her.

Outside, Owen pulled a dusty case from the bed of his truck, and then, after waffling for a second or two, the long, narrow bag nestled behind the seats. He returned to his office and set the items down.

"I'll feel a lot better about this if you two close up the office and act like no one's here." He handed the thin bag to Kisima and told her, "Morgan will show you how to use this."

She took it gingerly, already wary of what it might contain.

Owen knelt down and unpacked the other case, and in moments had a wide camp cot erected for Morgan. He wadded up a jacket hanging on the back of his door for her to use as a pillow, and Kisima procured a length of soft mud cloth from her bag to drape over her like a sheet.

Morgan laid down and closed her eyes, breathing raggedly as she tried to find a comfortable position. It wasn't an ideal set-up, but it was the best he could do for now.

"Kisima, let me show you that rifle before I fall asleep," she whispered. "I'm fading fast."

Kisima looked uncomfortable at the prospect, but Owen had no doubt she'd do what she had to, to keep her charge safe. "You'd better go," she told him. "There isn't much time."

He nodded, watching Morgan a moment longer. At last, he forced himself to move. "I'll get back as soon as I can," he said over his shoulder. "You probably won't have to use that rifle, but if you do…don't hesitate. You hear me? Not for one second."

The woman nodded, her eyes wide.

"Don't forget to lock up behind me."

Owen turned and trotted out to his truck, mind spinning. The whole situation felt eerily similar to his last hurried drive away from town, and it sent his nerves into a tailspin. He had to keep reminding himself that Morgan wasn't alone this time, nor was she out in the middle of nowhere.

She was safe, but that didn't change his need to get this over with as soon as possible. The Shadey Inn wasn't a straight shot from the Preserve office, and time was clearly of the essence.

He took several turns that carried him past the outskirts of town, then pulled onto a thoroughfare that would take him most of the way there. He would figure out the rest once he got closer.

Almost immediately, however, a steady presence popped up in his rear-view mirror. It was unusual to see other vehicles on this particular stretch of road, but it wasn't unheard of—and Owen had definitely grown paranoid these last few weeks.

He tried not to overreact, but as he raced along the road the other car tracked him steadily, staying far enough back that he couldn't discern the make or model through the dust he was kicking up, but keeping pace, nonetheless.

By the time he neared the first turn-off for the inn, he'd started considering evasive measures. Kisima might have been circumspect about why her cousin had summoned him, but she'd also sounded…ominous. He had no idea what he would find in Stephen Thorpe's room, and adding another variable to the equation would be pure stupidity.

For one thing, Owen could be walking into an ambush. Thom might also be long gone by the time he got there—and the last thing Owen needed was for some clueless bystander to hold him accountable for whatever asinine thing Hannity had done.

With that in mind, Owen doubled back on his route a few times, then hung out in the lee of an abandoned building for as long as he dared. Nothing moved out near the road but a few birds, so Owen put the truck in gear and made the final left toward the inn, winding through scrubby grass and bushes for nearly two kilometers.

Once the road straightened out again, he watched his mirrors, but the other car didn't appear. Whether he'd managed to lose it or merely bought himself some time, the end result was that the coast seemed to be clear.

Convenient, too, since the Shadey Inn's drive was just ahead, its little painted wood sign hammered into the ground at a remote intersection. Instead of turning in, Owen drove past and pulled onto the dirt track that met the road around the corner, no doubt meant for employees and deliveries, rather than guests.

The path wound around the side of the squat buildings and ended in a small car lot behind them. A couple of cars were parked there, Thom's dented blue coupe among them.

Owen parked near the fence, then stepped from his truck and listened carefully. The place appeared to be deserted, the only sound coming from the cicadas humming in the heat.

He threaded his way carefully through the compact, pastel-painted buildings. They were set close together but nothing else protected them from the afternoon glare, not like the place's name implied.

Looking down the walkways that branched off on either side, Owen didn't see any activity, but he did catch the quiet strains of a radio or television coming from one of the rooms. This did not feel like Thorpe's kind of place at all.

Owen had no clue which room he was looking for, and if anyone spotted him wandering around like this, it was sure to raise some eyebrows.

Fortunately, a moment later Owen spotted a cleaning woman pacing anxiously in a breezeway, not too far from the inn's office. He stopped and whistled softly, and sure enough, she frantically waved him over.

"Miss Charlotte?" he murmured, once he got closer.

"Thank heavens you're here," she whispered, dragging him by the sleeve toward the nearest room. "Mr. Thorpe checked out this morning, but when I went in to clean the room I found…something bad."

She unlocked the door and began turning the handle, then stopped and swallowed nervously. "I didn't know what to do. Kisima said I should wait for you before I told anyone else."

With that, Charlotte swung the door wide, stepped back, and looked resolutely away.

The hairs on the back of Owen's neck stood on end. There was dreadful, suffocating silence emanating from the interior of that room. He had an unnerving suspicion of what he was about to see, and it didn't increase his desire to walk through the door one bit.

He had to, though. People were counting on him. *Morgan* was counting on him.

Charlotte peeked at him. "I have to call someone soon," she said. "He's already been here way too long. After what happened before, the manager is going to go crazy."

Owen nodded and forced his feet to move, one in front of the other, until he was standing inside the motel room. He spotted Thom immediately, which was hardly surprising given that he was splayed out in terrible Technicolor across the bed.

Owen's stomach lurched dangerously, so he turned to grasp the doorjamb and close his eyes for a second. He pressed his forehead against the pastel green stucco and made himself breathe regularly, in…and out. In…out.

He was going to have to take another look—this time at closer range—if he was going to be sure of what had happened here. But when he opened them, Owen's eyes danced around the room instead, taking in different details so they could avoid the horror.

Someone had clearly searched the room, presumably Thom. Most of the empty drawers and cabinets were still ajar in some form or another. After that…well.

After that, it appeared that Hannity had parked himself on the end of the bed and stuck a gun in his mouth. There was no way to tell from here whether that was actually the case, however, or whether someone just wanted it to look that way.

With unsteady steps, Owen poked around the room and bathroom. He was careful not to leave any prints, but there was nothing to see—nothing except Thom, the gun, and the blood.

He stepped out into the breezeway and took a big gulp of muggy air into his lungs. Charlotte was fidgeting near her cleaning cart, still avoiding eye contact.

Owen asked her, "Did you hear the shot?"

She shook her head. "No. It must have happened before I got here." Then she really looked at him, and her eyes welled up. "The manager could have, but I think he would have checked if he had."

Owen took a deep breath, hating every second of this. "Okay. Go ahead and call the police now," he told her. "Tell them you just found him, and maybe…don't mention I was here."

"Are you…all done?"

Poor Charlotte was obviously shaken, and now she'd have to face the cops, too. Owen would have to find a way to make it up to her, but he doubted a bunch of flowers was going to cut it.

"Wait—" He straightened from the wall, a sudden thought occurring to him. "His car is still here, isn't it?"

"I don't know. There are some in the lot," she said, closing the door with a determined yank, then wiping her hands on her skirt.

He'd seen Thom's car when he'd driven in. Owen was sure of it. "Listen, can you give me just a couple more minutes before you ring the police? I want to have a quick look at his vehicle."

Charlotte nodded, so Owen turned and trotted toward the parking area out back.

"Mr. Hargreave?" Charlotte called.

Owen spun around, walking backwards. "Yeah?"

"I'm really sorry. This must be hard for you." The maid's eyes were soft with sympathy. "Kisima told me he was your friend. Before all this stuff started happening, I mean."

Owen looked away. Eventually, he managed to say, "He was," but the past-tense words nearly choked him. With a little more composure, he tacked on, "Thanks again for calling. I really appreciate it."

Then he took off for the lot and went over to Thom's car. The interior was a mess as usual, but nothing seemed out of the ordinary, aside from the open windows. The doors were unlocked, too, so perhaps Hannity hadn't intended to stay long.

Owen used his shirttail to open things up, then unlatched the trunk. Thom had pretty standard gear stashed in the boot—field supplies and a pack amongst the other detritus a game preserve worker tended to accumulate.

Owen didn't see any other guns, but there were two shovels caked in dirt.

"Where the hell did you bury the rest of them, you fucking punk?" he muttered, abruptly furious with the man.

He slammed the trunk shut and went to peer inside the car again. This time, Owen noticed the sheets of printer paper on the passenger-side floorboard. He reached in to snag them, then scanned the pages.

Once it became clear what he was looking at, Owen glanced around quickly, then ran for his truck. Thom had come to this place with three travel itineraries in his possession—he had to have realized that he was going to be the one left holding the bag once all the ringleaders had flown the coop.

If Owen wasn't mistaken, Sir Mark Thorpe, along with Thom's erstwhile girlfriend Carol, had departed for Heathrow by way of Milan yesterday afternoon. Had Thom been aware of that relationship? It hardly mattered now, he supposed.

The bigger problem was that Stephen Thorpe wasn't scheduled to leave the country for another three days. After a brief stay in England, he'd return to Africa and his hometown of Johannesburg, where he'd be well beyond the reach of Joseph Teleki and the rest of his TANAPA cohorts.

An awful lot of trouble could be made in three days.

Owen got behind the wheel and shoved the papers under the loose seat belt beside him. He'd already started the engine and begun pulling away when the printed line at the bottom of each page finally sunk in.

He slammed on the brakes, grabbed the itineraries, and looked closely at the fax coding again. They'd been sent to Nigel's machine in the Preserve Office just yesterday morning.

But Kisima had said she hadn't seen anyone all week. Was that true? He'd left her back there, alone with Morgan and armed. His heart threatened to slam right out of his chest before he reminded himself that he trusted her. Morgan would be safe. It was okay.

At the sudden sound of an engine nearby, Owen looked up and spotted a car racing away from the inn. Had it been Charlotte, or the manager, perhaps?

Owen's heart jumped into his throat when he remembered the car that had trailed him here. Maybe they'd found him after all?

He didn't think either car had been a black Mercedes, so unless Stephen had switched vehicles, it probably hadn't been him. Didn't mean it couldn't have been one of his thugs, however.

Owen's scrambled brain chose that moment to offer him up an image of Morgan, sleeping on that camp cot he'd set up for her, damp hairs sticking to her forehead and her cheeks prettily flushed.

She'd taken pain medicine before he left and was undoubtedly incoherent by now. Would Kisima be able to work that rifle after one disjointed lesson?

Owen's mind reeled, weighing the what-ifs. He had to find Joseph, and soon. But he needed to get back to Morgan and Kisima first, and move them to a safer location.

As he pulled onto the road that would take him back to Victoriaville, he glanced back at the Shadey Inn just in time to see Charlotte give him a small wave before she entered the office to call for the police.

Chapter Thirty-Nine

OWEN LOOKED HAUNTED when he finally returned from the inn. Morgan could see it clearly, even through the dusty front windows.

He unlocked the front door and stepped in cautiously, no doubt hoping he wouldn't have his own gun pointed at him. Kisima had spent the last couple of hours sitting beside Morgan, but at the sound of his footsteps she jumped up, worry etching her soft features.

When she realized who it was, she rushed out to him with a finger to her lips. "Morgan's been asleep this whole time," she whispered, and then, heading off the next predictable question, she added, "Don't worry. No one's been here but us."

Owen sighed, and sank into a chair with obvious relief. "That's good." He popped back up again, staring down like he'd sat on something. "What's all this?"

There seemed to be stacks of paper piled everywhere. Morgan felt as confused as he looked—none of those had been there when she'd sacked out earlier.

"I ran out of things to clean and I couldn't just sit here waiting for you," Kisima explained sheepishly, "so I tried to sort out some of the post that's been accumulating all week. I hope that's okay."

"Kisima, it's more than okay," Owen laughed, squeezing her shoulder. "This is so helpful. Thank you." He picked up a pile and leafed blindly through it, but his gaze slid toward Morgan, on her cot in his office.

She squeezed her eyes shut and pretended she was still asleep. She couldn't say why she did it, except that she suspected he'd be more candid if he thought she wasn't listening.

Owen was protective that way.

"What about Mr. Hannity?" Kisima wondered.

"Dead. I assume you knew that?"

Morgan held her breath and risked a peek through her lashes. Kisima nodded and Owen scowled off into space. *Thom Hannity was dead?*

After a while, Owen muttered, "I just can't figure out how it came to this." He dropped the papers he held onto Thom's desk. "What happened to him?"

"*Bwana*, I hope you'll forgive me for saying this, but you've always had a blind spot when it came to that man." She said it gently, like she didn't want to scold him—for the moment, anyway.

"You're probably right." Owen moved the stack of mail from the chair and sat down again. He didn't seem sad, so much as perplexed. "I guess, on some level, my relationship with him has been based on nostalgia for a while now."

The look on his face broke Morgan's heart. She couldn't feign sleep any longer, not if she could help him through this. She sat up and stretched, then wandered out to the front room, blinking in the strong afternoon sun.

"Hey, I heard your voice," she said. She looked from Kisima to Owen, and went with the obvious question. "How'd it go?"

Owen shook his head and asked Kisima, "You didn't tell her?"

Kisima played with her new braids, which grazed the tops of her shoulders and showed off her cheekbones. Morgan had passed out before she could compliment her on them before. She'd do it now, if the timing weren't so awful.

"She was asleep, remember?" the woman pointed out. She turned away, moving papers from one pile to another while she announced, "Morgan, Thom Hannity is dead." There was no inflection to soften the bald statement.

After a moment of silence, she muttered, "God help him," under her breath.

"Dead? What happened?" Morgan gripped the doorjamb, suddenly a little dizzy.

Owen was at her side in an instant, wrapping his arm around her waist and helping her to the nearest chair.

"It looked like he might have shot himself," he told her.

Morgan winced. "You sound as if you're not sure."

"I could've misunderstood what I saw," he said. "It's possible someone else did it, then arranged it to look like a suicide. It wouldn't make a ton of sense, but then again, none of this has."

Morgan struggled to shake off the grogginess still dogging her. "But…why would Thom want to kill himself? Even if he thought you were going to catch him, that seems extreme."

Owen shrugged. "I'm speculating, but it appears Carol ran off with Thorpe the elder," he explained. "I don't think she and Thom were deeply in love or anything, but maybe that was a bit of a blow."

He cut a glance at Kisima, who raised a cynical eyebrow at him.

Owen went on, "On the other hand, Thom could've suspected the Thorpes were planning to skip town, then pin everything on him once they were gone."

As she thought about that, Morgan fanned her face with a couple of envelopes she grabbed from the desk. The heat had gotten a lot more oppressive as the day had worn on, and it wasn't helping her brain fog at all. In an instant, Kisima moved behind her, gathered her hair off her neck, and began braiding it down her back.

Owen watched the process in utter fascination. He liked to run his cheek along her hair before they fell asleep. He'd told her that he liked to be surrounded by the scent of it, of her— that it made him feel like everything would be okay.

Kisima tied off Morgan's braid with a stray rubber band she snagged off Thom's desk and patted her back. "Wait…did you say *the elder?*" she asked suddenly, intruding on Morgan's reverie. "Not Stephen?"

"No, his father, Sir Mark. I assume Thom must have introduced him to Carol at some point, but who knows? I wasn't even aware the man was in town until recently."

"No one ever saw him?" Morgan wondered.

She remembered that locked door in Thom's bungalow, and the cough she'd heard behind it. And then she thought about the cultured-sounding man who'd threatened her so calmly as she lay scared and bleeding on Owen's floor.

Could they both have been Sir Mark? If so, she wouldn't trade places with Carol in a million years.

"No," Owen replied. "I was starting to doubt he was really here."

His eyes lingered on Morgan's fingers, and she realized she was toying with her locket again. At the market, Malaak had ripped out that horrible photo and made a production of thoroughly cleaning and polishing the necklace before giving it back to her. She'd only put it on so she wouldn't offend him or lose it in the confusion, and Owen looked surprised to see her wearing it.

Morgan dropped her hand to her lap and tried not to think about it. She hated that her sister Meg's gift had been tainted so thoroughly. It felt like a lead weight around her neck now, chafing against the healing cuts.

Owen pulled his phone out of his pocket and said, "I should try Joseph again. I need to tell him about Thom."

As it had been doing all week, the call went straight to voicemail. Owen hung up and looked too exhausted to do anything but sit for the moment.

Morgan looked from him to Kisima. "Do you suppose Christine knows her sister left?"

"I think she suspects," she mused. "She called here looking for you while you were gone, *Bwana*. I forgot to tell you. She said Conrad was out with another tour group and she couldn't find Carol. I wonder if she was bluffing, though."

"Christine's not that devious," Owen said, pushing out of his chair. "And listen—we ought to get moving. It's possible someone was following me on the way up there, and I'd rather not get caught here unaware."

"Oh, now you tell us," Kisima groaned.

He looked at Morgan. "How are you feeling? Any better?"

Morgan felt hot and dizzy and totally out of it from her nap. She needed to eat, but she was still queasy from the pain medication. Even so, she assured him, "Much better. I'll be able to get home, no problem," since that was clearly what needed to happen.

However, Owen hadn't said where they were going, had he? She'd assumed, because as far as she knew, they didn't have other options. Still, when he hesitated, Morgan asked, "*Are* we going home?"

"Yeah, for now," he decided. "I've got to figure out how to reach Joseph. It's been too long since we've spoken." He walked into his office to pack up the cot and the rifle, calling, "Kisima, we'll drop you at home on the way back."

She studied Morgan with a critical eye. "Just take me as far as the park road and I'll walk the rest of the way," she said. "It's not far, and then you'll get home faster."

"Okay." Owen emerged with the cases in his hands and glanced around. "Everyone have what they need?"

Morgan gathered her market bags and nodded.

Kisima retrieved the cloth she'd draped over Morgan earlier and stuffed it into her tote. "There's one more thing I need to show you before we go. When I put Mr. Cotton's mail on his desk, it was lying right on top. It might explain where he is." She lifted a piece of paper from a nearby pile and handed it to him.

Owen scanned it. "Okay, so TANAPA asked for a meeting with him in Dodoma. On…looks like yesterday afternoon. If he kept that appointment and Sir Mark and Carol made their flight, that means we still have Stephen Thorpe in the wind. Where the hell is he hiding?"

Kisima scowled. "Why do I have the sinking suspicion we'll find out soon enough?"

Morgan eyed the front door of the office warily. "Maybe we can discuss that in the truck," she said. Her voice came out higher than it should have. She took a few deep breaths and tried not to let her growing anxiety gain any traction.

Owen walked around, peering at each pile of paper Kisima had made before selecting two and tucking them under his arm. Then he herded them outside, set the cot and the rifle down on the sidewalk, and rooted around in his pocket for his keys.

Morgan scanned up and down the block, while he locked up the office. It was empty this late in the day, but her skin still crawled with how exposed she felt.

She wasn't sure she'd recognize the other men involved in her attack if they were sitting across the street at the café, or even if they approached her on the sidewalk. So many of her memories of that night were blurry and haphazard. The man named Chagga was clear as a bell—but the rest could probably waltz right up to her before she realized what was coming.

Kisima must have noticed her discomfort, because she reached out and took Morgan's arm, then huddled close like a mother hen. Owen unlocked the truck, loaded the gear, and held the door while they got in.

His eyes were alert, watching for any sign of something out of the ordinary. Morgan should have found that comforting, but his wariness only put her more on edge. Not much worried a man of his size and skill set, but Owen was worried now.

Before long, he was swinging the truck around and heading for home. The small plume of grit they kicked up floated in the windows and dusted her skin, making Morgan long for a shower and a real bed even more.

She couldn't wait to return to the cocoon of safety that sheltered them when it was just her and Owen. Perhaps that was naïve, given how easily their little bubble had been invaded—but Owen exuded that kind of assurance. She needed his confidence, after the unsettling day they'd had.

Morgan needed to hold him and be held by him, and they needed to talk, too. Thom's demise couldn't have been easy to talk about under the glare of Kisima's dislike of the man, but on some level, Owen had to be grieving.

Once, the men had been friends, and she hoped Owen wouldn't blame himself or second-guess his role in Thom's last days. Morgan was already doing that enough for both of them.

Perhaps Owen and Kisima were having similar thoughts, because the three of them rode in uneasy silence for most of the way. Owen checked his rear-view mirrors every couple of minutes, and Kisima checked her watch.

At last, they passed the turnoff for the road heading north into the Preserve, and Owen pulled his truck onto the weedy shoulder beside the pavement.

"It's ridiculous for you to walk," he complained, even though Kisima was already halfway out of the cab. "We can have you home in ten minutes."

"Nonsense," she fired back. "It would take you twice that long, and you know it. I'm completely fine. Besides, Morgan flinches every time you hit a bump. You need to get her out of this truck."

Kisima was no dummy. She knew that was her winning card, and as soon as she played it, she smiled smugly. Right on cue, Owen's gaze flew to Morgan's face.

"When you said you would be able to get home, no problem..." he began.

"I might have been exaggerating," she admitted.

Her forehead felt clammy, despite the warm sun, and even though she'd been braced from the worst of the ruts when they stuck her in the middle seat between them, it was still rough going. It seemed pointless to deny it now.

Owen sighed and leaned around her. "Promise me you'll be careful," he told Kisima, "and call one of us the instant you're home safe."

Kisima gave him a jaunty salute, spun on her heel, and began to march off. Owen pulled slowly onto the road, and Morgan called out her window, "Bye, Kisima. Thanks for helping me today."

The woman turned, planted her feet, and shouted a reply. Owen took one look at her expression and hit the brakes.

"What did she say?" he asked Morgan. "Is everything okay?"

Morgan had scooted over to the passenger side when Kisima got out, but now she almost wished she hadn't. For one thing, she already missed the comfort of Owen's warmth pressed against her side.

And for another...if she'd hadn't moved, maybe she wouldn't have heard Kisima's words, either.

She stuck her head out of the window. "Should I—?"

Kisima cut her off. "You'll know when to tell him," she called, then gestured impatiently for them to drive on.

Owen started away slowly again, looking from the road, to Morgan, and back again. "What was that all about?"

Morgan hesitated. "She said...*Next time you see Tumelo, ask him how his wife died*," She sat back and watched Kisima's retreating form in the side mirror.

Owen frowned. "But that makes no sense. Everyone in town knows she had AIDS."

Morgan shrugged. She didn't know these people as well as he and Kisima did, so she was reluctant to speculate on the part she'd told him—or the part she hadn't.

"Why would she say that?" he wondered, lost in thought. "And why now?"

"I have no idea."

OWEN SPENT THE rest of the drive telling Morgan stories about how he'd met Nadra and Kisima, and about the way they enjoyed ganging up on him. From his chipper tone and hopeful smiles, it was clear he was trying to cheer her up.

Morgan braced herself on the dashboard and went along with it. He had to be going a little crazy, trying to strike a balance between getting home quickly and not hitting every pothole between there and Kenya. He didn't show it, though.

Owen simply kept up that easy chatter until they finally turned off the pavement and down the long drive that led to the cottage, nestled in its thicket of trees beside the lake.

It wasn't until he was helping Morgan down from the truck that they noticed the faded red hatchback, parked out of sight on the side of the house. Her heart leapt into her throat, pounding like a drum.

Owen's shoulders went tense and his hands gripped her waist, poised to whisk Morgan behind him in the blink of an eye.

The little car's door opened, and its occupant emerged. Owen sagged with relief. "Joseph! Thank god."

He steadied Morgan on her feet, then quickly kissed the top of her head before striding over to grasp Joseph's hand. "It's good to see you, *rafiki*. We were beginning to worry."

"I know. And I'm sorry I couldn't get to you sooner," Joseph said, in his characteristically soft-spoken way.

"Why don't we all head inside?" Morgan asked, since Owen was beginning to shift restlessly. "I'll make some tea and you guys can debrief each other."

She steeled herself for the walk up the stairs and took a few unsteady steps. Immediately, Owen dashed back to her side, circled an arm around her waist, and carefully helped her to the door.

Joseph followed, looking uncomfortable as Owen wheedled her into resting on the couch instead of letting her head straight for the kitchen.

Teleki dropped into the chair next to her. "Morgan, how are you doing? I was so unhappy to hear that you were hurt. I feel…responsible," he said.

"No, don't be silly." Morgan had to fight the urge to sink into Owen's side when he sat next to her. His reassuring scent and warmth were like a cozy blanket that she wanted to wrap around herself. "It wasn't your fault," she said.

She was out of steam, and still a little bleary from the pain meds. She wasn't sure whether she wanted that tea she'd promised them, a long hot bath, or to sleep for a week straight. Perhaps all three.

"Still, I never should've let you get involved in all this," Joseph murmured, pulling her attention back to him. He studied the bruises on her face and the cast on her arm and shook his head sadly. "I feel awful."

"I'm afraid I'm the guilty party here," Owen retorted, leaning forward to clap Joseph on the arm. "If Morgan had gotten a job with some respectable family in Arusha, she'd probably be snug as a bug right now."

Morgan sighed. "Guys, it's not a competition. Let's all agree that it was my fault for being too nosy, and move on. Okay?"

Joseph sat back, looking amused. "As you wish."

Owen smirked, too. "You're the boss," he told her, then had the temerity to wink. Apparently, he wasn't quite so worried about her anymore.

Morgan rolled her eyes and started to get to her feet. "I'll go put the kettle on."

Owen dragged her back down. "Oh no you don't. I'll put the water on. You stay here, or go lay down if you need to."

"Have I come at a bad time?" Joseph asked anxiously. "I should have called first. I'm sorry. I can always—"

"No, it's okay," Morgan assured him. "It's been a crazy few hours, and I'm a little worn out. Now that we're home, I'll be good to go in no time."

Owen snorted, but when he turned to Joseph the smile faded from his face. "Can I get you anything besides the tea? Something to eat, maybe?"

"No, thank you. I'm quite all right."

"I'll be back in a second." Owen looked jumpy as he darted for kitchen, the adrenaline from the day's events no doubt still coursing through him.

As Owen banged around at the stove, Joseph settled deeper into the chair beside Morgan and smiled at her, but he kept a careful eye on the front and back doors of the cottage. Morgan tried to get herself situated and to not groan too loudly in the process.

After a while, Owen sat back down and took a big breath. "A lot has happened since we last spoke. I tried calling, but…" he trailed off, then murmured a careful, "Anyway."

"I know. And I did get your messages, but then I was pulled in a different direction when the dominoes started falling."

Morgan watched Owen nod, accepting the vague explanation for now. She rested her head on the soft couch cushion and fought to keep her eyes open, afraid she might miss something.

Joseph continued, "I suspect Cotton and the Thorpes were very nervous about what you knew and what you might do with that knowledge. It's the only explanation for why they kept striking like they did—first the shots at you directly, and then the attack on Morgan." He glanced at her and shrugged. "Who knows what else they may have tried, that we aren't even aware of yet?"

"Seems like those two things were plenty," Morgan muttered.

Owen nodded. "Agreed."

"I did wonder, though," Joseph said. "When the men came here, did they find anything to link you to TANAPA's investigation?"

Morgan and Owen shared a long look before he answered, "We don't think so. I had a file hidden in the house, but Morgan had discovered it, and already moved it to a better spot. When those goons tossed the place, they didn't find it," he explained. "We got lucky." He looked so proud of her that Morgan had to blink back tears.

Joseph nodded approvingly. "Excellent. Then we'll hope they're satisfied and will leave you both alone—at least until we get the rest of them into custody."

"Hope seems like un unreliable defense," Owen said, as the kettle began whistling. He got up and went to the kitchen for their tea.

"True, which is why we've also been keeping an eye on the house, just in case," Joseph called. To Morgan, he added, "They got past me once. I promise you it won't happen again."

"I appreciate that."

Owen returned carrying a tray with mugs, a jar of honey, and the teapot. She'd never seen it before, which probably meant that he'd bought it while she recuperated to replace the one that had been smashed in the break-in.

"Morgan recognized one of her attackers today," he said, once he set everything down. "I imagine that counts as a falling domino. Did you hear about that?"

They'd wondered earlier if Joseph would get wind of what happened at the market, given the scene they'd made.

Joseph smiled, "I did, and we had a stroke of luck on that score, too. Andrew happened to be at Miss Lenah's when you two arrived at the market. After you left, he and Mrs. Chagga had a nice long chat. Coupled with Cotton's falsified reports and what we found in Stephen's motel room, she was very helpful in rounding up her husband and some of the others."

"I bet she was good and mad that he gave her a stolen necklace," Morgan said, accepting the cup Owen handed her. When she took a sip, she wanted to moan with happiness—he'd added a healthy slug of whiskey to hers, and it tasted like heaven.

"Oh, she was," Joseph agreed. "And I can't blame her."

Owen frowned as he topped off his mug. "Some of them, you said. Not all?"

"Not yet. If we follow the money, as Morgan so helpfully suggested, there appears to be a couple more in the network that we haven't flushed from the weeds yet."

Owen sat back and tilted his head. "Maybe that's who was following me today."

He seemed to realize Joseph might not know what he meant, so he explained, "Kisima's cousin called me back to the Shadey Inn after we left the market. On my way out there, I think I picked up a tail."

Joseph set down his cup and chuckled. "Sorry, that was us. We started keeping tabs on the inn once we learned the Thorpes were staying there. Our agent called for backup when he heard the shot this morning—but the closest team turned out to be the one assigned to you. You brought them right where they needed to be," Teleki said. "Very efficient. Thank you."

Owen looked incredulous. "You had guys on me?" he asked. Then, after scowling mightily for a moment, he muttered, "I was sure I'd lost them."

Morgan snorted, and he glared at her.

Joseph grinned at his consternation. "Don't be angry. We were simply trying to be prepared in case Thorpe came for you again. Now that we have enough to detain him, we hoped he might get reckless."

"There's reckless," Morgan said, "and then there's—"

"—murder," Owen finished.

Joseph turned serious quickly. "We didn't know if Hannity or Thorpe was the one who'd gotten shot this morning, or if neither of them had. Thorpe vanished afterward and Charlotte was working so hard to keep the manager and the other maids away from the room. We had our hands full trying to help her while we got the proper people in place. Incidentally, at least a few of those employees must have been paid to keep quiet. Even though all of them probably heard that shot, not one called the police."

"It was Thom. Who got shot, I mean." Owen's voice sounded flat and expressionless. Morgan reached over to squeeze his hand.

"So, we discovered," Joseph said. "I'm sorry. I know that you were friends, once."

Owen sighed. "Thom has…he's changed over the years. I don't know why. But then the Thorpes came to town, and it was like he became a different person altogether."

He peeked at Morgan, and there was guilt and sadness in his eyes. She longed to comfort him, to remind him that Thom's sins were Thom's.

There was an awkward pause, then Joseph continued, "Cotton has been detained in Dodoma. He came to us claiming that the entire Rathbone herd was dead and demanding a change in status for the Preserve—but thankfully, we had all those altered scouting reports to nail him with."

"I was wondering about that," Owen replied. "Kisima found the letter requesting the meeting at the office."

"I'll be honest. The bosses were amazed when he actually turned up, right on schedule. Acted like he didn't see it coming at all—but hubris does seem to be a talent of his. Anyway, they've built a pretty good case on him down there. With our help, they'll have a lock on the others, too."

Joseph straightened the creases of his khakis, then refilled his mug, clearly anticipating more questions.

Morgan was happy to oblige. "What about Stephen Thorpe? Do you guys know where he is?"

"We do not," Teleki sighed, obviously frustrated. "We can't find him anywhere. It's very strange. We know he's supposed to join his father—"

"And Carol," Owen interjected.

"Yes, and Miss Connelly—in Britain in three days. He can't have gone far, but he hasn't turned up at any of his regular haunts. There's no way he's hiding out in the bush, either. You saw the man. He'd sooner die than rough it for an hour, much less a few days. I'm almost starting to wonder if he's crossed the border to hide out somewhere else until his flight leaves."

Morgan asked, "But you guys won't let him on a plane, will you?"

"Of course not."

She wasn't terribly reassured by Joseph's casual tone, but figured the man probably knew more than he was permitted to say. She took another big swallow of her boozy tea, letting it thaw her suddenly icy hands.

Owen blew out a long breath. "When Conrad hears about that girl, he is going to have a bloody fit."

"He already knows," Joseph shrugged.

That was surprising. "Really?" Morgan asked, "How?"

"Our man Twospeak has been of enormous assistance to TANAPA lately," Joseph told them. "Under the auspices of his company, he enabled us to evacuate the remaining gazelles to Arusha National Park before anyone else could get to them. We paid handsomely for the favor, mind you, but we still felt obliged to inform him when his sister-in-law left the country as she did."

"You're—you're kidding," Owen sputtered.

Morgan couldn't blame him. Conrad and Christine had visited them a few more times since the attack, but neither had given any indication that he was involved in this whole mess.

"Not at all." Joseph's phone chimed quietly in his breast pocket, and he pulled it out to examine the screen for a moment before replacing it.

"How long has Twospeak known about the investigation?" Owen demanded.

Morgan understood his confusion. Every time they thought they'd found their footing with the situation, the sand shifted beneath their feet again.

She just hoped he didn't suddenly decide that it wasn't safe for her to stay with him any longer. It would be exactly like him to try to send her someplace else—like home to Boston. He already believed that he'd failed her once. He'd never take the chance of it happening again.

"We approached him some time ago to help with the animals," Joseph explained. "But Twospeak isn't aware of the full scope of the investigation. Not through us, anyway." He picked absently at a loose thread on the hem of his shirt and even though he was pretending to be unconcerned, his question was clear.

Owen scowled. "Not through me, either. But Conrad's a smart man. After we found Morgan that night, it's possible he put two and two together."

"True," Teleki conceded. "Even so, we're in his debt for helping us preserve the remaining herd. Tanzania's future depends on nurturing its treasures."

Joseph's pride in his work—in his country—rang loud and clear in his words.

In the hands of men like him, the natural wonders sheltered by Tanzania's park system would have a real chance to flourish, despite the encroachment of the wider world.

Owen looked pensive as he poured himself more tea. "Did anyone ever spot Sir Mark around town? I never laid eyes on him."

Teleki nodded. "He kept a pretty low profile but if I'm not mistaken, he stayed at Thom's house fairly often," Joseph said.

"We think he must have been the man who came and threatened Morgan after Chagga's thugs attacked her."

Morgan shivered, remembering that cold, emotionless voice. Owen set down his cup and put his arm around her.

From the breast pocket of his shirt, Joseph's phone rang again.

"Forgive me," he murmured, clearly embarrassed. "Something must be…" He trailed off as he pulled it out and tapped the screen.

"Yes?" he said. He listened intently for a moment, then sprang to his feet, shoving the phone into his pocket with a wild look.

He dashed for the door. "Stephen Thorpe is at my house," he blurted over his shoulder in dismay. "Patricia's there alone. I have to go help her."

Chapter Forty

WHEN CONRAD TWOSPEAK entered the British liaison office on Royal Avenue in Victoriaville, it was with a messy mixture of curiosity and concern. The eminent Dr. Bing had called him earlier that day, and one did not ignore a summons from the dignitary.

Bing only rang a person up for good reason, and a wise man made it a point to discover what that reason was—especially if, as happened on occasion, the liaison did not immediately make his purpose clear.

Conrad had not made it this far by being stupid, however, and he wasn't about to start now. So, here he was.

The elderly man met him in the waiting room and, after a burst of polite chit-chat, escorted him into the graciously appointed back office. Conrad sat across from Bing and eyed all the opulent colonial décor while he waited semi-patiently for the liaison to speak his piece.

The man was rolling something thoughtfully in his palm, back and forth. "Mr. Twospeak, once again I do thank you for stopping by on such short notice."

Conrad sighed. Dr. Bing was known throughout the region as the soul of gentility. It got to be irritating after a while.

"It's no trouble, I said," Conrad told him. His knee bounced, marking the minutes until he could discover why he'd been called in front of this monstrously large, polished desk like a recalcitrant child. He had better things to do. Opportunities to pursue, as it were.

"What can I do for you?" he prodded.

Bing blew out a breath, but his gaze was sharp. "I've been trying to finalize the paperwork on the American woman who died on your tour. Get a few things cleared off the old desk, you know. But…there are a few small details that keep knocking around in my head. Things that don't fit the puzzle." At that, he smiled apologetically. "I'm an old man."

"Okay," Conrad said, wary now. The liaison's age was irrelevant. He was still sharp as a tack, and everyone knew it. So why play that card? "How can I help?"

The man abruptly stopped toying with the object he was holding and held out his hand. Conrad leaned forward and when he saw what it was, his veins ran cold.

Dr. Bing noticed. When he dropped his bomb, his voice was no longer genteel—it was as blunt as a cudgel.

"Know anyone shooting this type of shell lately?" he asked.

Conrad did. And he wasn't about to spread that information around.

OWEN STOOD NEXT to his desk, paralyzed by indecision. His first instinct had been to race after Joseph, but he'd only gotten as far as the front door before he'd frozen in his tracks.

He wanted to help Teleki if he could. The man had done his best to include Owen—and by extension, to look out for

Morgan—while investigating the Rathbone deaths. He'd been under no obligation to do that, and Owen was grateful.

However, leaving Morgan here alone didn't feel like an option, and she was in no shape to come along. She'd been through enough already, and it could be dangerous.

Morgan hadn't moved from her spot on the sofa while he dithered. She just sat there quietly, watching him and waiting for him to decide.

Owen growled, pacing into his room, and back out again. He was gritting his teeth so hard, his jaw felt like it was going to crack.

Morgan called softly, "Owen. Take a deep breath and think through the steps."

He spun and blinked at her. Her words were eerily similar to what his mother used to say when he was a young man and about to hare off on some half-cocked crusade or another, and it knocked him back a step. His legs hit his desk chair, and he sat in it heavily.

Joseph had said it himself, he thought. TANAPA had someone keeping watch on the cottage, and they'd rounded up nearly all of the bit players. The most dangerous entity—Stephen Thorpe—had a confirmed location, as well. He was at Joseph's house. *Now.*

Besides, no one had any proof that Owen or Morgan knew a thing—Morgan had deftly seen to that.

She shifted on the couch. "I think you know what to do," she said.

"No," Owen replied, "I don't." God, he missed holding her. His chest felt tight with yearning, and love, and separation anxiety.

"Come here," she murmured. A command he would never refuse, Owen thought.

He went and sat beside her. "Did you see his face?" he asked. "He looked frantic." He sighed and rubbed his eyes. "Don't get me wrong, Patty can take care of herself. But if it was you…when it was you…"

"Word has it, she prefers Patricia," Morgan corrected, smiling gently.

Owen smirked, despite himself. "Is now really the time?"

She shook her head, and then she shoved him. "Go, Owen. You know you have to—so, do it. I'll be fine."

"I think you'll be safe," he said uncertainly. "Joseph said they were keeping watch."

"I know."

She stroked his arm lightly, and he tried to ignore how the brush of her fingers sent heat lightning streaking across his skin. It had only been a few weeks since they'd been together, but it felt like an eternity. Owen ached for her.

Her warm, feminine scent drifted around him as she leaned against his side, and he breathed it in hungrily. He didn't want to leave, but he had to, and he hated it. Every second he hesitated could mean the difference between life or death—for Joseph, for Patricia, and for untold others.

Owen turned and pressed a kiss to Morgan's forehead, and then to her lips. What kind of coward went after his enemies' women? Owen wanted to strangle Stephen Thorpe with his bare hands, and Joseph could just queue up after him.

"I'll keep this," Morgan said, reaching under his shirt and unsnapping the holster he'd strapped there before their trip to the market. She slid the gun out and dropped it with a heavy thump on the cushion beside her.

"You remember how to use it?"

"I do. And you still have the other one." It wasn't a question, but Morgan still glanced at his ankle, making sure.

Owen nodded. A man who worked around big game was usually armed, but Owen had been packing more heat in the last few months than ever. Fat lot of good it had done him, though—or Morgan, for that matter.

"What if you fall asleep?" he asked. "What if someone…what if…" Owen couldn't make himself finish the thought. He clenched his fists on his thighs and hung his head.

"I'm not going to sleep," she said, calm and matter of fact. "And you can't wait any longer. Joseph and Patricia need you."

"Call me if anything seems amiss. Promise me," he instructed. "I can get back here before you know it."

"I will."

Owen kissed her lightly again. He'd been aiming for her cheek, but Morgan tilted her face at the last minute, catching his lips with hers and lingering there. He drew back once to study her face, then kissed her again—and tried to pour everything he hadn't yet told her into it.

Then Owen pushed himself up and walked away from her before he could change his mind. He broke into a run as soon as he hit the porch.

Behind him, Morgan called out, "Be careful." And then, almost too quietly for him to hear over the roaring in his veins, she said "I love you."

OWEN TRIED TO put Morgan's bombshell out of his mind as he raced toward Joseph's house, dialing Teleki's phone in case there'd been some confusion, or the situation was already resolved. The man didn't answer, though, so Owen left him a quick message and pressed on.

Joseph's parting words had been somewhat cryptic, he reflected. Owen had no idea who'd alerted him that Thorpe was at his house, or why he'd been so sure that Patricia needed help. Owen could be walking into anything from a stakeout to a shootout, and he doubted any of the parties would be expecting him.

He couldn't be more than ten minutes behind the man and with any luck, he'd arrive before things could get too hairy. Owen wished he hadn't sat on his couch lollygagging for so long, though. Ten minutes could feel like an eternity, when your woman's safety was on the line.

When he finally reached the edge of the Teleki spread, Owen pulled onto the shoulder and cut the engine. Instead of charging blindly in, he stayed in the truck for a minute, watching for some hint of what was going on. The place seemed deserted but for those same small goats, nickering in a dusty pen near the back corner of the house.

In the center of the property, the Teleki home was a simple concrete square, painted the color of salmon and raised up on blocks. Its simple design was softened by a tiled roof, wide wooden porch, and flowering shrubs planted around the foundation pillars, but its perimeter was mercifully free of hiding spots.

Owen scanned the yard, and his gaze hitched on a slight movement on the side opposite those goats. He relaxed a little when he realized it was Joseph, leaning around the corner and gesturing toward the barn.

Owen nodded, slipped his spare handgun from the glove compartment, and slid it into the empty holster under his arm. He reached behind the passenger seat and grabbed his rifle from its case, then shifted out of the truck as silently as he could.

He crouched in the dirt and weeds next to the door and tried to map out a route to the barn. Most of his options left him too exposed. There was no cover in front of the house, and he had no idea who might be watching.

Owen's only option was to make a dash for the porch, then work his way around the side of the house, where he could shelter beside a couple of small trees. He wished he knew whether there was anyone inside the house, but there was no way to tell from here.

Patricia could be in there, he supposed, if she wasn't in the barn. Thorpe would have his hands full, trying to subdue her— but he might have gotten lucky. Surprise could be a powerful advantage, even against someone as trained as Joseph's wife.

There was no more time to waste. Owen searched the yard one last time, then dashed quickly across it to the side of the porch. The sky hung gray and ominous overhead, the air thick with impending rain.

Owen crouched low and hurriedly wiped the sweat from his brow, then heard the porch creak near his head. He looked up to find an elderly woman peering over the edge at him. She cocked her head toward the front door, then glided back to hold the screen open for him.

Owen didn't hesitate this time. With one quick glance around, he crept up the steps and followed the woman inside. She took his arm and led him straight to the kitchen in the back, where another screened door opened onto a deep back porch.

The old woman held him still beside the opening, pointing first to the barn, then to the rear of the yard, with her gnarled, shaking finger. Owen catalogued the possible entry and exit points of the barn first, noting the slightly open door and the tall, cracked shutters on the windows. Joseph would be behind one of them by now if he hadn't made it into the barn itself. Patty could be there, too.

He couldn't make out much at the back of the property. There was enough uncultivated vegetation that ten men could be hunkered down there, but there was no telling whose side they might be on.

He couldn't imagine Thorpe tramping through bush that heavy—he might scuff one of his custom Saville Row loafers. So, perhaps that was where TANAPA had stashed a lookout.

The old woman tapped him and raised her finger again, indicating a small, decrepit shed off to the left. When he looked, Owen finally spotted Stephen Thorpe, inching his way around the side to get a good bead on the barn.

That bastard. So that's where he was. Nice of him to simplify their hunt.

Owen took the old woman's hand and raised it to his lips, then whispered his thanks. She twinkled up at him, giving him a wink and a coy smile before shuffling quietly back to the front room, where she sank into an armchair near the window and closed her eyes.

She'd done her part, and now she was trusting him to do his. Owen gripped his rifle in sweating hands and looked outside again. The porch was the perfect vantage, high enough to see everyone, with nothing to obstruct his sightlines.

Owen knelt low, hoping the railing would obscure him as he crawled over the threshold and onto the porch. Before he let go of the screen, he set his rifle beside him and withdrew the pistol from under his arm.

Hopefully, the door wouldn't scrape or creak when it shut, or reflect the sun off its metal frame. Owen needed a second or two to get into position before he caught Thorpe's attention.

No such luck—the hinges shrieked like birds of prey, Stephen swung toward the sound with his gleaming black revolver raised, and Joseph hurtled from the barn in an instant. Teleki got off two quick shots before Thorpe swung back and somehow managed to land a bullet in Joseph's leg.

Teleki went down, but one of his shots must have grazed Thorpe's shoulder. A bloom of red had sprouted on his sleeve, spreading rapidly. Owen fired to distract him, since Joseph was awkwardly trying to wriggle onto his belly to take aim again.

Thorpe recoiled when Owen's blast caught him just left of center, but then jerked and tumbled in the opposite direction when three gunshots rang out in quick succession.

Once he hit the horizontal, Patricia stalked from the barn, a scoped hunting rifle trained on Thorpe and the folds of her long mud cloth skirt snapping around her legs. Owen ran down the stairs and met her where their quarry lay sprawled in the dirt.

Thorpe gazed up at them, blinking and struggling for words, his hand flexing ineffectually on his weapon while the other patted at his bloody shirt front, searching for the damage. Patricia stared down at him like an avenging goddess, then kicked his gun out of reach.

From across the yard, Joseph bellowed, "Patricia!" When they turned and saw him struggling to get to his feet, he called, "Come away, *mke wangu*."

A groan at their feet returned their attention to the ground, however. A crimson stain was seeping across Thorpe's chest, and his eyes were becoming wide and unfocused. The man's body flexed, then abruptly went still.

Patricia let out a dismissive huff, then calmly walked to the porch and laid her rifle next to Owen's. Teleki had given up on getting upright, instead propping himself awkwardly on one hip so he could keep an eye on her. She trotted over to him, barking out rapid-fire orders in Swahili that soon had Joseph chuckling.

Owen checked for Thorpe's nonexistent pulse, then backed away from the body and holstered his gun. The Telekis were working to tear away Joseph's ruined pant leg, and the old woman emerged from the back of the house with a pan of water and some rags.

"You have a first aid kit?" Owen called.

Joseph nodded, his face contorted as Patricia bustled around him, her commands subsiding into worried murmurs. "In the washroom," he said. "Under the sink. *Bibi* will get it."

"My phone's in my truck," Owen said. "Let's get you onto the porch, and then I'll ring Dr. Mkwawa."

He'd made a point of programming the medic's number into his phone after Morgan's attack, and he had Conrad's guy in there too, now. They'd have options, if it came to that.

Patricia helped him lever Joseph onto his feet, and they made their way to the house, inch by painstaking inch. "How the hell did I go through this?" Owen laughed. "You've gone ten feet and you already look awful, aye?"

He and Joseph had struggled over a far greater distance when Owen had been shot. It seemed like a blur now, but Owen suddenly suspected he might owe Teleki more than he'd realized.

"Shot in the shoulder, not the leg," Joseph pointed out breathlessly. Then, he added with a grin, "Also...stubborn mule."

Owen and Patricia chuckled. They had to carry him bodily up the stairs, but soon had him settled in a chair in the shade. Joseph gripped the armrests while Patricia mopped at his wound, with rags the old woman soaked in water and handed to her.

Owen ran out to his truck, placed a quick call to Mkwawa, then fired off a short text to Morgan so she wouldn't worry.

When he returned, Patricia was wrapping bandages tightly around Joseph's thigh, but they weren't doing much to stanch the blood. Someone had cut off more of his pant leg, and the bowl of water on the floor was now bright red.

Patricia glanced at Owen anxiously. "I couldn't find the bullet," she said, reaching for her husband's belt, to wind around his leg. "Did you reach Mkwawa?"

"I did. She's not far away," Owen reassured her. "She promised she'd be here soon, and if she can't help, we'll bring him right to the hospital."

She stood and pointed at Joseph's face. "You stay there. I'll be right back," she told him.

When she disappeared into the house with the old woman, Owen dragged another chair over and asked, "Where does she think you're going to go?"

"Who knows." The goats began bleating, and he smiled over at them.

Now that the adrenaline of the last several minutes was wearing off, Owen realized he had some questions. "So, mate...couldn't help but notice that the little wife is pretty handy with a firearm."

Joseph smirked through his pain. "That surprises you? You know how we met."

"I don't, actually." Owen knew Patricia had served in the army, but her aim had been something else.

Teleki let out a sound that was half cough, half laugh. "*Rafiki*...Patricia was one of my marksmanship instructors in the TPDF. The woman lied about her age and volunteered when she was only fifteen. By the time I met her she'd been using privates as target practice for years."

"Fifteen? Blimey." When Owen was fifteen, he'd been hiking in the green hills outside Christchurch and obsessed with girls who did not yet return the sentiment.

Joseph shrugged. "Her father was very harsh, and she was anxious to leave home. The army was good to her. And it brought us together, so no complaints there."

"Still, cozying up to woman who knows her way around a rifle like that seems like it might be a little daunting."

Joseph smiled. "The trick is to not give them anything to complain about," he said. "And I don't know why you're joking. Your Morgan is coming along nicely with a weapon, herself."

"She hates it, though," Owen reminded the man.

She did not, however, hate him. As a matter of fact, he'd recently learned that she loved him...like he loved her.

"We'll bring her out to the reservist range with us," Teleki said. "She'll come around."

"Wait—you're still in the reserves?"

"Both of us are," he said mildly, examining his boots.

Owen tilted his head and studied the man. Had the TPDF planted reservists in the park service...on purpose? It made a certain kind of sense. Having moles in TANAPA would put them in an excellent position to suppress all manner of unwelcome situations.

In fact, Joseph's tenure as a scout at the Preserve began to take on an interesting new light. Owen stared at him, impressed.

"Why do you think Stephen came here today?" he asked, looking out at the body. "Was he looking for you, or hoping to orchestrate another attack like Morgan's?"

Joseph pondered it. "Maybe he was feeling desperate. Father's gone, Thom's dead. Can't reach Nigel, and his goons have mostly gone dark. Thorpe wouldn't have had to try very hard to find us here. Maybe he thought that if he took out Patricia, it would occupy me and my team long enough for him to get on a flight out of here."

Teleki closed his eyes and passed a shaking hand over his forehead. "Thorpe was a damn fool if he thought I'd let him board that plane."

"He was an even bigger fool to underestimate your wife," Owen commented. He angled his chair away from the body in the yard, but bumped Joseph's foot in the process.

The other man winced. "*Hiyo inaumiza.*"

Owen laid a hand on his arm. "*Samahani.* You okay?"

Patricia rushed out, glaring at him. "Joseph? Are you all right?" She squeezed his shoulder gently.

"He's okay. I just jostled his foot a bit," Owen admitted. "Sorry again, mate."

Joseph waved him off, but he had beads of sweat across his brow and was clearly struggling to stay alert. "Have you checked in with Morgan?" he wondered, scowling in concentration. "Is she still all right?"

"I texted her after I called the medic," Owen told him, "but I haven't heard back."

He slipped his phone out of his pocket and checked again, but there was still no response. Owen frowned, thinking of how small she'd looked, sitting on that sofa all alone.

Morgan had his gun, though, and she knew to call if there was trouble. Assuming she could.

The Telekis were looking at each other, conversing without words in the way that married couples sometimes did. Would he and Morgan do that someday, too? Speak to each other with just a look? He hoped so—and now that he knew she loved him back, it actually seemed like a real possibility.

Owen didn't ever want to let her go, but he had no idea if she wanted to stay.

"You should go home," Patricia announced suddenly. "Dr. Mkwawa will be here any minute, and you should be with Morgan."

"Joseph—"

"I'll be fine," the man assured him hazily, then tilted precariously sideways in his chair.

"Sure, you will. But, what about him?" Owen gestured to Thorpe's remains. "He's already attracting flies." At some point, the old woman must have covered him in a faded blanket, but he hadn't noticed her doing it.

"He can lay there forever, as far as I'm concerned," Patricia spat. "*Mtu mbaya.* How dare he try to best me in my own home? And with Joseph's mother here, too." She muttered a nasty-sounding imprecation that Owen couldn't quite translate.

Joseph smirked and cracked open one eye. "Even so, we won't want him littering our yard for long—he's bound to attract pests. I'll make a few calls to headquarters, while we wait for Amelia. Let them decide what to do with him. While they're at it, they can tell us whether they want to involve the police now or later, too."

"If you wish," his wife grumbled. "Now go on, Hargreave. Go home."

"All right," Owen shrugged, getting to his feet. "I can tell when I'm not wanted. You promise you'll call if you need anything?"

They both nodded, so he picked up his rifle and descended the back stairs, skirting the house on his way back to the truck. Joseph's mother met him at the front, laying her hand on his arm and reaching up to pat his cheek fondly.

Owen smiled at her and she motioned him closer. When he leaned in, she pecked his cheek, then shooed him away. "*Sawa,*" she croaked in a raspy voice. "*Kweda sasa.*"

Go now.

The whole exchange reminded him of Morgan's goodbye, and when Owen got behind the wheel his heart was already beginning to pound. Morgan had said that she loved him, but he hadn't had the chance to say it back.

She would be worried about him, and he was absolutely worried about her. Owen needed to hurry—back home, back to her.

He turned the truck around and pressed his foot to the accelerator, all the things he had to say clogging his throat in a mad scrum of emotion and want.

Chapter Forty-One

WHEN MORGAN HEARD the crunch of Owen's tires outside, she was ready for him. She'd gotten his first message while she'd been resting in bed, and once she knew he was safe she'd managed to nod off for a little while.

Now, she felt better than she had in weeks. She was ready to turn her words into action.

Owen might not have heard her say that she loved him earlier—he hadn't even broken stride on his way out the door— but she could show him. She *would* show him.

Morgan slipped from her bed and out of her room, the smooth planks of the floor feeling cool against her feet. The sensation made her shiver, though it was warm in the house.

It was hard to believe it was January, when the weather felt more like August did in Boston. Back home, her sister was probably wrapped to the gills in wool and slogging through shin-deep snow whenever she went outside.

Morgan didn't have time to worry about how Meg was faring, though. She had a man to entice.

She could tell Owen was trying to be quiet when he stepped lightly across the porch and turned his key in the lock. He probably assumed she'd passed out, after the shape she'd been in when he left.

He was going to be surprised to see her standing here. She'd have to coax him past that.

The door started to swing open, so Morgan looked down and began unbuttoning her shirt, slowly and deliberately, starting at the top and working her way down.

She was almost to the bottom by the time she worked up the nerve to check Owen's face. He'd frozen in the doorway, rooted in place and transfixed by her fingers.

Morgan must have undone the last few buttons, but she wasn't conscious of it. His gaze was all she saw, scorching her skin as she slid her shirt off her shoulders and let it fall to the ground.

She took a moment to scan him for injuries. There were a few spots of blood on his pant leg, but as far as she could tell, it wasn't his. Owen looked fine—a bit dusty and disheveled, but still whole.

As the seconds passed and he didn't move or say anything, Morgan began to wonder if she'd miscalculated. Instead of feeling brave and powerful, she only felt uncomfortable—like she'd accidentally managed to recreate a hackneyed love scene from a bad movie. Everyone seemed to have forgotten their lines, though, and maybe the entire script had been lost.

In any case, this was not the sensual and heartfelt encounter she'd envisioned.

She glanced around the room nervously. She'd obviously misunderstood the look on his Owen's face earlier. It hadn't been passion in his kiss, but adrenaline.

Morgan ran a hand down her leg and thought about putting her shirt back on. Retreat was going to be messy, but it had to be better than standing here in her bra like a half-dressed store mannequin.

But then, like he could hear her panic, Owen leaned down and placed his rifle case precisely on the floor. Without taking his eyes off her, he dropped his keys on the bag and straightened, contemplating her solemnly.

She couldn't read his expression, and her embarrassment grew. Morgan looked down and found her shirt, but Owen was in front of her in a heartbeat, his hands warm and sure on her waist.

"Don't do that," he murmured, searching her face.

"Are you sure?" she wondered, voice cracking on the words. She couldn't seem to muster any others. She felt swamped by her feelings for him, all of a sudden.

He closed the distance between them, cupping her face and kissing her desperately. Morgan melted into him, marveling as she always did at his unwavering strength.

Without warning, Owen bent and slipped an arm behind her knees, then lifted her effortlessly.

"*Ow*," she gasped, completely unprepared to hide how her healing ribs protested the movement.

Owen froze, his expression turning so horrified that an unplanned giggle bubbled out of her. She had clearly lost any seductive abilities she might have once possessed.

He didn't seem to mind, though, smiling and relaxing a bit. "Are you okay?"

"Fine. You surprised me, that's all." Morgan didn't want to lose momentum with more small talk, so she gave him what she hoped was a sexy look and tilted her head toward her bedroom.

Owen took a few steps toward the door and leaned in. There were multiple books and several pages from her journal spread across the bed, and not much room for two adult-sized lovebirds.

"Hmm," he rumbled, raising an eyebrow at her. Morgan bit her lip, and felt her face turning red. In her rush to pull off her dumb plan, she'd forgotten to set the *entire* scene.

Fortunately, Owen was undeterred. He simply turned and guided her carefully through his doorway instead, laying her gently on his bed. He knelt next to Morgan, untied the drawstring at her waist, and slowly smoothed her pants down her legs. Then Owen set them aside and sat up, contemplating her.

He ran his fingers lightly down her torso, from the hollow at the base of her throat all the way to her navel, and then lower, caressing the edge of her panties. Morgan shivered.

Two little lines appeared between his brows. "Are you sure about this?" he asked softly. "You still have so many bruises. I don't want to hurt you."

"I'm sure. We can be careful," she said. Morgan felt oddly nervous, though. Owen might have taken the bait she'd dangled in front of him, but could it last? What she wanted could be snatched away at any moment, leaving her with nothing.

Morgan didn't want to be protected, however, she wanted to be loved—and without taking a risk, there'd be no reward.

Owen leaned in close and brushed his lips against her ear. "That's what I'm worried about," he whispered, his breath deliciously hot. "It feels like I've been waiting an eternity for this. What if I'm too rough?"

As if to underline his words, he bit her earlobe, and Morgan's heart skittered wildly. "You won't be."

"What if I *want* to be?"

"What if I want you to?"

He chuckled. "Very clever, love, but I'm not falling for it. You know I won't let you hurt yourself."

"Spoil sport," she grinned.

He narrowed his eyes dangerously. "You're provoking me."

"I am." Morgan closed her eyes and sighed. "You're probably right, though. This was a bad idea. We should wait."

Owen drew back, and she could feel him studying her, trying to determine if she was serious. She held out as long as she could stand it but she cracked too soon, bursting out laughing so hard that her eyes teared up and her ribs started aching again.

Owen chuckled, too, but he had a predatory gleam in his eye. "Not a chance," he growled, closing in. "No take-backs here, aye?"

Outside the cottage, the storm that had been threatening all afternoon finally cracked the sky wide open, pouring sheets of rain against the windows and roof of the cottage like it had taken their jokes about being rough to heart. In contrast, Owen made love to her slowly and deliberately, his calloused palms inexpressibly tender as he stroked her skin and wound her tight.

When they came together at last, there were no fireworks—there was only a profound intimacy that shook Morgan to her soul. She breathed Owen in, grateful that he'd returned in one piece and that their nightmare was over. Grateful that—for now at least—he was hers.

The sounds Owen made were nearly lost to the thunder, but the emotion he poured into every touch—that, she heard loud and clear. It was a revelation, bathing her in a glow that could only come from one thing.

One *feeling*.

When it was over, Owen dropped his head to the hollow where her neck met her shoulder but soon after, he raised up to squint at her. Almost reluctantly, he trailed light kisses along her jaw, then planted a decidedly solid one on her mouth.

And then he announced, somewhat oddly, "I am a reprehensible human being." Owen didn't sound particularly sorry, and the corners of his mouth were quirked up in a smirk he was trying to fight.

"Because you couldn't resist my epic feminine wiles?"

"Yeah…something like that. If, by not resisting, you mean that I took advantage of a helpless invalid, and somehow once again perpetuated workplace harassment on my valued employee."

Owen rolled to his side and gathered Morgan close. "I'm not even ashamed, either. I enjoyed myself immensely." He stroked her side and hip happily. "One could even say that I loved it."

Morgan loved *him*, she thought. So much. "Who you callin' helpless?"

She laced her fingers through his and stretched Owen's arm over his head, using the leverage to roll him onto his back. Morgan straddled his hips and pulled his other arm up, too, so she could admire those thick muscles of his.

"Do I feel powerless? Or vulnerable?" she asked. She dragged her core along his length, velvet and hot and rebounding nicely, then eyed his face with satisfaction. When she moved again, she gripped his hands harder and watched his eyes squeeze closed in concentration.

Owen found his voice with effort. "You do not. Still, a man of my low moral character tends to retaliate when his victim tries to turn the tables," he explained.

Morgan stopped plying his neck and collarbone with licks and kisses and gave her hips another experimental shift. Owen groaned, low and long.

"There is no way I'm going to manage what you're asking for, love. Not yet," he said. "But damn, you make me want to try."

Hmmm. While she plotted her next move, Morgan tried to focus on the topic at hand. "You know, you should feel ashamed of yourself. No woman should have to work under these conditions. And I'm injured, too. I have even more rights."

She lost the thread of what she was saying, however, when she noticed the sexy tilt of Owen's lips. Morgan let go of his hands to cup his face and attempted to kiss him softly—but she ended up with more than she'd bargained for.

Owen gripped her hips and yanked her tight against his cock, hot and hard beneath her. "Back to my retaliation," he said, growling huskily when Morgan leaned in close to nip his shoulder. "I would rather endure a filthy house, and…and *hardtack* for dinner than…"

He was forced to stop when Morgan kissed him, deep and lingering. Owen gave it back to her in spades, then smacked her rear just hard enough to make his point.

She pulled back and smiled, feeling sassier by the minute.

"As I was saying," he continued, "I'd rather go hungry and live in squalor, than give up the right to do this with you all the time."

"All the time?" Morgan inquired, sweet as honey.

Owen adjusted himself, then pushed into her with one startlingly deep thrust. His jaw was set and his expression abruptly fierce. "All the time," he agreed, holding still inside of her. "You're fired."

"*Fired!*" Morgan stared down at him, stunned. "But…I mean…you'll help me find another job, right?"

Without a job, the work permit that allowed her to stay in the country would be useless, and Morgan would have to leave. Worry snaked through her system, dousing every ounce of ardor in its path.

Owen rolled her onto her back, agile as ever, then propped himself on his forearms so he could loom over her. Somehow, his cock was still buried in her body. "I have *brilliant* ideas for jobs you could do," he told her.

He kissed her, then went to work on her breasts, licking and sucking until Morgan was writhing and desperate for him. Once he had her mood rekindled, Owen began moving, thrusting in and out like he'd been born for it.

"*Owen*," Morgan moaned, hungry and confused and so in love with him her heart hurt.

"No worries, aye?" he gasped, "We offer a very generous severance package here at Hargreave Manor." He jerked his hips a little harder on his next thrust.

When Morgan snorted, he grinned crookedly at her, like he was enjoying keeping her off-balance. It was morning before she had either the time or the inclination to wonder what Owen might have meant by his words.

January 16

I missed having Owen's arms around me. But even though I managed to convince him that I'm healed enough to take all he has to give, it all feels twice as emotional as it did before.

Now, I just need to convince myself that getting involved with him to begin with was a good idea. I never meant to lose my heart to Owen, but now that I have, I need to figure out how I will survive the heartbreak of leaving him when the time comes.

That time is coming. Owen has begun hinting at it. It's happening far sooner than I'd hoped, though.

Chapter Forty-Two

OWEN WAS ALREADY sitting at his desk when Morgan awoke the next morning, the stack of mail he'd been reading set aside so he could watch her instead.

Dust motes swirled through the morning light slanting in through his window, casting a dreamy spell over the room. First, she stretched, and then she lay still for a bit, her eyes drifting lazily around like she didn't know he was there.

Owen wondered what she was thinking about. Did she feel at home, or did it still feel strange, even alien, after keeping house here for months?

Morgan turned her face into his pillow and breathed in deep, making him smile.

When she sat up and slipped from his bed, she looked reluctant to leave. Soon, however, she padded toward him, wearing one of his old t-shirts and not much else. Owen's smile turned into a smug grin.

"Now, that's a sight I could get used to," he told her.

Morgan mumbled something that sounded like, "G'morning," and gave him a sleepy smile.

Owen was about to pull her into his lap when his phone started ringing. Baffled, he said, "Hang on," and turned to see what it could be about.

While he talked, he eyed Morgan's long legs, beckoning her closer so he could run his palm up her thigh. However, the wild story Christine Twospeak was spinning kept distracting him.

His hand fell away and Morgan wandered off in search of coffee. He'd made it hours ago, though, and knew it must have gone cold by now. Sure enough, Morgan was soon brewing a new pot, and industriously starting in on the dishes he'd left in the sink.

Knowing her, she'd try to apologize for sleeping so much later than him. She'd probably make a fuss that he'd fixed his own breakfast, too, and spend half the day trying to make up for it.

He couldn't wait to stop talking about who was supposed to do which job, so he could start playing house with her.

At a pause in his conversation, Morgan came over and whispered, "Did you really fire me last night?"

Owen grinned and nodded. *Damn straight, he had.*

She frowned and looked so adorably confused that by the time he was able to hang up, Owen couldn't help laughing at her.

"Is everything all right?" she asked.

"Fine," he chuckled. "Christine just wanted to let me know that Carol came back."

Morgan set down her mug with a loud thunk. "Already?"

He snorted. "Would you believe, Sir Mark neglected to mention that he's a married man?"

"Uh-oh."

"Lucky for us, Miss Connelly has vengeance on the mind. She apparently took some of Thorpe's papers before she made her escape, and she wants me to turn them over to the authorities for her."

"You're kidding," Morgan exclaimed. *"Hell hath no fury,* I guess."

Owen nodded. "Quite right. Carol's mad as a wet hen."

Morgan grabbed his cup, then stepped back into the kitchen to pour them both fresh coffee. When she returned, Owen picked up the letter that he'd been perusing earlier and showed it to her.

She gazed at him quizzically. "What's that?"

Owen placed her mug on a stack of envelopes, then guided her onto his lap. He wrapped an arm around her waist and tapped the letter with his fingers. "Looks like I'm out of a job, love," he replied. "Much like yourself, aye?"

"What happened?" She was trying to play it off, but the dismay in her voice was clear.

"Sir John wrote me, and—"

Morgan peered at him and shook her head.

"Sorry. Sir John Windsor Kelly. The Preserve's been in his family for ages. I've no idea how the bloke's managed to hang on to it for so long after independence, even with the special charter he has. Knows someone high up, I guess."

"Okay."

"Anyway, with Nigel in the clink and the Rathbone case wrapping up, Kelly's decided to cut his losses, as they say."

"By firing you?"

"Yes and no. He's actually going about it rather smartly, transferring the entire parcel to the Mount Meru Forest Reserve. I think they'll be able to annex the Preserve without too much trouble."

She frowned. "But…won't they still need your help? That's a lot more land, and more animals, too."

"Well, they'll probably keep on some of our scouts, but they have a solid infrastructure already. They'll be able to absorb the administration of the Preserve into that without too many headaches. Plus, Sir John will undoubtedly funnel a monetary donation or two their way to help smooth things along. He feels dreadful about the Thorpe debacle."

Morgan studied his face. "So, what will you do? Try to work for Mount Meru, or go somewhere else?"

Owen sighed and stroked a hand up and down her spine. This was where things got a little tricky. "You know," he said, "I've been here a long time, and…I've missed a lot back home. Weddings, babies…funerals, too. I think…I think it might be time for me to head back."

"*Back*. To New Zealand?" she asked, her voice a tad shrill.

Owen nodded, watching her face carefully. "Just outside Christchurch," he clarified. "My mum and sisters will be over the moon when I tell them."

Morgan turned her head and stared out the back windows, blinking rapidly. He couldn't read her expression. Was this the end of them—or, as he hoped, the beginning?

"What about you?" Owen held her loosely in place and buried his nose in her hair. He couldn't bear the thought that he might not be able to do that for much longer.

"Me?" Morgan opened her mouth, then promptly shut it again. No other words seemed to be forthcoming.

"Yes, you," he prodded. "What do *you* want to do?" He held his breath and waited to see what she'd say.

Morgan shook her head and looked confused. "I don't know," she said, swallowing hard. "This is a surprise. But I guess…if you won't be here, I'll need to go home, too."

"Morgan," he said gently, "my parents are getting older. My youngest sister and her husband have a baby on the way, and I feel like it's time for me to be with my people again."

He tried to keep his words soft, but the more he said, the more certain he felt. The only thing he wasn't sure of was what she was going to do about it.

Tears welled in her eyes, but her small, broken voice was what really did him in. "How long have you known all this?" she asked. "And why didn't you tell me?"

"I only read the letter this morning," he assured her, "but I suppose I've been wondering for a while if it was time for me to leave. This just seems like the nudge I was waiting for," he shrugged, tapping the letter again.

"I see."

Owen stroked her cheek so she would look at him. "What about *your* family, love? You've been here for months and they must miss you terribly. Don't you miss them? Your sister, perhaps, or your mum and dad?"

Morgan bit her lip, then blurted out, "No. I don't. I know I probably should, but…" She grimaced a little, then explained, "I don't really have anything to go back to. My sister Meg has been staying in my apartment, but I was only in it for a little while after my divorce. It was just a place to sleep. It wasn't a home."

Owen tried to tamp down the wild flare of hope rising in his chest. "And your parents?"

"My parents." Morgan let out a scornful sound and scowled over his shoulder. "My parents did not make things easy for me during the divorce. My dad especially."

Owen wondered about that. Up till now, they'd only spoken of their families and pasts in a superficial way. Perhaps there were bigger reasons she'd holed up a continent away from her home—reasons that went beyond her friend's untimely demise.

"And your mum?" he prompted.

"My mother is…" Morgan trailed off, exhaling hard. "God. I hate this part."

"What part?"

"My mom is an alcoholic, actually," she told him bitterly. "She crashes through life like a bull in a china shop, and just expects me, Meg, and Dad to clean up her messes. As long as we do that, she doesn't care what else we accomplish. She never has. Even when I lost the baby, you would've thought I'd only lost my car keys, for all the emotion she showed."

Morgan froze then, blinking at him with eyes as wide as full moons over the savannah. Tears rolled freely down her cheeks, and it was clear she'd taken herself by surprise with that admission.

Well, she'd said it now, and Owen, for one, was happy that everything was finally out in the open between them. "I'm sorry to hear that," he murmured, taking one of her shaking hands and kissing it gently. "You did not deserve to be treated that way."

"You have no idea what a relief it's been," she continued, "all this time away from my stupid, stalled life. No disapproval from my father or trying to catch the interest of my mom. No worry about protecting Meggie from them, or suffocating sense of failure about everything else." Her voice was hoarse, but she still barreled on.

"When I'm with you, I'm just Morgan," she said. "And Morgan is a good person to be here. My share of blame feels like a fair one. A *manageable* one."

Owen smiled a little at that and gathered her close to his chest. "That's good."

"Thank you for being so understanding. I didn't mean to spring all this on you. It's just…the thought of going back there…"

It was now or never. Owen steeled himself and said, as reasonably as he could, "Boston doesn't sound like the most compelling place to return to."

"It isn't," she muttered into his chest. "When it comes to me, it's a disaster zone."

"Well, that explains why you're still here, I guess." He hoped this meant she didn't intend to ever go back, because the thought of saying goodbye to her for good felt like brambles under his skin.

However, asking Morgan to traipse even further across the world, to yet another new country, seemed like the height of presumption. Owen needed to use the right words, but it felt like they were all backing up in his throat, blocked by a wall of nerves.

She looked abruptly resolute when she leaned away from him, though. "It's not the *only* reason I stayed," she said. "And if I have to go, I may as well swing for the fences, now. So, Owen…you have to know that I can't walk away with you thinking I don't care."

The lump in his throat got bigger. "I don't think that."

"How are you so calm right now?" she laughed. "I'm trying to tell you I love you. So much it hurts."

Every taut muscle in his body released at once, like Morgan had released a painful knot with her words. It felt like the sun breaking through the clouds after a storm, like flowers blooming in the spring, like…*life*, suddenly returning to him.

Owen grinned. He ran his thumb along her cheekbone, wiping away her tears. "I was hoping you would say that. I love you, too, by the way. To a completely ridiculously degree."

He kissed her, then pulled back and studied her face. But after a long, awkward pause, he knew he had to dive in and trust the well was deep enough.

"I've been wondering if someone else's rather spectacular hometown might suit you better than Boston." He didn't take his eyes from her face, and he didn't feel the least bit calm—Owen was a basket case, and he knew no answer had ever mattered so much to him.

Morgan cleared her throat and swiped at her cheeks. "Whose spectacular home did you have in mind?"

He swallowed back the ball of nerves climbing his throat. "Well, you know—New Zealand is gorgeous this time of year. It's common knowledge."

She laughed at his bravado. "I've heard that."

"Have you really?" He sat up straight. *That was lucky.*

Morgan rolled her eyes, those pretty hazel pools he could swim in for a lifetime. "No, Owen. I haven't."

"Ah. Toying with me, in your precarious position, aye?" He jostled her on his lap, pretending to spill her off.

Morgan gave a little shriek, then cut it off when he steadied her again. He smoothed a hand up the silky skin of her thigh, but she swatted him away. "I'm sure it's true, though," she giggled.

"I promise it is," he vowed. "Listen. I know it's a lot to ask, and it's a really big step…but I'd love for you to move home with me." He gripped her hips and stared into her eyes, willing her to want it as much as he did. "Please. Just…think about it, all right? I…have the best of intentions, if you get my meaning. And I'll do everything in my power to make it easy on you. I swear."

"I will. And thank you. For wanting me. And everything else."

"My pleasure, believe me."

Morgan cocked her head and scanned his face, and her expression turned somber. "This is not a great time," she announced, "but I hate that it's hanging out between us. I have to tell you something."

That didn't sound good. "What? Whatever it is, we'll figure it out. It doesn't change how I feel about you, or my offer."

Morgan took another deep breath. "It's not about that. But…remember when we dropped off Kisima yesterday? She told me something when we were about to drive away."

"Yeah. *Ask Tumelo how his wife died*, wasn't it?" Owen couldn't imagine where this was going, or how it applied now.

"That's not precisely all she told me." Morgan admitted, wincing.

"Okay. So what did she say? Precisely?" He shifted his legs under her, bracing for…something. He had no idea what.

Morgan looked pained. "Well, uh…I didn't tell you the rest."

"Tumelo's wife had AIDS," Owen said. "What more is there?"

"Apparently, she got it from Thom," Morgan explained, looking wan. "I'm sorry I didn't tell you right away. I knew you were upset about the way he died. I didn't want to—"

"Wait. What?" he sputtered, stupefied. "Thom and...Tumelo's wife?"

"Yes. According to Kisima," she said, "Thom was the only person who could've infected Tumelo's wife."

"Well, she would know." Owen ran a shaky hand through his hair. "*God,*" he breathed, "That's just a whole new layer of *what-the-fuck,* isn't it?"

Morgan levered herself off his lap. "I'm sorry I kept it from you last night. It seemed like too much to pile on you at once, and then after that, there wasn't exactly a good time to bring it up again."

"It's all right," he assured her. "I wish Kisima had told me herself, and long before now. Maybe I could have done something to help."

Suddenly, though, a sickening thought occurred to him. "Christ, love—Thom's been mowing a path through the women in this town for years. There could be others."

Morgan grabbed her cup and eyed the cold coffee in it. "And, if not for you, I might have been one of them." She set the cup down again. "Owen, I feel like an such idiot. If you hadn't come home when you did, I'm not sure I could've stopped him. Would he have said anything to me? Or even used protection?"

Owen sighed. "I have no idea. I hope he wouldn't have endangered you like that—or anyone else, for that matter. But clearly I was wrong about him in a lot of other ways, so who knows."

"I should've known better than to get so drunk," Morgan said forlornly. "I knew he was paying me too much attention, but I kept hoping if I got him talking, he'd tell me stories about you."

Owen tilted his head. "You…were interested? Even then?" There was something reassuring in the notion that he hadn't been the only one carrying a torch day after day.

Morgan rushed to agree. "Of course I was, and I'm sure you could tell, too. I was mooning around this place like a preteen with her first crush."

Owen snorted. "I didn't have a clue. Might've made things easier, if I had."

"Maybe," she smiled, then grew serious again. "Do you think Thom's illness might have had something to do with him killing himself? If people knew about Kisima's sister-in-law, I'm surprised he was able to keep it a secret for so long."

"I am, too. And that's definitely a conversation Kisima and I will be having soon."

Morgan's eyes were welling up again, so Owen stood and wrapped his arms around her. "I've been beating myself up ever since she told me," she admitted. "I already felt awful that you had to intervene that night, and that you two ended up in such a fight over it. But realizing how much worse it could've been, I…"

"Slow down," he told her, rubbing his hands up and down her back. "What-ifs aren't important. The main thing is that you're fine. *We're* fine," he said. "Thom made his choices, and we can't change that. But you and I—we are going to be okay from here on out."

Owen now knew that Morgan had lousy parents, and that she'd lost a child in addition to weathering a contentious divorce. He had saved Morgan from his supposed friend—who had turned out to be the worst kind of ingrate—then nursed her back to health after a traumatic attack. Owen knew how she grieved, and how she turned brave as a lioness when the chips were down.

Owen knew how Morgan cried, and laughed, and came. And he knew, in the marrow of his bones, that he'd never let her go.

He loved her and would for a lifetime. Morgan gripped him tight, loving him back.

Okay was the very least of what they were going to be.

Chapter Forty-Three

A S THE INVESTIGATION into Thom's death progressed, Morgan had a front row seat to Owen's surprise and dismay over each new revelation. That was the way things went with old friends, though. Over time, you stopped seeing them as others did. You blurred the edges.

When a person died like Thom had, however, the harsh outlines had a way of reasserting themselves—and Morgan hated to see the way it affected the man she loved.

At least Ruth hadn't had some secret life she'd been keeping on the down low for years. She remained the same person in death as she had been in life.

Owen wasn't nearly as lucky. Thom had listed him as his next of kin on every official record from Victoriaville to Dodoma, so he was left with the burden of trying to locate Thom's family to inform them of his passing.

He soon discovered, however, that Hannity did not have relatives in Boonah, Queensland, as he'd always alleged—and might not have come from Down Under at all. It was as if Thom Hannity hadn't existed at all before he'd arrived in Victoriaville, as much a riddle in death, as in life.

The task that kept Owen up most nights, however, was trying to track Thom's most recent romantic liaisons. Thom's autopsy had confirmed that he was HIV-positive, and Carol had told them he'd been taking medication for about two years. That left far too many assignations that could potentially be problematic.

Owen had finally enlisted Nadra and Kisima to help spread the word and hoped it would be enough.

The authorities had raised other questions about Thom's demise, of course. Owen could hardly address those head-on, since his visit to the motel still remained a secret, and their contacts at TANAPA hadn't given them much guidance about what they could say to whom yet.

Joseph was still recuperating at home and in his stead, the Temba brothers had been doing their best to run interference. For that, Morgan was grateful.

It was hard to watch him suffer, and have no real way to help him, but Owen didn't seem to care that Morgan was pretty useless. He simply did what he had to regarding Thom, vented when he needed to, and cheered himself up by making arrangements for his return to New Zealand with his dog and his girlfriend in tow.

The puppy had been a surprise, to say the least. When he'd crept out of his carrier that first day, he'd slunk right to Owen's feet, curling into a quivering ball on top of his boots. He looked skinny, but his shaved fur was growing in silky brown, with black patches here and there.

Morgan took one look at him and proclaimed, "*Aw*. He looks like a cookie."

"Cookie is a girl's name," Owen declared, but he scooped him up, studied him carefully, and decided Biscuit would serve just as well. The puppy shadowed them everywhere, adoration all over his inquisitive little face.

Morgan was very attached to her boys. So, yeah—she was going to New Zealand, too. She'd found the love she'd always dreamed of, and she wasn't about to let it go.

She'd learned the fates could be charitable when you were dense and stuck. They gave you as many signs in a row as you needed, to let you know it was time to move forward—and sometimes they even shoved you into taking the first step.

She had a feeling she was going to thanking them for it for the rest of her life.

MORGAN RECEIVED AN unexpected piece of mail in the next day's post—an official-looking letter from Dr. Bing, the British liaison in Victoriaville. As soon as Owen handed it to her, she sat down on one of the packing crates accumulating in the living room to read it.

Inside that particular crate, she knew, were some of Owen's most-loved books. Morgan had never found the passage he'd marked for her in his favorite one. Just as she'd never talked about the violet petals he'd hidden in her locket, or recognized his lingering looks for what they really were.

In the end, none of those things had been necessary, though. Love, like life, found a way no matter how ineffectual its participants were.

Owen paused over the box he was packing to prompt her, "What's it say?"

Morgan looked down at it and frowned. "It's…about Ruth's death certificate," she told him. She scanned the words a second time, but she was still confused.

"Shouldn't they have sent that to her family already?"

"They did, but this says it's been amended. The medical examiner received new evidence, I guess." The letter in her hand was shaking, just a little.

Owen noticed. He moved to her side and began reading over her shoulder. "What kind of evidence?"

Morgan handed him the notice and looked up at him, feeling unsteady. "They traced the bullets that killed her to someone else's gun," she said. "But how—"

Owen interjected, "Whose gun?" He scanned the letter, but Morgan already knew what he'd find.

"Would you believe Christian Chagga's? How is that possible? I didn't even know you or Joseph then." Her voice was shrill but *come on*—panic was starting to wind itself around her chest like a vine.

"The thug who came here?" Owen's hand dropped to her shoulder and settled her with its warm weight.

Morgan rubbed at the locket around her neck and nodded grimly. "Dr. Bing says they're treating it as a homicide now. Owen—they're rolling it into the Rathbone investigation." She watched his face for his reaction. As revelations went, this was a big one.

"*Good god*," he breathed, turning pale. "I can't bloody believe I haven't heard about this yet." He stared grimly off into space, then asked, "Would you mind if I give the old bloke a call?"

"No, of course not. I'm just…I'm kind of in shock." That was a bald understatement, Morgan realized. She was so shellshocked she didn't think she'd be able to stand up if she had to.

Owen squeezed her shoulder. "I believe that. Let me see if Bing has any more information."

The letter had somehow thrown her back into the mindset she'd been in when she'd first gotten here. Morgan gazed out the back windows and tried to remind herself that she wasn't alone anymore. She wasn't damaged and she wasn't vulnerable. This was only…a bump in the road. That was all.

Owen grabbed his phone from the corner of his desk and made the call. Morgan listened numbly while he talked to someone, and when he hung up, he told her, "Dr. Bing didn't go in today, but his assistant told me we've got Conrad to thank for this."

"Conrad? Why?" She turned away from the sight of egrets picking their way through the tall reeds at the edge of the lake. It had stopped raining for the moment, giving the shore birds a chance to fish for their breakfast, but judging from the angry gray clouds rolling in, more storms were on the way.

Owen set his phone down thoughtfully. "Apparently, the liaison smelled a rat with your friend's case, and kept a shell or two so he could look into things himself," he explained, coming back over.

"Very Sherlock of him." Morgan tried, in vain, to reconcile that idea with the kindly old gentleman she'd met after Ruth died. She could picture Dr. Bing being interested in his grandchildren, and maybe a garden. Murder mysteries was stretching it, though.

Owen shook his head. "Don't be fooled. Bing was a sharpshooter in Korea and Vietnam. He knows his guns."

"Seriously?" He'd seemed so kind every time Morgan had dealt with him.

"No joke, love," Owen smiled. "He showed me his medals one time. Keeps them in the top drawer of his desk, aye? For easy access."

"But he's...so *sweet.*"

"Right." His eyes crinkled at the corners with amusement. "Sweet, and bloodthirsty."

Morgan pushed herself to her feet and paced away, nervous energy forcing her into motion. "I still don't get it," she muttered. "What does that Chagga guy have to do with Conrad's tours? Why would he even care about clueless tourists? We wouldn't have understood the first thing about what they were doing."

"I don't know. Conrad was supposedly doing a side job for TANAPA when Bing gave the shells to him. I guess that's how they got the ballistics match and made the connection."

"Don't you think that's strange, though? Our group wasn't in the Preserve when…it happened. Why would Dr. Bing think Conrad could help?"

"Beats me. My guess is the Thorpe crew was going farther afield to dispose of the Rathbone carcasses at first. It would've bought them some time before they stepped up their efforts and the scouts started to catch wind of what they were doing. Maybe your friend picked a bad time to wander off and saw something she shouldn't have."

"Ruth didn't *wander off*," Morgan cried, wheeling on him. "She just had to pee!"

Owen only shrugged and watched her sympathetically. *Immaterial*, he seemed to say.

"This is weird," she said again. "I mean—Conrad? And Dr. Bing? How many people in this town have secrets and…and *skeletons* rattling around? Nina kept saying that nothing made sense, but I thought she was crazy—that she couldn't accept the facts." She swiped angrily at her tears with her palms. "Turns out, I'm the crazy one."

Owen grasped her arms, holding her still so he could look into her face. "You're not crazy," he said firmly. "It's the situation that's crazy."

"What does it say about me, that I was so ready to believe Ruth would kill herself because she was sick?" Morgan cried. "She was tough. Ruth was a fighter. She would have tackled her illness just like she tackled everything else in her life, and I didn't give her credit for that."

"I'm sorry she had to go the way she did," Owen said simply. "But you can't berate yourself for believing what the police told you. You were in shock, love, and in the moment, it made sense."

"You're right," Morgan mumbled miserably. "I'm sorry for losing it. I don't know why I'm so emotional." She wound her arms around Owen's waist and rested her cheek against his chest. His heart thumped steadily, and it calmed her.

"Speaking of the Twospeaks, I should probably go over and say goodbye. I want to thank them one more time for taking me in and helping me find you."

Owen's hands stroked up and down her back, soothing her even more. "I'll take you," he said. "We can call them later to arrange a time."

His phone rang again, and he pulled away with a frown. When he answered it, Morgan watched his expression shift from curiosity to horror, and alarm rose like bile in her throat.

"What happened?" she demanded, as soon as he hung up.

"*Jesus.*" Owen sat heavily at his desk and stared at her. "The assistant liaison just got a call from Bing's daughter."

"Is he okay?" Morgan could feel the hysteria trying to claw its way out of her, and she struggled to push it back.

"No, he's not. He's dead."

OWEN HAD BEEN fielding calls for most of the afternoon, but his phone rang again as they pulled up to the Twospeak home. With one hand on his mobile and one on the wheel, he awkwardly tried to park the truck.

He didn't tell Morgan who he was talking to, and his brow was knit in concentration. It took him a minute to realize she was waiting for him.

When he finally did, he whispered, "Go ahead in. I'll join you as soon as I finish up. Five minutes, tops."

As she got out of the truck, she tried to figure out what he was up to. He'd been making calls and talking to people for hours, but they still had no idea what had happened to Dr. Bing.

He wasn't saying much, though, so Morgan swung her door shut and made her way around the truck. There were two ways to reach the kitchen door out back, the preferred entry point for the family. A narrow dirt path along the left side of the house, favored by the Twospeaks—and a less-used walkway on the right, overgrown and known for its proliferation of spiders and mosquitoes.

Owen had parked on the right. Steps from Insect Alley. Morgan hesitated, trying to decide. Maybe she should just knock on the front door. It felt too formal, but then again, she didn't live here any longer.

Birds chirped happily all around her, enjoying the sun and the brief respite from the rain. Morgan searched the trees, but all she could find was a pair of mourning doves nestled on a corner of the roof, heads together and cooing softly.

Morgan sighed and made her decision. *Front door, it was*. Her future was taking shape and pulling her away from this place. She'd be a visitor here forever, soon.

As she moved toward the steps, however, she spotted something through the tangle of overgrown ficus and olive trees on the right side of the house—something that looked a lot like fire.

She peeked back at Owen, but he was digging through his glove compartment as he talked and didn't notice her. His call was obviously important, and besides, people burned trash and brush around here all the time. That was undoubtedly all this was.

Except…Morgan didn't remember *Conrad* doing it, especially back there. So, instead of knocking on the front door, where Christine was probably waiting with cold lemonade and warm wishes, Morgan picked her way carefully along the side of the house, slapping at the bugs that landed on her arms and watching warily for the larger critters that might be lurking in the shade.

During the first week of her safari, a bird snake had dropped from a tree directly onto the shoulders of Irish Kevin. Morgan shivered. She'd never heard a grown man make such a sound. The memory of it made the hairs on the back of her neck rise in warning.

Fortunately, she made it to the back without getting mauled by tree snakes, where she discovered a rusted metal barrel containing the blaze and keeping it from spreading to the surrounding vegetation. The top of the container had a shiny, jagged edge, like it had been sawed off pretty recently.

Morgan edged forward and peered inside. A carefully arranged pyramid of wood was sending up sparks and occasional bursts of flame. Strewn across the sticks and branches were the ashes and curling remains of many sheets of paper—but it was the fancy crest on the letterhead of one in particular that caught her eye.

Frowning, Morgan leaned over and darted her hand in between the flames to fish it out. She waved it around to dispel the heat and looked closer. The distinctive royal insignia of the Preserve was embossed at the top of the smooth, rich paper.

Why was it here? And more importantly, why was Conrad destroying it?

Morgan quickly scanned the handwritten note, heart thumping hard in her chest. But the breeze shifted, sending stinging smoke into her eyes and nose. Morgan spun around, searching for the truck, and Owen.

He wasn't behind the wheel any longer, and she had to show him what she'd found right away. Morgan took a step in the direction of the truck, then heard an unmistakable click.

She froze and felt the gun's muzzle press hard into her back.

Chapter Forty-Four

OWEN HUNG BACK and watched as Conrad gripped Morgan's arm and roughly pulled her back, hooking an arm across her chest and holding her tightly. Like he was using her as a shield.

The urge to charge from the shadows and demand that he unhand her was nearly overwhelming, but he resisted in the off chance that Twospeak thought she'd come alone.

The task was not made one bit easier when the man hissed, "You've been a pain in my ass since the day you landed here. Why can't you be a good girl and *just go home?*"

Morgan was staring up into the trees overhanging the house, but she didn't say a word. Conrad jerked her, trying to elicit a response, but all she gave him was a small grunt of annoyance.

She was still holding that singed piece of paper, and Owen watched in admiration as she worked a little more of it between the buttons of her shirt every time the fire popped or sizzled.

She was a quick thinker, he'd give her that. Now Owen just had to keep her safe until Conrad showed his cards and they could get her free.

He shifted his weight, ready to lunge forward if the opportunity presented itself, and prayed there weren't any dry twigs to snap under his boots.

"Thommy told me all about his plans for you, Morgan, my love," the guide sneered. "Maybe I ought to take up where he left off, eh?" He shook her again, his voice distorted by an ugliness completely at odds with his usual jocularity. "Teach you some manners for sticking your nose in where it isn't wanted, and making me have to torch all my research."

"Don't," Morgan said softly.

Owen tamped down his frustration over how badly they'd all misjudged the man. Morgan had told him all about the aftermath of her friend's death, when Conrad had apparently given them such avuncular support. He'd stuck close when they'd given their statements, she'd said, and been endlessly patient when Morgan and the other girl had agonized over the incident.

Morgan had thought Conrad kind, but Owen had always suspected he was worried about how an untimely death would affect his business. He'd never considered that the guide had been trying to determine how much the women knew. In retrospect, it seemed so obvious.

And now, the bastard had somehow managed to take Morgan by surprise. If Owen hadn't spotted her creeping through the bush and gone after her, she'd be in real trouble right now.

He breathed in slowly through his nose, and let it out through his mouth, striving for calm and focus. The sun kept shining and the birds kept squawking as Morgan struggled against her captor, making this all feel surreal.

From inside the house, he heard Christine call, "Conrad? Sweetie?"

The guide hissed, "Shhh," in Morgan's ear, pulling her away from the window above them, and toward the front of the house—toward Owen.

"Good work bringing your boyfriend's truck," he told her. "It'll come in handy when I get rid of that fucking boy scout later. After I'm through with you."

Morgan's eyes went wide and wild. She tossed her head and struggled even harder. As they came closer, Owen backed further into the shade so she wouldn't spot him and give away his position. He hated how scared she looked, but it would only put her in more danger if he had to take a shot.

Two feet past his hiding spot, Morgan stumbled on a tree root and fell to her knees. Owen swore silently, knowing it had to have hurt her.

The screen door at the back of the house creaked open. Christine called, "Sweetie? Did you forget that Morgan is coming over soon?" a little louder, then paused a long moment before going inside again.

Conrad yanked Morgan to her feet, but the distraction had been the golden opportunity she'd needed. Fast as a mamba, she tucked the hem of her shirt safely in her waistband, securing that paper and hiding it completely.

Twospeak snatched her closer and swung her around, prodding her ahead of him as they neared the front yard. After a quick glance out, he pushed her toward Owen's truck, yanking open the door, and shoving her in.

Morgan climbed up and Owen relaxed a fraction. She was out of that fucker's clutches, at least, but Owen had the keys. When she couldn't produce them, what would Conrad do?

She slid clear across the bench seat, then immediately went for the handle on the passenger door, like she intended to bolt right out the other side. Owen smiled at her cleverness, but Conrad saw it, too.

"Don't you dare," he growled, pointing his gun at her head. "Give me the keys. And stay quiet." He put a heavy boot on the running board and gripped the doorframe, but his aim shifted when he hoisted himself up.

Owen didn't have a second to lose. He burst from the trees and got off a shot before the guide could swing into the seat, knocking Twospeak back onto the dirt. The crack of the blast reverberated off the house and Morgan cowered, holding her ears and ducking below the console in a delayed reaction.

Christine burst out of the front door a second later, calling frantically. "Owen? Oh my god, what happened?"

Morgan peeked at him from the passenger seat. She looked pale, but at least she was safe. Conrad was writhing on the ground, holding his wounded leg and cursing a blue streak. He looked surprised—and not a little brassed off—to see Owen standing there.

Christine ran over and skidded on her knees in the bloody dirt, trying to pull her husband's hand away so she could see his wound. "Jesus, Owen—did you *shoot* him?" she cried.

"Why don't you tell her why I did it," he told her husband. He watched Conrad's every move, but he didn't try to get closer yet. Twospeak might be in pain, but he still had his gun.

"Where did you think you were going to take Morgan, anyway?" he wondered.

She was kneeling next to the driver's side window now, fingers gripping the window frame and a determined look on her face. "How can I help?" she asked him.

"*How can I help?*" Twospeak mimicked, then groaned and rolled his eyes. "*Please.* You romantic idiots make me laugh." He gasped and swatted at his wife's fluttering hands. "Just like fucking Hannity. He and Carol thought they were Bonnie and Clyde, but they were so bloody easy to get around. Once I convinced them to deal me in, I didn't even have to get rid of them myself. I only had to look out for number one while they self-destructed."

"Conrad. Sweetie. What are you saying?" Christine demanded, sitting back on her heels in confusion.

"That the Thorpes have more fucking money than sense," her husband snarled. "Why else would they get into bed with such morons? And why shouldn't they spread some of the largesse around? Look at Cotton—that asshole was so bloody sure he could spin everyone with his poacher line of crap, and that he'd be living the high life within a month. He deserved to get caught."

Owen watched the man's fingers flex on the gun's grip and asked, "And Thom?"

"*Thom.*" Conrad laughed sourly. "Oh, Thom. He just knew you wouldn't believe he was capable of such dastardly deeds. What a joke. But you—you, Hargreave, were the biggest dunce of them all. You and your little TANAPA buddies were so busy running around in circles, you never got close to me."

Christine made a squeak of surprise, launching herself back onto her husband, attempting to silence him and get him to lay still.

He pushed at her and kept his eyes on Owen. "I was so *helpful*, remember? And all of the fools were out of the way. All of them! In a few more months, everything would've died down and I could've gone back in under the cover of the tours, to take what was rightfully mine."

"Stop it," Christine demanded, "Stop it right now."

"No one would've been the wiser," Twospeak sneered. "And I would've put the money from those stones to good use. Been a real *philanthropist*—better than any of you lot, anyway. Not one of you knows shit about what's right for this country. Nigel and the Thorpes didn't, and for all your piousness, you don't either, Hargreave."

"Don't I?" Owen asked. The longer Conrad rambled on, the looser his hold on that gun became. His eyes were getting glassy, too, darting around in an unfocused way that had Owen hoping he was wearing himself down enough to pass the hell out.

At least it would put an end to the movie villain soliloquy.

"No. And you know why?"

Owen shrugged, not caring one bit.

"Because this isn't your country. It's mine. You and your little whore are visitors, in and out once you're done *protecting the Rathbone*s, or whatever other blessed cause you come up with. Couple of real savior complexes, you know that? You're perfect for each other."

Christine had stopped fussing, stunned into silence as she stared at her husband.

Owen had been listening to Twospeak's diatribe mostly impassively, but he couldn't resist commenting, "Now I know why it was so easy for you to find a match for those bullets Bing gave you. You knew exactly whose gun had fired them, didn't you? I'll bet he did, too. Is that why you killed him?"

Conrad's eyes burned, but he didn't answer right away. He only turned to stare up at Morgan and point an unsteady finger at her face. "If this irritating little twit hadn't shown up today, of all days," he snapped, "there wouldn't have been a single piece of evidence pointing to me at all."

But all of a sudden, he raised his gun and pointed it at Owen's chest, and there was nothing unsteady about it. Owen's pistol was up and aimed a heartbeat later, but Twospeak did the unthinkable—he swung his arm in a wide arc, until he sighted on Morgan.

Owen didn't waste time on threats. He just fired.

Christine shrieked but he ignored her, kicking the gun away from both of them and looking over at Morgan. "Are you okay?" he asked.

She blinked at Conrad, laying still and silent in the dirt. Christine forgot all about stanching the blood seeping from either of his wounds, and simply begged him to open his eyes.

"Is he dead?" Morgan wondered, looking dazed.

"Unlikely," Owen told her. "But I should call someone to make sure. Wouldn't want him to kick off before he can give a proper statement."

He took out his phone and dialed the police dispatcher, then called Sully Temba.

Morgan stared at him. "Why do you sound like you're ordering a pizza?" she muttered. "Does this sort of thing happen to you often?"

Owen sighed, relief coursing through him that she was safe and unhurt. "Almost never. I promise."

He could hear the note of panic creeping into her voice, though, so Owen left the Twospeaks, fetched Conrad's gun out of the grass, and walked around to the truck's passenger door. Morgan slid over and let Owen pull her into his arms.

She clung to him like a vine, burrowing into his chest and...smelling him? He stroked her hair. "Are you all right?"

"Forget about me. You're the one getting into gunfights. How did you know I was in trouble?"

"Joseph called me when we got here. The higher-ups at TANAPA finally brought him and his team in on all the details of the investigation. They discovered that the last Rathbones in the Preserve never made it to their destination, and there seemed to be only one explanation for it."

"Is that why we came here?"

"No, total coincidence on that score. But when I looked for you and saw the fire back there..." Owen cleared his throat and looked away. From now on, he wasn't going to let her out of his sight. *Ever.* "Anyway."

"I'm sorry about those poor little gazelles," she said sadly, then turned to eye Christine when the other woman let out a loud sob. "Are they all dead now?"

"Unless we find some stragglers in one of the neighboring parks—which is certainly possible—the Rathbones are probably gone from the wild," Owen told her. "There are a few of them left in zoos, though. Not enough." He looked over her shoulder and sighed again. "Hang on."

He walked around the truck and squatted beside Christine, putting an arm around her shoulders and reassuring her, "Help is coming any second now, love. Don't worry. Your man's only passed out. He'll be fine."

Just to make sure, he reached for Conrad's neck and checked his pulse. It felt steady, and by the looks of things, that second shot had merely grazed him. Perhaps he'd fainted, or perhaps the leg wound was worse than it appeared. Owen tugged the guide's belt from his waist and wrapped it tightly around his thigh.

"There. That should do it."

Christine watched him with a confused frown. "Owen, I don't...I don't know what's going on right now," she stammered. "Why did you *shoot* him? What was...what was Conrad talking about?"

Her face was blotchy and red, and streaked with tears. Her eyes were bewildered, but even though Owen had shot her husband—twice—she still didn't seem to fear him. Either she was the best actress in the world, or she truly had been in the dark.

"Hey, Morgan?" he called. "Maybe you can give me a hand down here."

She'd been watching him through the driver's side window, and to her credit, she didn't hesitate to nod and swing the door open. It wasn't until she realized she couldn't get down without stepping on the wounded man—or his blood—that she halted.

Owen stood and lifted her over the mess, then pulled Twospeak's gun from the back of his waistband, unloaded it, and laid it in the bed of his truck. He dropped the bullets into his pocket and turned to find the guide glaring up at him.

"For Christ's sake, you're not bloody Mother Teresa," Conrad gasped, his tone malicious and completely at odds with the way he'd always presented himself. "Would you give it a fucking rest already? I can take care of my wife. We don't need you."

He tried to sit up and push Christine away, but she kept her hands on him, holding him down. Still, he continued, "If you didn't act so bloody superior all the time, you might remember that you couldn't even protect your own woman."

He sneered and rolled to find Morgan with his red-rimmed gaze. "I'll tell you what—you had it coming, sweetheart. All you got, and more."

Owen dove for him. "Go back to sleep," he growled, trying to deck Conrad without inadvertently hurting the man's wife.

For a moment, Christine seemed conflicted about whether she should keep holding Conrad down, or try to fend Owen off. She only succeeded in getting in the way, however, and soon Morgan was gently urging her back.

Twospeak, it appeared, had found his second wind. "And your precious Preserve—what does it accomplish, except bring in tourists that drop their garbage everywhere before they leave again? Don't think we don't notice that their money leaves, too, Hargreave—straight into greedy British hands. Meanwhile, people can't farm that land…can't hunt that land. At least a diamond mine…" he stopped to catch his breath but didn't seem able to, "it…would've let them earn a decent living. Have some control over things."

"There aren't any diamonds there, you tosser," Owen fumed, grappling with the guide to keep him prone. "And even if there were, do you seriously believe that the Thorpes would've left a single shilling to the locals—or to *you*—for helping them? If so, you're a bigger fool than I am."

Conrad spit out, "Screw Thorpes. I didn't…need…any longer." He was battling for every breath. "I only needed…find a few stones and…could've done…all myself. Christine and I could've…managed things. We could've…" He blinked rapidly, narrowing his eyes as he tried to maintain focus and explain his grand plan. His head lolled, though, his strength deserting him.

Morgan tapped gently on Owen's arm, murmuring, "I think I hear the ambulance. If we can put that fire out, maybe we can salvage some of the papers in the barrel. Prove what he was up to."

Owen nodded and got to his feet. Conrad had thrown down quite a few gauntlets, however, and he couldn't resist one last parting shot. "You're wrong, you know. This isn't your country any more than it's mine. The best thing any of us can do is to just get the hell out of the way."

He took a few steps, then stopped. "And you better believe I can protect what's mine." Owen grabbed Morgan and hauled her close, and when her pretty lips fell open in surprise, he pressed a hard kiss to them.

As he stalked away, the driveway began filling up with emergency vehicles, TANAPA agents and medics spilling out and barking orders, with the police detectives hot on their heels.

Owen tried to wrap his mind around what he'd heard. Most of it was irrelevant now, and maybe, on some level, he ought to be thanking Conrad.

If the guide hadn't helped Morgan stay, Owen might not have so much that was worth protecting—so much worth fighting for. Whether he was a boy scout, a savior, or just a man in love—he wasn't ever going to stop fighting for her.

Chapter Forty-Five

AS OWEN MOVED in and out of the cottage, Morgan watched him load their bags in the back of the truck and tried to keep Biscuit from getting underfoot. With the exception of a few of the largest pieces of furniture, most of their possessions had already been crated and shipped to Christchurch to await their arrival.

When he'd paused to assess his progress, Morgan asked, "When is Kisima moving in, again?"

"I told you, love—later this month. Tomorrow, her husband will bring some workmen to add on another room. Then they'll have enough space for Tumelo to stay with them full time."

"And you're sure the scouts can use the truck?"

"Yes. They said they'd pick it up from the airport, after our flight leaves." He gave her a reassuring smile and waited, no doubt wondering if she had more repetitive questions lined up.

As their departure had drawn closer, Owen had been so patient about answering everything she'd come up with, even when she promptly forgot it.

"And the Preserve office—" she began.

"The sale went through with no problem whatsoever. By this time next week, Kisima and Nadra will be the proud proprietors of Victoriaville's first temp agency."

"I'm sorry we're going to miss that."

"You and me both."

Morgan sighed and toyed with Biscuit's leash as she led him around the empty rooms one more time, searching for anything they might have missed.

"I'm still sad we have to leave this pretty armoire," she told the dog.

"We took photos," Owen said from the doorway. "It shouldn't be too difficult to have someone make a copy once we're settled."

Morgan turned to him. "Are you sure Joseph is going to be okay?"

"More than okay," he assured her. "When I talked to him, he said he's graduated from the crutches to a cane and earned a nice promotion when he linked Conrad to the case with those bank records we saved."

"Follow the money."

"Exactly. He even hinted that they might try for another kid next year."

Morgan smiled, trying to picture it. "I wish we could've seen Nadra and the baby one more time."

"She promised to send photos."

"At least no one gave her and Kisima a hard time for helping with the investigation."

"Agreed. And I promise they'll be okay. They'll *all* be okay. It's you I'm worried about, aye?"

Morgan believed that. She'd been absent-minded and flitting around like a nervous nelly for days, and what they'd just discovered had only made the man more protective.

Owen wrapped his arms around her and pulled her close. "Now, tell me again," he said, brushing his lips against her ear and sending a shiver of pleasure down her spine. "What've you learned about sheep?"

She smiled into his chest as Biscuit promptly wound around their legs, trapping their ankles with his leash. "Let's see...the breed you like is called Coopworth and you want to buy a ton of them. We can make good yarn from their wool." She thought for a minute, then tacked on, "You know, I used to have a pair of sheepskin boots that I loved. Don't those come from New Zealand?"

"I think we can rustle some up," Owen chuckled against her hair. "And find some wee ones for the babe, as well."

His big, warm hands slipped under her shirt and smoothed across her stomach. Soon it would begin changing. Growing.

They'd been careful, but not careful enough, it seemed.

Nothing about this pregnancy felt like the last time. Morgan had been so stunned when she'd realized what was going on, she hadn't even considered coming up with a good way to tell Owen. She'd simply met his gaze in the bathroom mirror and blurted it out.

And unlike Chip, Owen was completely over the moon about it. He'd dropped to one knee right there next to the sink and proposed so fast he was lucky he hadn't hurt himself.

It was all good, though. As Owen had told her repeatedly, it was all going to be good, because they both knew they were meant for each other.

Morgan smiled to herself, thinking maybe escapism wasn't such a bad plan, after all. She felt whole, in a way she'd never experienced before. She felt...fulfilled. If she hadn't fled her old life, she might never have found this one.

She linked her arms around Owen's neck and pulled him down for a kiss. "I have one more quick thing to do," she said, "And then we can get going."

Owen's lips lingered over hers for a long moment. Then he grabbed a couple of bags piled against the wall, untangled the dog, and left her alone.

Morgan pulled her old journal from her carry-on and scribbled a quote in it that she'd come across a few days ago.

"You are alone with everything you love."
~Novalis

She dated the entry and contemplated the words, marveling over how such a simple sentence could encompass her feelings so perfectly.

She and Owen, and their future child, would be a family now—their own little world, no matter what happened in the wider one around them. Knowing that was a comfort, and an unburdening.

She closed her journal and zipped it back into her bag.

Owen strolled back in, grinning with anticipation. "Well, love? Are you ready?"

Morgan looked around one last time, trying to commit the cottage to memory, then nodded. He picked up her bag and took her hand, quickly kissing her knuckles before leading her through the door.

Morgan followed her man—soon to be her husband, and the father of her baby—outside. Biscuit sat in the truck, paws on the window and panting happily.

When her feet hit the grass, she shut her eyes and turned her face to the sun.

She might've taken a winding path, but she'd finally found the home she'd always longed for—but she could bring this one with her wherever life took her.

Epilogue

OWEN STOOD BY the big picture window in the family room, watching wisps of clouds drift past the bay in the distance. The sky stretched vivid blue over the rolling hills of their farm, but beyond the next rise it would plunge down to the water to mix with the steel gray of the waves.

A breeze had kicked up, making the long grass at the edge of the garden bend and sway. It was a sight he'd loved from the moment he was big enough to stand and peer over the sill, and one that he'd hadn't enjoyed for far too long.

He couldn't get enough of it, now. Once he'd come back, new family magically in tow, his parents had immediately retired to a cozy new condominium in town, like they'd been holding out for exactly that situation. He and Morgan had taken over the family farm, and Owen got to live on the land that had nurtured him and countless other Hargreaves for generations.

He got to raise his own family here—the biggest gift of all.

When he turned, the sun caught the diamond on Morgan's hand, and made it flash as she knit in his grandfather's rocking chair. Owen had put that stone on her finger nearly a year ago, but he could still feel his chest puff out with pride and contentment whenever he realized she was his for good.

Over in the corner, the Christmas tree twinkled, but it couldn't compete with the joy on his wife's face when she broke off humming a carol and looked up at him.

"I can't believe I'm using yarn from your sheep," she gushed for about the hundredth time. "How cool is that?"

Owen laughed. Morgan's enthusiasm for his birthplace had taken root the moment their plane had entered the airspace over Christchurch last year, and she found new things to gush over nearly every week. It was easy to get swept up by it and—coupled with his long years living abroad—had him viewing so much with fresh eyes.

"*Our* sheep," Owen corrected her.

Morgan grinned and did a cute shimmy in her chair. "I have *sheep*," she whispered, like it was the best secret she'd ever heard.

He went over and sat near her feet, pulling her sheepskin slippers into his lap with a smile of his own. The woman was obsessed with the things—refusing to take them off, even in the dead of summer.

"You have many sheep." He touched the knitting taking shape on her knees. "This is soft. Old Mavis is doing well for us, isn't she?"

Morgan hesitated, then nodded. He squeezed her feet and winked, knowing she had no idea which animal he meant. That was okay, though. She'd already learned so much, and before long, she'd learn how to tell the sheep apart, too.

Morgan dropped her needles in her lap with a faint look of alarm. "My…slippers didn't come from an animal with a name, did they?"

"Oh, now you ask?" Owen snorted. "But no. Just the yarn, aye? And Mavis and her sisters will grow you even more wool, next year. I promise."

A sudden burst of rustling erupted from the bassinet beside him, so Owen reached out and lightly touched the nose of their baby boy, napping *somewhat* peacefully. He was rewarded with the adorable scrunching expression Ollie made when he was concentrating very hard on sleeping, and Owen tried very hard not to swoop him up for a snuggle right then.

Biscuit's curious face popped up on the other side of the cradle, and the pup gave his buddy a sleepy sniff.

The little brutes had been up half the night with their shenanigans, after all, and Biscuit, at least, recognized that they now needed to rest.

Morgan watched them and sighed, sounding as tired and happy as Owen felt. He leaned against her legs as she stroked his hair, and his eyes fell on the beautiful quilt she'd made him all those months ago, now folded neatly across the back of their couch.

Sometimes Africa seemed so close—just under the skin, perhaps, or a breath away. Maybe someday they'd go back to visit, but for now, the calls and emails they exchanged with their friends were enough.

Owen and Morgan had discovered, rather blissfully he thought, that life—their real, till-death-do-us-part *life*—was here, on the sheep farm he'd grown up on. They were, at last, home.

Review

Did you enjoy **Finding Home**? If so, please consider leaving a review at the retailer where you purchased this title.

Book reviews can be as simple or as detailed as you wish, but all of them help authors sell more books, and assist other readers in finding the stories they want to read.

Almost any book can be reviewed by simply logging into the website where you purchased the title, then scrolling to the bottom of the title's product page to find an area called "Leave a Review."

Up Next

Finding Love

Lost & Found, Book Two

A year ago, he gave her his heart. Now he wants it back.

Meg never expected to find the love of her life sitting in a coffee shop. It wasn't like life was good right then, and she knew she wasn't any great catch. But handsome Edward, with his sexy British accent and irresistible kisses, was very persuasive. Meg handed over her heart without much resistance and expected it to be for keeps. When Edward suddenly disappears, though, she is forced to confront her deepest fears. Has she been a fool?

Months later his brothers appear, begging for Meg's help and telling a story that is almost impossible to believe. Caught between the love she once shared with Edward and the demands of his new, agonizingly different persona, Meg is faced with a choice. His family is counting on her to get through to him, but only she can decide whether to stick it out, despite the uncertain outcome—or cut her losses and move on.

Can Meg break through Edward's barriers, and remind him of all that they've lost? Or will he refuse her help, and force her to live a life without him?

Finding Love

Chapter One

SHE'D STARTED TO notice him a few months ago, another regular, who always sat at a table behind, and just to the right, of hers. They made eye contact only occasionally, but the first time they had, it had given her a little thrill, a little stutter, right in the center of her chest.

He hadn't appeared to be similarly affected, and he wasn't always there, but he'd begun showing up with increasing regularity. Her neck positively prickled with awareness when her mystery man was in attendance, every brush of her hair across her neck and shoulders feeling like a caress. It was unnerving and exciting—about the only thing in her life these days that she could say that for.

Meg parked herself at her table, and arranged everything the way she liked it. Until her food arrived, she liked to people-watch. There were the other regulars, like herself, though by mutual agreement they didn't really acknowledge each other with more than the barest of nods, because all the creatures of habit had their routines. There were also the occasional tourists, and the harried students and professors. And, naturally, if the day was promising and the stars aligned just right, there might, gloriously, be *him*.

She glanced quickly around the café again. He still wasn't there. Her cappuccino arrived, and she took a quick gulp, scalding her mouth. Her knee bobbed restlessly, up and down. Why was she so antsy today? She couldn't seem to settle down. And now, she had to pee.

Meg sized up the girl at the next table, taking in her unhealthy pallor and enormous textbook. Deciding she was likely a pre-med student, she leaned over and asked her to watch her stuff, then threaded her way through the other tables toward the back wall and the restrooms. As she paused for a departing knot of boys to gather up their backpacks and cups, her eye was caught by the instantly recognizable pink pages of the *Financial Times*. Uh-oh. She furtively peeked down at the table next to her, right into her mystery man's face, raised to hers in inquiry. Meg was stunned. He was there? *He was there!* How had she missed him? He smiled a little, and she felt herself flush beet red. Meg forced her feet into motion, hurrying back to the bathrooms in numb shock. She'd made eye contact with him. He had smiled. And now, she'd have to go back *out there*. Why was she such a wreck all of a sudden? It must be because he'd startled her, that was all. Oh god. She was being such a nerd. This was what she'd *wanted*.

Meg second-guessed her entire lavatory visit. Was she rushing? Was she taking too long? What would he think if she took too long? And when she finally admitted to herself that she had to get back out there before someone ate her breakfast or stole her stuff, she felt like her legs had been removed and reattached wrong. She walked clumsily past him, her movements feeling jerky and awkward. She stubbed her toe on a chair leg, recoiled, and bumped the corner of his table. In her peripheral vision, she thought she saw him reach out to steady his coffee cup, but she couldn't look at him. She just couldn't. Finally, gaining the sanctuary of her table, she slumped in her chair, and was never more thankful to be facing away from him. Her cheeks were flaming, and the fraternity guy next to her had swiped her paper's sports page.

"Sorry," he grinned sheepishly, trying to return it.

"No, it's okay," she said, flustered. "You keep it." She lifted her mug, peered into it and decided it looked unmolested, then took a deep gulp.

Right then, she felt a soft touch on her shoulder, and heard a polite little throat clearing. Meg closed her eyes, said a silent prayer, and forced herself to look up. Up, and not at the belt buckle situated disconcertingly right at eye level.

Even prepared, it was still a shock to see him standing there at her elbow, smiling warmly down at her. He was even more attractive up close, with thick light brown hair and tawny hooded eyes that crinkled charmingly at the corners. His eyelashes seemed preposterously long for a man.

Meg realized with a start that he must have just spoken to her and she had no idea what he'd said. She was too busy staring like a loon, for god's sake. She blinked at him in confusion, speechless and tongue-tied. Willing herself to speak, to say something, anything, to acknowledge his presence, she only got as far as opening her mouth to speak. Sadly, no sound emerged.

Gamely, he tried again. "I said, I'm sorry to bother you. It's just," he shrugged, adorably. "The curiosity is killing me."

Meg was momentarily stymied by the fact that he sounded British, but it was an odd enough opening gambit that she discovered she actually knew what to say to him: "About what?"

"For weeks, I've been back there," he gestured to his accustomed spot, as if she didn't know exactly where it was, "Wondering how a girl who looks like you developed the taste in literature that you have."

Meg frowned slightly, glancing down at the book on her table. *Slowness*, by Milan Kundera. "Uh..." she stalled. There was a lot going on in his statement, and she was trying to decide which part to tackle first.

He continued standing there, waiting, for an excruciatingly long minute. Then he looked fleetingly, but significantly, at the chair opposite her.

Meg smiled and nodded, then managed a polite little, "Please."

Happily, he settled in, arranging his coat and bag against the wall without a second's hesitation. A server arrived then, and Meg was relieved by the further delay, so she could *think*.

He looked up, and the other girl just melted before Meg's eyes. "She'll have another..." he peered into her cup. "Cinnamon latte?" She nodded, amazed that he'd gotten even that close. "And I'll have the same." He turned to her. "Have you eaten yet?" he asked, solicitous and elegant with his fancy accent and impeccable clothes.

"Not yet," she replied. "But I already ordered."

"What did you get?" he asked, just as Poppy stalked over to hand a plate to the server.

She dropped it unceremoniously on the table, right on top of Meg's newspaper, before intoning robotically, "Everything bagel, toasted, butter and cream cheese, with tomato and onion." So it wasn't just Poppy, thought Meg, they *all* hated her order.

Her mystery man looked quizzically at her plate, then up at her. Meg shrugged and nodded, as if to say, *Sure. It's not like it'll kill you.*

"For you?" the server asked, pulling his attention back to herself, and preening a little once she'd secured it.

"Oh, why not? I'll try one, too," he smiled up at her.

"How did you do that?" Meg breathed, once the server had left with a swish of her ponytail. "The rest of us mortals have to order at the counter!"

"I know," he admitted, bashfully. "I've seen you."

"Am I really that obnoxious?" Meg asked, pained, suddenly, by her behavior with Poppy earlier.

"Not at all," he demurred. "Just...noticeable." He looked away for a minute, then seemed to collect himself. "Now, about these books you've been reading."

Considering last week's edition of *The Highlander's Reluctant Bride*, Meg was grateful that today's volume was a tad less dazzling. Frantically, she tried to remember every other title she'd read in the past year, but couldn't think of a single one. "Yes?" she said.

"At first, I suspected a literature class of some kind, but I can't imagine one that would encompass the scope of what's crossed this table," he began.

Inside her head, Meg was screaming: *What is his name?!* But she managed to find her normal voice, somewhere. "I'm still stuck back on what you meant by 'a girl who looks like you'," she admitted. It was shameless fishing, she knew, but what did he expect when he dropped bait like that into the water?

He raised an incredulous eyebrow at her. "Surely you've had your appearance commented on before."

There was something so easy-going about this guy, and he seemed so utterly cheerful about whiling away the morning with her. Meg felt herself relaxing steadily, and with that, the words came easier.

"Well, I have, on occasion, been called 'cute'," she began. When he started to look a little smug, she hurried on: "*But,* never with your particular emphasis. And, to be precise, you didn't exactly specify *what* I looked like."

"No, I did not," he agreed. He smiled at the server who sidled up, thanked her for their fresh cups of coffee, then handed her Meg's empty one to take away.

Oddly, the girl didn't seem to find that annoying, even though patrons were generally expected to bus their own tables here. "Your bagel will be ready in a minute," she purred, before departing again.

He shot Meg a look of exasperation. "So, you're taking a class..." he prompted.

"Nope," she said.

"Are you a book reviewer of some kind?" he persisted, studying her.

"No." Meg was enjoying this, but she knew she couldn't drag it out forever.

"Then...?" he prodded.

Meg shrugged. "I just really like to read. Good stuff -" she glanced helplessly down at her book, a redeeming one today, at least. "And I like a lot of junk, too." She turned pink. The highlander's bride hadn't *exactly* been that reluctant last week, and she wouldn't have been either, given his skill set.

"I see," he said, looking unconvinced.

His bagel arrived, delivered by yet another server, this one a pale blonde Russian girl new this semester. Apparently the kitchen was going to send out all its big fish, in an effort to snag him. He didn't appear to notice, paragon that he was. Meg turned back to study her own plate, wondering how to consume something so large and messy with a modicum of delicacy. But he dug into his with enough gusto that she decided to give up on dignity and just go for it. She was starved.

He winked at her, licking his lips in approval, and said around a mouthful, "It's not bad!"

Meg blinked, chewing mightily. Even with his mouth full, he was so beautiful it was actually a little difficult to look him in the face for very long. And the way he was searching *her* face, eyes roaming intently over her features as they ate, was incredibly unnerving. Suddenly, he snorted.

"Oh god, I am such an arse," he groaned.

Meg was confused. "You are?"

"I'm Edward," he grinned, wiping off his hand and holding it out to her. "Edward Hughes."

"Oh! Hi," she shook his hand, his long graceful fingers and broad palm, warm and strong. "I'm Meg. Flynn. Meg Flynn."

"Meg," he repeated. She had to admit, her name sounded really, really good on his lips. "I'm sorry. I should have led with the introduction."

"It's okay," she allowed, bashfully.

They finished eating, and an awkward silence threatened to descend. It wasn't lost on Meg that he had deftly managed to change the subject of her appearance, even though he'd been the one to bring it up in the first place. Who only knew what that might mean? As he busied himself paying the check Svetlana brought him, Meg gazed out the front windows at the glorious fall day underway out there. He hadn't asked for her number, and she was a little discouraged that things looked like they were wrapping up here. She only realized she had zoned out for too long when she felt his disconcerting eyes trained on her face once more. He turned in his chair to look outside too, then turned back to her.

"I expect you probably have other things to do today, but," he paused, trying to gauge her mood. He seemed to steel himself, then continued, "I don't suppose you'd like to take a walk down to the Commons with me? It looks wonderful outside."

Was he serious? They couldn't do that! Except...her mind flickered briefly to the desolate afternoon that would otherwise be looming before her. If she went shopping, she couldn't buy anything anyway. If she went home, she'd end up doing something riveting, like dusting her nonexistent possessions. So, with barely any hesitation, she found herself shrugging yet again. "Sure," Meg agreed. And handsome Edward looked as pleased as he could possibly be.

To read more, please purchase *Finding Love* from your favorite bookseller!

FREE BOOK

Get a glimpse of Morgan, Meg, Molly and Mina—*before* their happily ever afters take place!

Sign up for the author's Reader's List and get a free copy of the Lost & Found prequel novella "Girls Night Out."

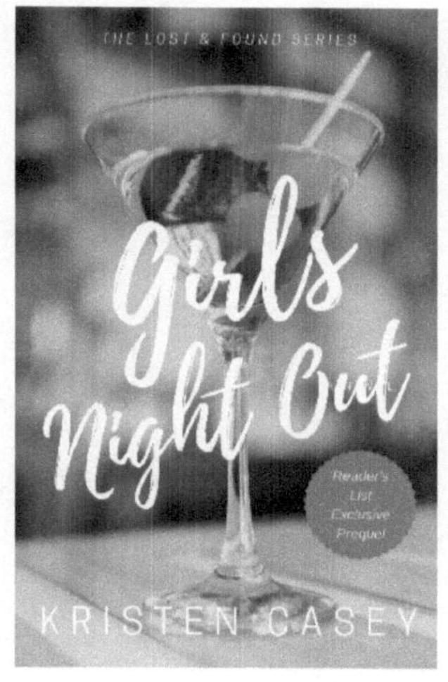

Visit Here to Get Started:

http://eepurl.com/ctGk1j

Also by Kristen Casey

The Triple Threat Series

The Titan Was Tall

The Doctor Was Dark

The Hero Was Handsome

The Masquerade was Magic

The Hero's Brother

The Triple Threat Box Set

The Black Watch Security Series

False Flag

Heat Seeking Missile

Brothers in Arms

Fight or Flight

Search and Destroy

Squared Away

Acknowledgements

People often like to point out that "you don't know what you don't know." That was never clearer to me than when I made the decision to return to the book that started my career as a romance author, in order to give it a full makeover. I've learned so much about how to tell a story since I wrote it. I knew I could make it better.

I thought I would blow through, clean up the writing and editing a bit, and then move merrily on to my next project. What *actually* happened was…unexpected. I waded into Finding Home and discovered that it needed far more revising than I'd anticipated. Instead of a brief dusting-off, I ended up completely overhauling the book from the foundation to the rafters—reconstructing chapters, scenes, and sentences until I was sure I had each thought exactly the way I'd intended them. I got about halfway through, and then…

You know what happened? The entire world shut down. 2020's stage director called, "Cue the pandemic!" and what was already a long and involved process suddenly became a Sisyphean grind that I despaired of ever finishing.

Like so many creatives across the globe, I suddenly had no peace, no privacy, and no focus to work. And yet, the year from hell eventually came to a close, and we are still here—surviving and looking together for the light at the end of the tunnel.

Finding Home is done at last, too. I think it's better than ever. The ones who helped make that happen know who they are, and how much I love and appreciate them. Thanks, you guys.

About the Author

Kristen Casey writes the kind of heartfelt, steamy books she loves to read—full of relatable characters and delicious dialogue. She lives in Maryland with her husband, kids, and assorted cats, and in her free time, she enjoys all things crafty—especially projects she finds on Pinterest.

Sign up for her newsletter to receive exclusive free content and the inside scoop on sales and new releases—all emailed right to your inbox.

You can also follow her on social media for behind-the-scenes tales, character and setting inspiration, book reviews, and more:

Goodreads: Kristen_Casey
Facebook: AuthorKCasey
Twitter: AuthorKCasey
Pinterest: KristenCase0461
Instagram: Kristen.Casey.Books
BookBub: Kristen Casey
TikTok: KristenWritesRomance

Reading Order of Kristen's Books

The Lost & Found Series

Girls Night Out (Prequel exclusive to subscribers)

Finding Home (Book 1)

Finding Love (Book 2)

Lost in Love (Book 2.5 – Includes *Lucky in Love*)

The Flynn Sisters Box Set (Includes *Christmas in Cambridge*)

Finding a Husband (Book 3)

Finding Forever (Book 4)

Forever and a Day (Book 4.5 – Includes *Forever Starts Now*)

The O'Connell Sisters Box Set (Includes *Heroes & Husbands*)

The Triple Threat Series

The Titan was Tall (Book 1)

The Doctor was Dark (Book 2)

The Hero was Handsome (Book 3)

The Triple Threat Box Set (Includes *The Masquerade was Magic* and *The Hero's Brother*)

The Black Watch Security Series

False Flag (Book 1)

Heat Seeking Missile (Book 2)

Brothers in Arms (Book 3)

Fight or Flight (Book 4)

Search and Destroy (Book 5)

Squared Away (Book 6)

www.ingramcontent.com/pod-product-compliance
Lightning Source LLC
Chambersburg PA
CBHW061336190726
48288CB00005B/1470